A BOOK WITH SEVEN SEALS

A Victorian Childhood

A
BOOK WITH
SEVEN SEALS
A Victorian Childhood

◆

Agnes Maud Davies

With a Preface by
Martin Secker

1974
CHATTO & WINDUS
LONDON

Published by
Chatto & Windus Ltd
42 William IV Street
London WC2N 4DF

*

Clarke, Irwin & Co Ltd
Toronto

First published at the Cayme Press 1928
Reprinted by Martin Secker 1931
This edition of Part One first published 1974

© The Estate of Mrs. Agnes Maud Douton,
1928 and 1974
Preface by Martin Secker © 1974

ISBN 0 7011 2027 4

Printed and bound
in Great Britain by
REDWOOD BURN LIMITED
Trowbridge & Esher

PREFACE

There are some books which refuse to die and *A Book with Seven Seals* is one of them. It was originally published anonymously in 1928 by the Cayme Press, a small publishing firm which soon closed down. In 1931 I re-issued it, again anonymously. Now it can be revealed that its author was Mrs Agnes Maud Douton.

She was the daughter of the Rev. Robert Henry Davies and was born in 1858, three years after her father had been appointed incumbent of Chelsea Old Church, a position which he was to hold for the next 53 years. She married one of his curates, the Rev. George William Douton. There were no children of the marriage. She died in Chelsea in 1934 aged 76.

When the Cayme Press closed down it was necessary for her to find a new publisher, and I well recall her visit. Her mode of address was alert and forthright, and she came straight to the point. She had come to me, she said, because she liked my style of publishing and it was her wish that my name should appear on the title page of the book. She also explained that while she was not its author she controlled the publication rights. When the time came for the preparation of an Agreement it became necessary to alter laboriously throughout the phrase as printed in the preamble "hereinafter called the Author" to "hereinafter called the Owner of the Copyright." This fiction, since the book was clearly autobiographical, persisted to the end of our association.

In appearance she was tall, spare, upright and, beneath a somewhat formidable manner I detected kindness and a great sense of humour. During one of our conversations she found it necessary to rebuke me. Once I said to her impulsively, "Mrs. Douton, why don't you write a sequel to your book?" She sat up in her chair and regarded me sternly. "Mr. Secker," she said, "you forget yourself." But there was a twinkle of humour in her eyes.

She disliked the telephone and always communicated with me by letter. On some later occasion when she was recovering from an illness in Westminster Hospital she wrote to ask whether I would care to come to tea. The Hospital was within easy walking distance of my office in the Adelphi and I accepted gladly. We had tea in a private room, and I think perhaps this was the last time that I saw her. Looking back I am glad now that I accepted that invitation, and I remember her with affection. I think her latter years were lonely ones, for she was beginning to outlive her contemporaries and she had offended many of her former friends by their portrayal in her book.

One of the most difficult tasks which faces a publisher is to re-issue successfully a work which has appeared in the not too distant past. The publicity given by its reviews is over; it is not likely to be reviewed again, and further readers can only be gained by personal recommendation and word of mouth. But *A Book with Seven Seals* has already made many friends, not only among the public, but in the book trade also. Years ago when my traveller used to call on a bookseller on the south coast, as he did twice yearly, he could always count on an order for half-a-dozen copies, since, as the proprietor said, this was a book which he could always sell. And there were others who thought the same.

So now Mrs Douton makes her appearance for the third time, and I believe she will continue to make fresh friends and take many new readers back into a world which, although we all had far less money, no motor cars, no television, was perhaps on the whole a happier one.

MARTIN SECKER, August 1973

CONTENTS

"Many an old age is sweetened and brightened by the memories of early years. They are wise who in their happy youth-time fill their hearts with pure and pleasant things: they are laying up blessings for old age."

J. R. MILLER, D.D.

"Why is the past so beautiful? The element of fear is withdrawn from it, for one thing. That is all safe, while the present and future are all so dangerous."

THOMAS CARLYLE

"I believe that if the history of any one family, in upper or middle life, could be faithfully written, it might be as generally interesting, and as permanently useful, as that of any nation, however great and renowned."

LOCKHART'S *Life of Sir Walter Scott*

"My friend, the times which are gone are a book with seven seals."

GOETHE

I. THE HOUSE OF MEMORY

" He that getteth a wife, getteth a possession ; a help like unto himself, and a pillar of rest."—ECCLESIASTICUS.

I

ON a fine Sunday morning in the month of May, two generations ago, a young Parson brought his bride for the first time to the Old Church by the river, on his appointment to which, the year before, he felt himself to be in a position to marry.

It was full early when they entered by the little door in the chancel, and he placed her in the large square pew hung with red curtains. Only a few aged members of the congregation had as yet assembled.

The lady was tall, and carried her crinoline with a swaying grace. A Paisley shawl hung from her shoulders in rich folds over the full-flounced skirt of lavender silk, which set off her elegant figure to advantage. A coal-scuttle bonnet completely covered her head, adorned with delicate sprays of lilac blossom, as befitted the season ; and a veil of fine Brussels lace fell lightly over her face.

Henry Danvers felt a proud man as he closed the panelled door of the pew, then stood for a moment looking over it, a smile of satisfaction lighting up his genial countenance, while his young wife seated herself, and laid the new Church Service which she carried upon the book-rest. It was a present from her Sunday-school class in the village where she had spent her girlhood, and she was using it for the first time.

After a few minutes spent upon her knees, Mrs Danvers

settled herself in a corner of the large old pew, spreading the flounces of her dress on either side, and smoothing her white satin bonnet-strings with long slim fingers, conscious that the pew-openers were hovering near by to catch a glimpse of the Parson's bride.

She raised her veil, and cast her eyes around, glancing at the tablets on the chancel wall. Peeping between the faded curtains that surrounded the pew, she could see into a small chapel beyond, where the white marble effigy of a woman appeared to be in the act of rising from the dead. It arrested her attention until someone passing by peered in at her and audibly said " country bumpkin." This in-quisitive spinster had wasted her affections in vain upon the young Parson and parish work : she was bound to give vent to her feelings ; but Mrs Danvers was in no way discomposed by the intrusion, for she belonged to a county family, and considered herself superior to a " cockney."

While she sat waiting for the service to begin, her thoughts strayed back to the happy Sundays in her country home, and the beautiful church in the eastern village where her father had been Rector and Squire ; to whom her husband came as curate, and had won the esteem of her parents as well as the affection of their numerous family.

But when it came to a question of marriage with the second daughter, she was sent for by the Rector and lectured in his library on the folly of falling in love with a curate.

" By gad, my dear Agnes," he exclaimed, " I did not know that you were so fond of bread and cheese. But that will probably be your portion in life if you persist in this silly attachment. Nevertheless, I have a great regard for Henry Danvers, and he may succeed in obtaining good preferment. When that is the case I will not withhold my sanction to your marriage." He then took snuff and dismissed the nervous maiden from his presence.

Seven years had passed since then, but the loving pair had been patient. In the meanwhile the " Squarson " had brought his years to an end " as a tale that is told," and Agnes inherited her small share of his fortune. So she and the curate began their life of bread and cheese together upon the slender preferment that he had at last obtained, little guessing what a long future lay before them in the quaint old waterside parish.

2

The home to which Mr Danvers brought his bride stood at one end of an old row built in Queen Anne's reign. "A right old strong, roomy brick house, built nearly a hundred and fifty years ago, and likely to see three races of these modern fashionables fall before it comes down." He furnished it, bit by bit, from second-hand dealers in the neighbourhood, but allowed his wife to exercise her taste and discretion at her own expense in the best parlour.

A visit with her husband to a fashionable warehouse resulted in a carpet that resembled moss bunched all over with full-blown roses, and two hearthrugs to match. A rosewood suite was also selected, consisting of six elegant chairs, a sofa and a settee, upholstered in green damask. A large looking-glass was chosen to fill the space over the mantelpiece, and a marble-topped chiffonier surmounted by a mirror added to the general effect by reflection.

The room was well proportioned though not large, and Mrs Danvers did not consider it complete without a circular table of walnut wood, and a grand piano. Damask curtains with tasselled testers framed the high windows, and a polished steel fender and fire-irons adorned the hearth.

The Parson's mother took up her abode in the house before he married, and arranged all domestic details. She was a widow of economical habits, who felt it her duty, for

the sake of her son, to stay on awhile and take the in-
experienced young lady in hand. He had a second mother
not far off who had made up her mind to do the same ;
this was the wife of the Rector at the new parish church.
She had been pleased to house Henry Danvers in the big
old Rectory while he held the office of curate to her husband,
and had learned to regard him in the light of a son. She
was anxious therefore to welcome his bride as a daughter.

Paying an early morning call most days, she lectured
young Mrs Danvers on parochial and social duties, and
when she acted contrary to the wish of her husband by
declining an invitation to dine with the parish doctor, in
preference to one received from some fashionable friends
of her own who were in town for the season, she was severely
reproved by the Rector's wife and made to understand that
parishioners must always come first, and their acquaintance
must be cultivated.

This caused a temporary coolness, and was the first
difference of opinion between husband and wife. But the
bride was amiable, and yielded gracefully to the well-
meant interference of her elders.

The Parson's mother prolonged her visit at the request
of her son, since she had no settled home of her own ; but
when his first child was born she stayed no longer than
to see it " britched," which was her term for short-coating ;
then went to take up her abode with her married daughter.

In the course of a few years the good old Rector of the
parish died, and his widow went to live with a son in the
country, who was a great man in a little place. She had
done what she considered to be her duty to Henry Danvers
and his wife, by bestowing upon them the full benefit of
her parochial experience, and by standing godmother to
their daughter.

Young Mrs Danvers was now deemed fit to reign supreme
in her own domain.

3

In mid-Victorian days the waterside parish was little more than a row of picturesque houses and trees facing the river, with a few narrow streets in the background, leading to the King's highway. Wharves and mud banks and barges formed the foreground. Overlooking these, and out of their midst, rose the massive square tower of the ancient Church.

Long years ago the place had been a village of palaces owned by great men. Kings and queens, courtiers and statesmen, had dwelt there. Barges of a gayer kind, bedecked with pennons, conveyed them to and fro for pleasure or prison as the case might be.

In later days the poor and the maimed had taken refuge where people of notoriety and fashion once made merry. But the quaint Walks and Rows were still frequented by men of art and learning, who loved the spot for its interests and associations with bygone days. And the glamour of the broad, winding river, with its many tides ebbing and flowing, continues the same, yesterday, to-day, and for ever.

In olden times a sweet peal of bells rang out across the water from the red brick tower, and " a lyttel bell " had solemnly tolled for daily Mass. There were worshippers of high degree then, whose names had not perished with them, for they were engraven with epitaphs and eulogies on tablets of brass and stone upon the walls of the Church, both outside and in.

Beneath the floor lay the illustrious dead, encased in leaden coffins. And one bell alone survived of the " good ring of eight bells which called the parishioners to divine service."

In the Evangelical days of the early sixties this bell was swinging briskly on a Sunday morning in November.

Nearly a decade had elapsed since the new Parson brought his bride to church and placed her in the family pew.

During those years many changes had taken place. An old gallery had been removed and a new one erected. Square pews were cleared away, and rows of long ones filled the spaces that they had occupied.

Dirt had been effaced by whitewash, and gas had taken the place of candles. A brighter aspect reigned within and without, for the Parson was popular with his people and an impressive preacher.

At the corner house of the old Row three more babies had been born since old Mrs Danvers had taken her departure.

Upon this Sunday morning two little girls were descending the old staircase with dignity, dressed for church-going. They were feeling impressed with a sense of importance, for on that Sabbath day they wore crinolines for the first time, and their full-gathered skirts were as much uplifted as themselves.

The elder child went in advance of her sister, who was slow in her movements and followed sedately. They wore their hair crimped, and spread over their shoulders under round pork-pie hats which were held secure by black elastic beneath their chins.

One carried her Mamma's big Church Service with the gilt clasps, the other held in her fat little hands a small black prayer-book with silver corners, which included Tate and Brady's version of the Psalms.

They were coming from the nursery at the top of the house to the dining-room on the ground floor, where they expected to find their Mamma, and be surveyed by her critical eyes before proceeding on their way to church.

The door stood open, and they entered the room. Mrs Danvers was seated by the fire in a horsehair arm-chair, attired in a velvet cloak and a spoon bonnet, looking as though she sat upon a throne.

A white-faced little boy occupied her lap and her attention ; she was feeding him with small pieces of sponge cake dipped in port wine.

The children stood in the presence of their mother, who addressed them as follows : " Come here, Harriet and Mary Anne, and let me see if you are neatly dressed."

They advanced towards her hand-in-hand as she dipped a morsel of the cake into the wine-glass, and sopping up the dregs with it said to her son :

" Now, my pet, take this tiny bit more."

The boy opened his mouth like a fledgling, and drained it to the last drop.

His sisters eyed each other and muttered ; this indulgence aroused a feeling of jealousy within their breasts.

" Why shouldn't we have cake and wine too, before we go to church ? " the elder child said in an undertone to her sister, as she leant up against the table with a defiant air, making her crinoline bulge out on one side.

" Roger is much too young to go," the younger one retorted. " Nurse says so."

Mrs Danvers rose, and placed the little boy upon his feet.

" I forbid you to repeat nursery gossip," she said. " You forget yourselves, and display jealous dispositions. Your brother is delicate and may not live to grow up. Then you will be sorry to have treated him thus."

So telling was the reproof, that tears welled up in Mary Anne's eyes and Harriet hung her head. They loved their little brother dearly, and the idea of his early death had not occurred to them before.

Mrs Danvers saw that she had created an impression and said no more. She put a large white hat trimmed with ostrich plumes upon the child's head, and tied it with ribbons under his chin. This hat was a source of envy with his sisters, who wore no feather in theirs.

At this moment a whiskered face appeared at the door smiling at them.

" Now Pussy and Polly, are you coming with me ? I must be off, and Mamma can follow at her leisure with the son and heir."

Mrs Danvers told the children to get their goloshes, as the pavement was damp.

" I can't wait," said their Papa, and he vanished from sight.

By the time the goloshes were found and put on he was well on his way to the Church ; so down the length of the quiet Row the little girls went hand-in-hand, their Mamma following in stately measure with their brother. When they came to the river a damp haze hung over everything. The tide was out . . . the pleasure boats and big black barges lay high on banks of mud.

4

The Old Church clock said eight minutes to eleven when the family filed in at the chancel door to the Parson's pew. It was no longer square, or curtained, but of a length to seat eight persons in a row, and distinguished by a mitre carved upon the centre panel. In bygone days this decorated a pew belonging to bishops, who had owned a palace near by.

The three children knelt on hassocks for a few minutes with their hands folded and their eyes closed. Then there were places to be found in books with long ribbon markers, which it was Harriet's business to hand to each one from a locked cupboard under the shelf. She was glad to be there in good time to do this, and to see the congregation assembling.

In those days pews were only for those who could pay for them, and free benches were ranged down the nave. These were occupied by the respectable poor ; and old Miss Milman, who claimed kinship with King George the IVth, was now seating herself on the foremost one under the pulpit and facing the reading-desk where her failing sight and hearing would not be overstrained. She was clad in a rusty black silk dress and bonnet, with a frilled tippet to match, and a pair of old kid gloves, the fingers of which were nearly double the length of her own. This attire was a mark of real respectability in the eyes of Harriet and Mary Anne, because Nurse wore the same on Sundays.

" Old George " always shared the front seat with this lady of royal descent, being hard of hearing too. Nurse declared that he was half daft, whatever that might mean ; but what did it matter, since he performed such delightful duties as milking the cows kept in a yard at the top of the row, close onto the corner house ? And came twice a day from there carrying two shining cans slung on a wooden yoke round his shoulders, crying out " Milko " at the area gate. He wore a clean white smock frock on Sundays, which lasted throughout the week, and presented a contrast to Mr and Mrs Flood, who sat just behind him, looking remarkably like the big sacks of coal and potatoes which filled up the space in their greengrocer's shop.

The cobbler's wife was the next to arrive. She came squeezing herself and her crinoline between the pews and the benches to the chancel steps, where there were other free seats in a more exalted position. There she settled herself upon the ancient tomb of a Lord High Chancellor of England, obliterating it by her gigantic hoops. Mrs Tite was a woman of importance in the eyes of the children because she came once a week on Saturdays to the corner house, and did duty as charwoman.

B

The crinoline had been bestowed upon her in part payment after a visitation from the sweep. Nurse called her a vain hussy, because possessing no natural attractions she resorted to artifice. Her round face resembled a crumpet, being pitted all over with smallpox. It was topped up by an elaborate headpiece of dusty black crape, and profusely ornamented with bugle beads which jingled as she walked up the aisle, like the chandelier candlesticks on the parlour mantelpiece.

Her husband came close behind her, his spare figure tightly buttoned into a shiny frock-coat. He carried a superannuated chimney-pot hat that had once been the Parson's, and which acted, like the crinoline, as a stimulant to regular attendance at church.

Daddy Tite was a great favourite in the nursery. He came every day to fill the scuttles and carry the coals from the cellar to the top of the house ; he mended their shoes, and soled everyone's boots.

Then there was Mr Turke, the beadle, who was a carpenter by trade, but he looked quite imposing on Sundays in his uniform with the collar and cuffs of red velvet trimmed with gold braid, and a row of gilt buttons down the front of his coat. He could do all sorts of things that Daddy Tite could not. Short of stature and slow of gait, he paced up the nave and down again in his official capacity, before the clock struck eleven, to see that everything was in order, and that the Charity children seated round the altar rails were behaving themselves. Then he finally disappeared to help Mr Danvers into his surplice.

In the chapel facing the Parson's pew, a little door opened on to the churchyard. Through it now came Mr Coulston, the City Missionary, who bolted himself into a box that only held one person ; then stood for a whole minute praying into his hat, which he presently hung upon a wooden peg above, and disappeared like a Jack-in-the-box behind the red curtains, which were a relic of the past.

By the same doorway Ellen and Maria Swan, both well known in the nursery, followed close upon his heels. They held their heads high as befitted their position, for their father drove the local omnibus and their brother was the conductor. In their opinion this was equivalent to owning a carriage and pair, with a coachman and footman.

It is recorded in an old chronicle that the Princess Elizabeth attending the church from the Queen's House, " entered to her seat by the same door under the window, not choosing to enter with the common folk."

The two Miss Swans were aware of their importance as they made their way in single file through the narrow passage of the little chapel to the chancel steps, and seated themselves on a bench facing Mr and Mrs Tite. Both considered themselves vastly superior to that worthy couple, though they shared the same old house in the narrow lane that led up from the wharf, crowded with vessels laden with coal.

It was one of several roomy residences once occupied by men with great minds, who bathed in the clear running river from a pebbly shore where barges now lay upon the mud. The atmosphere of their marvellous mentality had clung but little to the panelled interiors.

That a Dean far-famed for wit and learning some centuries ago had spent his leisure hours writing satire where Daddy Tite now sat daily cobbling shoes, was a matter of no concern to the cobbler. . . . And if Mr Swan's slumbers beneath the oak beam in the room above were never disturbed by the ghost of a well-known divine wearing a nightcap very similar to his own, it could only be said that he had no imagination.

But it was hard work with long hours driving a pair-horse omnibus in all weathers. The box seat might be an

enviable position to a city man on a fine morning, when he
would tip the coachman a fourpenny piece for the privilege
of sitting beside him ; but to remain there most of the day
and a good part of the night, come hail or rain, snow or
fog, in the bitter east wind or baking hot sun, was another
matter.

" I plasters myself all over with brown paper to keep
me warm, sir," said old Swan to the Parson one cold
day at Christmas time. " I lay it on under my weskit,
three or four sheets thick, whenever there's a nor'easter
a-blowing ; and my son David he does the same."

Another nursery favourite was now seating herself on the
bench just alongside the family pew. This was Mary-Ann
Knight. She had been coming on fine mornings to wheel
the perambulator, until Sarah Turke, the beadle's daughter,
was engaged to enter service at the corner house as nursemaid.

Mystery was attached to Mary-Ann, for her left arm
consisted of wood instead of flesh and blood. An iron hook
did duty for a hand, which miracle placed her on a pinnacle
in the eyes of the children.

The pew which faced the Parson's, on the other side of
the reading-desk, was always filled by a long row of young
ladies and gentlemen with a stout middle-aged mother.
The little girls called it the Paradise pew, because their
Papa had told them that the good people who occupied it
so regularly every Sunday were the proprietors of Paradise
Gardens, where the fireworks went off and kept them
awake in the summer-time. Harriet and Mary Anne
would creep out of bed if Nurse was downstairs having her
supper, and stand at the window watching the rockets
shoot up into the sky, and the many-coloured balls falling
in the darkness.

They envied the young people in the pew opposite, who
could go to Paradise Gardens whenever they pleased. But

their Papa told them that it was not a nice place, in spite of its name, which puzzled them ; for it sounded so beautiful when they sang the hymn about it in church.

Colonel and Mrs Lindsey were now coming up the aisle, preceded by Miss Barbara, their daughter, and followed by Mr Hugo, their son. . . . They lived next door to the corner house, and had a nice large garden where the Parson's children were welcome to play whenever they liked. These arrivals were of more interest to them than others whom Mrs Cobb and Mrs Webb, the pew openers, were showing in and shutting up with a good deal of bustle and going to and fro.

The organist began to play the Voluntary, and presently Mr Danvers appeared, preceded by the beadle, who conducted him to the reading-desk and then seated himself on a small bench under the pulpit, from which he could keep his eye on the Charity school.

Harriet's head went round to look at a tall gentleman with three children like themselves who were entering the pew behind. They were objects of pity, for they had lately lost their Mamma, and were all in deep mourning.

The service began with a hymn of praise.

> " Through all the changing scenes of life,
>   In trouble and in joy,
> The praises of my God shall still
>   My heart and tongue employ.
> O magnify the Lord with me,
>   With me exalt His Name ;
> When in distress to Him I called,
>   He to my rescue came."

The sun shone out through the mist while they sang, and lit up the dark corners of the old building with its dusty monuments to the dead.

" I will arise and go to my Father, and will say unto Him, Father, I have sinned against heaven, and before thee, and am no more worthy to be called thy son."

The Parson's strong natural voice rang out like a call to action. Hymn-books were laid aside, prayer-books were opened, and the business of Sunday began. . . . There was much to be gone through in those days before they settled down to the sermon, which was looked forward to as a period of rest after the vicissitudes of the Church Service.

Harriet and Mary Anne were allowed to stand on hassocks and raise themselves above the level of the pew while the Psalms were being read. They took this opportunity of making the most of their new crinolines for the benefit of the two little girls behind them, whose heavy black dresses hung in straight folds to their ankles.

It was the duty of the Parson's children to set a good example to others in the congregation by kneeling straight up during the Litany, with closed eyes and folded hands, and to repeat the responses audibly.

But their hearts were far from it, because their Mamma had seated their brother on the large round hassock at her feet and was feeding him with almonds and raisins from her pocket.

Harriet's spirit rebelled within her : the Litany was so long and dull, and what was it all that they were praying to be delivered from ? And why should they keep on beseeching God over and over again to listen to them ? Was it because He was so very far off and not likely to hear them at once ? But Papa had told her that He was always near.

Mary Anne was too young to understand what beseeching meant, but she repeated it to order like a Poll parrot. Every now and then she opened her eyes and glanced down sideways at her little brother who was behaving very badly, helping himself to a store of sweet things placed inside the book-box for his benefit. Mamma had her eyes shut and was taking no notice. The patience of the gentle-

man in the pew behind was sorely tried. It was such a
bad example to his own children.

His long arm presently stretched across and administered
reproof. The child turned his head in surprise at being
touched and put out his tongue. Only Mary Anne had
seen what was happening, and she pondered over the
audacity of it all through the Ten Commandments, and at
intervals during the sermon.

Sermons were very long in those days ; but the little
girls had learnt by experience when it was coming to an
end.

Mamma's touch was sure to be felt if their eyelashes
came in contact with their cheeks, though Roger was
allowed to go to sleep in her lap.

5

Another hymn was sung while Mr Danvers changed his
surplice of fine linen for the voluminous black silk gown
in which he preached, with the delicate bands of white
lawn arranged on an elastic beneath his stiff cravat, which
Mrs Danvers had stitched so beautifully with her own hands.

The pulpit stood on the left side of the pew, and when
the Parson, discourse in hand, mounted the stairs that led
up to it, Turke climbed behind and shut the door tight.
His family could no longer see him, but they were expected
to attend to all he said and commit the text to memory.

Down again on their knees they went, and buried their
faces in their kid gloves for the long preliminary prayer.
Then the trial began of sitting still for at least half an hour
—generally forty minutes.

Mary Anne's short fat legs dangled from the seat, and
were subject to attacks of pins and needles. Harriet's
longer limbs reached down to the hassock, but they were
seldom at rest.

It was the custom of the congregation when the text was given out, to find it in their Bibles, but the Parson would repeat it several times in order to impress it on his hearers.

Harriet knew the headings by heart. " Firstly " seemed unending, " secondly " was followed by " thirdly " in due course, and " lastly " did not always bring the sermon to a conclusion. But a double-barrelled sneeze from Miss Milman, which usually occurred at that point, had a rousing effect upon the slumberers.

Mary Anne would amuse herself by counting the heads that had their eyes shut, and watching for the lids to open ; but no one really bestirred himself until it came to " finally, my beloved brethren," which meant about another five minutes to the finish.

Then there was a finding of places in hymn-books and a feeling in pockets for purses if a collection had been announced, which was only on special occasions, however.

The little girls were expected to repeat the text at the dinner-table when grace had been said, but this depended on its length.

Mary Anne, sitting still as a mouse to begin with, would say it over and over again to herself like a parrot, but her thoughts wandered when the pins and needles set in. To keep her eyes open when they felt inclined to close, she would fix them on the white marble lady opposite, rising from her sarcophagus of black stone in the dim recesses of the small chapel : or she would make up stories in her mind about the family of boys and girls in Elizabethan costume who were kneeling like ninepins with their parents on the same wall.

The Charity children were more attractive to Harriet for they were made of flesh and blood, and given to fidgeting like herself. Daddy Turke would create a diversion by tip-toeing round the altar rails in his creaky boots to display his authority as beadle.

Sometimes a loud snore like a pig grunting would escape from the snout of "old George," whose red poll could be seen sinking downwards till such chin as he possessed was buried in the smocking of his frock . . . for the Parson's excellent discourse was far beyond the limits of his intelligence. But Miss Milman's sneeze acted like an alarum upon him or anyone else who dozed, and it never failed to come off punctually.

When at last the organ burst out a general bustle began. . . . Pew doors, carefully fastened by Mrs Cobb or Mrs Webb, were flung open by imprisoned parishioners, who marched forth to the music, exchanging friendly nods or greetings in their progress down the aisles.

Not until all the pews were empty was the Parson's family released. Then Mrs Webb came curtseying up and unfastened the catch on the door to let out the little girls, who were followed by Mrs Danvers at a dignified pace, leading Roger by one hand and carrying his hat in the other.

" I hope I see you well, ma'am ? " Mrs Webb would say.

" Yes, thank you, Mrs Webb, and I trust you are the same."

To the children this polite interchange of remarks was a regular part of the service. They met the beadle in the porch, who saluted them with a broad grin, and touched his forehead to Mrs Danvers.

" Good morning, Turke," she said graciously. " I am glad to be able to give a satisfactory report of Sarah. She is improving in her work, and Nurse speaks well of her behaviour."

" Thank you, ma'am," replied the beadle, with a second touch to his forehead. " She's a good girl, and I'm sure she will do her best."

" By the bye," continued the Parson's wife, " a pane of glass has been cracked in the nursery window and it lets in a draught. Come to-morrow morning after breakfast, if you please, and mend it."

" Thank you, ma'am," said Mr Turke. " I will endeavour to do so."

Then the family left the porch and set out for home. Mary Anne was bursting with the desire to tell her sister what had happened during the Litany, and she found a ready listener in Harriet as they walked ahead of their Mamma.

Arrived indoors, the two little girls scuttled up the stairs together, regardless of their crinolines, eager to repeat the story to Nurse, who was their confidante and adviser on the top floor. She was standing at the head of the staircase awaiting them with a big brown baby in her arms.

" Well, young ladies, you are late home this morning," she remarked. " But I suppose that is your Papa's fault for preaching a long sermon. Now be quick and take off your coats and hats, and let Sarah brush your hair. Dinner must be ready."

" Oh, Nurse, you must listen ! " began Harriet. " What do you think that Roger did in church ? He put out his tongue at the gentleman who sits in the pew behind because he reached over and boxed his ears."

" No, no ! " cried Mary Anne, " he only poked him while Papa was praying the Litany."

" Yes, yes ! " protested Harriet, " don't interrupt . . . and Roger was eating almonds and raisins on the floor, which Mamma gave him. . . ."

" And he turned right round and put out his tongue, I saw him do it ! " exclaimed Mary Anne triumphantly.

" My word ! " said Nurse. " And what did your Mamma do ? "

" She never saw," replied Mary Anne, " because she was saying ' Our Father ' with her eyes shut."

" And so ought you to have been," decided Nurse.

" And it ain't Master Roger's fault when he is taken to
church so young and given things to eat there. He knows
no better, but you do. Now look alive both of you, the
dinner-bell will be ringing in a minute and you won't be
ready. Kneeling and praying don't do you much good
if you come in from church telling tales of one
another."

This was a turning of the tables quite unexpected by the
sisters. In their opinion Nurse was always right, whoever
else might be wrong. So no more was to be said, and the
little culprit was heard now slowly climbing the last flight
of stairs that led up to the top floor.

" Come along, Master Roger ! " called Nurse. " Sarah,
give him a hand ; I can't put the baby down or she'll
begin bellowing again. She has kept me awake pretty
nigh all night with her teeth, the baggage. I've never had
one like her for worriting, and I hope I shall never meet
with the likes of her again."

Sarah Turke was getting out clean pinafores from the
linen drawer.

" Aren't we to wear our silk aprons on Sunday ? " asked
Harriet.

" Well, be quick and find them then," snapped Nurse.
" They are in the top long drawer, Sarah ; and tie their
hair with the black and white velvets. There now, there
goes the upstairs bell ; run along do."

Away skipped the two little girls downstairs, smoothing
their aprons as they went. These were a source of pride,
like the crinolines, for they were a promotion from pinafores,
and possessed a pocket each side.

They found Mrs Danvers waiting in the dining-room
alone, for their Papa never partook of a midday meal.
Phœbe, the parlourmaid, assisted them on to the chairs by
lifting their crinolines behind. Her mistress having said
grace, cut a slice from the cold shoulder of mutton and

minced it up finely ; she mixed it with some mashed potato and sprinkled it with salt. It was then ready to send to the nursery for Roger.

" It isn't fair that he should be helped before us," muttered Harriet.

Mrs Danvers glanced at her first-born and told her to repeat the text that her Papa had preached upon that morning.

" For it is written that the elder shall serve the younger," replied Harriet promptly.

" So you shall have the privilege of taking up Roger's dinner instead of Phœbe before you have any yourself." Then turning to the maid she said, " Now you may cut up this mutton for Miss Mary Anne, and mix it with bread and vegetables."

When Harriet returned she found a similar plate of food awaiting her, and Mary Anne was relating what had happened during the Litany.

Mrs Danvers took a different view of the matter from Nurse. That anyone should have dared to correct a child of hers in the sanctuary of the Parson's pew, or to question her authority as to what was fitting behaviour in church, was beyond her comprehension.

She reproved Mary Anne for being so eager to proclaim the faults of others, and declared that she must have been mistaken in what she saw.

" If your eyes had been closed in prayer, as they should have been, you could not have imagined such a thing. And it is not possible that so young and innocent a child as Roger could have been so rude unless he had seen you do it first."

Phœbe, who was standing behind her mistress's chair, put out her tongue and wagged it to and fro to the discomposure of the children, who began to giggle.

" What do you mean by laughing ? " said their Mamma.

"Instead of being sorry it seems that you are vulgar. I see that I shall have to punish you."

Phœbe was vexed when she found that she had got the " young ladies " into trouble. " Please, ma'am, it was my fault," she said.

" It has nothing to do with you," observed Mrs Danvers. " You can remove the meat now."

It was replaced by a cold apple tart and a firm white blancmange.

Phœbe carried the dishes down to the kitchen and told the cook what she had done. Mistress had worried her over the dusting that was to be done on Sunday, she declared, and she couldn't help making a grimace behind her back.

When dinner was finished the little girls said their grace with hands folded and eyes closed. Mrs Danvers then administered the punishment.

" Mary Anne, you may go upstairs and tell Nurse to bring your brother and the baby to the drawing-room as soon as she is ready to go to church. But you will not accompany her this afternoon. I wish you to learn the Church catechism with Harriet, in addition to the collect appointed for the day."

6

Nurse had entered service in the Parson's house when Mary Anne was born. The little girl loved her dearly. To go with Nurse to afternoon service was a Sunday treat that she always looked forward to.

A small chapel near by was Nurse's orthodox place of worship, though it was not given over to Dissent, as its name might imply.

Mary Anne was allowed to go to sleep during the sermon, which was often longer than her Papa's. Then she would wake up fresh and bright to sing " Sun of my soul, Thou

Saviour dear, It is not night if Thou art near ! " and " Abide with me, fast falls the eventide, The darkness deepens, Lord with me abide." . . . Later on she would trot home in the dark, clasping Nurse's hand, to a cosy tea by the nursery fire.

Mary Anne couldn't bear the idea of staying indoors and learning collects and catechism. So by the time she arrived at the top of the house with her Mamma's message her eyes were full of tears.

Nurse was putting on her black silk dress for Sunday afternoon, and her gold watch and chain with the little round locket attached to it, which she only wore for best. The baby was asleep in the wicker cradle behind the door.

" Please, Nurse," began the little girl . . . " Mamma says she wants Roger and baby in the drawing-room when you are ready . . ."

" And you have come to put your things on," said Nurse, contemplating herself in the small mirror that stood on the top of the big chest of drawers, while she fastened to her bosom a large oval brooch which served as a frame for a marvellous plait of grey hair from the head of a relative.

" Well, just run down again and tell your Mamma that baby had best be left where she is. I've had such a job to get her off, and now p'raps she will sleep all the while I'm out, there's no telling. Make haste up again, like a good girl, it's nearly time to start."

But Mary Anne suddenly burst into tears.

" Why, whatever is the matter, my precious ? " said Nurse. " 'Ush 'ush ! You will wake your little sister. There now, come into the next room and tell me all about it. What is it then ? Got to stay at home and learn your collicks, have you ? Well, well, that's what comes of telling tales out of church, no doubt. Never mind, my pretty,

Sunday will be round again in a week, and Park Chapel won't run away, nor shall I."

She stroked the golden head and wiped the wet eyes and washed the tear-stained face of Mary Anne before sending her downstairs with Roger. Then Nurse went to the cupboard in the corner and took from it a band-box which contained her Sunday bonnet. It was a neat composition of ribbon and straw, with a curtain of black silk behind, which covered her black plaited hair. She found a fat Church Service in the small top drawer, a present from her mistress when Mary Anne was baptised. Equipped with her black kid gloves and cotton umbrella, she sallied forth to the afternoon service at three.

As she walked along, turning to the right and then to the left, she missed the little hand that was always in hers when she wended her way to the chapel. But the weather was damp and foggy, so she thought it was just as well that Miss Mary Anne had stayed at home.

Meanwhile the two little girls were standing in front of their Mamma, who held Roger in her lap, while they endeavoured to repeat the collect for the twenty-fourth Sunday after Trinity.

" I wish you to understand the full meaning of this prayer," said Mrs Danvers. " A more suitable one could not have been chosen for you to learn, since you have both offended to-day. What does the verb to ' absolve ' mean, Harriet ? "

" To melt," replied the child.

" No, you are thinking of to ' dissolve.' ' He pardoneth and absolveth all them that truly repent.' Now think again before you answer."

And Harriet quickly replied, " Forgiveness."

" That is better," said Mrs Danvers. " ' That through thy bountiful goodness we may all be delivered from the bands of those sins which by our frailty we have committed.'

Now, Mary Anne, what does frailty mean ? " But this was beyond the limits of the little girl's understanding, and her sister answered for her.

" Now, in order that this collect may be especially impressed upon you both, kneel down and say it after me," said their Mamma, and she substituted the word " children " for " people."

Roger was amusing himself by mocking his sisters, who were told next to sit down and read a Bible story in the Sunday picture book which Harriet brought from the chiffonier cupboard. The crimson cover was decorated in gold outline by the funeral car of Jacob, which resembled a haystack on wheels drawn by six horses. Mrs Danvers turned over the leaves until she found the history of Joseph and his Brethren. This she related, dwelling on the helplessness and innocence of Joseph and the jealousy and ill-nature of his elder brothers.

It was indeed a second sermon to sit through, and intended to soften the hearts of her little daughters towards their brother. But it had a contrary effect on Harriet, who wriggled when it came to Joseph's dream, where all the sheaves made obeisance to his sheaf ; and her heart became hardened, like that of Pharaoh, King of Egypt.

The pictures of Joseph in the pit, and his brethren bringing the blood-stained coat to Jacob, were pointed out with meaning by Mrs Danvers' long forefinger. Mary Anne was moved to tears, but Harriet leaned against the sofa on which her Mamma reclined, and bulged out her crinoline defiantly.

The baby was heard crying upstairs. Mrs Danvers rose in haste and left the room.

Harriet at once assumed maternal authority, and leaving the objectionable story of Joseph unfinished, she quickly turned over the leaves of the book in search of a picture portraying Elisha the Tishbite being mocked at by children, who cried out to him, " Go up, thou baldhead—go up, thou baldhead."

" What is a Tishbite ? " asked Mary Anne.

" A prophet, of course," replied Harriet.

" A man without any hair, like the one you put your tongue out at this morning, you naughty boy," said his sister. " We saw you. He was quite right to correct you for setting a bad example to his children ; and Elisha punished those boys and girls for mocking him by telling two bears to come out of a wood and eat them up. They will come and eat you up as well if you mock us as you were doing just now when Mamma wasn't looking."

" I didn't," whimpered the little boy ; " and I didn't mock any baldheads."

" You did ! " exclaimed Mary Anne. " You put out your tongue at one."

" I didn't put out my tongue, I curled it round like this," declared Roger as he illustrated the action.

" Now you are telling a lie," said Harriet, " and that is worse than being jealous like Joseph's brethren, because if you don't mind you will fall down dead the next minute like Ananias and Sapphira in the picture here," which she found and triumphantly pointed out to her little brother.

" Harriet ! How dare you be so wicked ! " exclaimed Mrs Danvers, who had entered the room unheard with the baby in her arms. " Go up to the nursery at once and remain there. Take your prayer-book with you and learn a portion of the Church catechism to repeat to me when Nurse returns."

Harriet left the room delighted with herself. She went singing all the way upstairs, and slammed the nursery door when she got to the top. There she proceeded to amuse herself by turning the contents of the big chest of drawers upside down, and afterwards laying the cloth for tea.

When Sarah Turke came in from her Sunday visit to her

c

parents, she found all ready and the kettle singing on the hob.

"Well, Miss Harriet, you have made yourself useful for once!" she exclaimed. "Why ever don't you always try and help like this?"

"I shall if I like, and I shan't if I don't like," was the little girl's offhand rejoinder. "But I've turned all the drawers topsy-turvy in the night-nursery."

II. THE NURSERY

" The street runs down upon the river, which I suppose you might see by stretching out your head from the front window, at a distance of fifty yards on the left."—CARLYLE.

I

WHEN the beadle arrived the next morning to mend the window-pane in the nursery, he found the children alone.

Nurse was busy getting the clothes ready for the laundry woman, and Sarah was helping Phœbe to make the beds.

The high fireguard was hung with a row of cloths to dry, and Harriet sat before it with the baby in her lap.

Mary Anne and Roger were amusing themselves by turning out the toy cupboard. This was a remarkable piece of furniture, which consisted of a washing-stand above and a roomy receptacle for everything beneath. It was painted yellow, and had a large lid which covered the top part. The lower half was divided into two separate cupboards, one of which was used for stove and blacking brushes, dusters and dish-cloths, and in the other one the children kept what few toys they possessed.

On this particular morning the contents of both cupboards were emptied on to the floor, and Mary Anne was busy cleaning her button-boots with stove polish, meaning to be helpful.

Roger, equally busy, was scrubbing the interior with a blacking-brush when Mr Turke entered the room, carrying a workman's hod over his shoulder. His face lighted up

29

when he saw the children, and they gave him a warm welcome.

" Have you seen Sarah ? " asked Harriet.   " She's going to settle down comfortable here, and Nurse says she will do for the present if she behaves herself."

The beadle grinned from ear to ear as he deposited his tool-bag on the floor.   He looked quite a different person from what he did on a Sunday.

Roger at once deserted the washstand and went to examine the contents of the tool-bag.

" Be careful there, little master ! " warned Mr Turke. " Them tools will bite if you touch 'em."

" Sarah tells us lots of stories in the firelight when Nurse is putting baby to bed," said Mary Anne.   " I like the ' Mistletoe Bough ' best, where the lady gets shut into the chest of drawers and no one can find her."

" It wasn't a chest of drawers ! " said Harriet.   " It was a big wooden box like Mamma's for going away with ; Nurse said so."

The beadle took off his coat and set to work in his shirt-sleeves and carpenter's apron.

" What's this ? " asked Roger, holding up a soft lump of something he found in the bag.

" That's putty, what I'm going to mend the window with," said Mr Turke, " but it's not for you to be eating of."

Nurse came bustling into the room.

" My word ! " she exclaimed when she saw the muddle on the floor.   " I declare I can't turn my back a minute but you're all up to some mischief or another.   Now tumble all them things into the cupboard again this minute, and come and get ready to go out."

Turning to the beadle, she said " Good morning," and enquired for his wife.

" Please give her my respecks, and next time we come along your way for a walk I'll look in for a minute. It's a pity she's so ailing. I s'pose she misses Sarah, but she's got Sophie to do for her, and she's getting a big girl now."

Nurse took the baby from Harriet and prepared to leave the room.

" How long will you be over that window ? " she asked. " Sarah's got to clean it when you've done, and tidy up here. She isn't quick, but she's getting on all right, and she's willing and good-tempered, which is the best of her."

Daddy Turke never had much to say for himself, his mind worked slowly, but he always replied to everything with a grin and diligently did his duty.

2

The little girls wore no crinolines to-day. Their full-gathered stuff dresses hung in folds to their knees, showing white short socks and bare legs. They put on warm shag coats and felt hats shaped like mushrooms, with thick black elastic under their chins to keep them firm on their heads.

Nurse attired Roger and the baby in pelisses, then they all went downstairs together, leaving the beadle in possession of the nursery.

They found Mrs Danvers in the parlour writing the weekly orders in the tradesmen's books.

The little girls stood by her side looking on while she wrote as follows :

1 lb. tea	..	4s. 6d.	2 lbs. loaf sugar	..	1s.
1 lb. rice	..	6d.	1 lb. cheese	..	1s. 8d.
2 lbs. brown sugar		10d.	1½ lbs. butter	..	2s. 6d.

Harriet interrupted her by saying, " Please, Mamma, may we have some treacle for tea ? The butter is so nasty."

Mr Danvers was seated in the horsehair arm-chair reading his Bible, as was his custom every morning after breakfast. He closed it now and said, " What is that I hear ? Little girls who call things nasty mustn't have treacle for tea."

" Oh, Papa ! " cried Harriet, turning to the fireside where he was sitting, " it is nasty."

" No, no," he corrected, " it may be disagreeable, but that is a long word for little people to use. Suppose we say the butter is so nice that we do not want any treacle."

" It wouldn't be true," said Harriet decidedly.

" Then in that case," replied the Parson with a twinkle in his eye, " you may ask Mamma to order some treacle."

Mary Anne was looking out of the window through the wire blind, to which height she just reached. She saw Nurse wheel out the perambulator, into which she lifted Roger and the baby. They were then strapped in and covered with an apron of black leather.

A man wearing a chimney-pot hat stopped to pat the children's cheeks, and ran up the doorsteps.

" Here's Mr Coulston ! " cried Mary Anne.

The next moment a tap was heard at the dining-room door, and he entered. The little girls rushed at him.

" Oh, please Mr Coulston, throw me up to the ceiling," they both cried out, and the good man, who was a City Missionary, and called every morning to see the Parson on parish matters, took them in turn in his arms and did as he was requested, laughing in a squeaky way all the time.

" Pussy, fetch that parcel of tracts from my library table," said Mr Danvers to Harriet, " and untie the string. Before I forget it, Coulston, these have been sent from the Religious Tract Society, and I want you to leave them wherever you call this week."

Harriet busily unpacked the parcel and began reading out the titles and looking at the pictures on the papers.

" Price one penny," she said. " Will Father be a goat ? "

" Oh, Papa, how funny ! May I have one to read ? "

" Certainly you may, my dear, but I don't suppose you are old enough to understand the meaning of it," replied Mr Danvers.

" Oh yes I am," said Harriet confidently. " It is about the sheep on the right and the goats on the left, isn't it, Mr Coulston ? "

" Yes, my dear, I expect so," replied the Missionary

" Papa won't be a goat, will he ? " asked Mary Anne, with round eyes gazing at him.

" No, my dear, that I'm sure he never will ! " said the good man. " 'E 'as such a 'uman 'eart, and 'e is as full of the 'oly Ghost as an egg is full of meat."

The little girls both burst out laughing, and their Mamma reproved them, remarking as she did so : " I do not wish you to read tracts, Harriet, they are only for the poorer classes. Leave them all as you found them for Mr Coulston to distribute in the parish. Now take these books for the tradesmen, and go for your walk at once."

Nurse came in and called them, and they all set out down the Row in the direction of the grocer's shop, which was round the corner facing the river.

They left the perambulator at the entrance and went inside.

A little man with a big nose was beating butter into pats with a pair of wooden bats. He was Mr Chaine, the grocer, and his sister was busy at the counter weighing out pounds of brown sugar from a tub. The shop boy was twisting blue paper into cones, into which each pound went as it left the scales.

These performances always interested the little girls, and when they went to the shop on their weekly visit, Mr Chaine's mother would emerge from the back parlour and give them biscuits from the row of tin boxes in front of the counter. Then she would stay and have a chat with Nurse.

This morning she went to the shop door and looked at the little ones.

" Don't she grow a big girl ? " she said of the baby.
" How old is she ? "

" Getting on for a year," replied Nurse, " and she'll
have her nose put out of j'int before long, though her Papa
says she ain't got no nose to speak of."

" Mr Chaine has . . . Mamma says so," remarked
Roger as he munched his biscuit.

" We've all got noses," said Nurse quickly, " and yours
is always wanting wiping, so the sooner you learn to do it
for yourself the better I shall be pleased." She whipped
out her handkerchief and applied it with such vigour that
Roger was rendered speechless.

" Now, young ladies ! " she called to Harriet and Mary
Anne, who were absorbed in the sugar and butter business.
" Come along, we must be going."

Nurse was very particular with her little charges when
they walked out, keeping one on each side of her by the
perambulator, which took up most of the narrow pavement.
The road also was narrow in those days, between the river
and the houses. Posts connected by iron chains, and a
row of tall trees behind them, were the only protection
there was from mud and water.

The children liked to run across and swing on the chains,
but they did not dare to do so with Nurse. Miss Margery
Manners, who came every afternoon to teach them sewing,
and their scales and exercises on the piano, was the only
person who permitted such a scandalous breach of deportment when she took them for a walk after tea.

" No, no, now, don't worrit me ! " Nurse would say
when Harriet took it into her head to be rebellious. " I'm
not going to bring a bylim of rapscallions out along with
me . . . and whatever should I do if you got run over or
fell into the river I should like to know ? " So there was
an end of the matter.

They crossed the road at the end of the wide street

which ended with a pier, from which the steamboats started. Proceeding on their way by the fine old residences with a frontage of handsome wrought-iron gateways, they would meet some of the people who lived in them.

There was that black-faced foreigner who in Nurse's opinion was only fit to be a bat and come out in the dusk, flitting up the walk and in again to hide away from the sun in his great big house, where he painted pictures and kept a lot of poets and other wild beasts, so she had been told. " She wasn't going to have the children frightened by the likes of him," she declared, and when she saw him coming she would turn up a side street.

Bookworms and musicians, painters and poets, and all kinds of queer-looking objects were to be seen out for a morning stroll.

Then there was the prophet, or the pessimist, as the Parson sometimes called him, who lived in the same row as them-selves, and was always to be seen by the river. He went out regularly after breakfast, and came stumping along on his homeward way clad in a large cloak and a slouch hat, which made him look like a conspirator. Nurse would wheel the perambulator aside and give him a wide berth because he scowled at the children.

To-day they left the riverside and went up a street past another row of old houses in one of which Miss Manners· lived with her parents. They were on their way to call on fat Mr Flood and his wife, who dealt in coals and potatoes. This brought them into the King's Highway, which con-sisted of shops and noisy traffic, though there were two or three nice old houses with trees, where Mr and Mrs White-head and their three daughters resided ; and Sawbone, the surgeon, next door to them.

Opposite was an arch leading into a yard, from which the omnibus started for the City every twenty minutes. Mr Swan happened to be driving out his pair of horses just as they passed by, with his son in a shiny black hat on the step behind.

Nurse nodded, and went into the oilmonger's to buy a pound of " dips " which hung in bunches from the ceiling. A few doors further on was a hosier and haberdasher's where a leash of crinolines was tethered above the entrance like air-balloons. Nurse was needing some white knitting-cotton with which she made her own strong stockings sooner than trust her hardened feet and legs in the fine hosiery to be bought ready made.

Mary Anne went inside with her, and Harriet was left in charge of the children. As soon as Nurse's back was turned she wheeled the perambulator on to the corner shop at the next street, where photographs of Mr Danvers and others of the neighbouring clergy were displayed in the window for sale, as well as valentines when in season. There were books and note-paper and pencils and fancy goods of many kinds besides.

Harriet peeped inside and saw Mr MacArthur behind the counter. He was a regular attendant at church with his family, which consisted of two sons and three daughters ; besides which he acted as " sidesman " and handed round the plate when there was a collection. So he was an important personage, and Harriet was fond of going into the shop with her Papa and listening to their conversation on parish and politics.

By the time Nurse had completed her purchases it was nearly eleven o'clock. They turned the corner down the wide street that they had crossed at the other end, and the first turning to the right took them home again. There they found Mr Danvers standing on the doorstep, and the children ran to him.

" I am just going across to the farmyard," he said. " Would you like to come with me ? Mamma wants a drive this afternoon, and we will see if old Silvester can take her." The Parson clasped a hand of each little girl in his, and they crossed the narrow roadway to the opposite corner.

"COLLEY . . . COWKEEPER" was painted in large white letters upon the double gateway that confronted them. It stood ajar, and a strong odour of stable manure was wafted from within. The Parson pushed it open, and there stood "old George" busy with a pitchfork.

He grinned at them and pulled his carrotty forelock.

"Morning, George," said Mr Danvers. "Well, what was my sermon about yesterday, eh?"

The little girls ran across the yard and peeped into the cowshed lest they should be appealed to if George's memory failed. Mr Silvester, a lean, wiry little man, appeared at the back door in his waistcoat and shirt-sleeves. He was a fly proprietor in a small way of business, and shared the stables with Colley the cow-keeper.

"Good day, sir. Yes, sir," he said. "I'm not engaged for this afternoon, and I will bring the carriage round at three o'clock punctual. Well, little ladies, do you want to go in and see the cows?" and he unfastened the lower half of the shed door.

The hens were clucking about in the straw, and one of them had just laid an egg. It was quite warm, and to the delight of Mary Anne, Mr Silvester made her a present of it to take to her Mamma. Then they stepped across the road again to the corner house, and Mr Danvers opened the door with his latchkey.

"May we go for a drive too?" asked Harriet, to which her Papa replied,

"Run in and ask Mamma, and tell her to be ready to start at three o'clock." Then he shut himself out, and set off into the parish.

3

Three o'clock that afternoon found Mrs Danvers and her little daughters all arrayed in their best attire. Harriet and Mary Anne wore pelisses of blue velvet and bonnets to match, which had been given to them by their Uncle Roger, who lived in rooms in London, and often came to dinner.

Silvester looked quite a different man in livery, with silver buttons and top boots. He held the door of the brougham open for Mrs Danvers to enter, and lifted the two little girls onto the back seat. They were out to pay calls, and he was directed to drive to a house in Kensington.

The old horse went his own pace, but it was an excitement to the children to go for a carriage drive, as Nurse called it.

If the ladies happened to be at home Mrs Danvers took them into the houses in turn, and they would compare notes afterwards as to what they had seen and overheard

The Miss Tregunters were out, so they drove on to see Miss Speergrove, who lived near by, and was at home. Harriet went in with her Mamma. Mary Anne was left alone for a long time and she fell asleep.

Harriet was in high feather when they appeared again, and exclaimed triumphantly :

" Miss Speergrove has promised to give me a doll because I said I hadn't got one, and its clothes are to take on and off ! "

This piece of news struck deep into the intelligence of her sister's small mind, for there was only an old rag image in the toy cupboard and it was common property. When the carriage stopped at a large villa not far off it was Mary Anne's turn to go in, and her hopes rose high. But no such luck awaited her. Mrs Gilston and her three daughters were all at home, and made much of her, kissing her chubby cheeks and admiring her golden locks—but when cake and wine were brought in she was not offered any. So she returned to the back seat a disappointed and saddened child.

The next lady they visited was out, and then came a call that Mrs Danvers preferred to make alone, so the little girls were left together.

Harriet was very lively and excited, but she found her sister in no humour for fun. In fact, Mary Anne was inclined to be sulky, and was brooding over the doll that was not to be hers.

" Never mind," said Harriet, with gracious good humour, " you shall have it to play with sometimes ; but you must take great care of it."

The little girl longed for a doll of her own and did not respond to this suggestion.

" We can make some clothes for it with Miss Manners," said Harriet.

Then she began to unfasten her sister's things to see how they were fashioned. Mary Anne was usually quiescent, and when Harriet promised that she should have a joint interest in the doll and play with it in turns, she allowed herself to be completely undressed.

Her sister shut both the windows and drew the blinds down to their lowest limit.

" Now let's pretend you are the doll, and see what clothes we shall have to make. Mamma is sure to be ever so long before she comes out, and we can't sit still all the time."

So one by one Mary Anne's little garments were taken off, examined, and set aside, while she sat on the floor of the carriage shivering with cold.

Silvester was nodding on his seat outside, and when he descended to open the carriage door for Mrs Danvers to enter, the little girl was revealed to view with nothing on but her bonnet and socks.

The astonishment of both knew no bounds, and indignation succeeded it. Mrs Danvers took the child on her lap and told the man to drive home. Harriet was lectured while her sister was being re-clad. "It is bad enough to give her a severe chill," said her Mamma. "And your undisciplined behaviour makes me disinclined to bring you out driving. You get into mischief the moment my back is turned. You are eight years old now and you ought to know better. The eldest of the family should learn to set a good example to the younger ones. I am ashamed of you."

This reproof was delivered in such scathing accents that Harriet hung her head and was silent.

When they arrived home Mrs Danvers ascended to the nursery with Mary Anne and ordered a hot bath for her at once, and a powder at bedtime.

The little girl dreaded that nightly potion almost as much as the day of judgment. But Nurse did her best to make it palatable by mixing it with a teaspoonful of strawberry jam, and stirring it with a pin.

"Come now, dearie," she coaxed when it came to the time to be taken. "Open your mouth and shut your eyes, there's a good girl. Just go to sleep and forget all about it."

But Mary Anne never forgot. And long years after she tasted the powders whenever she took strawberry jam.

4

It was the last Sunday in Advent. The tolling of the Old Church bell could be heard rising and falling on the fitful gusts of wind to call the parishioners to evening service.

Nurse was bustling about in the night nursery preparing for the children's bedtime by the light of the fire and a tallow candle stuck in a large tin candlestick, which was set on the tall chest of drawers.

The baby was asleep in her cradle in the corner, and Sarah Turke had gone downstairs to fetch a can of hot water from the kitchen.

Three little nightgowns were hanging in a row on the high fireguard to air. A bath shaped like a coffin was in front of the fire with sponges and soap and towels. Nurse's low wooden chair stood near it, all ready for action, while she busied herself by cutting rounds of coarse brown paper and smearing them liberally with tallow from the end of a dip warmed at the fire. This form of plaster was her infallible remedy for coughs and colds.

The wild west wind blew hard against the windows, rattling the old frames into which Nurse next proceeded to wedge little pieces of firewood. Then she made some sugary butter for Mary Anne's special benefit, because her cough kept her awake at night.

Her Papa would give her lumps of liquorice to suck, but it was not nice like the mixture of butter and sugar, and Nurse said, " Nasty black stuff, messing the pillows," and put it in the slop-pail.

When Sarah came upstairs again with the bath water and had turned back the bedclothes of the three iron cribs that stood in opposite corners of the room, she was sent off downstairs again to fetch Master Roger.

" And tell the young ladies to come up quick and not to keep me waiting," said Nurse.

It was not long before they were all upstairs, for their Mamma was tired and wanted to be quiet. They had been wrestling with the Advent collects, and Mrs Danvers had required Harriet and Mary Anne to repeat all four from memory.

The first one inspired them with awe, like their Papa's course of sermons dealing with the Last Day and the Final Judgment. Harriet had got it quite by heart, but Mary Anne was slow of understanding. She had been to the Park Chapel with Nurse in the afternoon and the congregation had sung with much fervour " Lo, He comes, in clouds descending, Once for favoured sinners slain." Her little soul was filled with terror lest this should really happen.

Mr Danvers had taken for his next text that morning in church " The day of the Lord cometh as a thief in the night," and as she crept up the dark staircase Mary Anne felt afraid to go to bed.

But Harriet was talkative as usual, and her mind was full of the delights of Christmas, which was coming so soon. She had heard her Mamma making arrangements with Mrs Cobb and Mrs Webb after service that morning about decorating the church, and a larger hamper of holly and evergreens had come the day before from an uncle in Norfolk, with lots of rosy apples packed underneath for their benefit.

When the ladies came for the choir practice on Saturday morning Mrs Danvers had asked them to help her at the church on Christmas Eve, and Harriet was hoping that she would be allowed to go too and make herself useful.

Roger was in the bath when the little girls entered the room, and Sarah was waiting to undress them. Nurse, seated on her low chair, was sponging the naked little boy and saying :

" He's a funny old gentleman with a long white beard, and he wears a brown coat like your Papa's dressing-gown, and he carries a staff in his hand and a sack on his back."

" What's in it ? " asked Roger.

" Why, it's full of toys and sweeties for good little girls and boys. Now, out with you, and don't make a splash or he won't bring you anything."

" Oh, Nurse ! " cried Harriet, " are you talking about Father Christmas ? "

" I shan't say a word more till you get undressed and let Sarah plait your hair," replied Nurse as despotic on her wooden chair as her mistress was when seated on the horse-hair throne in the dining-room.

" May Sarah sing us the ' Mistletoe Bough ' ? " asked Mary Anne.

For the sake of peace and progress the nursemaid was allowed to raise her cracked voice to the tune, and when it came to the chorus they all joined in, until the baby woke and began to scream, so there was an end of everything until she was quieted with a feeding-bottle.

When they were all clad in their well-warmed night-gowns and ready for bed, Nurse said :

" Now kneel down and say your prayers like good children."

Upon their little knees they knelt in a row before the fire, and began :

> " Jesus, tender Shepherd, hear me,
>   Bless Thy little lamb to-night ;
> In the darkness be Thou near me,
>   Keep me safe till morning light.
>
> Through the day Thy love has spared me,
>   And I thank Thee for Thy care ;
> Thou hast clothed and warmed and fed me ;
>   Listen to my evening prayer.
>
> Let my sins be all forgiven,
>   Bless the friends I love so well ;
> Take me, when I die, to Heaven,
>   Happy there with Thee to dwell."

Little Roger was already half asleep, and Nurse lifted him into his crib and covered him over.

When Harriet and Mary Anne rose after saying the Lord's Prayer they were not allowed to utter another word. Sarah helped them to climb into their cribs, and bared their chests for Nurse, who came and clapped a tallow plaster on to each as they lay there. Then she brought a

D

saucer with the sweet butter, and popping a piece into Mary Anne's mouth, she kissed her saying :

" Good night, and go to sleep quick like a good girl."

" Nurse," whispered the child earnestly, " will he come to-night ? "

" Who ?   Father Christmas ? " asked Nurse.   " Not likely ; he isn't due till Christmas Eve."

" No, I don't mean him," said Mary Anne shyly.   " ' Lo, He comes, in clouds descending,' you know, Nurse, like a thief in the night."

" Never fear ! " said Nurse, and then she added, " you just turn over and think about Father Christmas, and guess what he's going to bring you in his sack, and see if you don't dream about him."

Then she tip-toed out of the room and went downstairs to the kitchen for her supper.

But Mary Anne laid awake a long time listening to the wind howling outside, and sometimes it rose to such a pitch that it rocked her little bed which was in the corner by the window.

> " Wild, wild wind, wilt thou never cease thy sighing ?
> Dark, dark night, wilt thou never wear away ? "

The rain came and beat against the panes of glass until they sounded like the crack of doom.   The pigs in the farmyard at the back squealed loudly every now and then as they stirred in their styes, trying to cuddle up against each other for warmth.

It was all terrifying to the little girl, lying awake by herself, for Harriet was soon in a healthy slumber.   She tried to remember the collect she had been learning about the works of darkness and the armour of light, until Nurse came to bed and undressed by the dim light of the dip. Then she felt safer and fell asleep.

5

When Daddy Tite came to carry coals to the nursery next morning Mrs Danvers asked him to take the hamper of holly that had come from the country and put it in the church porch on his way home.

After dinner Harriet and Mary Anne were told to get ready to accompany their Mamma, and make themselves useful at the decorating.

This they were delighted to do, and although the day was dark and a fog hung over the river, they set off in high spirits.

It was only a short distance to go, and as they walked along their Mamma explained in what way she wished them to help her.

" I shall require a number of nice pieces of holly with bunches of berries on them. You may use these scissors, Harriet, to cut off the sprigs. Then put them in this basket for Mary Anne to take to the ladies who are making wreaths, and remember to keep two nice pieces to take home."

" What for, Mamma ? " asked Harriet.

" For the plum pudding and Father Christmas," replied Mrs Danvers.

" Is he coming to-night ? " enquired Mary Anne eagerly.

" Yes," replied her Mamma.

" Shall we see him ? " asked Harriet excitedly.

" No, you will be in bed."

" Oh, mayn't we sit up, Mamma ? " pleaded Mary Anne.

" No, he comes too late, but you will meet him at breakfast to-morrow, and perhaps he will bring you something nice," replied Mrs Danvers as they entered by the big western door and found the porch full of evergreens.

The ladies who came every Saturday morning to the choir practice, which Mrs Danvers conducted herself in her drawing-room at home, sang in the gallery on Sundays.

They were now busy inside the church, where all was bright with gaslight.

Stout Miss Speergrove and thin little Miss Sumner were in a pew together fastening sprigs of holly at intervals along the top of the woodwork with the aid of a hammer and staples, so that whoever attempted to lean back on Christmas Day during the sermon would find it necessary to sit bolt upright.

The two Miss Tregunters were pricking their fingers to distraction by tying bunches of holly to the altar rails, which would have the same straightening effect on the Charity children.

Miss Margery Manners and her sister were converting the fine old carved pulpit into a Jack-in-the-green with ivy, when Mrs Danvers came to the rescue, and asking Miss Margery to go and help Harriet and Mary Anne in the porch, she tactfully dismantled and continued the pulpit with Miss Esther.

Mrs Cobb and Mrs Webb were bustling about with brooms and dusters to get the church cleared up for Christmas Day, and grumbling together at the mess ladies made.

Miss Manners found the little girls very busy over the holly boughs.

" We are to keep a nice piece with berries on for Father Christmas," said Mary Anne ; " he is coming to-night."

" Mamma says we shall be in bed," declared Harriet, " but I mean to sit up and watch for him."

" Will he come in clouds like our Saviour does ? " asked Mary Anne.

Miss Margery laughed. " He is more likely to come in soot," she said, " since he has to crawl down the chimney."

" Or in snow through the window," remarked Harriet. " I've seen pictures of him doing that."

" Oh, that's only in the country where the snow lies on

the ground," replied Miss Manners ; " but in London all the windows are barred and shuttered up to keep out the fog, so he can't get in, and he is obliged to come down the chimney. Now the basket is full of sprigs ; you can take it to Mamma, and we must be quick and fill it again."

There was no time for more talking, and it was not until the little girls were tucked up in bed that Father Christmas came into their heads again. But they were both so sleepy that before they were aware of it their eyes were closed by the fairies, as Sarah said they would be, if they tried to keep awake to see him come down the chimney.

" He takes good care not to be seen on his errands, young ladies, so it's no use your trying to keep awake," remarked Nurse as she kissed them good night.

But Harriet felt sure it was not much later when she woke up with a start and heard the cocks crowing in Cook's ground. She jumped up to peep out of the window into the darkness.

" It must be Father Christmas coming," she said to herself, " and he has disturbed the fowls."

But the door opened the next minute, and there was Sarah coming in with a candle to call Nurse.

" A happy Christmas to you all ! " she said. " It's ever so late."

" Well, we have slept sound ! " declared Nurse as she hurried into her clothes. " Even baby didn't wake and worry for her bottle."

" That shows the fairies did come after all and seal up our eyes," said Mary Anne as she rubbed them with her fat little fists.

Harriet was perplexed. " Has Father Christmas arrived ? " she asked.

" Yes, he's here right enough," said Sarah, " and he sends you all his good wishes."

" Oh, where is he ? " cried Mary Anne.

"He's in the parlour waiting for your Pa and Ma to go down to breakfast," replied the nursemaid.

"Oh, Nurse, can't we just run down and shake hands with him?" asked Harriet.

"What, with nothing on but your chimmies!" exclaimed Nurse. "I'm ashamed of you, Miss Harriet. He don't want to see no naked little girls this cold weather. Make haste and get your clothes on now, and help your sister into hers while Sarah lays the breakfast. Now, Master Roger, wake up and let me dress you," she said, lifting the sleepy little boy out of his crib. "It's that dark this morning we might be getting up in the middle of the night."

"There's a thick yaller fog outside, what Father calls a stinker," said Sarah as she pulled up the blinds. "I'm just wondering how Father Christmas has managed to find the right chimney-pot."

Then she went into the day-nursery, and while she was laying breakfast and putting the kettle on to boil they could hear her crooning the " Mistletoe Bough."

The children were anxious to begin breakfast and to go and greet Father Christmas, but the baby was screaming and had to be fed first.

Little Mary Anne stood waiting before the tall fireguard, and watching a thick slice of fat bacon sizzling in the frying-pan. That was Nurse's own particular relish on Sunday mornings, which she provided for herself from her store of good things that she kept in the nursery cupboard. This and the fact that they had put on their best frocks and were going to church, made it seem like the Sabbath, as Mr Coulston called Sunday, though their Papa generally referred to it as the Lord's Day.

But Mary Anne had been told that this was Father Christmas's Day, and she stood thinking it over in her little mind as to what was the difference between them, while Harriet was teasing Roger for want of something better to do, and the milk boiled over on the hob because Sarah's back was turned while she cut up the bread for the children's bread and milk.

When at last they all sat round the table silence reigned for a time. Nurse forked her slice of bacon from the pan and replaced it with a slice of bread to fry in the fat.

Harriet gulped down her bowl of bread and milk quickly, and, jumping up, said she was ready to go downstairs.

" You just sit down again and wait then, until the others have finished," commanded Nurse, who was revelling in her fried bread and bacon. " You won't see Father Christmas any the sooner for being in such a hurry."

Mary Anne was always slow, and little Roger had to be fed by Sarah, so Harriet's impatience was sorely tried. But at last they were all ready, and were sent running down to the dining-room, where they found their Mamma seated on one side of the table behind the big silver teapot, and their Papa facing her with a dish of sausages before him.

But where was Father Christmas ?

" I see him ; there he is ! " cried Harriet, pointing to the figure of a little old man with a long white beard, which stood in the centre of the table.

He was holding in his hand the large sprig of holly that Mary Anne had carefully carried home.

" Why, he's not a man at all ! " exclaimed Harriet in disgust.

" He is good old Father Christmas whom we all love," said the Parson, " and he has got something under his coat for each of you : come and see." So saying, he lifted off the top of the little old man, who came in two, and revealed inside his lower half three sugar pigs and three small drums made of cardboard, containing carraway comfits.

" He isn't at all sooty," remarked Mary Anne in bewilderment.

" Perhaps he had a bath before breakfast like me," said
her Papa.

" I don't believe he came down the chimney at all ! "
exclaimed Harriet, disillusioned. " Didn't Miss Speergrove
send him, Mamma ? "

" Yes, dear, he is a present to Roger from her," replied
Mrs Danvers.

" Not to all of us ? " asked the little girls.

" You have your share of the good things he has brought,"
said their Papa, " isn't that enough ? "

But Harriet was jealous and Mary Anne's faith was
shaken. Father Christmas was only a toy after all, and
Nurse and Sarah had told stories about him.

Later on, when they were in church singing—

> " Hark, the herald angels sing,
> Glory to the new-born King——"

Mary Anne was more puzzled than ever, for it seemed that
old Father Christmas had suddenly become a baby again.

Mr Danvers took for his text, " Unto you a child is born,
Unto us a Son is given." And the City Missionary had told
them that what their Papa preached in the pulpit was
Gospel truth. She wondered how that differed from home
truth, or any other kind of truth. It was all very mysterious
to be sure.

6

The following February Mary Anne added another year
to the six that she had already travelled along the rainbow
path of childhood ; and when she went with Harriet into
her parents' bedroom before breakfast on this eventful day
to say her prayers, she received a special blessing from her
Papa, who was still in bed with his nightcap on. But the
solemn words he said to her lost none of their significance
on that account.

Roger was already praying at the dressing-table, which with its candles lighted on either side resembled a high altar, while Mrs Danvers sat before the looking-glass combing her hair.

His childish voice was lisping out the well-known hymn :

> " Gentle Jesus, meek and mild,
> Listen to a little child ;
> Pity my simplicity,
> Suffer me to come to Thee.
>
> Fain I would to Thee be brought ;
> Gracious Lord, forbid it not.
> In the kingdom of Thy grace,
> Grant a little child a place."

His sisters knelt down together before the ottoman at the foot of the big wooden bedstead, and next repeated the morning hymn :

> " Glory to Thee, who safe hast kept,
> And hast refreshed us while we slept.
> Grant, Lord, when we from death shall wake,
> We may of endless life partake."

This was followed by confession of sin and a desire for clean hearts, and the renewing of right spirits within them.

Blessings were then invoked on their parents, grand-mothers, uncles and aunts, ending up with the Lord's Prayer after a special request that the old Adam might be cast out, and a new Adam installed within them.

The two Adams were a mystery to the little girls. Not that Mary Anne thought much about what she was saying. She was more intent on the jam-pot full of treacly stuff that stood upon the dressing-table with a spoon beside it, from which they were sometimes given a portion for health's sake.

It was Harriet who had the inquiring mind, and who wanted to know the meaning of everything. Mary Anne

said her prayers as well as her lessons like a parrot, and
when she knelt down her mind was absorbed in counting
the little white oyster shells which formed the diametrical
pattern on the dark green chintz that covered the ottoman.
Her Mamma's face wore an anxious expression as she listened
with closed eyes to the petitions while arranging her back
hair in a large chenille net. Then she warmly embraced
Mary Anne and presented her with an illumination by her
own fair hand in large letters :

" THOU GOD SEEST ME."

The card was framed to hang up beside her bed and greet
her waking eyes. The text was terrifying to the little girl,
for she possessed the simple faith that believeth all things
in a literal sense.

At breakfast she found on her plate several parcels. One
contained a bookmarker from Harriet with the words
" Many happy returns of the day " worked in silk letters
on perforated cardboard and sewn onto a blue ribbon.

For some time Nurse had been knitting on four steel pins
a pair of little white cotton stockings, like her own, and
Sarah Turke presented a pincushion upon which " Mary
Anne Danvers " was spelt out in pins, surrounded by a
prickly border of flowers designed in the same style. This
was, to the child's mind, a wonderful work of art.

When Miss Manners came in the afternoon she brought
her a doll, with clothes that took off and on, so the little
girl's happiness was complete. Instead of doing lessons
that afternoon as usual, and hemming dusters, Miss Manners
took them for a long walk across the old wooden bridge into
the park on the other side of the river, and home again
over the new suspension.

It was almost dark when they came in, and they kissed

Miss Manners at parting on the doorstep, and ran upstairs to take off their hats and coats.

A bright fire was burning in the nursery, and the black iron kettle was singing a cheery song on the hob. Mary Anne loved to listen to it while she stood warming her cold little hands over the tall fireguard, her heart in tune with the blaze.

The table was laid all ready for tea, and on it was a plain dripping cake and a pot of Nurse's home-made jam, in addition to the usual loaf and salt butter. Sarah was drawing down the blinds and lighting the tallow candles on the chimney-piece.

Mary-Ann Knight had been invited to tea for the occasion. She was now seated on Nurse's low chair with Roger in her lap, reading to him from a rag picture book. It was his favourite, " Who killed Cock Robin ? " and she was saying, " Who saw him die ? I, said the fly, I with my eye, I saw him die." That was certainly conclusive. But the little boy was absorbed in the mysteries of her wooden arm, which ended with an iron hook instead of a hand, and she sat smiling and trying to persuade him to shake hands with the hook.

Harriet was full of curiosity about the wooden arm because it seemed as much alive as the other one ; and she pulled up the sleeve to see where it began.

Then Nurse came in from the night nursery with the baby who had just woken up. She set her down on Mary-Ann Knight's other knee facing Roger, and the wooden arm went round and held her tight.

" Now go and take off your boots, there's good girls, and let poor Ann be," said Nurse, while she warmed the teapot and made the tea.

" And Sarah, you just run downstairs to the kitchen and ask Cook if she can spare us a bit of dripping. Now be quick up again, and don't stay talking, then we'll have some toast for a treat," and she began cutting slices of bread.

" There now, who's going to make the first round ? "

" I will," said Mary-Ann Knight, drawing nearer to the fire. " I with my hook, I will be cook, I, Mary-Ann."

" Come along then, Master Roger, and have your pinafore on," said Nurse. " Now, Miss Molly, reach down the toasting-fork and give it to Mary-Ann."

" I don't want no fork," declared Miss Knight. " My hook'll do as well."

But when Molly saw the slice of bread stuck onto the hook she felt she couldn't touch a morsel of the toast.

" Now, Miss Hetty," called Nurse, " get your pinafores and tie on Molly's, and come and sit down to table."

Hetty and Molly were nursery names bestowed upon the little girls by Nurse, who only gave them their proper titles when she tried to stand upon her dignity like her mistress.

Sarah came panting upstairs with a plentiful supply of good dripping which soon disappeared on the thick rounds of toast.

Nurse bustled about between the fire and the tea-table, spreading and sprinkling, and piling the slices on top of each other until the plate was full ; then she stood it inside the tall fireguard to keep hot, and took the singing kettle from the hob to pour some more water into the teapot, and fill up the children's mugs of milk.

Sarah placed the chairs round the table, and they all sat down to tea feeling very comfortable and cosy.

When the toast was finished came slices of bread and jam, and the little girls were allowed to have tea with sugar in it instead of milk and water because it was Molly's birthday.

Lump sugar was a luxury in those days, so there was only a basin full of coarse brown molasses.

Harriet imitated Nurse, who stirred her tea and left the

spoon in her cup, pouring half into the saucer to cool. She had never seen her Mamma do that, and she was told :

" No now, Miss Hetty, I'll have no messing just because you've got a spoon and sugar."

" Why shouldn't I ? " asked Harriet. " The tea is so hot, and you do it."

" Them as asks questions will hear no stories," snapped Nurse. " You've got milk in your tea to cool it and I haven't. Sarah, you just pour it back again for her."

Nurse had taken the baby on to her lap and was feeding her with a spoon, so the child was unusually quiet and stared about from one to the other with her big brown eyes.

It took quite a long time, with so many good things to eat, before they all gathered round the fire, and Nurse poked it up into a lovely blaze while Sarah cleared away the tea-things.

" Let's tell stories ! " cried Hetty eagerly. " Mary-Ann shall be the first to start."

" I don't know no stories," said Mary-Ann Knight, smiling inanely in the firelight. Nevertheless she was fond of cackling, and she began a long rigmarole about the man who went round every day calling out " Rabbit skins, hare skins ! " with a lot of them suspended on a pole across his shoulders.

" Cook sold him a hare skin the other day," said Molly. " I saw him go down the area steps when I was looking out of the dining-room window. Uncle Charles sent it to us from Norfolk."

" She got fourpence for it," remarked Hetty.

" How do you know ? " asked Nurse.

" Because I asked her, and Mamma said she ought to put it in the Missionary box."

" Whatever for ? " exclaimed Nurse.

" Because the hare was sent to Papa and Mamma for a

present, and so the skin wasn't hers to sell," replied Hetty quickly.

" Stuff and nonsense," said Nurse. " Your Papa and Mamma ate the hare, but they couldn't eat the skin as well. It was Cook's perquisites, and it ain't any business of yours, Miss Harriet, to go telling tales from the kitchen. If I hear any more such stories you shan't have any more of my goodies."

Nurse was a farmer's daughter, and hidden away on the top shelf of the nursery cupboard was a store of farm-house produce from her home in the country, which always arrived at harvest time and lasted through the winter months for her private benefit.

The children knew of a large piece of very fat home-cured bacon from which an occasional rasher was cut on Sundays, and a pot of honey as stiff as cheese, a bottle of elderberry wine, and several jars of jam, one of which had been on the tea-table that very afternoon, besides a stock of nuts and apples which Nurse ate in bed at night.

The supply was getting very low now as it was the end of February, but it was sometimes replenished in the spring by a mysterious little hamper which came by Parcels' Delivery directed to Ann Dane, and was put away in the nursery cupboard, and not unpacked until the children were all in bed and asleep.

Sarah was washing up the tea-things and listening to all that was said. She now began a tale of how her sister Sophy had told her that Father Turke and Daddy Tite had a few words at the church door last Sunday morning.

" It was all along o' Mrs Tite's crinoline," said Sarah. " There was father in his beadle's coat and hat a-standing outside of the church door, as was his rightful place, saying good morning to the people as they went in, when up comes Mrs Tite a-flaunting her crinoline, and she says to father, ' Let me pass ! ' says she, seeing as how her crinny was so big she couldn't get by, though father he is but a little man, as you know."

"They think a lot of themselves, those Tites do, when they're dressed for church," remarked Mary-Ann.

"Well, father said he wasn't going to stand aside for anyone but Mr Danvers and his lady, so she took and swung her crinoline against him and nearly knocked 'im over."

Miss Knight vouched for the truth of this statement, and waving her hook, cried out :

"Yes, that she did ! she just swep' 'im out o' the way with 'er 'oops, for I was a-comin' up behind 'em and I saw 'er do it. She 'as the face for anything, all marked as it is with the small-pox."

"Well, poor thing, she can't help that," said Nurse, "though there's no need for her to show it off so with them bugles on her bonnet."

Sarah proceeded with her story by saying :

"And there stood 'er 'usband be'ind 'er, with 'is top-'at in 'is 'and, and 'e 'ad the himperance to tell father 'e was only a tinker on week-days for all 'e was a beadle on Sundays, and so no better than anyone else. Father, 'e was that taken aback, 'e called Daddy Tite a dirty old cobbler and only fit to patch other people's shoes. And there they 'ad to stop, for all of a suddent round the corner comes Mr Danvers ; and the Tites they squeezed by and took their seats in church. But father says as 'ow 'e ain't going to be insulted by people as wear cast-off clothes ; and Sophy, she's been and written to Mrs Tite and told 'er she'd better 'pologise at once."

"What's 'pologising ? " asked Molly.

"There's a nice question for Sarah," said Nurse, not sorry that the story had come to an end.

"I know ! " cried Hetty. "It's saying you are sorry."

"You won't make Mrs Tite do that in a hurry," clacked Mary-Ann.

" We 'pologise to God when we say our prayers, don't we ? " asked Molly.

" Mayn't Mrs Tite wear her crinoline again until she's 'poligised ? " asked Roger.

" She wouldn't go to church without it ! " snorted Sarah. " She's that ugly, she must be in the fashion."

" She'll have to tell God all about it, and 'pologise to Him if she stays away from church, won't she, Nurse ? " said Molly.

And Hetty said, " I shall ask Mamma not to give her any more crinolines if she behaves like that to Father Turke."

There was a knock at the nursery door, and in walked Maria Swan. This was a pleasant surprise, and both the little girls jumped up and ran to her.

Maria had removed her bonnet and was attired in a neat black dress with a turned-down collar of white embroidery. She also wore a cap and apron. Her hair was arranged like the ears of a spaniel, which covered her own, and her mouth was shaped like the slit of a button-hole.

" Has Mamma got a dinner-party to-night ? " asked Hetty, for on those supreme occasions Maria always came to wait at table.

" Come and tell stories round the fire with us," cried Molly, dragging her into the circle. " We're just in the middle of Mrs Tite."

" Oh, them Tites ! What about her ? " exclaimed Maria, who lived in the same house with them. " The airs she do give herself to be sure, and she only a charwoman ! "

Maria allowed herself to be drawn into the conversation for a minute, then she said, " But I must not forget that Mrs Danvers sent me up to say as she can't have the children downstairs this evening."

" Oh, why not ? " cried Hetty, " and on Molly's birth-day ! It's too bad ! "

" Your Mamma's busy putting out extra silver and glass

from the pantry cupboard," said Maria, " and I must run down and help her."

" Is there going to be a dinner-party ? " asked Molly. " Shan't we go down to dessert ? "

" No, not to-night," replied Nurse. " There's no company, only your aunties and Grandmamma Jackson, and they will be too tired to see little girls and boys, because they have been travelling all the way from Rome, and will want to go to bed early."

' ' Where are they going to sleep ? " inquired Hetty.

" In a hotel, I suppose," said Nurse, " and so they won't stay long, you may be sure."

" Shan't we see them then ? " pouted Hetty. " Oh, Maria, please tell Mamma not to forget that it is Molly's birthday."

Mary-Ann Knight began tying her bonnet-strings and wrapping her black shawl round her wooden arm. She had come to help wash up in the kitchen as there were " extra " to dinner, and it was time to go down and begin to make herself useful.

The fire had burned low, and the baby was getting restless.

" Why, it's six o'clock, I do declare ! " exclaimed Nurse, consulting her gold watch. " There's no going downstairs to-night, so get out your toys and picture books, there's good children, and be quiet while I put baby to bed."

This seemed a very tame ending to a birthday, Molly thought, but she set about undressing her new doll, and put it to bed in the wicker cradle where the old rag doll reposed.

Nurse went into the night-nursery and undressed the baby, who shrieked all the time and was stretching herself out stiff with passion.

" She's that obstinate," said Nurse to Sarah, who was getting the bath ready for the others, " there's no doing anything with her."

E

And that was all the notice Nurse took of such vagaries.

Then came Roger's turn for a tubbing, and Sarah fetched him to be undressed. The little girls were left alone with their dolls until Sarah was ready to crimp their hair.

This was done in the day-nursery, accompanied by a great deal of lively chattering. They had divested themselves of their frocks and were standing before the fire in their little list stays and short flannel petticoats when the door opened and in walked Grandmamma Jackson, followed by their Mamma and two tall aunts who all wore such gigantic crinolines and full-flounced skirts that the room became completely filled by their presence.

Silence fell at their majestic entrance. Even Nurse appeared small in her own domain when she followed them a minute later.

Grandmamma Jackson was a tall and stately dame, with a Roman nose. She advanced towards Hetty and Molly and laid across the bare shoulders of each little girl a striped silk scarf of many colours, which brought Joseph's coat to their minds at once.

"A present from Rome for my granddaughters," she remarked, smiling graciously upon them. "Your dear Mamma is going to spare you both to come and stay with me in the country next week."

The tall aunts stooped to kiss their little nieces, and told them that they would have lessons together when they came to Davenport Hall.

"Miss Manners is our governess," said Hetty, quickly recovering her tongue.

"Miss Manners will have a holiday while you are away," said her Mamma. "And you are very fortunate children to be going on a visit to the country. I hope you will behave yourselves properly. Now thank your kind Grandmamma and say good night. We must just see little Roger in his crib. Is he asleep yet, Nurse? And by the bye, don't forget to give Miss Mary Anne a powder to-night, she looks flushed."

They all swept away into the next room, leaving Hetty grinning and Molly making grimaces, for Hetty was contemplating the visit in prospect, and Molly the taking of the powder.

"Oh, Sarah, I can't swallow it ever!" she complained.

"Perhaps Nurse'll forget all about it, so don't worry, dearie," soothed Sarah.

Harriet didn't care, for she never had to take powders. She began to clap her hands and jump about the room.

"Don't be a baby, Molly," she cried. "What fun we'll have in the country! Grandmamma lives in Suffolk, and we shall see and do all sorts of things we don't here. There's baby crying! They've woken her up, and she's frightened of Grandmamma, like everyone else. Are you frightened of her, Sarah? I'm not, and I don't intend to be."

Nurse came bustling into the room and said the ladies had all gone down to dinner, and a good job too, "For they've woke up the baby just when she'd dropt off, and I must rock her to sleep again, the baggage. And now you both be quick and undress; Sarah must bath you. And just please be as quiet as lambs and no talking."

Mary Anne hoped that Nurse had forgotten all about the powder, but as soon as their nightgowns were on and baby was quiet again she saw her go and fetch the strawberry jam from the nursery cupboard.

Molly watched the process of emptying the contents of the slip of paper into the teaspoon, and the mixing of it with jam by means of a large brass pin which Nurse took from her apron. It didn't seem fair on her birthday, she thought, and why shouldn't Hetty have to take one as well?

Her little soul rebelled at the injustice; but when Nurse approached, holding out the spoon, she meekly opened her mouth and gulped it down.

The children talked in whispers about the coming visit long after Nurse had put the candle out and left the room.

Just before they fell asleep who should peep in but Maria Swan.

" Are you awake, dearies ? " she said.   " I just ran up to tell you such a lovely bit of news.   Your Grandma has asked me to go to Davenport Hall and see after you.   That will be nice, won't it ? "

" Oh, Maria, what fun ! " exclaimed Hetty.

" Yes, won't it be ?   And now I must run down again and take coffee to the drawing-room, or Phœbe will be after me.   But I thought I'd be the first to tell you.   So good night and pleasant dreams."

She gave each little girl a kiss and left the room.   Harriet soon fell asleep, but Mary Anne still tasted the powder, and she woke up in the night with a pain inside.

III. DAVENPORT HALL

" Gather instruction from thy youth up : so shalt thou find wisdom till thine old age."—Ecclesiasticus.

I

THE two children, in charge of Maria Swan, were driven to the station in Worby's cab one wet morning the following week, and sent off to Suffolk. The aforesaid vehicle was a very capacious four-wheeler, and Worby, its proprietor, was a fine old grey-beard, who wore a rough beaver hat and a huge overcoat of thick drab cloth with three graduated capes which covered him to the middle ; that being the fashion in those days amongst cabmen and watchmen to protect them from the inclemency of the weather to which they were exposed.

Mrs Danvers' large black wooden trunk containing the wardrobes of the little girls was carried downstairs on this portly man's shoulders and thrust on to the roof of the cab, where Maria's humbler box in its neat holland case already occupied a small space.

Nurse was hugged upstairs, Mamma was kissed downstairs, and stood waving her hand at the dining-room window while their Papa tucked them up in a rug, for it was bitterly cold, and with fond farewell injunctions he shut the door of the old hackney coach. Worby hoisted himself on to the box, and away they drove.

Harriet was far too excited to mind much about leaving home, but Mary Anne was very silent. The train was slow, and they arrived at their destination late in the

afternoon, tired out with the journey. After tea they
went to bed, according to their Grandmamma's direc-
tions.

The next morning they awoke to a " white world," as
their Aunt Anna said at breakfast. Snow was lying on the
ground, and it felt very cold after smoky London.

But before they returned home at the end of the month
the primroses were peeping out in the hedges and the birds
were singing in the woods, telling of such delights as the
two town-bred children had no idea of.

When Maria came to their bedside and said it was time
to get up, and that they were to breakfast with their Grandmamma and aunts, Harriet was out of bed at once, and
pulling sleepy little Molly after her.

" Mamma said we were to wear our linsey dresses every
day," she dictated to Maria while her stockings were being
dragged on.

" And you'll find them none too warm in this cold place,"
Maria answered with a shiver. She had unpacked the big
black box overnight and laid everything neatly in the
drawers of a large bureau in the bedroom.

Harriet now turned them all topsy-turvy in a vain search
for a new pair of garters she had knitted for herself with
Nurse's help.

Maria's sister Ellen was a sempstress, and she had been at
work for the past week getting the little girls' clothes in
order for the visit.

A voluminous black silk skirt of their Mamma's had been
turned and made over into pelisses for Sundays, and aprons
were also contrived out of it, trimmed with white-edged
ribbon velvet, to take the place of pinafores.

This was a great promotion—Hetty declared that
pinafores were only fit for the nursery.

Mary Anne was also allowed to wear stockings and garters
for the first time instead of thin white cotton socks, and she

was so long putting them on that Hetty hustled her through the rest of her toilet and upset her equilibrium.

" Now, now, Miss Harriet dear," remonstrated Maria, " just let Miss Mary Anne alone, and she will be ready as soon as you are."

" She is such a slow-coach ! " exclaimed Hetty. " That's what Papa calls her, and she must learn to be quicker."

Maria Swan had been carefully instructed by Mrs Danvers to give the young ladies their full titles while on this visit, and never to omit the " Miss." She felt the importance of it while staying in such a grand house, with a retinue of servants, and was inclined to give herself airs in consequence.

" Shall we have to go to Grandmamma's room and say our prayers to her ? " asked Mary Anne, realising that it was the first time in her little life that she had been separated from her Mamma and Nurse.

" No, lovey, I'll hear you say them," replied Maria, as she tied the narrow velvet ribbon around the fair hair which was now crimped out all over Molly's shoulders.

" We shall say our prayers to God, not Grandmamma," remarked Harriet.

Now kneeling at Maria's knee in strange surroundings, Mary Anne's lip quivered and her little voice trembled when she came to " God bless my dear Mamma and Papa." But she was not going to cry, since Hetty didn't seem to care, for she was pattering glibly on to " for ever and ever, Amen."

Then up she jumped, saying, " Oh, Maria, we have forgotten to put on our new aprons ! I thought of them just as we were saying, ' Give us this day our daily bread.' Mamma said we were to wear them always at meals."

" Yes to be sure, so she did ! " said Maria, going to a drawer to find them. " Lor ! whatever is that awful din ? "

The big clock in the hall was striking nine as the sound of the breakfast gong rang through the house. It startled them all, for they had not heard a gong before.

2

Maria Swan led her two young ladies into the large dining-room, which was flanked at the entrance by four marble pillars, and opened through French windows on to the garden at the further end.

Grandmamma was seated, very upright, at the head of the long dinner-table which was laid for breakfast. A large Bible and prayer-book lay open before her. Two aunts sat facing her from the window, and each called a little niece to a vacant chair at her side. " Come, ye children, and hearken unto me," Mrs Jackson began, when she noticed them ; " I will teach you the fear of the Lord."

A wooden bench was carried in by the footman and placed between the pillars. Maria joined a line of servants, who filed in and filled it, leaving no room for her. She was allowed to sit upon one of the brown leather chairs with a duster spread over it.

Then the Family Prayers began, and Mary Anne thought they would never come to an end.

Mrs Jackson prayed in measured tones from the open book before her. " Blessed Lord, who has caused all Holy Scriptures to be written for our learning " was the pre-liminary. A chapter from the Old Testament and one from St Luke followed. Then all stood up to read verses from the Psalms in turn. It interested the little girls to hear the servants making mistakes and being corrected by their aunts.

Next came a sudden whisking round of crinolines, and the whole household went down upon its knees while Mrs Jackson repeated collects and said prayers " like being in church," as Hetty afterwards remarked to Maria.

It was a relief when at last they stood up again and sang a hymn, which was led off by Miss Jackson in a fine soprano voice :

" New every morning is the love
Our wakening and up-rising prove ;
Through sleep and darkness safely brought,
Restored to life and power and thought."

Harriet and Mary Anne knew the whole of it by heart and joined in the singing, which won the approval of their aunts.

When all was ended and the servants had left the room, followed by Maria, the footman quickly reappeared, carrying a leather post-bag on a tray which he presented to Mrs Jackson, who produced a key from her chatelaine and unlocked it.

Letters were handed round, and Grandmamma called the little girls to her side and told them to read a chapter from the Bible until breakfast was ready.

" Molly can't read yet," said Harriet.

" Then it behoves her to listen while you do so, and apply herself to learn," replied Mrs Jackson.

To Mary Anne this seemed unendurable, and she began to yawn for want of food. At home the nursery breakfast was early, and she longed to be there. But Hetty was showing how well she could read, and was feeling no pangs at being promoted to meals with her elders.

At last the footman entered the room bearing a tray with hot coffee and milk and boiled eggs and toast. There was home-made bread and brawn upon the table, to a slice of which each child was helped by their aunts. But Mary Anne did not like either. Her Aunt Anna perceived that the bread tasted of tallow and she rang the bell sharply.

" Charles," she said when the footman came in answer to the summons, " remove this loaf, it reeks of tallow fat, and bring another one quickly."

" He's laughing," remarked Hetty as the man left the room.

" Little girls are to be seen, not heard," said her Grandmamma, who was reading her correspondence.

When Charles returned, bearing another loaf on a tray he said :

" Please, ma'am, Cook sends her respects, but this one will be as bad ; she had the misfortune to drop a dip into the yeast pan yesterday, and it has flavoured the whole batch."

" I will speak to Cook about it later on," said Mrs Jackson sternly. " You can leave the room."

" Extremely careless ! " declared Miss Jackson. " We had better drive into Southbury this afternoon and bring back some bread from the baker. I also require a few things at the draper."

" Doesn't the baker call like he does at home ? " asked Harriet.

" No, my dear, we bake our own bread in the country, and what we can't make we sometimes have to go without," said her aunt.

" I had rather go without, please," said Mary Anne.

" My dear, nobody asked what you preferred," said Mrs Jackson, laying aside her letters.

Molly was compelled to finish the brawn and bread that she would fain have left on her plate, while Harriet, having eaten hers, was fidgeting on her chair.

When they were allowed to rise from the table the clock was striking ten, and they were told to run away and look for Maria.

" You may come back again in half an hour," said Aunt Emma, " and we will do some lessons together."

Away from Mrs Jackson, Harriet found her tongue again, but Mary Anne was silent and shivering with cold.

" Grandmamma doesn't wear a crinoline, does she ? "

said Hetty ; " but Aunt Emma's is immense, bigger than Mamma's Sunday one. I don't see why we shouldn't wear ours as well as our aprons every day while we are here. We look so flat without them."

" Your aunts are finely dressed ladies and no mistake," remarked Maria. " Silk robes and gold lockets, with streamers reaching from neck to heel, to come down to breakfast in to be sure ! But there ! They've been travelling about a lot, and have picked up grand notions and foreign ways no doubt ; and your Grandmamma must be a rich lady. Now come along, and we will have a look round this fine house."

The little girls had never been in such a big place and would have lost themselves if they had not met another aunt on the stairs who had been breakfasting in bed.

She took them into her room and showed them her drawings and books.

" It is too cold to go out this morning," she said, " while the snow lies on the ground ; but if you are well and strong that is the best way to get warm."

" Molly has chilblains," said Hetty, " and she can't bear her feet to be wet and cold, but I don't mind in the least."

" Poor little Molly ! " said her aunt. " Never mind, we will stay indoors to-day."

When it was time for lessons she took her little nieces downstairs to the morning-room where the two other aunts were practising duets on the piano.

The noisy overture to *William Tell* came to an end as they entered. Miss Jackson turned round on the music-stool and regarded her nieces.

" We must have some system in teaching these children," she remarked, " in order that they may return home with their minds improved. I think it would be the best arrangement for us to take them in turn for different studies."

Mary Anne shook in her sandal shoes while her aunt continued to say :

" For instance, if Anna instructs them in reading, writing and arithmetic this morning, Selina and I might take them to-morrow for drawing and the piano. By that means we shall all be freer to follow our own inclinations while they are with us."

This was agreed upon as an excellent arrangement, and the youngest Miss Jackson at once led off the little girls, who were overawed at the prospect of so many instructresses.

They found their Grandmamma sitting in a very upright armchair by the fireside, and she was knitting some very thick wool into strips on long wooden pins. A Bible largely printed lay open in her lap.

" Well, my dear children," she said, looking up as they entered the room, " has Mamma taught you how to knit ? "

" No, but Nurse has," replied Harriet quickly, " though it's not a bit like your knitting, Grandmamma."

" What sort of knitting is it then ? " asked Mrs Jackson.

" She makes her own stockings on four steel pins with white cotton, and she has knitted herself a bed-quilt as well."

" Indeed ! " remarked Mrs Jackson. " And you must be very clever little girls if you can do the same."

" Oh, but we can't ! " explained Hetty. " We can only knit our garters. I made a pair for Mamma at Christmas, and Molly made some for Nurse."

" And are you being taught the use of the globes ? " enquired Mrs Jackson.

" What are they ? " asked Harriet.

Grandmamma lifted her hands in astonishment.

" I fear your education is being sadly neglected if you do not even know what the globes are," she said. " Anna, you must really see that dear Agnes's children are properly grounded in geography while they are with us, and they had better take the globes back with them."

"But we do learn geography with Miss Manners from 'Stepping-stones.' Won't they do as well as the globes?"

"Nothing can equal the use of the globes," replied Mrs Jackson. "Let us hope that during the short time you are here you may advance considerably in knowledge."

"Mamma said that we were going to stay a whole month," said Hetty.

"That's a very long time," sighed Molly.

"It may seem so to little girls," said Aunt Anna as she laid two slates with pencils and two copy-books with pens and ink upon a table in the window. "But time is never long enough for all you have to learn."

Mary Anne heaved another big involuntary sigh. She was thinking of dear Miss Margery Manners and her easy questions and answers to be repeated every day by heart, with sometimes a new one committed to memory.

The children were told to seat themselves on chairs placed for them at the table. Their aunt observed:

"Now I must first find out how much you know, and then how much you don't know."

Mrs Jackson continued to knit by the fireside. She was heard to remark that a child of Harriet's age ought to be able to read and spell properly, and to repeat the multiplication table by heart; and that Mary Anne, having been taught with her sister, should be equally proficient according to her years.

Molly was an observant child. Being always too shy to enter into conversation and to answer questions as Hetty did, she nevertheless took notice of all that was said. Under her placid exterior lay a wildly beating heart, and when it came to her turn to repeat "twice one are two, twice two are four," although she knew it like a parrot from beginning to end she could only stare at her sister, who made signs with her fingers and tried to help her, to no purpose.

If only Grandmamma had not expected so much!

Harriet was delighted with herself, and whispered to Mary Anne not to be stupid.

" Now we will have some reading, if you please," said their aunt ; and she opened a book called *Mrs Markham's History of England*.

" We have that at home," said Hetty, " but Molly can't read it."

" Then she can hold the back-board and listen," said Aunt Anna, taking up an instrument of wood with holes and pegs in the handle-bars for adjustment, which she proceeded to fit on to Mary Anne's back like a cross.

" Stand up now before me," she said, " and pay attention while Harriet reads aloud, for at the end of the chapter I shall question you both on what it is about."

In this strange new attitude Molly's mind was less receptive than ever, and the only question she could have answered correctly was given to Hetty, being the date on which William the Conqueror came to the throne.

Writing in the copy-books came next, with penholders that had little pedestals for their thumbs and fingers. Mary Anne was praised for her pot-hooks, and Harriet was blamed for making blots.

Sums were then set on the slates, and Aunt Anna went to warm herself at the fire while they were being done.

" Harriet is intelligent," she remarked to Mrs Jackson, " but I am afraid Mary Anne is a little dunce." And Molly overheard it.

3

At the end of the time devoted to lessons Harriet had won approval, and Mary Anne had given but a poor impression of her abilities.

Mrs Jackson called her to her side and said solemnly :

" My child, it is your duty in life to improve your mind. If you are not so quick as your sister in learning

your lessons, it behoves you to be all the more painstaking."

The tears came into Molly's eyes. Had Miss Manners
been there she would have declared that if Mary Anne was
slow to learn she was persevering and never idle.

The little girl longed to escape, but she was detained by
her Grandmamma, who said :

" My dear, it is not a fit morning for you to go out. You
may stay by the fire with me, and I will show you how to
rub my knees ; they are very stiff and painful. It is your
duty to be useful as well as intelligent."

She produced a piece of yellow brimstone from her silk
pocket and gave it to Molly, whose little hand went up and
down under Mrs Jackson's black crepe skirts until her
arms ached and her knees were sore with kneeling.

" I trust you are being taught to read your Bible every
day, my dear," said her Grandmamma as she closed the
book upon her lap and laid it aside. " All Scripture is
given by inspiration of God, and is profitable for doctrine,
for reproof, for correction, for instruction in righteousness.
The beautiful collect that I always repeat at Family
Prayers says that God caused all Holy Scriptures to be
written for our learning. We must therefore learn to read
and mark inwardly, as it bids us, and try to digest them
with His Almighty help. Can you say the collects by heart ?
Then you may repeat this one to me while you are rubbing
my knees."

But to do two things at once was never possible to Mary
Anne without failing in both. The little arm flagged when
the small brain began to work by trying to remember how
the collect began.

" Blessed Lord," prompted her Grandmamma, " Who
has caused all . . . Holy Scriptures . . ." and so on all
through Molly stumbled and stuttered to the end.

Harriet had left the room with her aunt when the lessons

were over, and Mary Anne was longing to be released too. She thought she had never spent such a dull morning before.

Now Hetty was really enjoying herself, and looking forward to being taught by three different aunts in turn. At this moment she was in the morning-room seeing them play battledore and shuttlecock. It was much more exciting than having only Miss Manners day after day, and learning to hem dusters.

The first morning at Davenport Hall was over.

Punctually at three o'clock that afternoon Mrs Jackson's barouche, drawn by a fine pair of grey horses, came round to the door to convey her to Southbury. This was the nearest town for shopping, and it was six miles away. The little girls who accompanied her thought it a very dull place indeed. They went to the draper's shop, " which was nothing like so large and important as Mr Peters' at home," said Harriet, " where Mamma buys all our things." Miss Jackson took her inside with her, leaving Mary Anne with her Grandmamma in the carriage.

They drove to the baker to get some bread, and then went to the grocer, where Mrs Jackson ordered a long list of goods. A number of empty pickle-bottles were put under the seat, and Molly wondered what they were for, but she was not inquisitive, and seldom asked questions as her sister did.

The drive back seemed long and tedious, in spite of the pair of horses, which were fat and well-fed, and only proceeded at a measured pace.

The little girls soon learned that every day in the country was more or less alike. Occasionally they were taken for a drive, but it was not so enjoyable as going with their Mamma through the streets to pay calls, or into the Park. Oftener they walked on the wet country roads with Maria.

They had not been at Davenport a week before they made friends in the servants' hall, and Harriet's high spirits ran away with her below stairs. She was soon on intimate terms with Charles the footman, and got quite beyond the control of Maria, who did not approve of her young ladies " making so free," as she called it, with the servants.

" Whatever would your Ma say ? " she complained. " You will get me into trouble, Miss."

But Hetty only replied, " I don't care ; I shall do as I please."

4

The time of day that the little girls liked best while they stayed at Davenport Hall was when, after having had tea with Maria, they were allowed to spend an hour in the drawing-room with their Grandmamma and aunts until the gong sounded for dressing before the late dinner.

With the lamps alight and the shutters closed, the heavy crimson curtains drawn across the large windows, and the fire piled up with logs of wood, blazing brightly, all went to make a very pleasant interior.

The aunts would be occupied in doing Berlin wool-work, and Grandmamma continued her knitting. Sometimes Miss Jackson read articles from the newspaper aloud, or she would sing old plantation-songs, in the chorus of which they all joined.

" I'll bet my money on de bob-tailed nag, do-da, do-da, do-da, day " was the one Hetty liked best, but Molly's favourite was the same as her aunt Anna's :

" 'Tis the song, the sigh of the weary—
    Hard times, hard times, come again no more !
Many days you have lingered around my cabin door,
    Oh, hard times, come again no more ! "

The little girls were allowed to do much as they pleased during this restful hour ; the ladies would unbend in their

F

manners, and laugh and talk with them while they worked, and ask them all about home.

Aunt Selina showed them how to do the wool-work on canvas, like the chairs about the room, which were covered with the handiwork of their aunts, done in bunches of red roses like the carpet at home.

Mary Anne would amuse herself on the hearth-rug with the solitaire board and its pretty glass marbles, which she was allowed to take from its place on the large round rose-wood table in the centre of the room.

But Harriet never cared to play by herself, neither was she capable of remaining quiet like her sister for any length of time. So she was not sorry when the dressing-bell rang and good-night was said.

It was the signal for Maria to appear in her best cap and apron, and fetch the young ladies to bed, when their elders went upstairs to array themselves in evening attire.

One night when the gong was sounding for dinner, and Mrs Jackson and her daughters were sailing down the wide staircase clad in black bombazine and coloured silks, two little figures in red flannel dressing-gowns and list slippers emerged from their bedroom at the end of a long corridor to peep at the ladies.

Quick as lightning Hetty darted to the top of the staircase, followed by Molly, with Maria at their heels.

Charles was making such a noise on the gong that they could not be heard, and they were careful not to be seen as they peered through the banisters.

" You naughty little girls, what are you doing here ? " said the lady's-maid, who came out of Mrs Jackson's room behind them.

" Oh, Miss Pratt ! " exclaimed Maria starting round, " aren't they tiresome ? Miss Harriet won't mind a word I say, and she leads her sister into all sorts of mischief. They wanted to see their aunts dressed for the evening."

" We just caught sight of them as they went into the dining-room and Charles shut the door," cried Hetty. " Aunt Emma wore a low dress with all her shoulders bare, didn't she, Pratt ? and Aunt Selina had on a white lace skirt with flounces, and a shawl to keep her warm, hadn't she, Molly ? "

" Yes, and Aunt Anna went in first, although she is the youngest, and so we couldn't see her properly. What did she wear, Pratt ? Do tell us."

" Well then, since you must know," laughed the lady's-maid, " she put on blue silk all trimmed with black lace that she's very fond of, because she was much admired in it abroad. It does become her and no mistake ; and they are expecting some company after dinner. It has had a lot of wear," she went on, turning to Maria. " When it's done with I shall have it dyed a dark plum and it will do me nicely for Sundays, turned over. I shan't get the lace, however, it's real Spanish, and will go on to a new dress, no doubt. Well, good-night, young ladies ; now go along with Miss Swan like good children," and Miss Pratt disappeared down the back staircase.

Instead of returning to bed Harriet popped into her aunts' room, dragging Molly with her. There they found a crinoline on the floor and the discarded afternoon dresses lying on the beds.

Intent on diversion, Harriet quickly put on some of these garments and began twirling round before the long pier-glass, regardless of Maria's persuasive promises to sing them to sleep.

Maria had hold of Mary Anne firmly by the hand, and threatened to go and fetch Miss Pratt again if Miss Harriet " didn't come along this very minute."

" I don't care for Pratt ! " laughed Hetty as she whisked round and round to make the silk skirt bulge out like a balloon.

" Then I'll just go down to your Grandma ! " declared

Maria in a rage. But Hetty knew that she would never dare to disturb them at dinner, so she continued to romp about in her aunts' clothes, calling on Molly to put on the crinoline.

" I'd just like to know what your Ma would say if she could see you ! " exclaimed the worried woman. " I shall write to her to-morrow and say as I'm going to leave you here alone because you won't mind what I tell you."

" There now," she added, seeing that her threat had taken effect ; " are you coming to bed like a good girl ? "

" Not unless you will sing us to sleep as you promised," replied Hetty.

" It's more than you deserve then," retorted Maria, seeing that she had gained the day, for Harriet was disrobing herself, and the crinoline was once more reclining on the floor.

" I wonder why Aunt Anna didn't wear it to-night," remarked Mary Anne.

" Because of her flounces, I expect," replied Harriet. " We've got flounces on our new dresses, haven't we, Maria ? But I mean to wear my crinny all the same." And away she skipped, darting along the passage, followed by Mary Anne.

When they had said their prayers and were tucked up together in the big bed, Miss Swan seated herself on the edge of it, and began singing the evening hymn in a loud nasal voice, which the little girls admired because they could hear it in church above everyone else.

The six verses lagged to an end, and she started off again with " Nearer my Gawd to Thee, nearer to Thee, E'en though it be a cross that raiseth me——" becoming very flat as it drew to a close.

Maria liked to hear her own voice raised in spiritual song, and she was about to begin another hymn, but the children were getting sleepy and gave her no further encouragement ; so she kissed them, being in quite a good humour again, lit a night-light on the wash-stand, and left them.

5

The following evening when Miss Swan went to fetch her young ladies from the drawing-room, she had recourse to tactics by quietly turning the key of the door as she followed them into their bedroom. But Hetty was unusually docile, and Molly seemed sleepy.

They had apparently forgotten all about the frolic of the evening before. Even the sound of the gong for dinner did not awaken Miss Harriet to action.

Nevertheless Maria prided herself on her forethought and laughed in her " leg-of-mutton " sleeve.

" Maria dear," wheedled Hetty while her hair was being brushed, " please don't do it in so many plaits to-night, we are so tired."

" Dearie me then, what have you been doing to tire yourselves ? You've only been for a drive with your Grandma this afternoon."

" But it was such a long, dull drive ! " sighed Hetty. " All the way to Southbury again, and shut up tight inside. And Molly was nearly sick sitting back to the horses."

" Yes, I was," put in Mary Anne, " and Aunt Anna was cross because I had to change over and sit between her and Grandmamma."

" Well, I think I had better be giving you one of those powders then," said Maria.

" Oh, no, no ! " cried Molly. " I feel quite well again now ! "

" Well, well, we'll see. And what did you do in South-bury to tire yourselves so ? " asked Maria while she braided the golden locks.

" We went to the undertaker," said Hetty, " and took some pieces of silk to be pinked out for Aunt Anna's new dress, you know, that Pratt is making. And then we went to the grocer, and Charles told him to come to the carriage door and take the orders."

" We didn't go in the shop, like we do at home," said Molly, " and we ordered pounds and pounds of sugar and tea and coffee and currants and raisins and peel, and all sorts of things ; much more than Mamma ever does from Mr Chaine."

" And then Grandmamma asked if he had any more empty bottles to fill with tea-leaves for the poor," said Hetty. " They must be horrid to drink."

" So I should think," observed Maria, " but poor folks can't afford to be particular, they have to put up with the crumbs that fall from the rich man's table."

" Is Grandmamma rich ? " asked Molly.

" Well I dare say she's a deal better off than many people, living as she does in this fine house, and travelling abroad when she chooses," remarked Maria.

" I mean to be rich when I grow up," said Harriet, " and have a lot of silk dresses and lockets like Aunt Emma, and a gold watch and chain like Nurse."

" Come now and have your face washed, Miss Mary Anne," called Maria. " And you, Miss Harriet, kneel down and say your prayers, and don't forget to ask Gawd to give you a clean heart, for you've not been behaving as your Ma would wish."

Very soon both the little girls were in bed, and Maria, seating herself upon it, began to sing :

> " Abide with me, fast falls the eventide ;
> The darkness deepens, Lord, with me abide."

This was her favourite hymn, and she drawled it out in a high-pitched key, which seemed too much for Hetty's nerves ; she wriggled about and said she wanted to go to sleep.

Maria lit the night-light, remarking crossly, " I can't

think what's the matter with you to-night ; but after all it's better than if you were tearing up and down the passage with me after you."

Saying this, she softly unlocked the door and went down-stairs to her supper in the servants' hall.

A minute later Hetty slipped out of bed and put on her dressing-gown.

" It's all right, she's gone at last. Come along, Molly, and be quick." So saying, she ran to the washstand and picking up the night-light, led the way out, and along the corridor to their aunts' room.

She had inspired her sister during the dull drive with a desire to take part in an escapade.

" Hetty, you are a story-teller ! " whispered Molly. " You said you were so sleepy, and you are not a bit."

" Well, I'm not now, and it will be such fun," replied Harriet. " You shall dress up as Aunt Anna and I will be Aunt Emma. But we must be ever so quick, while Pratt is having her supper, or she will be coming up to tidy the room."

They shut themselves in, and Hetty lit the big wax candles on the fine dressing-table which was a charming arrangement of white muslin and lace, like their Mamma's at home.

Everything was lying about just as their aunts had left them, and Hetty was soon arrayed in the voluminous brown silk dress that Aunt Emma had cast off, while Mary Anne was struggling with Aunt Anna's crinoline before putting over it the black and white check silk gown that she had been wearing that day.

Finishing touches were added at the looking-glass with the lockets and brooches that were lying there, and blue ribbon streamers all complete.

Harriet quickly unplaited her hair and stuffed it into a large chenille net that lay on the dressing-table. Then she went to the wardrobe to see what more she could find. She fetched out a pork-pie hat with a red ostrich feather and a long gauze veil, with which she crowned herself.

A pink parasol with a fringed border and a folding handle was brought to light from behind a lot of dresses, and thrust into Molly's hand. With a final survey of themselves in the long pier-glass, they opened the door and sallied forth.

Harriet led the way in the direction of the back stairs.

" Where are you going? I don't want to come," remonstrated Mary Anne.

" Don't be a goose," said Hetty sharply ; " you can stay here by yourself then ! "

But that idea did not commend itself to Molly. There was no alternative. She must follow her mischievous sister.

" Now you must hold your tongue and tread on tip-toe," said Harriet, " and mind you don't tumble downstairs."

They stood whispering for a moment at the top of the short flight, then, gathering up the full skirts around their little figures, down they crept.

The footman came at that moment through the red baize door which led from the dining-room to the kitchen premises. He was carrying an empty tray, which fell to the floor with a clatter.

" Lawk-a-mercy ! " he exclaimed on catching sight of the little girls.

" Charles, Charles ! " whispered Hetty gleefully, " be quiet and don't say a word. We are coming to the kitchen if Pratt isn't there. Do go and see for us."

The footman was convulsed, but he managed to say, " It's all right, miss, she's sitting at supper with Miss Swan in the servants' hall."

" Then give me the parasol, Molly, and follow me," said Harriet, dropping her skirts as she opened the sunshade.

But Mary Anne was left behind, for Aunt Anna's crinoline

proved quite unmanageable, and finally shed itself on the
passage floor.

In fits of laughter Charles lifted the little girl up without
it and carried her bodily into the august presence of the
cook, who was in the act of making a cheese omelet.

Harriet, who was in advance, held the pink parasol high
over the red feather and the pork-pie hat. Then she elon-
gated her back and strutted into the kitchen.

" Well I never ! " exclaimed the cook, throwing up her
hands. " What's become of Miss Swan ? If you ain't the
living image of Miss Jackson ! "

The housemaid and the kitchenmaid laughed and clapped
their hands.

" Hush, hush, don't let Pratt and Maria hear ! " said
Hetty. " They are in the servants' hall."

" Please, Charles, throw me up to the ceiling to make
a balloon like Mr Coulston does at home," cried Molly,
who was getting as excited as her sister. And up she went
the next moment in the arms of the footman, laughing and
screaming, followed by Hetty, who laid the pink parasol
on the floor.

" 'Tisn't very nice for your aunt's silk gownds to be
trailing about the kitchen," remarked the housemaid,
picking up the parasol.

" The floor's as clean as the parlour carpet ! " declared
the kitchenmaid indignantly, " or I should know it soon
enough."

The dining-room bell rang sharply.

" Lor' bless us, the omelet ! " cried the cook ; " I've
clean forgot all about it," and she turned to the pan to find
it burnt to a cinder.

" Now what's to do ? " asked Charles in dismay. " Caroline will be after me if I don't look sharp."

" Oh, we don't want her here, do we ? " said Hetty.
" She gives herself such airs," and she began to take

off the parlourmaid for the amusement of the other servants.

The cook clapped the omelet on to a dish and covered it over quickly with parsley.

" There ! " she said, " if they say anything about it, tell 'em we want a new frying-pan."

" Oh, what a story ! " exclaimed Molly.

" It's gorspel truth, missie," said Cook, " for the bottom is burnt right out of this all along o' your pranks. Now you'd best be off upstairs to bed or we shall have Miss Swan comin' in to see what's all the noise about."

" Oh, please give us something nice to eat," pleaded Mary Anne.

" That I will," said the good-natured woman. " Here's a jam tart for each of you. Why, we haven't had such a laugh in the kitchen ever since I come to live here, God bless your dear little hearts. I hope you won't get into trouble." And she gave them each a hot hug, following them to the door just as Charles, on his way to the dining-room, was in the act of falling over Miss Anna's crinoline, which was lying in the passage where Molly had left it.

For a second time the omelet came to grief, and while the footman was disentangling himself the bell rang sharply again, and the parlourmaid appeared at the swing door in a flurry.

" Sakes alive ! " she exclaimed, " whatever are you up to, Charles ? The ladies are that impatient ! "

" There's the omelet," said the footman, pointing to the floor. " You can say I was a-coming along with it when I met the family ghost walking in a crinoline, and it wouldn't let me pass."

He proceeded to fasten the hoops round his waist, and taking hold of the cook, who was looking on at the doorway, they whirled round together for the amusement of the little girls, who were peering down into the passage from the top of the stairs.

" Oh, Charles, please give us the crinny ! " whispered Hetty. " We must take it back. Oh, do be quick or we shall be caught."

6

Miss Pratt and Miss Swan were seated together at the table in the servants' hall discussing their mutual interests over bread and cheese and a jug of beer.

" Dear me," remarked one to the other, " what a noise they are making in the kitchen, to be sure. What can be going on to make 'em so merry ? "

But they were more interested in their own concerns, feeling themselves somewhat superior in their position to vulgar kitchen jokes.

" It's that Charles, I'll be bound," said the staid Miss Pratt. " I declare he's a regular merry-andrew."

Presently when all was quiet again and they had finished their supper, the kitchenmaid entered and laid the table afresh for the other servants.

Of her they took no notice, but when her majesty the Cook came in and sat herself down in a Windsor arm-chair, they felt that their *tête-à-tête* was ended.

" You've been making merry in the kitchen to-night," observed Miss Pratt.

" Yes, we've 'ad visitors callin' on us," replied Cook, still breathless. " And one of 'em left 'er crinoline behind."

" Lor ! " remarked Maria primly, " and 'ow did that 'appen ? "

" It come right off on the floor," continued the cook, " and Charles he dressed himself up in it and led me a fine dance down the passage. I ain't got me breath back yet," and she went on laughing. Presently she added, " You'd best go and see if your young ladies are a-bed, Miss Swan, for Charles declared they'd been walking in their sleep."

This she said to get rid of Miss Swan, whom she found too prim and pious for her taste.

Maria, flustered and apprehensive at the bare idea, made off at once, and was soon followed by Pratt, who went to get her ladies' rooms ready for bedtime.

There was no cause for alarm. All was quiet ; the night-light burning dim on the washstand, and peaceful breathing came from under the bedclothes.

Maria left the room, having satisfied herself that her young charges were asleep, and went along the wide corridor to see if she might be allowed to help Miss Pratt.

" There's rather a bad tear in this new silk dress Miss Jackson was wearing," observed the lady's-maid, holding it out for Maria's inspection. " Just look, it's all out of the gathers too ! However can she have done it ? She ain't one for climbing over stiles with that long straight back of hers."

" I wonder she don't get married," remarked Maria as she helped Miss Pratt tidy up. " Such fine-looking ladies as they all are, and seeing the world too, as they've been doing."

" It ain't for want of offers, so I've heard tell," replied Pratt. " Miss Anna is as good as engaged to a gentleman she met in Rome ; but Miss Jackson, being the eldest— well, there is such a thing as going through the wood and picking up a crooked stick at the last."

Uttering this mystic sentence, Miss Pratt whisked across the corridor into Mrs Jackson's room to perform her duties there, and Maria followed out of sheer curiosity.

The overpowering feature of this apartment was the bed. It had the appearance of a royal hearse, with four massive posts of turned mahogany, and hangings of purple damask, enclosing almost completely the coverlet of patchwork made in octagonal sections of pieces of satin.

Miss Swan had never seen such furniture before, and she was also interested in the gossip.

The lady's-maid was standing in front of a gigantic mahogany wardrobe with deep drawers and rows of shelves above them, in which she was replacing her mistress's caps and laces. On either side were spacious hanging-cupboards, where all the gowns of silk and satin and crêpe that Mrs Jackson possessed were suspended. The wardrobe was large enough, in Maria's estimation, to hold clothes for a life-time.

" Yes, it's a fine piece of furniture, but too heavy for my taste," replied Pratt.

" I should feel suffocated if I had to sleep in that bed," remarked Maria, turning towards it. " The old lady's had a large family in it, hasn't she ? Didn't you say as there were more married daughters than single ? "

" That's so," replied Pratt as she folded the white cash-mere shawl that Mrs Jackson had worn during the day. " There's your Mrs Danvers, and Mrs Rashlegh, and Mrs Musgrave as died not long ago, poor thing, leaving six little ones ; then there's Mrs Ingram : she's an officer's wife out in India, so we don't see much of her, but I believe she's coming home shortly with her babies. They do say as she is the liveliest and handsomest of the lot."

" And how many sons is there ? " asked Maria.

" The eldest died, and there's three left," said Miss Pratt.

" Two of them often comes to dine with Mr and Mrs Danvers," remarked Maria. " I've seen them when I've been waiting at table there; such nice, good-looking gentle-men they are, to be sure. I suppose they live in London."

" Yes, they don't come here except when there's some shooting on," said Pratt. " And then there's Mr Harry ; he's the youngest of them all, and he's going to be a hofficer."

" Ah, that's a fine thing to be, so long as there ain't a war," was the complacent comment of Miss Swan.

" There now, I've finished, and here comes Louisa to turn down the beds," concluded Miss Pratt. " I must go and get this dress mended ; it's sure to be wanted to-morrow. Good-night, Miss Swan." And Maria felt herself dismissed.

7

A few mornings later, prayers being over, Mrs Jackson unlocked the post-bag and produced a letter addressed to herself from Mr Danvers.

Anxiety was depicted on her stern features while she opened it, but they relaxed into a smile of relief when she read the news it contained. Her three daughters stood round her, and looking up at them Mrs Jackson said :

" All is well, I am thankful to say. Dear Agnes has another little son."

The envelope was found to contain a second letter, which was addressed to the little girls.

" My dear children," said Mrs Jackson, turning to them, " here is a letter for you from your Papa. You may read it aloud to me instead of the chapter in the Bible, Harriet."

Hetty took the letter eagerly and opened it.

" Let us all hear the news he has to tell you ! " said the aunts, pressing forward to listen. And Harriet began :

" My dearest Pussy and Polly,

What do you think ? God has given you another little brother. Perhaps you will want to come home at once on purpose to see him, but we cannot have you yet awhile for Mamma is ill in bed, and Nurse has plenty to do with two babies to look after instead of one. I know you will be good children and try your best to please your kind Grandmamma and aunts as long as they are good enough to keep you. Here is a kiss for each of my pets x x,

From your loving Father."

Mary Anne's eyes were wide open with wonder. The news was too marvellous to be digested all at once by her small understanding. Another baby and another brother both together !

Harriet's perception was much quicker, and she clapped her hands and danced round the room exclaiming :

" Hip, hip, hooray ! Now Roger's nose will be put out of joint ! "

The aunts couldn't help laughing, but Mrs Jackson was shocked at the behaviour of her grandchild, and said peremptorily :

" Be quiet at once, you noisy little girl ! Explain the meaning of your vulgar expressions."

Harriet came to a standstill and said, " I heard Nurse say so to Mrs Chaine, but it was baby's nose she meant."

" Papa says baby hasn't got a nose," Mary Anne broke in.

" No, only an excrescence he calls it," observed Hetty. " But I mean Roger's nose, because he is the only boy, and Mamma spoils him."

The footman now entered the room bearing the breakfast tray. Harriet rushed towards him, calling out :

" We've got a new little brother, Charles ; there's a surprise ! But mind you keep it a secret, and don't go and tell Maria."

Charles was covered with confusion, and an ominous silence reigned until he left the room. Then Mrs Jackson pronounced sentence.

" Come hither, Harriet ! " she commanded, and the naughty child drew near to her majestic presence.

" If you desire to be on such familiar terms with the footman I think you had better go and have your breakfast in the servants' hall."

But Aunt Selina drew the offending little girl to the table by her side and bade her be seated.

Aunt Emma began to cut some slices of the home-made brawn, which always appeared on the breakfast table, and she put one slice on Harriet's plate and another on Mary Anne's.

The little girls had never seen brawn until they came to Davenport Hall, or even heard of it, except in the Psalms.

At first they ate it out of curiosity, but Molly disliked it exceedingly. She found it full of big lumps of fat and gristle, and in its solidity and circumference it resembled the liver-coloured marble columns that supported the ceiling at the entrance to the dining-room.

But Mrs Jackson declared it to be nourishing, and constrained her to finish every morsel on her plate.

" Was David obliged to eat it too ? " she asked the aunt by whose side she sat.

" What a funny question ! " said Miss Jackson. " What do you mean ? "

" Because I don't think he liked it either ; he said so in the Bible."

" My dear child ! " exclaimed her aunt, " it is only dainty children who don't like fat, and if little girls can't eat what is given to them without quoting the Scriptures they will have nothing but dry bread in the future for breakfast."

" But I didn't quote the Scriptures. I only remember——"

" Well, what did you remember ? " asked Aunt Anna. " I have noticed that you forget a good many things that you ought to remember when you are saying your lessons."

" Papa says she only remembers things like a parrot," laughed Harriet.

" Well, well," remarked Aunt Selina, seeing Molly's face redden and look perplexed. " She is very young yet to understand the meaning of things, though she may be right in saying that David disliked brawn, because he likened it to the hearts of proud people who imagined evil against him."

" Then I trust, my dear Mary Anne," said her Grand-mamma gravely, "that you will also agree with the Psalmist in his love for God's law."

Molly was quite out of her depth now, so she buried her face in a mug of lukewarm milk and water and washed down the brawn.

At last the little girls were free to rise from the table and run away to Maria.

" I hope Charles hasn't told her," sighed Hetty impatiently, as she wriggled off her chair.

" It will be a fitting reward for ill-manners if he has imparted the news to the maids," observed Mrs Jackson. " It is very unseemly for a young lady to address a man-servant familiarly, and in the presence of her elders. Now you may leave the room, and go quietly."

Most sedately the little pair marched out hand-in-hand. But once through the door, Harriet rushed upstairs, closely followed by Mary Anne, calling :

" Maria, Maria ! Such a piece of news ! What do you think ? You will never guess ! "

Maria met them in the corridor above. " Is it anything about a new baby ? " she asked.

Hetty looked at her and said, "There ! I do believe Charles has been and told you after all. You don't seem a bit surprised."

" Grandmamma said it would serve you right for telling Charles about it," observed Molly in a virtuous manner. " Oh, Maria, I do wish we were going home to-morrow ! "

" Well, it's certain you can't do that, lovey," said Maria. " Besides, to-morrow is Good Friday, and not a day to be travelling in railway trains. You will be going to church with your Grandmamma and aunties."

" I don't want to go home yet," cried Hetty, "it's fun being here."

8

Punctually at half-past ten o'clock on Good Friday the big barouche rolled round to the hall door with James the coachman and Charles the footman in sombre livery, side by side.

Maria Swan had been instructed to have her young ladies dressed ready for church, and they stood waiting in the hall when their Grandmamma and aunts came sailing down the broad staircase like a fleet in full rig. They were heavily attired in black silk gowns and mantles.

The little girls wore their plain linsey dresses, with loose coats made to match that were warmly lined with wadding. They were annoyed that Maria had not allowed them to put on their new silk pelisses and crinolines.

" But it ain't Sunday, nor yet a day to be making yourselves smart," Maria had declared while getting them ready. " And if you wear your fine clothes to-day you will have nothing new for Easter ; then sure enough the crows will punish you."

This was a country mystery which required explanation before they were reconciled to their everyday dresses.

" Well, I don't see why we shouldn't wear our crinnies at all events," grumbled Harriet. " You see, they would be underneath."

" And how then are you going to squeeze into the carriage I should like to know ? " said Maria. " It ain't as though you was coming walking along with me and the maids. We are doing the two miles on foot, for Mrs Jackson is most particular about church-going, same as your Pa, and quite right too. This isn't a day to be thinking so much about your clothes, Miss Hetty, and of going to church to be looked at. Think of our dear Lord upon the Cross, who died to save us all, and never mind your crinolines."

" I wonder if Mrs Tite will wear hers to-day," remarked Mary Anne. " I heard Papa say it was part of her religion, so I s'pose she must."

The packing into the barouche was quite a business. Charles opened the carriage door wide and let down the folding step. Caroline followed the ladies from the house and manipulated their skirts and crinolines with practised hands. Then she wedged one little girl in between the flounces and furbelows on the front seat, and the other between the two younger aunts on the back seat.

Charles closed the door and mounted the box beside James, who touched up the horses with his whip and away went the carriage solemnly down the drive, past the lodge, where the coachman's wife stood curtseying as she held the gate open, and out along the muddy road towards the village.

The five-minutes bell was tolling when they drew up at the lych-gate, where a row of school-children stood bobbing while Mrs Jackson and her daughters alighted and entered the church by a little side-door.

They were closely followed by Harriet and Mary Anne, who scrambled in after them, and up a narrow staircase which led to a large curtained box above. Aunt Selina shut the door, and they all proceeded to arrange themselves on the hassocks in prayer, while Harriet and Mary Anne took the opportunity of peeping out between the curtains.

They found they were looking down upon the congregation beneath, and facing the organ loft, where rows of children were seating themselves with a good deal of noise.

The church was filled with large square pews below, in which the occupants were screened from observation by faded red curtains.

Hetty could see the Hall servants hurrying into a similar

box just beneath as the Rector took his place in the high reading-desk, above which towered the pulpit.

Had it not been for the bad behaviour of the school children, the little girls would have felt the service to be very long and dreary.

There were none of the interests connected with their own old church to absorb them ; but the antics and grimaces of the elderly schoolmaster in his endeavour to keep the children quiet and orderly were an attraction to Harriet.

The aunts saw that their prayer-books were open before them, but the two pair of eyes were wandering through the aperture where the curtains had been drawn aside sufficiently to enable the family to take part in the service.

When the hymn before the sermon commenced the aunts tried a trio in part singing, reading the music from their hymn-books with " pianissimo " and " crescendo " and much rolling of " r's."

> " We may not know, we cannot tell
> What pains He had to bear ;
> But we believe it was for us
> He hung and suffered there."

Mary Anne knew the hymn by heart, which gratified her Grandmamma as she listened to the clear little voice uplifted like the faint trill of a robin :

> " He died that we might be forgiven,
> He died to make us good ;
> That we might go at last to Heaven,
> Saved by His precious blood."

A high-pitched soprano was wafted from below, lagging in long slurs behind the rest of the congregation. Harriet ventured to lean forward and crane her neck over the edge of the pew to see where it came from, though she recognized the voice.

Her eyes looked down upon the top of Maria Swan's spoon bonnet which was swaying to the tune :

> " There was no other good enough
> To pay the price of sin ;
> He only could unlock the gate
> Of Heav'n, and let us in."

In the last verse, when melody had reached its fullest limit, and emotion was beyond control, Harriet dropped her hymn-book over the ledge and it fell upon the footman's head.

The aunts were too much occupied in their music to notice this catastrophe as they burst into a final fortissimo :

> " Oh, dearly, dearly has He loved,
> And we must love Him too ;
> And trust in His redeeming Blood,
> And try His works to do."

Then they all knelt down ; and when the long prayer which preceded the sermon was ended, Mrs Jackson beckoned Mary Anne to her side and bade her be seated on the hassock at her feet.

The aunts drew the curtains close round the pew and composed themselves for sleep.

The sermon was long and dull. Mrs Jackson soon yielded to the soothing influence of Molly's little hand as it gently rubbed first one knee and then the other.

But presently the golden head and pork-pie hat dropped into the black crêpe lap of her Grandmother and lay there with eyes shut until a snore like a trumpet awoke her with a start, and Mrs Jackson, frowning, bade her remember she was in church.

Harriet was the only wakeful person in the pew, and she was never at a loss to amuse herself. She softly drew aside the curtains when all were dozing, and the panorama kept her interested all the time.

The Rector, clad in black gown and bands like her Papa, was raised to the same level as herself in the top-heavy pulpit, which reminded her of a Punch and Judy show with the school children looking on.

While the text was being given out she observed James and Charles slink from the pew below and she resolved to know the reason why. In those days such a proceeding was regarded as a grave offence to the preacher.

When all was over, and they were packed into the barouche again, Hetty declared :

" James and Charles went out when the sermon began."

" How do you know they did ? " asked Miss Jackson.

" Because I saw them go," replied Harriet.

" Then you ought not to have been looking," said her aunt.

" James had to put the horses in," observed Aunt Selina.

" And how did you manage to see them, I should like to know ? " asked Miss Anna, " for the curtains were closely drawn."

" I peeped through," said Hetty reluctantly.

" For shame ! " declared her Grandmamma. " You should have been listening to the sermon. The curtains were closed in order that we might be enabled to keep our attention fixed on what the Rector was saying."

" But your eyes were all closed too," said Harriet.

The aunts sat reproved, though they tittered, and Mrs Jackson tried to turn the conversation by observing :

" If what Harriet says is to be relied upon I shall certainly reprimand Charles. It is highly improper that he should leave the church before the service is over, even if it be necessary for James to do so."

9

When they were all assembled in the dining-room for luncheon, Mrs Jackson began by administering reproof to the footman, which made Harriet feel sorry that she had told.

A dish of cold hard-boiled eggs, reposing in a nest of watercress, formed the repast, followed by a hot suet pudding anointed with gravy and sprinkled with salt.

Mary Anne choked, and Charles was told to take her to Maria, who was at dinner in the servants' hall.

There Molly quickly overcame her indisposition and settled down to a hearty meal of bubble and squeak, which smelt very appetizing.

Cook and Caroline, Miss Pratt and Maria with Mary Anne all sat round the table and partook of it. Later on they were joined by Charles, who told them of the " wigging " he had received from the mistress for leaving church before the sermon.

" I just wonder how she knew anything about it," he said.

" Hetty told her," said Molly. " She peeped through the curtains and saw you." Then she stuffed her little mouth full of bubble and squeak.

" That was mean of Miss Harriet, after dropping her hymn-book on top of my head too," declared Charles. " I shan't play any more games with her."

But Hetty was very penitent. When she was released from the dining-room she came running to look for Molly.

" You are a little sneak ! " she declared ; but she told Charles she was sorry and would never tell tales out of church again.

" Maria, we are to be got ready to go out with Grand-mamma," she said. " We are going to take tea-leaves to Miss Tinkler and Mrs Billings and old Mother Bugge."

" I don't want to go," complained Mary Anne, who was

feeling fat and lazy after her full meal. " Can't I stay with you, Maria ? "

" Not if your Grandmamma wants you," replied Miss Swan, who was looking forward to a quiet afternoon walk with Miss Pratt.

" And we are to have tea in the dining-room because it's Good Friday," Hetty went on.

" Shall we have hot cross buns ? " asked Molly.

" Yes," replied Cook, " because I've had to make 'em."

" Papa won't let us have them at home," said Hetty, " so I s'pose we mustn't here."

" Why ever not ? " exclaimed Cook.

" Because they would be a treat, and he says this isn't a day for treats."

" Well, if you don't have 'em to-day, you shall to-morrow, warmed up and buttered for your tea with Maria ; I'll see to that," declared the good-natured woman. " But if your Grandma lets you have 'em to-day, you can't eat 'em and have 'em to-morrow, so that's all about it."

" Won't they be hot-buttered to-day ? " asked Mary Anne greedily.

" Oh no, my dear ! " laughed Cook. " I specks it a bit o' religion to eat 'em dry."

At three o'clock the little girls were ready dressed for their walk to the village, and a basket containing the bottles of tea-leaves was in the hall for them to carry.

As they trudged through the mud by the side of their Grandmamma she discoursed to them on the duty of giving to the poor. " He that hath pity upon the poor, lendeth unto the Lord ; and look, what he layeth out, it shall be paid him again."

" What do they want the tea-leaves for ? " asked Mary Anne.

"To sweep their floors with, like Phœbe docs," said Harriet.

"My dears," said Mrs Jackson, "they are too precious to be wasted for that purpose. With tea at the price it is, I find that very few of the poor people can afford to buy it : and some are thankful to receive what we have already made use of, which is better than having none at all."

"But don't you ever give them any real tea, Grandmamma ?" enquired Harriet.

"No, my child," replied Mrs Jackson, "it would not be right to encourage the working classes to indulge in luxuries which are beyond their means. It would only make them discontented with their lot."

"But they haven't got a lot—only a little," said Mary Anne.

"I shouldn't like to drink old tea-leaves, would you, Grandmamma ?" said Hetty.

"My dear Harriet," replied the upright old lady, "you are too ready with your tongue. If I lived alone in one room, like Miss Tinkler, for instance, I hope I should be thankful for any small mercies." And she came to a standstill at a garden-gate.

"Now, this is the cottage wherein Mrs Bugge resides with her married daughter. Run up and knock at the door while I wait here."

"What a funny name !" observed Mary Anne, who stayed with her Grandmamma at the gate. "We have bugs at home, but they are insects that bite."

"My dear !" admonished Mrs Jackson, "such things are never mentioned. You ought to know nothing about them."

"But I do," persisted Molly. "Nurse catches them and Papa says they live in the wooden walls."

"I am shocked indeed to hear it !" exclaimed her Grandmamma. "That is one of the evils of uncleanliness in former generations, for which we have to suffer."

Old Mrs Bugge now appeared in answer to Hetty's summons. She was crippled with rheumatism and came slowly, curtseying down the path.

" Good day, Mrs Bugge, are you pretty well ? " enquired Mrs Jackson graciously. " I and my little grand-daughters have brought you something to make yourself a cup of tea. You seemed to appreciate the last I sent."

" Aye, thank you kindly, ma'am, and so we did," replied the old woman. " My daughter, she boiled up a kettleful of water, and when her man come home from his day's work in the fields, we and the children sat down and had a cup o' tea-leaves for our supper."

" Ah ! " responded Mrs Jackson with satisfaction, " they have not the harmful effects of beer, especially in their weakened condition. I trust he keeps out of the public-house now ? "

" Well, my lady, a man must 'ave somewhere to go of an evening, when the children's all inside and the washing a-drying in the kitchen ; for we can't put it out o' doors this damp weather. But won't you kindly step inside, ma'am ? My daughter's just finishing off her ironing."

" No, I thank you, not to-day," replied Mrs Jackson. " We must say ' Good afternoon,' as we have others to visit. Mary Anne, hand one of those bottles to Mrs Bugge —or perhaps she would like two—since there are so many of them in family."

Mrs Bugge curtseyed her thanks and retreated up the path carrying the gracious gift, while the little girls lifted the basket again and pursued their way along the road with their Grandmamma.

As they crossed the village green to Betsy Billings' cottage, they passed a group of children at play. The game ceased when Mrs Jackson approached, and they stared at Harriet and Mary Anne.

" Where are your manners, young people ? " demanded the stately lady, as she stood towering above them.

The merry party, inspired with awe, put their fingers in their mouths and stared harder.

" What game are you playing, that makes you so noisy on this solemn day ? " enquired Mrs Jackson.

A small girl with shrewd eyes thrust out her hand at the question and replied, " Fewl, fewl, go back to school, and learn your A B C."

" The first thing you should be taught at school, is to curtsey to your betters," said Mrs Jackson. " Now let these young ladies see if you have learned to do so, for if not, you have certainly come home fools."

The three elder girls proceeded solemnly to bob down and up again.

" That is right. Now show your little sisters how to behave to ladies when you see them—so—like good children," said the old lady. " Why do you not go into the woods and make yourselves useful by gathering primroses and daffodils for Easter Day ? You would be better employed than in playing games on Good Friday. It is not the day for noise and mirth."

With this reproof Mrs Jackson proceeded on her way.

" Oh, Grandmamma ! " cried Hetty, " mayn't we go too ? "

" You would find the woods too wet and muddy, my dear ; besides, you are helping me this afternoon. But perhaps to-morrow, if it is fine, Maria may take you there."

Mrs Billings was gossiping with a neighbour at her gate. She invited the ladies to walk in ; but Mrs Jackson was not in the habit of entering the cottages she visited. A few words in season, exchanged outside, on the important questions of health, cleanliness and godliness, as the case demanded, and a request that the pickle-bottle might be returned when empty, for further favours, sufficed for the occasion.

" Mrs Billings is a born grumbler," she remarked, as she wended her way to Miss Tinkler, a few doors further on. " She is never satisfied with the weather or her condition in life, and is seldom grateful for what she receives."

Mrs Billings had declined the tea-leaves with thanks, having been presented with a quarter-pound packet of real tea the day before by the Rector's lady.

Miss Tinkler lived alone with her cat in a tiny two-roomed cottage. She took in sewing and mending for the neighbouring gentry, and was proud of having been lady's-maid to former tenants at the Hall.

Mrs Jackson considered her a very superior person ; so she allowed her grandchildren to go inside and stroke the cat.

They found the animal the contented mother of two kittens, and Molly's heart went out to them at once as they lay all curled round together in a basket on the hearth.

Miss Tinkler conversed with her august visitor at the door and gratefully accepted what was bestowed upon her, without mentioning the fact that she had also been the recipient of a small packet of the precious beverage from the Rector's wife.

" Oh, Grandmamma ! " interrupted Hetty, as she ran to the door, " do come and look at these dear little kittens."

" Not to-day, Harriet ; we must be getting home now. Tell Mary Anne to come."

Whereupon Miss Tinkler said :

" Would the young ladies like to have one of the kittens to take home with them ? They are old enough to leave their mother now."

To which Mrs Jackson replied :

" I am surprised that you are able to support a family of cats in your straightened circumstances, Miss Tinkler ;

but indeed I do not think it at all likely that these children's parents can afford it either, unless there are mice to render it a necessity in the house."

" Oh yes, there are lots of mice, Grandmamma," said Hetty. " They eat the candles in the nursery cupboard, and Nurse has to set traps to catch them."

" Well, you must write and ask Mamma's leave before I can grant it," replied Mrs Jackson. " Remember you have another baby at home now, so you don't want a kitten as well."

The children had not forgotten this, although their daily life in the country had taken their thoughts off affairs at home.

Harriet talked about the new little brother all the way back, wondering what name would be given him at Baptism : but Mary Anne's thoughts were entirely absorbed in the family of cats, and she was busily composing a letter in her little mind, as she trotted along by her Grandmamma's side, which was to appeal to her Papa, that she might be allowed to have one of the kittens for her very own.

Maria was confided in while she tied on their aprons and brushed their hair ready for tea in the dining-room ; an event which had not taken place before.

" Why are we going there to tea ? " asked Mary Anne petulantly, because she preferred Maria's society and wanted to talk to her about the cats.

" Shall we have to say collects and hymns like Sunday ? "

" I don't know about collects," replied Maria, as she tied the velvet ribbon round Molly's head. " But I dare say you will be singing hymns with your aunts. They don't expect any visitors as it's Good Friday, and your Grandmamma has had a long walk, and wants a good sit-down tea no doubt ; for they are not dining to-night, so as the servants can all go to church this evening."

10

It turned out very much as Maria had said. After tea, at which the little girls were allowed to have one hot-cross bun each, Mrs Jackson sent word to Maria that she could attend church with the rest of the household, as the young ladies would spend the evening in the parlour.

No toilettes were performed, and they all adjourned to the morning-room, where they sang hymns until it was dusk, while Mrs Jackson sat in the arm-chair and dozed.

When Charles brought in the lamps and closed the shutters which covered the long French windows, and drew the curtains across them, and made up the fire which had burned very low, Miss Jackson requested him to fetch a basket of eggs from the pantry, which the farmer's wife had sent up that morning.

"Now we are going to be very busy," said she, as she unlocked a cupboard beneath the large bookcase and produced a roll of red flannel, and a bag full of pieces of coloured material.

Harriet was all agog to see what her aunt was going to do. She was told to sit on the hearth-rug with Mary Anne, while the ladies drew their chairs up in a circle round them and the fire.

Molly was a little creature of habit and would have preferred to play with the solitaire board as usual ; but it was in the drawing-room with the Berlin woolwork and the three-volume novels.

There was other work to be done to-night. A basket containing as many as four dozen eggs was deposited in the centre of the group, and Aunt Selina brought forward a workbox which she set open upon a gipsy-table.

"You have heard of Easter eggs, I suppose ? " Aunt Anna asked her nieces while she put away the hymn-books and shut up the piano in a business-like manner.

" What are they ? " asked Harriet eagerly.

" Well, the hens lay them but we make them, and they would never know their own eggs if they were to see them again," said Miss Anna, as she settled herself into a comfortable chair.

Miss Emma was already cutting coloured flannel into strips, and Aunt Selina produced bright scraps of blue, crimson, purple and green stuffs from the piece-bag to be similarly dealt with.

" Mayn't I cut some too ? " asked Hetty.

" You may hand us the eggs as we need them," replied her Aunt Anna ; " and woe betide you if you let one fall ! You would forfeit it on Easter Day."

Needles and thread were busily plied sewing the eggs into coloured coats, while the little girls looked on, and laid each egg as it was covered on to a tray.

" What is going to be done with them all ? " asked Harriet, who was longing to do something more.

" The cook will boil them hard to-morrow, and when they are cold we shall take their jackets off and you will see the result of our labours."

" Now, this one will be unusually smart if it turns out a success," remarked Aunt Anna, handing it to Mary Anne, done up in various gay stripes.

Molly had the misfortune to drop it.

" Butter-fingers ! " cried Hetty. " Now you won't have one on Easter Day."

" You careless child ! " exclaimed Aunt Anna. " Fortunately it has fallen on the wool rug, but it may be cracked, and if so it will be spoiled, after I took such pains to make a pretty one."

Mary Anne did not think it looked at all pretty. She sat silently longing for Maria to come in and take her to bed. She was tired of doing nothing but watch her aunts sewing away like the three Fates. It was as dull as rubbing her Grandmamma's legs.

But Harriet managed to find amusement in it, and was allowed presently to have a needle and thread on her own account.

Molly began to yawn. Her walk in the mud had tired her, with the heavy basket, and she was suffering from indigestion after eating " bubble and squeak." Sitting on the hearthrug with her back to the fire made her feel hot and uncomfortable, but she was too shy to say so

Aunt Selina noticed that she looked flushed, and kindly called her to her side.

" Is anything the matter, dear ? " she enquired ; but Molly was silent.

" I know what it is," remarked Hetty, " she ate too much at dinner."

Fortunately for Mary Anne the door opened at that moment and Maria appeared. The eggs being just completed, no notice was taken of Harriet's remark and they went off to bed. But while they were undressing Hetty teased her sister and told her she deserved to feel sick because she had been greedy on Good Friday.

Maria produced one of the odious powders and administered it as directed by Nurse, only without any jam, to counteract the evil effects of too much " bubble and squeak."

II

The snow was gone, the sun shone, the wind blew softly from the south, the daffodils nodded their heads with satisfaction, and the primroses peeped cautiously out in the hedgerows, on Easter Day.

When Maria went to call her little ladies the birds were tuning up outside for the first time, and the rooks cawed vigorously in the tall elms down the drive, threatening to punish anyone who did not put on something new, as Maria observed.

" But they won't trouble you, dearies," she went on, " for Miss Pratt and I worked hard last evening after our supper, and we finished the Garibawldies, so you have got something smart to wear. See ! here they are " ; and she held up two little scarlet bodices trimmed with black feather-stitching, like those worn by their aunts, who had brought the fashion from Italy.

When shopping in Southbury Miss Jackson had purchased the red cashmere, for she considered it advisable that Maria Swan should be suitably employed in doing some needlework during the mornings while the little girls were at their lessons. And Pratt was requested to cut out the Garibaldies and to be responsible for the fitting of them.

The result was that Hetty and Molly went in to Family Prayers on Easter Day swelled out with satisfaction above and crinolines below.

While Mrs Jackson was reading aloud the chapter from the Bible, their eyes went wandering from one aunt to another to see if they were also a match for the crows.

When prayers were over, Aunt Anna, arrayed in a wonderful new gown, admired the Garibaldies but con-demned the crinolines.

" It is absurd to dress up children like their elders," she maintained. " I wonder that Agnes has not more sense."

" Where did you get these silk skirts ? " asked another aunt.

" Mamma had them made for us to come here in," replied Harriet, feeling rather crestfallen.

" The stuff frocks were all you needed," said Miss Jackson, " and the Garibaldies will do very nicely to wear on Sundays."

" Come hither and let me look at them, my dears," said their Grandmamma. Regarding the bodices closely, she remarked :

H

" I am sure Maria Swan did not do all that feather-stitching."

" No, Pratt did it," replied Hetty, " and they both worked hard to get them done last night so that we should have something to keep the crows off us to-day."

" To do what ? " exclaimed Mrs Jackson.

" And we have new stockings on as well," boasted Mary Anne.

" And new skirts, so it seems," remarked Aunt Selina, smiling.

" Well, not exactly," explained Harriet, " because they are only made out of Mamma's old dress, you see."

" How proud we are, how fond to show our clothes and call them rich and new ; when all the time your mother wore this very clothing long before ! " quoted Aunt Anna, laughing.

" There won't be room in the carriage for all to drive, that's certain," remarked Aunt Emma as they seated themselves at the breakfast table. " It was a crush on Good Friday, and to-day we are wearing our new gowns. As it is a fine morning, I think Harriet and Mary Anne might walk across the fields with Maria to church. And they must also return on foot, as we are staying to Holy Communion."

This was considered a good suggestion, and the little girls liked the idea.

" Maria must see that they put their goloshes on," said their Grandmamma. " Agnes asked us to be sure that they did not get wet feet."

" May we sit in the servants' pew ? " asked Molly, hopefully.

" Certainly not ! I never heard such a suggestion," exclaimed Miss Anna.

Mary Anne pouted with vexation because she disliked the prospect of rubbing her Grandmamma's knees during

the sermon. But it proved to be of shorter length than on
Good Friday, when all the terrors of the Crucifixion had
been entered into and enlarged upon.

As the little girls left the church with Maria they fell in
with Miss Tinkler, who invited them to come and see the
kittens.

Maria Swan was pleased to make her acquaintance, and
she promised to call again another day and have a gossip.

After dinner the eggs which had been released from their
bindings the evening before, were to be distributed among
the school-girls, who came to a Sunday afternoon class held
by Miss Jackson in the servants' hall.

Harriet and Mary Anne were desired to be present to
learn the collect and repeat hymns by heart with the village
children, in order to set them a good example.

When the class was over they were told to give each girl
an Easter egg and to choose one for themselves.

The eggs had emerged from their wrappings dyed all the
colours of the rainbow, and as chocolate and sugar eggs
were unheard of in those days, they were eagerly accepted,
though quite uneatable.

The servants had one apiece, Maria included, and still
there were some left over.

" You must take them home with you," said Aunt Emma
to her little nieces. " There's a red one for Papa, and a blue
one for Mamma, and a yellow one for Roger, and a striped
one for your little sister."

" May Nurse have one, please ? " asked Molly.

" And Sarah Turke and Phœbe ? " cried Hetty.

" And Miss Manners ? " put in Molly again.

" And how many more ? " laughed Aunt Selina. " That
makes eight, and there are nine eggs left. Who shall have
the odd one over ? "

" Oh, I know ! " cried Hetty. " Mr Coulston."

" And who may he be ? " asked Aunt Anna.

" He is a Missionary, who throws us up to the ceiling just as Charles does."

" My dear, what do you refer to ? " asked Mrs Jackson with a shocked expression.

But Harriet only ran round the room, tossing her egg into the air and catching it again.

" If you have been getting familiar with the manservant it is time that you returned home," remarked Aunt Anna severely. " I must speak to Maria Swan. She ought to know her place sufficiently to keep you under restraint when you are not with us."

" We had hoped to send you home with your manners much improved," said Aunt Emma. " You did not come here to run wild."

" Hadn't they better go and get ready for tea ? " suggested Aunt Selina gently. " It is past four o'clock, and they are to have it with us in the dining-room to-day, you remember."

So the little girls ran off to find Maria, who brushed out their highly crimped hair and tied on their ribbons afresh, and fastened their black silk aprons with the pinked-out frills and pair of pockets apiece.

When tea was over Harriet asked if she might write a letter to her Papa. But this was not permitted, for Aunt Anna sat down to the writing-table in the drawing-room and began a voluminous correspondence.

Mrs Jackson was conducted to the arm-chair by the fire, which she always occupied. Aunt Selina lay at full length on the uncomfortable-looking sofa with the hard bolster. Aunt Emma seated herself upon a straight-backed chair and took up a book of sermons to read.

" Aren't we going to sing hymns ? " asked Harriet, who, like Maria Swan, enjoyed hearing her own voice upraised in song.

" Presently," replied Miss Jackson. " You may open the piano quietly and put out the hymn-books."

Mary Anne cast longing glances at the solitaire-board, with its variety of glass marbles, which she liked to run round the edge of it. But she did not dare to venture into its vicinity. Instead, she sidled up to the table where Aunt Anna was writing and began to examine the contents of the handsome silver inkstand with its tray of quill pens, and its bowl of shot, and the wafer-box, and the sticks of black and red sealing-wax.

Every now and then she heaved a heavy sigh She attempted to remove the little silver candlestick with the miniature red wax candle from its pedestal between the inkpots. This action disturbed her aunt.

" Now, Mary Anne," she said, dipping her quill into the ink again and sending it swiftly squeaking along the sheet of note-paper, " go and get your prayer-book and spell out the Epistle to yourself by the fire. Then you may come and help me seal my letters for the evening post. But don't let me hear any more sighing, for goodness' sake ! "

" I should think not indeed ! " remarked Mrs Jackson from the depths of her comfortable chair. " You are very fortunate little girls to be allowed in the drawing-room at all, and your aunts cannot always be exerting themselves to amuse you. Come to me, Mary Anne," her Grand-mamma continued, beckoning the child with a rigid forefinger. " Bring that footstool and sit at my feet while you rub my knees."

She produced the biggest piece of brimstone she could find in her silk reticule and began repeating aloud the collect for Easter from memory, with her eyes shut, telling her grandchild to say it after her.

Mary Anne was never able to do two things at once, so she incurred Mrs Jackson's displeasure.

When her aunt's letters were ready to be sealed it was Hetty who was at her hand to light the little red candle with a spill from the vase, and to press the big seal onto the hot wax, for Molly was detained by her Grand-mamma.

" It is a great privilege to know the prayer-book by heart," she said to the little girl. " And if you are spared to live as long as I have been you will feel thankful that it has been instilled into your mind during your early years, my child."

In after life Mary Anne remembered these prophetic sayings, and dimly associated her Grandmother with the Psalmist, who said :

" From my youth up, Thy terrors have I suffered with a troubled mind."

12

The month spent at Davenport Hall did not pass quite so quickly as Mary Anne could have wished. But when at last the day came for going home, Harriet at all events was sorry to leave.

Lessons with their aunts had been a very different affair from the afternoon instruction imparted by Miss Manners.

" They will certainly go back with their minds improved," remarked Aunt Anna as she replaced the books they had been using on the shelf in the morning-room. " Mary Anne can read quite fairly now, though I must say she is woefully ignorant compared with her sister."

" Harriet is quick, and ought to have a more advanced governess," Aunt Emma observed. " I must write to Agnes about it when she has recovered from her confinement."

Maria Swan packed the big black box and fixed on the label firmly with paste. It was carried down the back stairs and lifted on to a fly with Maria's holland-clad trunk, while the farewells were taking place.

Saying good-bye in the kitchen was a much more demonstrative affair than it was in the parlour. Hetty hugged the cook, and Molly clung to Charles, while Maria clasped hands and vowed eternal friendship with Miss Pratt.

When the little girls entered the morning-room ready dressed for the journey, the aunts ceased playing their duets, and rose from the piano, and Mrs Jackson, sitting by the fire in the dining-room, laid aside her knitting and embraced her grand-children, sending fond messages to their mother. Kisses were exchanged in the hall, and wishes for a pleasant journey.

Packets of sandwiches had been made of bread and brawn and secreted in a basket containing the Easter eggs.

The globes were sharing the back seat of the fly with a roll of umbrellas strapped to the backboard.

Harriet screamed at the sight of them, " We don't want these horrid things ! who put them in ? "

" The Mistress's orders," said Charles, with a twinkle in his eye, as Miss Anna came down the door-steps to take a final farewell of her little nieces.

" Oh, Aunt Anna, must we take the globes and the backboard ? " said Hetty. " I thought we had done with them ! "

" On the contrary, Harriet, you have only just begun with them, and you are much indebted to us for allowing you the use of them. The globes are a very valuable present ; your Mamma will be grateful if you are not. She benefited by them when she was your age."

Mary Anne wriggled into position at Harriet's side, facing the old implements of torture, while Maria climbed on to the box by the coachman and away they drove.

Molly was pleased to depart, but she was silent with regret at not taking home one of Miss Tinkler's kittens.

Her Papa had given his consent, but the aunts decided that there were more than enough parcels to carry, and the kitten was considered superfluous.

When after a long journey they arrived at the big London Terminus, there stood the Parson on the platform, a prominent figure in his tall hat and stiff white cravat, looking out for his little daughters.

" Papa, Papa ! " cried Hetty from the window, out of which her head had been poked many times during the journey, in spite of Maria's remonstrances.

The next moment he had opened the door and she jumped into his arms. He was delighted to have them back again, and taking a small hand in each of his, he led them along the crowded platform to where Mr Worby was waiting with his cab, while Maria brought up the rear with the globes and the backboard.

Worby opened the cab door with a genial smile. He had on his coachman's coat with the three capes and the long whip in his hand, which was only for show.

When Maria had deposited her burden she went to look for the luggage, and Mr Danvers made some jokes about the backboard, and asked what had become of the kitten.

Mary Anne had almost forgotten about it in her delight at seeing her Papa again, and when they drove off into the busy London streets, Harriet could scarcely sit still for excitement. She chattered all the way home about what they had seen and done in the country.

But Molly only asked about the new baby. And then Mr Danvers began to tell them what had been going on at home during their absence.

" Mamma has been very ill, but she is better now," he said. " She is able to get up and lie on the sofa in the drawing-room, and there you will find her. You must be very quiet and help her to get well and strong quickly."

" What is the new baby like ? " asked Hetty.

" Oh Papa, is the old baby's nose out of joint ? " asked Molly.

" She never had a nose," laughed Mr Danvers. " But

she is just as impudent as if she had, and she gives Nurse much more trouble than the new one."

" What is his name to be ? " asked Hetty.

" Ah, that's a question I can't answer ; you must ask Mamma.

" Can't we call him Charles ? " said Molly.

" Why Charles in particular ? " enquired Mr Danvers.

" After the footman at Davenport Hall," urged Mary Anne. " He is such a nice man, Papa, and he played with us the same as Mr Coulston does."

" His name is Charles too," put in Hetty, " and he would be a nice Godfather for baby as well."

" I don't think Mamma would approve of that, quite, although she has a great respect for Mr Coulston," said their Papa.

A good deal more chatter ensued, until the cab turned the corner into the quiet Row and drew up at the dear old house.

Mr Danvers got out and opened the door with his latch-key. The little girls rushed in and ran straight upstairs.

Molly was soon being held in Nurse's warm embrace, while Hetty went to peer into the cradle, which was all done up afresh with white muslin and blue ribbons. But there was no baby in it.

In a corner by himself sat Roger, playing with a tin train that his Papa had given him on his birthday. He took but little notice of his sisters ; in fact he had almost forgotten them.

Nurse was in the middle of getting ready for tea and she didn't want to be hindered. So she said :

" Now run down to the drawing-room and see your Mamma before you take your things off. She has got the baby to show you, and you ought to have gone there first. Miss Charlotte is asleep in the next room, thank goodness, and mind you don't wake her as you go by."

" Who is Miss Charlotte ? " asked Mary Anne, staring at Nurse with round eyes.

" Why, your little sister to be sure ! " replied Nurse, as she cut up the loaf for tea. " She's no longer the baby, and she must be called by her christened name. Now go quietly, there's your Papa calling you."

Off they went downstairs on tip-toe, till they met Maria and Phœbe dragging the big box up between them and the Parson pushing behind.

" Ah, there you are ! " he exclaimed. " Mamma is waiting to show you your new little brother," and he led them into the drawing-room.

Mrs Danvers was lying on the sofa looking very delicate. On her lap lay a white flannel bundle, which squeaked and wriggled when their Mamma drew her little daughters towards her and kissed them.

Harriet wanted to take it in her arms, but Mary Anne shrank back and held her Papa's hand tight, feeling shy and strange in the new little presence.

" Oh Mamma, do let me hold him ! " cried Hetty. But the bundle objected loudly, and presently Mr Danvers was obliged to call Nurse, who came and carried it off, as well as the little girls, to the nursery tea.

During that meal there was plenty to talk about. Harriet never ceased her chatter, but Mary Anne sat slowly munching her bread and butter by Nurse's side, fully content to be near her again.

After tea there was the new baby to be washed and put to bed, which to Molly was an absorbing process. But Hetty began to tease Roger.

" I'm glad we've got another brother," she remarked, " because now perhaps Mamma won't spoil you so."

" She doesn't spoil me ! " cried Roger.

" She does, doesn't she, Nurse ? " Harriet went on, " and Papa said you were a milksop."

" He didn't ! " said Roger.

" And so you are," taunted his sister.

" I'm not a milksop ! " whimpered the little boy. " I'll go and tell Mamma what you say," and he began to climb down from his high chair.

" Now, Master Roger," said Nurse, " you sit still. Your Mamma don't want to be worrited with nursery tales. And you, Miss Harriet, be quiet will you and don't tease your little brother so. 'Taint his fault if his Mamma spoils him."

" There, Nurse says she does ! " cried Hetty, clapping her hands delighted. " There are two babies now younger than Roger, but he is the biggest baby of all."

Roger lifted up his voice and wept. The old baby and the new baby both began to cry also, and Nurse was so out of patience that she boxed Hetty's ears.

" A nice way to behave ! " she said, " coming home and upsetting the nursery like this. Be off now downstairs to your Mamma and don't let me see your face again till bedtime. I can't be bothered with such a bylim. Sarah, take Miss Charlotte into the next room and quiet her. And you, Molly dearie, go and comfort your little brother like a good girl."

Mary Anne would do anything for Nurse, whom she loved better than anyone at that period of her existence. But Harriet had made her jealous of Roger ; so it was with mixed feelings that she did as she was bidden.

Not a bit ashamed of herself, Harriet went down to the drawing-room and found her Mamma alone.

" What is all that crying upstairs ? " asked Mrs Danvers anxiously.

" The three babies all crying together," said Harriet, " and Nurse says she cannot manage such a bylim."

Mrs Danvers sighed. " Then you must try and help her," she said. " You are getting quite a big girl now,

Harriet, and you must learn to be useful in the nursery. You might keep Charlotte amused and quiet, and you could teach little Roger his letters. He is nearly old enough to learn them now."

" I could read when I was his age, couldn't I ? " boasted Harriet.

" Because I had more time to teach you," said her Mamma, although conscious that Hetty was unusually quick in understanding, besides being as imitative as a monkey. " And now I may as well tell you that there is no longer room for you in the night-nursery. You and Mary Anne are to share the bedroom next to mine, and Sarah will wait on you there ; but you will soon be old enough to attend to yourselves, since you have been away on a visit."

Harriet experienced a growing sense of importance as her Mamma talked to her, and the idea of being promoted from the nursery to a bedroom of her own gave her a feeling of responsibility. When shortly after, Mary Anne entered the room leading Roger by the hand, Hetty ran up to them and said with an air of satisfaction :

" We are going to have a bedroom to ourselves, Molly, and I shall show you how to keep it tidy."

Taking hold of Roger, she continued, " I am to teach you to read now, Mamma says so." But he tore himself away from her and ran to his Mamma, crying out, " I won't be taught by her ! I won't, I won't ! "

" Very well, darling, not now, then," said Mrs Danvers soothingly, for she was far from strong and feeling very tired.

Harriet and Mary Anne were whispering together behind the sofa. Their Papa entered the room and sitting down he took one on each knee and began to ask them all sorts of questions about their visit to Davenport Hall, and what they did with themselves all day in the country, and what they thought of the new baby, and whether they were glad to come home again, or would they rather have stayed with Grandmamma Jackson and their aunts.

Hetty nodded, but Molly nestled her little golden head against her Papa's black whiskers, and putting her arms round his stiff cravat, she clung fondly to him in reply.

IV. MISS MARGERY MANNERS

" Through wisdom is a house builded : and by understanding it is established : and by knowledge shall the chambers be filled with all precious and pleasant riches."—Solomon.

I

THE Corner House was none too large for the family it now contained, though of comfortable dimensions, being well-proportioned within, and well-constructed without.

They understood architecture in the reign of Queen Anne, as well as the art of making furniture, and both were lost sight of during the long reign of Queen Victoria.

Proofs of this were apparent in the Parson's house, furnished as it was in the latest style, with suites of upholstered chairs and couches, which perhaps looked out of place against the panelled walls. But they imparted an aspect of homeliness in the truest sense : there was nothing stiff or cumbersome. If the furniture did not harmonize with the house, it did with the family.

The advent of another baby caused several changes to be necessary in the household. The two little girls were promoted to breakfast downstairs with their parents, as well as to a bedroom of their own.

The Parson had Family Prayers every morning before he breakfasted. The bell that rang upstairs would tinkle, and Nurse would descend from above with Roger, who had partaken of bread and milk in the nursery, and remained downstairs on his Mamma's knee to be fed with tit-bits from her plate.

Harriet and Mary Anne, clad in holland pinafores, sat on either side of their parents, eating brown bread for the sake of their teeth. They soon discovered that promotion did not always mean pleasure. When breakfast was over they were required to bring their Bibles and read with their parents a long chapter from the Old and New Testaments, besides the Psalms for the day. Some of the verses perplexed Mary Anne; but there was no time for explanations before Mr Coulston arrived, full of parish matters, and the business of the day began.

Harriet's mind was more capable of grasping things than that of her sister, and she never troubled herself to ponder over meanings as Molly did.

Roger sat on his Mamma's knee and listened to his parents and sisters reading the verses in turn. Later on, when he had learned to read and was able to take part in this daily ceremony, the Parson made a point of alternating the Psalms of David with the Proverbs of Solomon for the admonition of his son.

While breakfast was being cleared away the little girls were sent to practise their five-finger exercises on the piano in the drawing-room, and when their Mamma had visited the kitchen and ordered the meals for the day, they returned to the parlour to read *Mrs Markham's History of England* with her, and to repeat the kings and queens in order, with the dates of their accession, while they took it in turn to hold the backboard.

During the recitation Mrs Danvers' hands would be occupied in various ways. She might be reclining on the couch engaged in needlework, or seated at the table cutting her correspondence into strips with the paper-knife to make into spills for the vase on the mantelpiece.

This always diverted Molly's mind and caused her to give the wrong date to William the Conqueror.

But when lessons were over her Mamma would produce a more absorbing pursuit by making little models of churches out of fine white cardboard, and Mary Anne would stand by her side interested as she cut the pieces with a penknife and joined them together with gum arabic.

A completed specimen stood on the marble-topped chiffonier in the drawing-room under a glass case. It was a miniature of the beautiful church in the village where Mrs Danvers had spent her girlhood, and near to it was a basket of flowers executed in wax of various hues on a black stand to match, and protected from the dust by a similar shade.

This was also the handiwork of Mrs Danvers, and Mary Anne had often overheard visitors expressing admiration at these works of art, and warmly extolling her Mamma's many accomplishments.

Molly was profoundly impressed by these marvellous attainments, but as yet she only aspired to the making of spills.

2

Miss Manners came regularly every afternoon at two o'clock to instruct the little girls, and if the weather was fine they went first for a walk by the riverside, or to play in the Rectory garden.

That was a dear old-fashioned place, enclosed by a high red brick wall with tall trees in front and a large green field at the back, where the Rector's cow could be seen grazing from the nursery windows of the corner house.

There was plenty of shade and sunshine in the garden, with gravel walks winding in and out through beds of bright flowers and rows of vegetables, and a spreading old mulberry tree on the lawn, which had been planted in the days of Queen Elizabeth.

A swing was suspended from the branch of a pear tree in the kitchen garden, which poor patient Miss Manners would have to keep going for ever so long, with first one child and then another, until it was time to go home and settle down to lessons and sewing for the rest of the day.

On rare occasions in the summer-time Miss Manners was granted an afternoon off, and Mary Anne would go out with Nurse and Sarah and the babies, but Harriet preferred a walk with her Papa.

Nurse would then take them for a treat to what she called the green lanes, which lay beyond the King's highway and Paradise Gardens. This was real country to the children, for there were hedges enclosing flat fields where market produce was grown, with stinging-nettles in profusion by the roadside.

Molly loved to gather anything that blossomed, and she would search diligently in the hedgerows for wild flowers to take to her Mamma, or to put in a jug on the nursery table.

Paradise Gardens was a haunt of mystery, and possessed fascinations of quite a different description. One was nature, the other artifice.

Along the busy high road Nurse wheeled the perambulator with Mary Anne on one side of her, and Sarah carrying the baby on the other, until they came to the " World's End Tavern " and the " Man in the Moon."

The entrance to Paradise faced these strange places, shut in all round with high green wooden palings, and tall tree-tops waving in the wind.

Nurse would pull up the perambulator near the entrance to the gardens, which was closed at that time of day, and they would take it in turns to peep through a hole in the barriers on the chance of seeing some of the enchantments within.

I

On one occasion a gateway happened to be open, and they got a glimpse of the fairyland beyond, with its smooth green lawns and rows of coloured glass lamps hanging from the boughs of the trees, which Mary Anne never forgot. In addition to this there was a background of painted scenery with dancing sylphs and cupids depicted thereon, against a pink and blue sky flecked with billowy white clouds.

" Does nobody ever go inside ? " asked Molly, as she gazed in with round, longing eyes.

" My word, yes ! " exclaimed Nurse, laughing. " There's people dancing there all night long."

And Mary Anne thought that must make the gardens more entrancing than ever. There were the gorgeous sky-rockets besides that often woke her up with a succession of bangs and explosions long after she had been tucked into bed and asleep ; she and Hetty would get up and watch them from the night-nursery window before Nurse came to bed.

During the summer months big balloons would come sailing over the house-tops from Paradise, and gay music could be heard when the wind set from the south-west.

" Father says it's a wicked place," said Sarah. Nurse and she had been talking about it in lowered voices as they went on their way to the green lanes beyond, while Mary Anne listened to all that was said and understood nothing.

" May be," said Nurse.

" Father has seen and heard enough, living close by as he does," Sarah continued. " Why, the whole place is ablaze with light, a-turning night into day, and the noise as goes on prevents respectable folks from getting any rest."

" So I've heard say," remarked Nurse ; " and on Derby night there's lines of carriages and cabs reaching the whole length of this road. Mary-Ann Knight told me as how she never see such a sight."

" Seems to be a nice place to finish up with after the

'orse-racing," Sarah went on ; " but Father, 'e says as 'ow one bad thing leads to another."

" Well, that's as may be," Nurse allowed, " but for my part I see no 'arm in 'orse-racing if you don't gamble and bet over it," for Nurse had cherished a secret longing to go to the " Durby," as she called it, ever since she came to town, and she was a farmer's daughter.

" P'raps not," assented Sarah, " but Father says as how there wouldn't be no betting if there wasn't any racing."

" Nor no racing if there wasn't any betting," Nurse argued ; " but there, never mind the Durby. Shouldn't you like just to go inside them gates and have a walk round one fine day ? "

" Yes," assented the virtuous Sarah. " 'Tain't the gardens as is bad, but what goes on there, I suppose. And Father says that those nice ladies and gentlemen as comes to church so regular every Sunday and sits in that long pew facing the Parson's family is the people as owns the Gardens."

" Well, it ain't nothing to do with them the sort of folk as goes to Paradise," remarked Nurse ; " and I dare say there's plenty of good 'uns along with the bad, just the same as there is the world over. We've all got to grow together until the harvest."

Molly, pondering over the parable of the wheat and the tares that her Mamma had read aloud from the Bible and explained to them only the Sunday before, likened Paradise Gardens in her little mind to a field of golden corn waving in the wind under a dark blue star-lit sky, and dancing with nodding red poppies all night long.

And then they would come home tired out, to tea in the nursery.

3

When Miss Manners arrived the next day, she had to endure being teased and questioned by Harriet as to where she had been and what she had done on her holiday. It was generally spent in some necessary shopping with her sister, or in going to visit some friends.

" You've got a new bonnet on ! " said Hetty. " Did you buy it yesterday ? "

" Yes," said Miss Manners, as she took it off and laid it down. " How do you like the colour ? "

It was composed of delicate mauve tulle on a wire frame, with a wreath of heliotrope and ribbons to match.

" Don't take it off," cried Hetty. " We are going for a walk, aren't we ? "

" No, not this afternoon. Your Mamma says we must make up for yesterday's lost time over lessons."

" But the sun is shining, and we should do our lessons better if we went out first."

Miss Manners smiled and replied, " Mrs Danvers said you were out too long yesterday, and had taken exercise enough for two days."

" I haven't if Molly has ! " declared Harriet. " Papa took me to see some parishioners, and I sat down half the time."

Miss Manners only smiled again, and opened the piano for a music lesson.

While her back was turned, Hetty seized the new bonnet in a fit of mischief and rammed it onto Molly's head. Then she turned it inside out and tossed it back upon the couch.

The tears came into Molly's eyes at such a wilful act of desecration.

" Oh, Hetty ! how can you be so wicked ? " she whispered, as she took the poor crushed thing in her little hands and tried to restore its shape.

" I don't care ! " grumbled Harriet. " It isn't half as nice as Mamma's new crinoline straw, which springs back into shape whichever way you turn it. I wanted to see if this would. She only came in it to show it off, and now she isn't going to take us out. It serves her right."

Molly wondered whether Miss Manners had seen and heard what was going on. If so she took no notice. She was accustomed to Harriet's pranks, and never scolded or punished her pupils. Her gentle ways and sweet smile endeared her to the little girls, and nothing gave them so much pleasure as when she obtained their Mamma's leave to take them home to tea with her.

Miss Manners lived with her parents and a sister and brother in another quaint old row of houses that led up from the riverside at the other end of the Walk.

Her father was always to be found of an afternoon, asleep in the dining parlour, with a bandana handkerchief spread over his face.

His wife, a woman of ample proportions, was usually reposing on a couch in the best parlour, where there were all sorts of interesting things for the children to look at and play with. Wax flowers and fruit under glass shades on rainbow-coloured mats made of Berlin wool-work ; boxes contrived out of numberless shells reposing on bead mats made by Miss Margery ; and photograph albums containing groups of Miss Manners' dead and gone relations, all of whom Hetty knew by heart, and Molly was never tired of looking at because of their remarkably outlandish costumes.

The walls were hung with stuffed fish and birds in addition to a number of wonderful water-colours painted by Miss Margery and her sister in their youth.

Gigantic sea shells adorned the mantelpiece, together with china ornaments and vases full of dusty everlasting flowers.

The little girls would take the shells in both their hands and press them against their ears to listen to the roaring of the ocean inside, and Miss Margery would repeat for

their benefit the lines written by the poet round the
corner :

> " Gather a shell from the strewn beach
> And listen at its lips : they sigh
> The same desire and mystery,
> The echo of the whole sea's speech.
> And all mankind is thus at heart
> Not anything but what thou art :
> And Earth, Sea, Man, are all in each."

There were cupboards on each side of the fireplace filled
with old books and toys connected with Miss Margery's
childhood ; and a doll's house stood in the opposite corner,
all fitted up inside with furniture, which Harriet loved to
turn out and set in order.

The old staircase had its fascinations too, for on the first
landing was a grandfather's clock with weights hanging
inside a mysterious little door, and on the wall outside the
bedroom where they took off their hats and coats, a bright
copper warming-pan was suspended.

When they looked out of the window of this room they
could see over the high brick wall opposite into the large
garden which belonged to the Italian desperado whom Molly
was afraid to meet, although Miss Margery said he wrote
the poetry about the sea shells.

But Nurse had told her that he kept wild beasts roaming
loose on the premises to frighten people away.

" Nurse says he looks like a wild beast himself," said
Hetty.

" He paints lovely pictures," said Miss Esther
Manners.

" What sort of pictures ? " asked Molly.

" Portraits of ladies with red hair, clothed in beautiful
colours and jewels."

" Perhaps it's a case of Beauty and the Beast," remarked
Mr Manners, for they were all seated round the table at

tea when this conversation took place. But Mary Anne
was much too matter-of-fact for fairy-tales.

Tea in the best parlour was the climax of delight. Mrs
Manners still reclined by the fireplace, while Miss Esther
poured out the tea ; and the novelty of sitting in a circle
at table instead of in a square, as at home, greatly added
to the charm for the children.

There was always a seed cake in the summer-time, varied
by dark brown gingerbread in the winter, and strawberry
jam to spread for themselves. But Mary Anne never took
the jam because it reminded her of the nightly potion
stirred with a pin.

A cat reposed upon the hearth, which Molly was allowed
to feed with a saucer of milk ; a comfortable old pussy who
periodically produced a kitten for her to nurse and play with.

Harriet pretended to be superior to these childish
pleasures, and liked to converse with her elders, who considered her a very precocious young lady. She would ask
Mr Manners unlimited questions as to whether he wore a
night-cap when he went to bed, as well as a handkerchief
when he slept in the day-time. And whether he went to the
City by the penny steamer or the penny omnibus, and which
took the longest to get there. Or why did he not go on one
and return by the other ?

When tea was over, Mr Manners would be wide awake
after so much cross-questioning, and usually went out up
the row and round the corner to the " Six Bells " for a
game of bowls if it was summer-time, or to sit in the bar
parlour with a few old cronies, playing dominoes and
draughts at other times of the year.

Miss Esther washed up the tea-things, while Miss Margery
told tales to the children until it was time to take them home,
pleased at the pleasure she had given, and promising to
invite them again soon if they took pains with their lessons
and tried to progress in what they were taught.

4

Soon after their return from Davenport Hall, the little
girls were doing needlework in the dining-room with Miss
Manners one afternoon.

Harriet liked her music lesson, but she hated sewing, and
sighed over the duster she was hemming. Mary Anne was
slow at crotchets and minims, but practised her scales and
exercises conscientiously. She showed considerable aptitude
with her needle, and was always relieved when the music
lesson was over and the hemming began.

Miss Manners endeavoured to keep their minds occupied
by reading aloud a chapter from *Dear Old England* and
asking questions in *Stepping-stones to Geography* while they
stitched.

Harriet seldom attended properly, and on this occasion
she replied, in answer to Miss Manners' gentle enquiry as
to the circumference of the earth :

" Oh, d'you know Mamma is going to give a party ?
I heard her talking to Papa about it this morning. It's for
baby's christening."

Miss Manners did not encourage conversation, but she
thought it was politic sometimes to humour Hetty, so she
asked what the baby's name was to be, and was told,
" Robert Charles."

" So we've got our way about Charles, though it's really
after our uncle in Norfolk, and not Mr Coulston," said
Mary Anne.

" Nurse says that one of baby's Godpapas is a rich man,
so perhaps he will give him a handsome present like ours,"
observed Harriet. " I've got a silver spoon and fork in a
case."

" Indeed ? " said Miss Manners, and she meekly enquired
the circumference of the earth again, but Hetty took no
notice, and rattled on :

" Miss Speergrove is going to be baby's Godmamma, and I heard Mamma say it would be a good occasion to invite the choir to a party, because Miss Speergrove is the leader, you know. At least she thinks she is, though Papa says she only squeaks like this——"

Hetty made a noise in her nose, and Molly burst out laughing, in which Miss Manners felt constrained to join softly.

" Your sister will be invited, of course, and p'raps you will too. What fun it will be ! " Hetty went on.

" You will be in bed," said Miss Manners.

" Oh no, we shan't ! If Mamma won't let us sit up we shall look between the banisters in our nightgowns, like we did at Davenport Hall, and see all that goes on ; and if you are there we shall call you upstairs to our bedroom, shan't we, Molly ? and you shall sit and tell us stories."

" Oh, indeed ! " laughed Miss Margery. " Then you had better be good now and go on with the geography."

" Aunt Anna says it's no use learning geography without globes," remarked Harriet, " and she made us hold the backboard all the time."

" So does Mamma now, every morning," observed Mary Anne, " till we ache all over."

" It's for your good," said Miss Manners, " so you mustn't grumble."

" To make us carry ourselves properly," the little girl remarked as she stitched away industriously.

" Like your dear Mamma," agreed Miss Manners. " Surely you would wish to be as elegant as she is when you grow up ? And as accomplished too ! "

" I don't care whether I am or not ! " declared Hetty, " and I hate holding the backboard."

" Now don't you think you can remember what the circumference of the earth is ? " insinuated Miss Margery, but Harriet continued :

" Papa says that Grandmamma Jackson must have held the backboard in bed, because she is as stiff as a ramrod, and looks as though she had swallowed the poker."

Miss Manners couldn't help laughing, though she gently reproved Harriet and told her to pay more attention to her needlework.

" Oh, bother this duster ! " exclaimed the little girl. " I can't go on hemming any longer."

A rustling of silk was heard outside ; the door opened, and Mrs Danvers entered, arrayed in her Paisley shawl and the bonnet of crinoline straw. She led little Roger by the hand. He was attired in his Sunday frock of black velvet, and a large hat set off with a white ostrich feather.

Miss Manners rose, and Mrs Danvers seated herself in the arm-chair, lifting the little boy onto her lap.

" I am going for a drive this afternoon," she began, " and as the carriage hasn't come yet, I have looked in to see how you are progressing with your needlework."

" Oh Mamma, mayn't we come too ? " cried Hetty jumping up.

" My dear Harriet, who gave you leave to rise ? " asked her Mamma. " Remember you are in the schoolroom, and be seated again."

Hetty obeyed with a rebellious face.

" Your little brother is going with me to have his photograph taken," said Mrs Danvers, regarding him fondly as she smoothed the broad white collar of point lace that encircled his neck.

" He looks just like that monkey with the organ-grinder when he wears his best frock and hat, doesn't he ? " Harriet whispered to Mary Anne, who sniggered into the duster.

" I hope to find a great improvement in your hemming, Harriet," said her Mamma. " You may both come and show me now what you are doing."

The little girls rose and went forward with their dusters.

" Take your thimbles off," said their Mamma. " Never wear them when you are not working ; only sempstresses do that."

" So does Nurse," remarked Mary Anne.

Mrs Danvers examined her hemming first and expressed approval, but Hetty's needlework never satisfied her.

" Really, Harriet," she said, " considering that you are nearly two years older than your sister it is quite a disgrace that your work is not neater. These stitches are like cats' teeth. I must ask you, Miss Manners, to give more time and attention to the sewing."

" But, Mamma," exclaimed Hetty, " I dislike needlework, and I shall never do it nicely."

" My dear Harriet," replied her Mamma, " it is not your business to argue, but to learn, and if Mary Anne can use her needle to advantage you also can if you try."

" Molly can't read music and play the piano like me," remonstrated Hetty, " and she never will ; she only does needlework nicely because she likes it."

" But she takes pains to learn music as well as sewing," said Miss Manners encouragingly.

" Just so," Mrs Danvers agreed. " If Mary Anne is not quick at her tasks she is very painstaking, and therefore in time she will make good progress. We all have to learn to do what we don't like, and needlework in all its branches is essential to the education of a young lady."

Harriet pouted and felt spiteful, so she gave Roger a sly pinch, which caused him to put out his tongue at her.

" Fie, Roger, fie for shame ! " exclaimed Mrs Danvers. " What do you mean by such rude behaviour ? "

" Hetty pinched me," he whimpered.

" Tell-tale tit, your tongue shall be slit ; every dog in the town shall have a little bit," said his sister vehemently, shaking her fist at him.

" Really, Harriet, where you pick up such sayings I

cannot imagine," sighed Mrs Danvers. "You must learn to subdue the Old Adam within you. I shall be much obliged, Miss Manners, if you will go through the Church Catechism this afternoon with her, and I wish you to teach both of them the prayer that was said for them at baptism in order that they may use it every day on their own account. They are quite old enough to understand the meaning of what was undertaken for them by their God-parents, and it would be as well that they should commit this prayer to memory before baby's christening. On Sunday I intend to read the baptism service through with them and explain it."

Miss Manners hesitated, and asked to be shown the particular prayer that Mrs Danvers referred to, for she had her doubts about it. Harriet was told to fetch a prayer-book from the bookshelf in the library.

Meanwhile Mary Anne was peering through the wire blind which screened the lower half of the window from the road. She observed a passing carriage and turned to her Mamma, saying :

"There goes Silvester, Mamma, with Mrs Pessimist ; he isn't coming for you to-day."

"Come away, Mary Anne," insisted Mrs Danvers ; " I cannot allow heads at the window, Miss Manners. . . . What will the neighbours think, I wonder ? "

" I was only looking for Silvester because you said you were going for a drive," pleaded Molly.

"And so I am," replied her Mamma. " Cousin Amelia is calling for me in her pony carriage."

" Oh, here she is ! " cried Mary Anne, as a lady in a four-wheeled chaise came round the corner and drew up at the house. " May I run and open the door ? "

" Certainly not," said Mrs Danvers. " Fryer will ring the bell and Phœbe will answer it. By the bye, Miss Manners," she continued, as she rose from the arm-chair,

" I meant to say that I shall be much obliged if you will
find time to teach little Roger his five-finger exercises. He
is showing some musical talent and a desire to learn. Soon
he will be old enough to join his sisters in their other lessons
as well."

Having said this, Mrs Danvers took her son by the hand
and left the room. Molly's eyes followed her Mamma's
graceful figure, full of admiration ; but Hetty was regarding
her brother with malice.

" We don't want him doing lessons with us, do we, Miss
Manners ? " she said. " He can't speak properly yet, or
sound his ' R's.' And boys needn't learn to play the piano.
Roger only bangs on it with both hands to make a noise,
and Mamma has had to tell him to be quiet, because it
makes her head ache."

Molly was at the window again, behind the wire blind,
looking on at the start and longing to be taken for the drive,
as she sometimes was, on the little back seat where the
coachman sat when he accompanied Cousin Amelia.

5

Miss Gingham was Mrs Danvers' first cousin. She lived
in Paddington, and frequently called in her pony-chaise.

Fryer, the coachman, was now lifting little Roger on to
his Mamma's lap, and tucking her crinoline away under
the rug.

Cousin Amelia always drove herself, and she made a
great pet of the fat little pony whose name was Tommy.

Miss Manners stood watching at some distance from the
window and Hetty went on chattering.

" Nurse says that Roger is too old to be wearing petticoats
now he is five. But Mamma likes to make a baby of him.
His legs will look like broomsticks in knickerbockers, won't
they ? "

Miss Margery smiled as she said in reply :

" You must not be ill-natured to your little brother because he is his Mamma's darling. Perhaps he needs petting, being such a delicate child. Now come back to work and we will try and find the prayer that Mrs Danvers spoke about."

" Oh bother ! " exclaimed Harriet. " I don't want to know who old Adam was."

" Well, never mind, nor do I, but we will try and find out," said Miss Manners sympathetically.

They seated themselves round the table again and took up the dusters, which by half-past four were finished and folded ready for use.

But Miss Manners after searching the prayer-book in vain, decided to leave the responsibility of the two Adams to the Parson's wife. It was time to go and she went to put on her bonnet. Molly sidled to the window again, to watch for her Mamma's return.

" There's Silvester come back," she said, as the brougham drove past the window and stopped at Number Five. " But there's no one inside."

Harriet was clearing the table and putting the lesson books back on the shelves.

" Mamma said you were not to stand at the window," she commanded. " Come away at once. It's an idle habit." And she made herself very busy at the book-cupboard.

" There's nothing else to do now," urged Molly, " and I want to see the pony and to open the door for Mamma. Perhaps she will let me give Tommy a lump of sugar."

" Miss Manners, please make Molly do as she is told," demanded Hetty, when the gentle little governess appeared at the door putting on her gloves, her pretty new bonnet all crushed out of shape.

Miss Manners never made anyone do anything, but she coaxed them into it.

"Oh, Molly," she said, "you know your dear Mamma disapproves and I am sure you don't wish to vex her. Come and be my looking-glass and try to put my poor bonnet straight. It seems all crooked somehow. I can't think what has happened to it. There, is that better? Thank you, dear," and she gave her little pupil a sweet kiss, which Mary Anne returned with a fond hug that nearly annihilated the bonnet again.

"Now come and open the front door and let me out, there's a good little girl. Your Mamma mustn't find you at the window, you know, when she comes home."

This artifice succeeded to the satisfaction of all, for as Mary Anne stood on the doorstep waving her hand to the governess, the pony-chaise turned the corner into the Row.

Silvester was driving into his yard at the moment. He drew up and leant forward to speak to Mrs Danvers.

Mary Anne waited at the open door. The carriage stopped there in a few minutes and Miss Gingham, with her long face full of concern, brought Mrs Danvers into the house. She looked very pale and took no notice of Molly.

"Please, Mamma, may I give Tommy some sugar and drive down the Row with Fryer while Cousin Amelia is here?" she asked.

"No, dear; shut the door at once," replied her Mamma. "Something very dreadful has happened since we started out. Silvester has just imparted to us the sad news. Is your Papa in the library?"

Harriet, all curiosity as to what was the matter, came from the dining-room.

"Our neighbour at Number Five has died suddenly this afternoon while she was driving in the Park," said Mrs Danvers, when she had seated herself in the arm-chair and untied her bonnet-strings.

Mary Anne thought of the empty carriage she had seen go by, and she wondered what had become of the poor lady's body when her spirit had so suddenly left it.

"I saw the carriage come back, Mamma, but there was no one inside," she said.

"No, my dear," replied Miss Gingham. "The coachman drove to the nearest hospital and left his poor Mistress there."

"Who killed her?" queried Mary Anne; "I saw her starting out in the carriage."

"She died of a shock," said Miss Gingham, "at seeing her little dog run over in the Park."

"Only think, Amelia!" exclaimed Mrs Danvers. "We started out for our drive at the same time this afternoon. We may indeed be more than thankful that we have been permitted to return home safely. If little Roger had been run over the shock would certainly have killed me!"

To which Miss Gingham replied:

"We may feel it is owing to an ever-watchful Providence, if I may venture so to express it, that nothing of the kind has happened, my dear Agnes, but if I may be allowed to suggest it, you mustn't give way to imagination, or let this sad event get on your nerves."

Harriet's quick and lively mind at once likened her little brother to the unfortunate lap-dog, and drawing her sister aside, she whispered it into her ear. But both the children were duly impressed by what had taken place and refrained from laughter.

Mrs Danvers leaned back in the arm-chair and removed her bonnet.

"I shall remain here until Henry comes in," she said. "I am sure he will feel the shock as much as I do. I hope you will stay with me, Amelia, and you must have a glass of wine. Harriet, ring the bell for Phœbe; go to the nursery now with Mary Anne and take Roger with you."

But the little boy was already on his way there, to convey the news to Nurse, who was saying to Sarah when Hetty and Molly arrived :

" Ah well, poor lady ! there's some as is ready to be took at any time. Let us hope she was ; though the Master said as how she never came to church. His mother was staying here when Miss Charlotte was born and she says to me one day that she never prayed the Lord in the Litany to deliver her from sudden death, because she thought it was the best way to die if you was prepared."

V. THE CHRISTENING PARTY

" O Merciful God, grant that the old Adam in this child may be so buried, that the new man may be raised up in him. Amen."

I

IN the early sixties, surpliced choirs were for Cathedrals only. Mr Danvers objected to modern innovations in an ancient church, and was oblivious to the fact that centuries ago the Lord High Chancellor, whose tomb in the chancel was effaced on Sundays by Mrs Tite's crinoline, had been found at the church to be "singing in the choir with a surplice on his back."

A select company of ladies and gentlemen now filled two long pews before the organ in the gallery, and conducted the singing in church. They came to the Parson's house on Saturdays for practice, when his wife would preside at the piano and take them through the canticles and hymns for the following Sunday.

They were personal friends of Mr and Mrs Danvers, who were of opinion that the baptizing of the baby was an occasion for an evening party, and so they were all invited to be present.

Miss Speergrove was looked upon as the leader of the ladies in the choir ; but her brother Horatio, a confirmed bachelor, was too bashful to do more than conduct his sister to church on Sundays, and retire into a back seat under the gallery. Being wealthy, as well as good church-goers, they were considered worthy to be sponsors ; a responsibility which they accepted with pleasure.

The eventful day arrived, and the Corner House was in a state of ferment from the kitchen to the nursery.

It was a gala day for the little girls. When they rose in the morning they put on their crinolines and best dresses, and at midday the whole family turned out to church in Sunday attire.

Mr Silvester's coach conveyed Mrs Danvers, Nurse and the baby, to the church, with Roger seated by his Mamma, and Charlotte by Nurse on the back seat.

The Parson having packed them all into the landau, took Harriet and Mary Anne each by the hand, and hurried off after the carriage.

They found the beadle in full uniform standing at the big west door, and quite a congregation assembled inside.

It was the first baptismal service that the little girls could be said to have taken part in, and as their Mamma had gone through it all with them in the prayer-book the Sunday before, they were expected to take an interest in the ceremony : especially when their Papa prayed that the Old Adam might be buried in the baby, and a new man be raised up in him.

This was quite beyond the limited understanding of Mary Anne ; although Mrs Danvers had made them commit the whole prayer to memory and repeat it each morning on their knees.

The baby slept peacefully through the ordeal, and opened his big blue eyes to smile on everyone when it was over.

But Charlotte was fidgety and raised her voice in a prolonged howl when she found that no notice was taken of her.

No lessons were to be done that afternoon, and when Miss Manners came as usual, she was requested to arrange the tables for supper, while Mrs Danvers reposed after the fatigue of the morning.

Harriet and Mary Anne, brimming over with excitement and delight, were allowed to help her, and her sweetness of disposition induced them to believe that they were indispensable.

Hetty could be very handy when she chose ; but poor little Molly was always slow at understanding what was required of her.

Maria and Ellen Swan had been hired for the day, and were both closeted in the pantry cleaning the glass and silver and extra china that were kept for state occasions.

There was the handsome dinner service with its border of red and blue, and the elegantly shaped green dishes for fruit, with the plates to match.

The little girls were sent running to the drawing-room to clear away the books and photograph albums that adorned the round walnut wood table, because Maria told them she was coming to spread a cloth upon it, and lay thereon the lovely white and gold tea and coffee service.

They put everything away into the chiffonier, and then took upon themselves to carry the chandelier candlesticks from the mantelpiece downstairs to the pantry for Ellen to wash. But she was much too busy to attend to them, so Molly unhooked the sparkling prisms and put them one by one carefully into a bowl of water, and Hetty, without waiting to dry them, carried them off upstairs again.

She found Phœbe on her knees before the fireplace, polishing the stove and ornate steel fender with all her might, until they shone almost as bright as silver.

The poker, shovel and tongs awaited their turn, and a gorgeous cascade of white horsehair and gold paper shavings was to be arranged over all, which the Parson's wife had purchased the day before from the woman who came along the Row twice a week, crying in a high-pitched voice :

" Ornaments for your fire-stoves ! "

" Doesn't it look lovely ? " cried Hetty, when she had

helped to suspend it from the hook up the chimney. " It is just like one of Mamma's evening dresses."

Away she flew to the dining-room to find Miss Manners and the Cook struggling with an extra leaf for the supper table ; and if the Parson had not come to their assistance from the library, the supper would not have been laid by the time that Mrs Danvers thought fit to appear upon the scene of action.

The folding-doors leading into the library at the back were thrown open, and Harriet helped her Papa to clear his writing-table.

Then Miss Manners and Maria unfolded two fine white damask cloths that were kept for dinner parties, and covered the tables in both rooms.

Mary Anne followed Maria like a shadow, as she watched her fold the dainty dinner napkins, transforming them into what she called Bishops' mitres ; and then she let the little girl place a dinner roll in the centre of each.

" Now, Miss Mary Anne, please," said Ellen Swan, coming into the room with a tray full of silver, " you must get out of the way and let me lay these spoons and forks."

So Molly retired to her usual post behind the wire blind. And from there she observed Mary-Ann Knight going down the area steps, to add to the general flutter below, and wash up in the scullery for Cook.

Mary Anne stood pondering in her mind as to how this could be done with only one hand and a hook.

Then her attention was attracted by old George coming across from the farmyard, wearing his yoke with the milk-cans suspended, full of new milk that he had just taken from Mr Colley's cows.

Cook had once told her that one can contained milk and the other water. So she observed him carefully when he stopped at the area gate calling out " Milko." And when

Cook came running up the steps with two large jugs in her hands, it was satisfactory to see that the milk all came from one can, without any water being added from the other.

There was a sound of jingling glass, and Molly turned to see Maria and Ellen Swan going the round of the tables together with a large tray full of tumblers and wine-glasses, while Miss Manners was arranging vases of flowers in the midst.

Delicious dishes, such as trifles and tipsy-cake, were making their appearance on the sideboard, with jugs of lemonade and claret-cup that Mr Danvers had been brewing in his den downstairs.

Mary Anne beamed with satisfaction at the sight ; and Miss Manners was just putting on her bonnet to go home, when Mrs Danvers entered the room and walked round both the tables, surveying them critically ; pulling a flower from one vase and sticking it into another, altering a spoon here and a fork there, placing a jug in the centre instead of at the side, just to see if it could not look better.

But Mary Anne coming away from the window when her Mamma appeared, did not think this was possible, and she threw her arms round her dear Miss Margery and kissed her as she opened the front door to let her out before she ran upstairs to the nursery.

Nurse stood calling at the top of the staircase.

" Where's Miss Harriet ? " she asked. " If she doesn't come at once she won't get any tea. You run down and fetch her, there's a good girl, my time's precious : I've got to put the babies to bed early, and get dressed for the party."

2

When tea was over, Harriet and Mary Anne were sent for by their Mamma who was engaged in arranging the furniture and setting out the tea-things in the drawing-room. The grand piano stood open, and tall silver candle-sticks were placed on the brackets. There were elegant vases filled with flowers and wild grasses upon the mantelpiece, between the chandelier candlesticks and an ormolu and gilt clock in the centre.

Phœbe was sent running upstairs to the bedrooms for more chairs, and Molly to the kitchen to ask if the dessert biscuits had come from Mr Chaine.

There she found Bella the parlourmaid from next door, who had just gone down the area with a silver teapot and a dozen teaspoons, as well as a calvesfoot jelly, with Mrs Lindsey's compliments.

Mary Anne carried this intelligence up to the drawing-room with the bag of biscuits ; and by going slowly she managed to eat one on the way. How delicious it was ! One of the very best mixed, with a sugary top ; and she knew the tin they came from in Mr Chaine's shop, having often fixed her longing eyes upon it.

When all was ready for the guests in the drawing-room as well as in the dining-room, Mrs Danvers seated herself on the sofa to rest and calling the little girls to her side, she said :

" Now Harriet and Mary Anne, I give you leave to be downstairs until nine o'clock this evening, so that you may make yourselves useful by handing the dishes ; but I forbid you to touch the teacups. Maria will take them round on a tray with the sugar bowl and cream. Go gently : there must be no rushing about and upsetting things. Be careful not to put yourselves forward in any way, but keep in the background until you see that your services are necessary."

" Yes Mamma," they assented together, pleased at the permission given.

" If you are spoken to, reply like little ladies : otherwise maintain silence.   Remember that children are only to be seen, not heard."

"Yes Mamma," they repeated with pursed mouths.

"When everyone has been helped, you may finish the bread and butter and have a slice of cake if there is any left," Mrs Danvers went on to say, "then you are to go to bed at once. Sarah will be waiting for you."

"Please Mamma, are we to keep on these dresses?" asked Harriet.

"Certainly not," replied Mrs Danvers. "You will wear your white embroidered frocks and blue silk sashes. Come at once to get ready. It is high time we were doing so."

The ormolu clock was striking seven, and with a final glance around the room, the Parson's wife ascended the stairs, followed by her little daughters. Before entering her bedroom, she went to the nursery above. All was quiet there. The two babies were asleep and Nurse was tidying up.

Roger heard his Mamma's gown rustling, and sat up in his crib.

"Mamma dear, may I have a piece of tipsy-cake?" he whispered.

"Yes darling, to-morrow you shall have what you like, if you are a good little boy and lie down now and go to sleep," she replied, stooping to kiss his white face.

Nurse was pleased with the policy of this remark, and also to see that Master Roger was inclined to do as he was told. For she had yet to array herself in her Sunday gown and black silk apron, and crown her braided·hair with a new cap made for the occasion on a front of narrow velvet rosettes. In this attire she was to be ready to receive the ladies in Mrs Danvers' bedroom when they arrived, and to relieve them of their shawls and bonnets.

Nurse was in high good humour that night, because the

chief sponsor had slipped a sovereign into her hand after the christening ceremony, and admired the baby, who was named after him.

" That's what I call being 'andsome," she had observed to Maria Swan in the pantry during the afternoon. " But of course it isn't everybody as can afford to be that."

" 'Ansome is as 'ansome does," was Maria's reply. " But I shan't get more than 'alf a crown for all this running up and down and waiting at table," she added with a sigh of regret.

3

The toilets were completed by eight o'clock, at which hour the guests were expected. Harriet and Mary Anne with necks and arms well scrubbed by Sarah, their faces shining with soap and satisfaction, their hair combed and crimped out over their bare shoulders, now stood on either side of their Mamma in low dresses and short sleeves, like a pair of wax dolls.

Mrs Danvers, seated on the sofa, certainly bore some resemblance to the ornament in the firestove, her skirts being composed of white grenadine and gold tinsel, with a lace shawl gracefully draped round her shoulders. Her neatly parted hair was covered by a lappet of real Irish crochet-lace.

Mr Danvers was still below stairs, engaged in decanting two bottles of wine ; and when the front-door bell rang, he was not in the parlour to complete the group. But before the first arrivals were divested of their shawls by Nurse, and shown in by Maria, he entered the room beaming and resplendent, with a new starched cravat wound round and round his neck, and tied in a stiff bow beneath his whiskers.

Harriet ran forward, and clasping his hand in hers, drew him to the sofa, where he had just time to seat himself by his wife and embrace her with affection, to the detriment of cap and crinoline, observing as he did so :

" A thing of beauty is a joy for ever ! "

When the first guests entered the room they proved to be Miss Barbara and her brother Hugo from next door, so they did not have far to come, and Miss Lindsey explained her punctuality by a promise made to pour out the tea and coffee.

Others quickly followed, and Phœbe was kept running up and downstairs for the next half-hour till all were assembled.

The size of some of the ladies' hoops filled Harriet with envy. She did not consider her own circumference of sufficient importance in comparison, and tried to swell it out by leaning against the grand piano.

The bright colours of the dresses, the depth of the flounces, the thick meshes of the ladies' hair-nets all engrossed her attention, while her sister was absorbed at the tea-table, which to her was more attractive, with its shining white and gold china and plenty of good things to eat. She was longing to hand them round, and strange to say, in spite of her angelic appearance, so cherubic, so innocent, so demure, Mary Anne had a greedy nature. One slice of cake, according to her Mamma's decree, was a very narrow limit to her capacity, with such a profusion of good things spread out before her.

While everyone was talking and shaking hands, she slipped a few selected sugared biscuits down the low-necked bodice of her frock, in the hope that while undressing later on she would be able to conceal them from Sarah and eat them in bed when Hetty had fallen asleep.

Maria now came laden to the table with a big bronze urn from next door, followed by Ellen carrying the silver tea- and coffee-pots on a tray ; and the pouring out began.

Barbara Lindsey and Miss Manners shared this responsibility between them, and the little girls each followed a maid as the cups went round the room, squeezing in and out between the crinolines and peg-top trousers.

Macaroons and mixed biscuits disappeared like magic. Mary Anne thought of her stolen store with sly satisfaction as she handed the elegant silver cake-basket to the guests, piled with slices of rich pound cake, none of which was left for her and Hetty.

The tea-things were cleared away, the wax candles lighted, and the buzz of conversation became louder. But Harriet had no intention of going to bed. She was engaged in conversation with Mr Manners, a brother of Miss Margery's, who had been invited to escort his sisters to the party.

Presently her Papa called across the room to her:

" Pussy, run and find Miss Speergrove's music roll. She has left it with her shawl upstairs."

Miss Speergrove lived with her brother at Brompton. His disposition was too retiring to permit him to be present on his own account at a party in pursuit of pleasure, but she obliged him to accompany her, and he was now concealed in a corner of the room behind a screen, while she was prominently rotating on the music-stool, the centre of attraction, surrounded by gentlemen in white waistcoats, with flowers in their button-holes.

Mary Anne wondered how so stout a lady managed to balance herself on so small a surface, as she twisted round from one to the other, talking to all at once.

Harriet found the bedroom empty. She tossed the hats and cloaks about in her hurried endeavours to find the music. Just as she discovered it on the ottoman, Sarah came in from the next room and pounced upon her.

" What are you doing in here, Miss ? " she exclaimed.

" I am waiting to put you and Miss Molly to bed now. Where is she ? "

But Hetty tore herself away and flew past her downstairs again.

Mrs Danvers beckoned to her as she entered the room and told her to say good-night. But Miss Speergrove smiled graciously as she handed her the music roll and asked as a special favour that the little girls might stay and hear her sing.

Mary Anne was longing to eat her biscuits. She hid herself under the wing of her dear Miss Margery, but no more was said about going to bed. When supper was served she squeezed in at the library table between Mr Hugo and Miss Manners, and was well looked after by them both. She soon began to feel sick and sleepy, while Harriet was chattering away at the other end of the table, and enjoying herself immensely, for she liked nothing so much as being taken notice of by grown-up people.

Very excited and wide-awake was she when the ladies retired to the parlour. Saying good-night reluctantly, she dragged Miss Manners upstairs, declaring that she would not undress until the ladies had been to put on their cloaks. But Sarah, who had been waiting so long, revolted and went to fetch Nurse, who was having her supper in the kitchen.

" My word ! What's all this I hear ? " She was heard breathlessly mounting the stairs from the bottom of the house to the top. " A fine idea indeed for you young ladies to be sitting up all night like this ! It's your Papa's fault I don't doubt. Fie, for shame, Miss Harriet, setting your sister such a bad example. See, she is half undressed already, like the good little girl she is."

At that moment there was a rattle of something on to the floor, and a shower of biscuits fell from Molly's unfastened clothes.

" Well I never ! What's this ? " exclaimed Nurse, while Hetty, taking in the situation at a glance, mocked her sister, saying :

"Good little girl, isn't she? Stealing biscuits and eating too much at supper. Sly little pig ! Make her eat them, Nurse, to punish her, then she will be sick, and serve her right ! "

Molly hid her face in Nurse's black silk apron, overcome with misery and fatigue. She had forgotten all about the biscuits until they tumbled to the floor. Nurse was sorry for her little pet. She told Sarah to pick up the biscuits and put them away in the nursery cupboard, saying :

" Miss Mary Anne must give them back to her Mamma to-morrow. Now into bed with you both, without another word," and she left the room, shutting the door behind her.

Molly dived down under the bedclothes, very sorry for herself, and was soon fast asleep. But Hetty was all on the " qui vive." She heard the fireworks beginning at Paradise Gardens, and getting out of bed, she went to the window and watched the rockets bursting in the dark blue sky.

When they were over she softly opened the bedroom door and stole part of the way downstairs. Some of the gentlemen were leaving the dining-room to join the ladies and she put her head over the banisters in the hope of attracting attention. Then she seated herself in a corner of the staircase and listened to the music, while the buzz of voices and the laughter went on unceasingly.

But after a while she got tired of her own company and reluctantly returned to bed, having made up her mind that in time to come she would rotate on a piano-stool like Miss Speergrove, singing and playing, while everyone else should look on and applaud.

VI. ALGERNON

" For the Lord hath given the father honour over the children, and hath confirmed the authority of the mother over the sons."—SIRACH.

I

THE summer slipped by too quickly, and winter came again without a welcome. Holidays were not taken into consideration at the Parson's house, but Miss Manners meekly asked for a week's absence in the New Year, which was granted, and Mrs Danvers engaged a respectable young person whose father kept a tavern close by, to be with the children in the afternoon, and do some dressmaking.

Harriet was growing too fast, and wearing out her clothes in half the time that Mary Anne did. The young person undertook to make a dress for her, while she helped Roger and Charlotte to decipher " Reading without Tears."

Hetty and Molly could be heard in the drawing-room practising duets on the piano while their Mamma counted " One, two, three ; one, two, three " in a high-pitched voice from the sofa on which she reclined, her hands employed in stitching embroidery for the children's frocks.

On New Year's Day a visitor was shown into their midst. The noise on the piano was so pronounced that the bell and knocker were unheard, and the family were taken by surprise.

" I have come to wish you all a Happy New Year," said the lady as she seated herself, " and to pay my perennial call."

" Harriet and Mary Anne, leave the piano and come and

say ' How d'ye do,' " commanded their Mamma, so they came forward and shook hands with the visitor, whom they recognized as Charlotte's Godmamma.

Mrs Leinster regarded the two little girls with interest.

" Dear me ! " she remarked. " How they have grown since last I was here. And where is my Godchild ? I should like to present her with this." She produced a small parcel from the interior of her sable muff.

" Ring the bell, Harriet," said Mrs Danvers. " I will send for Charlotte."

Mrs Leinster thought to herself that Harriet might have fetched her sister, but Phœbe appeared in answer to the bell and received instructions to see that Miss Charlotte was tidy and clean before she was brought into the presence of her Godmamma.

Roger, released from " Reading without Tears," came running into the room.

" Say ' How d'ye do,' dear," said his Mamma. " He is growing so fast, and needs great care. Is Algernon as tall ? "

" About the same height, and I am thankful to say he is healthy," replied Mrs Leinster decidedly. " I should have no patience with a delicate child. He is at home now for the holidays and rather lonely, so I wanted your boy to come and play with him ; but if he is not strong I should prefer that child." And she pointed to Mary Anne, who became shy at once on being singled out for notice.

" I think after all Algernon would like a nice little girl to play with. You see, he has no sisters, and she would teach him good manners."

Algernon was an only child and much indulged by his mother.

The door opened slowly and a sallow face with dark eyes peered in.

" Enter, Charlotte, and don't stand in the doorway,"
said Mrs Danvers. " Shut the door behind you." Charlotte
approached nearer.

" What a determined looking child ! " exclaimed Mrs
Leinster with a smile, by which she endeavoured to make
herself attractive. " Quite a contrast to Mary Anne. See,
here is a present for you, because you are my Godchild."

The little girl took the packet with a penetrating glance
from her big eyes and began to untie the string, while the
others looked on with interest.

A fat round pincushion was displayed to view, but it
was unfurnished and bare.

Charlotte looked at Mrs Leinster and observed :

" Molly makes pincushions, and she sticks them all over
with pins. I would like something better, like baby had
from his Godpapa."

" And what might that have been ? " enquired Mrs
Leinster in astonishment.

" A great big silver cup with his name on," replied the
child, staring the lady out of countenance.

" My dear Charlotte ! " exclaimed her Mamma, " I
am ashamed of your bad manners. Say ' thank you ' at
once for that handsome pincushion. She is too young to
know how to behave yet."

" Please don't be angry with her," laughed Mrs Leinster.
" She is quite an original child, I can see, and she has been
true to herself in not pretending to be pleased with a
present that is not acceptable. Now, my dear, if Molly
makes pincushions, perhaps she would be interested in
possessing this one, so you may give it to her. But to speak
as plainly as yourself, I have nothing else to give you."

Charlotte handed it reluctantly to her sister and left the
room at her Mamma's bidding. Big, silent tears rolled
slowly down her sallow cheeks as she returned to her
lessons.

" And may I take this child back with me for a few days ? " asked Mrs Leinster, with Molly's passive hand in hers.

" It is very kind of you," began Mrs Danvers, " but she would require a few things to be packed——"

" Then suppose I come and fetch her to-morrow in the brougham ? " said Mrs Leinster. " It will be paying you two visits instead of one, but Algernon is so naughty. I was anxious to bring him a playmate to-day, to keep him quiet."

Harriet stood listening and wishing that Mrs Leinster had chosen her instead of her sister. And so did Mary Anne.

After her departure, Mrs Danvers remarked to her children :

" Algernon Leinster is a very spoiled boy, but he is an only child and will inherit a very large fortune when his parents die. You have been invited, Mary Anne, not for your own pleasure, but for his. He has no sisters, you see, so you must make yourself agreeable to him and study to show yourself approved by his parents, that they may observe how carefully and well you are being brought up."

Charlotte appeared again now at the open door. She addressed herself to Harriet.

" Miss Crosskeys wants you to come and be tried on, Hetty."

" Come to me, Charlotte," said her Mamma. " You are a very rude little girl, and I am ashamed of you. It was very kind of your Godmamma to bring you that beautiful pincushion."

" I don't think it's beautiful, it's very ugly" replied the child. " Molly makes much nicer ones."

Mrs Danvers felt the direct truth of this remark and was nonplussed. Pointing with her long forefinger to the door, she dismissed the child and the subject, saying, " Leave the room. You must learn to behave yourself before you enter it again. You are in disgrace ; go to the nursery directly."

Mrs Danvers called Roger to her side and told Mary Anne she could continue to practise her scales while Harriet was absent.

Molly's mind was so full of Algernon and the pincushion, that it was not equal to guiding her fingers in unison on the piano, and she was banished to the dining-room for not taking pains to play her scales properly.

As she left the room, Roger made a joyful grimace at her, and ran to take her place on the music stool, where he was allowed to amuse himself while Mrs Danvers continued her embroidery.

Molly found Hetty wriggling and twisting her body about as Miss Crosskeys endeavoured to fit her. She could not be induced to stand still for a moment, and at length the young person gave up in despair.

" I shall be obliged to tell your Mamma that I cannot make the dress, and you won't have anything to wear."

" Yes, I shall," retorted Harriet. " I can borrow one of Mamma's skirts ; I am nearly as tall as she is now ; Papa said so yesterday."

Roger came running into the room with a message from Mrs Danvers, and upset the box of pins all over the floor.

Harriet turned round and hit him.

" Pick them all up again this minute ! " she cried in a temper.

" No, I won't ! " he screamed, putting his tongue out at her.

She took hold of him and shook him until he dropped on the floor, crying " I'll tell Mamma, I'll tell Mamma ! "

The doors which led into the library opened, and Mr Danvers entered.

" Here's a pretty kettle of fish ! " he exclaimed. " 'Tis dogs delight to bark and bite ; but little boys and girls were meant for something better. What is it all about, Miss Crosskeys ? I can't write my sermon in peace."

" Oh, sir ! " faltered the young person, " I do my best to keep them in order, but Miss Harriet is so masterful, she will have her own way ; and Master Roger is so spoiled, that I have no control over them." And she burst into tears.

The Parson's humorous countenance changed to one of gravity.

Hetty stood still, with her eyes downcast. Mr Danvers took her by the hand and led her into the library, shutting the door. What followed was kept a secret between themselves ; but she was a sadder and a wiser child for the rest of the day.

2

The next morning Mary Anne's best clothes were packed in her Mamma's black wooden bonnet box and Mrs Leinster came to fetch her in the afternoon.

It was the first time that she had been away from home by herself, and she felt shy and nervous, but anxious to please.

" You shall have her back at the end of the week," said Mrs Leinster, as she got into the brougham, " and I will take great care of her."

They drove off quickly to Bayswater, and came to their destination at Number Fifteen in a very tall row of big modern houses.

A footman deigned to carry in the small box, and Mary Anne was handed by the butler to a lady's maid, who took her upstairs to the very top of the tall house, into a tiny room next to her own, where she removed the little girl's hat and coat and proceeded to unpack her things without saying a word.

That being accomplished, she remarked :

" You can come downstairs now with me." And Mary Anne followed her to the ground floor, where she opened the door of a large, dreary room and looked in.

" Are you here, Master Algernon ? " asked the maid.

A low growl came from under the long table-cover and a small boy on his hands and knees thrust his head out.

" Here is the young lady who has come to stay with you," said the maid. " What are you playing at now ? Don't be afraid, Miss, he's pretending to be a bear."

" Get out of the way, Janet. We are in the Rocky Mountains and I am now going to carry off a lamb."

With a desperate pounce, which took Mary Anne's breath away, the boy seized her by her crimped hair, and after dragging her all round the room, he pulled her into his lair under the table.

" I told you I should ! " said he, " and I guessed you were a lamb ; you never uttered a sound."

Janet retired and shut the door behind her. Molly was left at his mercy.

" How do you like this game ? " asked the boy, as he crouched again on all fours. " I spring at everyone who comes into the room, but you are the first I have succeeded in dragging into my den. They struggle and fight desperately. But I knew you wouldn't the moment I saw you, you looked so sheepish. Mamma daren't appear again. She came to find me before she started in the carriage to fetch you, and I chased her round the table and pulled her all to pieces, because she wanted me to drive with her and I wouldn't. She was obliged to go upstairs and dress all over again, and Janet had to mend her mantle."

" She screamed and fought like a polecat," the boy added laughing, " it's always more exciting to battle with one's prey, you know, so I had some very good fun. What's your name ? "

Mary Anne, nervous and embarrassed by her encounter with this rude boy, every hair set on edge by being so violently pulled, did not answer him at once.

" Can't you bleat ? " he scoffed.

Molly's maidenly dignity had received a shock and she felt afraid at such treatment. She tried to emerge from under the table, but he took hold of her hair again and dragged her back.

Hot and ruffled, her dress disarranged, her fair locks dishevelled, she was on the verge of tears, when the door opened and Mrs Leinster appeared.

" Algernon, where are you ? " she called to him, " and where is your little guest ? Surely you have not taken her under the table ? Come out at once ! Remember she is a young lady, not a boy, and you must not be so rough."

She lifted the table-cover and was immediately seized upon.

" No, no, no ! " cried Mrs Leinster ; " don't come near me, you are to stop playing this silly game at once ! See how hot and untidy you have made this dear little girl, and she was the pink of perfection. Whatever can she think of you ?"

" I don't care what she thinks ! " declared the boy. " But I have had good sport this afternoon. A lion, that was Papa ; and a goat, that was Jones ; a polecat, that was you ; an antelope, that was Janet ; and lastly a lamb. Look at her golden fleece ! But she won't tell me what she calls herself."

" My dear Mary Anne, I hope you will try and teach my son better manners," sighed Mrs Leinster.

" Mary Anna plays the pianna, but she can't teach me better manners."

Mary Anne was in an upright position by now, and had recovered her self-possession sufficiently to say meekly, being anxious to appease him :

" You may call me Molly if you like ; that's my nursery name."

" Oh, you can talk, can you, though you are only a baby still." He carried her off to the pantry, where he said he was to have his tea.

" I get a fresh pot of jam from the store-cupboard, and plenty of cakes from the kitchen, and the goat doesn't mind me. When we have finished we will play at plundering. We'll sack the cupboards and carry off everything we can. Splendid fun it will be ! Why don't you clap your hands and say ' what sport ' ? You haven't got the spirit of a rabbit."

Mary Anne was relieved when Janet came and told Master Algernon they were wanted in the drawing-room ; so the plundering did not take place.

They went upstairs and found Mr and Mrs Leinster seated in front of a huge fire, in a very large room, which was illuminated by an enormous chandelier, hanging from the centre of the ceiling.

Mr Leinster was hidden behind the newspaper, but he lowered it to make Mary Anne's acquaintance ; and Mrs Leinster told Algernon to fetch a book of pictures to amuse his little guest.

In the presence of his Papa the boy became subdued, and Molly tried to amuse him with the pictures.

At half-past six the butler announced that dinner was served, and Mr and Mrs Leinster went downstairs arm in arm, after saying good-night to the children.

Then Janet appeared and took them both up to bed ; so there was to be no changing of frocks, or going down to dessert, after all, as Mary Anne had been led by her Mamma to expect. It was certainly very dull indeed.

Janet helped her to undress and put her hair into plaits for the night ; but she said nothing beyond asking one or two impertinent questions as to where she lived and how many servants they kept.

So Molly was glad when she blew out the light and left the room ; though she felt very lonely all by herself at the top of that big house, and she longed for Hetty's arms around her in the little bed.

3

The next day was wet and had to be spent indoors. Algernon chased Mary Anne up and down the staircase for exercise ; but he soon tired of her company, and she was left to amuse herself as best she could.

Molly thought there never could have been such a big, dull, gloomy house as the one in which Algernon Leinster lived. She felt very sorry for him when her mind reverted to her own small happy home, and all its pleasures and pastimes, so she began to make shy advances to the lonely boy.

While they were having their tea together she said timidly :

" Won't you come and see us all one day where I live ? Perhaps your Mamma will bring you in her carriage."

" She wanted to, but I wouldn't go," he replied.

" Why not ? " asked Mary Anne.

" Because I wouldn't," was all the answer he vouchsafed.

Molly sat munching a bun and pondering in her mind what next she should say, remembering that her dear Mamma had charged her to be affable ; but she felt sure that Hetty would have boxed the boy's ears and shaken him for his rudeness. After all, it was not his fault, for he had no brothers and sisters, no dear nurse, and no kind governess, however rich he might be in other things, and his parents did not seem to care for his company.

Mrs Leinster wrote letters in her boudoir all the morning, and her husband was like a lion shut up in his den.

The next day there was a thick fog, and again they were obliged to stay indoors. But Mrs Leinster drove out as usual by herself in the afternoon.

Mary Anne was standing at the window, just as she did at home, and feeling very despondent, when she saw her Papa coming up the doorsteps.

Her little heart gave a great throb of delight. She

rushed from the room, and the next minute she was in his arms. " Oh, Papa, Papa ! " she cried, regardless of the solemn figure of Jones, who had opened the door to Mr Danvers. " Have you come to take me home ? It is so dreadfully dull here, and there is nothing to do all day."

" Why, I thought there was a young gentleman to fascinate ? " said Mr Danvers, smiling. " Where is he ? Have you already deserted him for me ? "

" He won't speak to me because I don't like the rough games he plays," said Molly. " He hides under the table and pulls me about by my hair."

" That certainly isn't the way to behave to young ladies," replied her Papa, stroking Mary Anne's fair tresses fondly. " These golden locks ought rather to rouse in him a sense of chivalry. I must bring him to his senses."

Jones had shown Mr Danvers into the library, and so they were alone together, for Mr Leinster was not at home.

" I came to bring you this parcel from Mamma ; something left behind that she thought you might require."

" I don't want anything to wear," complained Mary Anne. " We don't dress and go down to dessert like we do at home, and Algernon has his meals with Jones and Janet, so I have to as well," she added disdainfully.

Mr Danvers threw back his head and laughed heartily.

" Well, I never did ! " he said. " So you think on the whole you would prefer to be at home again ? "

" Oh, Papa, I never wanted to come away ! Do take me back with you ! " pleaded Molly tearfully.

" What, run away and leave Master Leinster as you found him ? " said her Papa. " That would not be teaching him good manners, and what would Mrs Leinster say, I wonder ? No, you must not be impatient ; it is not like my little Polly. But perhaps to-morrow will be fine and you will go for a walk in Kensington Gardens, and forget how dull it has been indoors."

Mary Anne hung her head, for the tears would well up in her eyes, and she didn't want her Papa to see them.

" Where is the young ruffian ? Let us find him," said Mr Danvers.

Mary Anne opened the door and led the way to the dining-room ; but Algernon had disappeared, though Molly had left him playing ducks and drakes with pieces of coal from the scuttle.

" Fee-fo-fum ! I smell the blood of an Englishman !
    Be he alive, or be he dead, I'll grind his bones to make my
        bread ! "

growled Mr Danvers in a fierce voice, as he strode across the floor that was strewn with coal, and flinging back the heavy window curtains, he disclosed the frightened boy.

" What do you mean by behaving like a bear to my little lambkin ? " demanded Mr Danvers, pretending to be very stern. " You must learn to treat ladies properly, my fine fellow. You and I are old friends, are we not ? And I have been so kind as to lend you my little girl to play with for a week, and she tells me you have treated her roughly."

" Then she's a little sneak, and that's not behaving like a lady," declared the boy. " I hate girls, and always shall," he retorted. " You can take her away with you ; I don't want her here."

" I shall do nothing of the kind," replied Mr Danvers seriously. " I mean to leave her with you, and shall expect you to behave to her like a gentleman, which I am sure you will if you think. Now shake hands and say good-bye, until I come again to fetch her home."

Mrs Leinster came in from her drive just as Mary Anne and her Papa were parting in the hall. She was delighted not to have missed seeing her old friend, and she carried him off to the big drawing-room upstairs.

Molly was longing to follow them, but receiving no

invitation to do so, she reluctantly returned to the dining-room.   She found Algernon drumming on the window-pane, and as he took no notice of her, she began to pick up the pieces of coal that lay all about the carpet.

It suddenly occurred to the naughty boy to make an "Aunt Sally" of her, and each time she replaced a lump in the coal-scuttle he took it out again and shied it at her.

Mary Anne was not quick-tempered like Harriet ; her anger smouldered, and required a good deal of poking to bring it to a blaze.

Now it suddenly flared up, and she flew at Algernon like a little wild cat. He took refuge under the table ; then she dashed out of the room and up the wide staircase to find her Papa.

Jones, carrying a tray with decanters of wine and biscuits, was about to enter the drawing-room. He looked so impos-ing that she dared not venture to follow him in.

Her temper died down as suddenly as it had risen, and she crept up slowly to the top floor and shut herself into the tiny bedroom.

"Oh, I wish Papa would take me home with him, I do !" she moaned as the tears came thick and fast.

"Are you there, Miss ?" said Janet's voice a minute later as she turned the door-handle. "Mrs Leinster is wanting you in the drawing-room, and I have had to come all this way up to find you. Whatever is the matter ?"

She bathed Molly's red eyes and nose without another word, brushed her hair, and tied the velvet band on afresh. Then she sent her downstairs, remarking, "Now you look more respectable," and Mary Anne hated her there and then from the bottom of her heart.

Algernon was already in the drawing-room eating biscuits with a glass of sherry. Mrs Leinster began pouring some out for Molly, but Mr Danvers would not allow her to have it. He gave her his biscuits, while he held up a glass of port wine to the light and sipped it at intervals, declaring it to be of an excellent vintage.

" I am afraid it has been rather dull here for Mary Anne," said Mrs Leinster, " but we are going to take her to the pantomime before she goes home. I have been to book some seats this afternoon."

" It is very kind of you to wish to give her a treat, but we do not allow our children to go to theatres, or to be out late at night," said Mr Danvers decidedly.

" Indeed ! " exclaimed Mrs Leinster. " It has never occurred to me that there was any harm in a Christmas pantomime. Algernon always enjoys it, and I thought it would be good for Mary Anne."

" I hope that she will never regard it in that light," said her Papa. " My position in the parish makes it necessary to set a good example to others."

" But surely you do not consider it wrong ? " argued Mrs Leinster.

" Most assuredly I do, for young children," declared Mr Danvers. " In the first instance they ought to be in bed and asleep at night ; and in the next you never know what seed of vulgarity or indecency may be sown in their tender, impressionable young minds, never to be rooted out, or to what harmful cravings it may lead. When they are grown to years of discretion they must of course choose for themselves, but my motto is : ' Train up a child in the way he should go, and when he is old he will not depart from it.' "

" There, Algernon, you hear what Mr Danvers says," remarked his mother, " and I have a great respect for him. Are you willing to give up going to the pantomime ? "

" No," replied the boy. " If you don't take me I shall crave to go, and that would be harmful, I suppose."

" Very smart, young man, but not quite logical, I think.

There is another side to the question. Does the theatre do you any good ? "

That point of view had not occurred to Mrs Leinster, and Mr Danvers observed : " There is no harm in wholesome enjoyment ; but the Devil sows tares in the wheat-field as well as on the waste ground."

Mary Anne was secretly longing to go to the pantomime, and wishing that her Papa had not forbidden it. Again she felt in sympathy with Algernon, but Mrs Leinster changed the conversation by offering her friend another glass of wine, saying as she poured it out :

" It is quite a wholesome enjoyment, and cannot possibly do you anything but good. With that long walk home before you, at least it will not do you any harm."

Mr Danvers laughed, and allowed himself to be persuaded.

VII. DERBY DAY

*" We are a genteel neighbourhood. Two old ladies on one side,
unknown characters on the other ; but with pianos."*

THOMAS CARLYLE.

I

OLD Colonel Lindsey, who lived next door to the
Parson, was deaf and almost dumb. He had
caught a permanent cold during his campaign in
the Crimea, which made him asthmatic, and unable to
speak above a hoarse whisper. His ears were stuffed with
cotton wool, so the daily routine of scales and exercises,
which could be plainly heard through the wall, did not
trouble him.

There were older young ladies lower down the Row,
who practised duets vigorously all the morning, to the
distraction of the " Pessimist," as the Parson called another
neighbour who lived a few doors off ; but then his hearing
was nervously acute.

Colonel Lindsey wore a large military cloak of blue cloth
over his shoulders which had done duty with him at
Sebastopol ; and if the weather was too warm for it indoors,
he sat out in the summer-house smoking cigars all day long.

His wife and daughter had very kindly dispositions.
They loved the Parson's children, and often invited them to
tea and to play in their garden, which was larger than any
in the Row. It consisted of a square lawn with a big pear
tree growing in the centre of it, and a gravel walk all round.

Mr Hugo Lindsey rolled the grass every evening during

the spring and summer months to keep it in good order for croquet.

There were but few flowers because of the trees and shrubs that surrounded it, but the lilac and laburnum bushes made the garden quite gay when they blossomed.

One morning early in June the sun was shining bright and hot, and Mary Anne was peering as usual through the wire blind after breakfast. Mrs Danvers had gone downstairs to the kitchen to give her orders for the day, and Harriet could be heard in the drawing-room trying over tunes.

It was her birthday, and her Papa had made her a present of a hymn-book set to music. The noise she was making on the piano did not affect him, as he sat quietly studying his Bible in the arm-chair.

Molly saw a hansom cab dash round the corner and pull up suddenly next door. There was a hamper on the top and a gentleman inside, who was in the act of climbing out of the cab when Mr Hugo emerged from the house, and came down the doorsteps.

She observed that they both wore white waistcoats and grey hats with green gauze veils tied round them. Then she remembered that Nurse had said that it was a fine day for the " Durby."

Mr Hugo's bushy red whiskers shone in the sunlight as he stood on the pavement lighting a big cigar with a fusee, the scent of which came in at the window which was wide open.

The two gentlemen drove off down the Row, in the direction of the river, and Mary Anne heard Nurse coming downstairs with Roger and Charlotte and the baby, ready for their morning walk. She ran out of the room, for her Mamma had given a holiday in honour of Hetty's birthday, and she wanted to go with them.

" Now Miss Mary Anne, why aren't you ready ? "
exclaimed Nurse. " Don't keep me waiting a moment."
She strapped Charlotte and the baby in the perambulator
and wheeled it onto the pavement. Mrs Lindsey's cook
came from the area gate next door to wash the front steps.

" Ain't it a beautiful day ? " she remarked, " and ain't he
a beautiful boy ? " as she smiled at the baby. " Quite
cuts his little sister out, don't he ? and I dare say there'll
soon be another to cut 'im out, eh ? "

But it was beneath the dignity of Nurse to discuss family
affairs on the pavement ; so she turned the perambulator
sharply and wheeled it off round the corner, closely followed
by Mary Anne and Roger.

Mr Silvester was standing at the farmyard gates in his
top boots, and sunning himself in his shirt sleeves before
he donned his livery for the day.

" Good morning, ma'am," he said to Nurse. " Fine
weather for the Derby."

" For them as goes, I s'pose it is," snapped Nurse, for she
cherished a secret desire to see it herself. " Are you off
to it, then ? '

" Not I," laughed the old coachman. " My Derby days
are over. Why, the old grey mare would never get there."

Mary Anne perceived that Nurse was inclined to be
cross.

" Now Miss Molly, take hold of Master Roger's hand and
come along. We'll go and see all the people a-driving to
the Durby, if we can't go ourselves."

They went through pig's ground, as the children called
it, where the pigs squealed in their styes at night ; and
encountered Mr Coulston on his way to see their Papa.

Roger ran to meet him, and seized hold of his hand ;
Mary Anne, more sedate, shook the other one, saying
" How d'you do ? "

" Well, my little dears," said the good City Missionary,

" this is God's own sunshine, sent to bless Miss Hetty on her birthday, isn't it ? "

" It's for Durby Day too," declared Roger. " Nurse said so."

" The sun shines on the evil as well as on the good ; but it won't bring any blessing on gambling, my dears ; such deeds are best done in the dark : they have no need of the sun," said Mr Coulston. " But we can rejoice in it and so can Miss Hetty. She is a little ray of sunlight herself. I have a small gift for her here," he went on, tapping the breast pocket of his coat. " No, I am not going to show it to you," and he turned to take notice of the babies in the perambulator.

" What a beauty, to be sure ! " he remarked to Nurse, as he chucked Master Robert under the chin and provoked a sleepy smile. " I declare 'e 'as the 'ead of an 'istorian ! "

" What's a nistorian ? " asked Roger.

" A man who writes 'istory, like your learned neighbour in the Row."

" Well, I hope the baby won't grow up to look like him," said Nurse. " He's too pretty to turn into such an ugly old man."

Charlotte felt hurt that Mr Coulston had taken no notice of her : so she wriggled round and stretched herself stiff in one of her tempers. Nothing would pacify her but a peppermint which the good man produced from his pocket, and then they proceeded on their way towards the high road, which was alive with vehicles of every description, from a coach and four to a costermonger's cart.

" There will be fine goings on in Paradise Gardens to-night," observed Nurse, who was now in a better humour. " And a grand display of fireworks to begin with."

" Oh, may we sit up and see them ? " asked Molly.

" Who knows ? " said Nurse with a twinkle in her eye,

as she stopped at the egg and butter merchant's shop and went inside.

Roger ran in after her, leaving Mary Anne with the perambulator. There were numerous cases of eggs of all sorts, turkeys', ducks' and plovers', besides hens' eggs. And piled on top of each other were casks of all kinds of butter.

There were also the butter-merchant and his wife, Mr and Mrs Cooke, who were members of the congregation, and their young son John, and little Billy, who Roger liked to talk to.

Billy was generally to be found in the shop, clinging to the skirts of his mother, like a chicken hiding under her wing.

Nurse was once heard to say that Mrs Cooke had the features of a fowl, and Molly thought that Annie, their only daughter, was the image of a duck, for her nose resembled a bill and her skin was pale green like the shell of a duck's egg. But all this was not to be wondered at since, like fowls, their business in life was eggs.

Nurse soon appeared again with a basket of ducks' eggs for her Master's breakfast. Mrs Cooke followed her to the doorway to have a look at the little ones.

" What a contrast ! " she remarked. " No one would believe they was laid in the same nest, would they, now ? "

" No, that they wouldn't, as had anything to do with 'em, let alone what they look like." Nurse agreed. " This one might be a crow a-cawing day and night ; while that one is a wood-pigeon always a-cooing. Miss Charlotte will be a handful when she grows up, if she goes on like she does now ; and she cost her Mamma more to bring into the world than all the rest of 'em put together."

" Did she then ? " said Mrs Cooke. " Same as my Annie, I suppose. But I didn't mind what I went through to have 'er. Billy, come back here at once ! Do you want to get run over by all them cabs and carriages ? What a

M

day for the Derby to be sure ! They'll all be going to Paradise to-night, and there'll be no sleep for quiet folks like us."

Mary Anne stood listening to all that was said, and pondering in her mind the meaning of those mysterious words about Charlotte.

But the mention of Paradise dispelled them, and she determined to try and keep awake for the fireworks.

The egg-merchant himself now appeared at the door in his white apron, to see what was going on outside. He was one of the Churchwardens, and Molly regarded him in quite a different light when he handed the plate for a collection in church.

Nurse turned the perambulator to go in the other direction on the road.

" We must get some more powders for you at Gigner's, Miss Molly. You took the last one last night," she observed.

" Oh no, Nurse, please don't ! " begged Mary Anne. " I needn't take any more. Let's go home the other way."

But they had reached the chemist's shop already, and Nurse said :

" Now wait outside while I go in, and who knows but what I get you some acid drops as well to take the taste out."

Next door to the chemist were Mr Redburn's Printing Works. He was a Churchwarden as well as Mr Cooke ; but in his shop he wore a leather apron, not a linen one, and on his head a paper cap. Mary Anne often went there with her Papa on business, when long conversations would take place across the counter about printing and parish accounts, while the machines could be heard grinding away in the distance.

Mr Redburn was a very busy man. This fact had impressed itself on Molly, and when her Papa took for his text some Sundays ago :

"Seest thou a man diligent in his business? He shall stand before kings," her mind had reverted at once to the printer, for whom she had a great respect. She was just wishing she could run in and see him, when he came out and stood on the pavement looking about. He was not wearing his apron or the paper cap, but was clad in a black frock coat and a tall hat. When he saw the children he turned and spoke to them.

"Nurse gone in to Gigner's, eh? to get you some doctor's stuff?"

Mary Anne nodded her head sadly. "Are you going to the Derby?" she asked.

The Printer pulled his long red beard and laughed. "Well I never!" he said. "Me go to the Derby with all this riff-raff! I wonder where my business would be if I did such things!"

"But you've got your Sunday clothes on," said Roger.

"They'd be the last things I'd go to the Derby in, then," said the Churchwarden. "They are too respectable for that. I shouldn't ever be able to say my prayers in them again."

"Why not?" asked Roger.

"Because the Derby isn't a fit place for Churchwardens," replied the Printer.

"Then where are you going?" persisted Roger.

"Well, I was looking out for the omnibus to take me to the City on some business," he replied. "Here it comes, so good-bye, my dears, good-bye." The omnibus drew out from the yard just opposite, where it started on its route for Hoxton. The printer crossed the road and climbed in.

"I saw Mr Redburn talking to you," said Nurse, when she came out of the chemist's shop. "Where's he off to I wonder at this time of day?"

"He isn't going to the Derby," said Molly, "because we asked him."

"No fear!" replied Nurse. "He's a very busy man and knows right from wrong. If I make no mistake, he's that long-headed, he will die a rich one, too."

Mary Anne connected this in her mind with everything long about him. He was altogether a very long man. His face, his beard, his legs, were long, and now Nurse called him long-headed. Molly asked her if length had anything to do with riches, because she remembered reading about "Length of days and long life" in the Bible, which she thought might mean prosperity.

But Nurse only said as she turned the corner from the noisy road:

"Run along in front now, like good children; there's the church clock striking eleven, I declare."

When they arrived home, Bella the housemaid from next door was standing on the doorstep, with a three-cornered note in her hand.

The children ran up and greeted her warmly, for she was a great friend of theirs.

"I've brought a note from Mrs Lindsey for your Ma," said Bella.

"I'll take it to her," said Mary Anne, as Phœbe opened the door.

Nurse unstrapped the apron over the perambulator and lifted little Charlotte out. Then she took the baby in her arms.

"Here, Phœbe," she said, "take hold and don't stand gossiping there. Run along in, Miss Charlotte."

"Mistress has sent me to borrow some spoons and forks and a teapot," explained Bella, who was a fat person of some forty years and inclined to be lazy and cumbersome in a crinoline. Nurse could hardly get past her with the perambulator; but Bella went on to say,

"Miss Lindsey has got a croquet party this afternoon, and Mr Hugo is bringing his friends in to supper after the Derby."

"So you've got company, then," remarked Nurse, as she wended her way along the passage. "A good excuse for you to bustle round a bit. If I was you, I should take off that crinoline. You would get through your work twice as quick." But Bella only tossed her head in disdain.

Mary Anne came running from the parlour and told Phœbe to go in to her Mamma, who had instructions to give her about the silver that Bella would take back with her.

"Hetty has laid out her birthday presents on the table for us all to see," she said. "Nurse, do come and look."

There were pocket-handkerchiefs from her Mamma, which she was to learn to embroider with her initials as a relaxation from hemming dusters. Molly's present was a pincushion stuffed with paper and made by herself. Mr Coulston had brought her a textbook, and Phœbe had presented her with an hour-glass for boiling eggs. Molly had a fancy for that, but the thing she coveted most was the article she had helped Nurse to choose the day before at Albert Fish's shop, when they were out for a walk. A pin-tray was selected, which portrayed a china hen seated on her nest, the top of which lifted off and disclosed pins instead of eggs.

Nurse was fond of a gossip with Mrs Fish, who was a particular friend of hers. She was a buxom, smiling, kind-hearted woman, who had no children but loved to see them in her shop.

One winter's day when the snow was on the ground, while Nurse was selecting some knitting-needles and Molly was crying with cold feet, Mrs Fish had taken off the little socks and boots and rubbed her toes and chilblains until they were all of a glow. So Mary Anne felt very friendly towards Mrs Fish.

2

When Miss Manners arrived in the afternoon Mrs Danvers told her she might take the children to make hay in the Rectory field.

The Parson's wife had paid a call on the Rector's wife the day before, and an invitation was given, which seemed a suitable treat for Harriet's birthday. There was only the narrow road to cross that led from the Row into Pig's Ground, where there was a little gate in the wall which admitted them straight into the field. The sunshine made them dance with delight, and Miss Manners was pleased also not to have to spend the afternoon indoors brooding over history and hemming.

They found the Rector's children pitching the hay into cocks.

"You won't be much use without forks," remarked Eliza Church to Harriet.

"It should be raked into heaps," said Hetty officiously. "Go and get a rake."

But Eliza was not going to be ordered about in her own domain, and said it was to be tossed. So a pitched battle took place between them, which threatened to spoil the peace of the afternoon, had not Miss Manners poured oil on troubled waters.

Mary Anne thought she had never smelt anything so delicious as the scent of the hay. She was content to sit down in it with her dear Miss Margery and watch the others at play.

Presently the Rector came strolling down the garden and stood observing them for a while, then he went out through the little gate that led into the road.

Before long Harriet wanted to take the lead again, and she boxed the ears of the Rector's son because he took his sister's part.

This was not to be tolerated on their own premises, and the Rectory children went indoors to tell their Mamma.

Miss Manners mustered her charges and took them hot and tired to the seat under the old mulberry tree on the lawn.

There they sat quietly while she told them stories written by the sons of the former Rector, who was fond of sitting under the mulberry tree, which was said to have been planted by Queen Elizabeth.

" Their Mamma is my Godmamma," said Harriet, " and she had Papa to live here until he married Mamma. And d'you know she told Grandmamma Danvers that she loved him like one of her own sons. Nurse said so ! "

" There is nothing surprising in that," remarked Miss Manners, " when you know what a good man your dear Papa is. Everybody loves him."

" I don't believe Mrs Church does," said Harriet.

" Oh well, she is only one in a thousand then," laughed Miss Manners.

" What's being one in a thousand ? " asked Roger.

" Why, not mattering, of course," said Hetty promptly.

The Old Church clock struck four and Miss Manners jumped up.

" Your Mamma said you were to go through the duet before tea," said she.

" Bother the duet ! " exclaimed Hetty. " Molly will never learn to keep time, she is such a slowcoach. I am always two bars ahead of her."

Mary Anne did not like being found fault with.

" Well, you are two years older than I am," she remonstrated.

" Never mind, dear," Miss Manners said sweetly, " we are none of us quite so quick as Hetty, are we ? But after all, it's Slow and Sure that wins the race."

3

When the little girls went to their bedroom to take off their hats and get ready for tea, they looked out of the window and saw Miss Lindsey and her friends playing croquet.

" Look ! the party has begun ! " exclaimed Harriet. " There's Miss Speergrove and Carrie Gilston and Ellen and Georgina Tregunter on the lawn, and Miss Pryor and Mr Lambton sitting together on the garden seat. Mamma says they are going to make a match of it ; I heard her telling Papa so last Sunday."

" I don't know what it means," observed Mary Anne.

" I do," exclaimed Hetty. " I expect they will get married ; but never mind that now. Bella told Phœbe that a lot of Mr Hugo's friends were expected to supper after the Derby, and they are going to drink champagne, because all the glasses have been put out."

" I wish they would invite us in to hand round the cake at tea," said Molly.

" Yes, it would be fun," remarked Hetty. " Phœbe is going to help wait at supper."

" Shall we keep awake and see the fireworks to-night ? " asked Molly.

" Of course we shall ! " exclaimed Hetty. " I don't mean to go to sleep until they are over. We can pretend to be asleep if Mamma looks in." And then they ran downstairs to the drawing-room, where Miss Manners was waiting for them at the piano.

When the music lesson was over they sat down to tea in the dining-room with their Mamma, and Miss Manners went home.

Harriet's birthday was the only one which occurred in the summer-time, and instead of making a cake in honour of it, they always had the first ripe strawberries for tea.

Mrs Danvers had carefully selected the best punnet to be had at the greengrocer's, round the corner by the river, when she went for an airing in the sun before dinner.

She had arranged them nicely with leaves on a glass dish, and placed them in the centre of the table. The children looked at them longingly while they munched thick slices of bread and salt butter. Their Papa, who did not take tea, came in and smiled upon them.

" Eating again ! " he exclaimed. " It is such a hot day, I feel more inclined to drink. If you have a cup of tea to spare I will have it. And strawberries I declare ! They look refreshing to finish up with." But he refused to partake of them lest there should not be enough to go round.

" Would anyone like to come for a walk after tea ? " he asked, looking at Harriet.

" I want to water the garden," she said ; " everything is so thirsty and dried up."

" What about my Polly then ? " said Mr Danvers. She smiled assent.

" Don't take her far, Henry," said Mrs Danvers, " she has been out all the afternoon."

" But I was sitting still all the time," pleaded Molly, who loved a walk with her father.

" Then run up and get your hat, dear," said Mrs Danvers, " and don't keep Papa waiting."

The little girls left the room together, and the Parson said, " I am going to see my friend Parke, and I will get him to look at those two teeth of Polly's that are growing down over the old ones. I think he might be able to improve them. At any rate I will see what he says and take his advice ; they are spoiling her beauty."

4

Mary Anne walked sedately by her father's side with her little hand laid confidingly in his, and no idea of what was in store for her.

They went along the highway, past the shops where she had been with Nurse in the morning. She thought it would have been pleasanter by the river in the evening, for the traffic was noisy and the road dusty.

Her Papa had to make conversation for she was never communicative ; but he met many friends as he went along, and his habit was to stop and talk to everyone he knew. Molly was accustomed to this mode of procedure, and stood patiently listening to all that was said.

When at last they reached the Walk, at the corner of which was a shop, Mr Danvers said :

" Shall we go in and get some nice lozenges to suck ? " and Mary Anne agreed.

" Pharmaceutical Chemist " was engraved in large letters on the brass plate that ran the length of the expansive window in which were ranged a row of four huge caraffes of coloured waters : red, yellow, blue, green.

Molly often came here with her Papa to see Mr Parke, who sold the Spanish liquorice that was given her to suck when she had a cough in the winter. In the spring and summer-time they bought large lozenges of lavender and little ones of rose. In the autumn they changed into fat white peppermints, all of which were a pleasure to the children.

They entered the shop and found Mr Parke behind the counter and alone. He was an elderly man with a benign face and a black velvet skull-cap on his bald head.

" Good evening, sir ; pleased to see you," he said. He was a godly man, and enjoyed a chat with the Parson, though a frequenter of the chapel.

Mary Anne took no notice of what they said, for there were so many attractions under the glass case on the counter. She cast longing eyes at the pastilles and jujubes in the tall jars on the shelves, for on one or two occasions Mr Parke had given her a little packet of them all for herself, so she ˻elt as friendly towards him as she did to Mrs Fish.

Presently she heard her Papa say :

" I want you to look at my little girl's teeth and tell me if you can set them straight. The new ones are coming on the top of the old ones, which won't improve her appearance later on."

Mr Parke walked round from behind the counter to where Mary Anne was seated, and peeped into her mouth.

" I can soon set them right with the pincers," he said.

" Well," remarked Mr Danvers, " I was hoping you might be able to suggest another way."

" Nothing for it but that, I assure you, sir," replied the old man. " She has too many teeth for so small a mouth. They are crowding each other out. Better get rid of those two at once. The sooner the better : no time like the present."

Mr Danvers looked at Mary Anne to see if she understood what was said.

Mr Parke became all at once very brisk and bustling. He beamed on Molly and said :

" Will you walk into my parlour at the back of the shop, my dear, and look at all my pretty things ? "

He led the way into a little room where there was a tap and a sink, like her Papa had in his den at home, and a basin, and all sorts of strange contrivances. Mary Anne began to feel nervous and frightened in this queer apartment ; it was so unlike a parlour, though it contained a sofa and an arm-chair very like her Papa's, and a round table in the centre. Some verses she had been learning by heart with Miss Manners during the week suddenly came into her mind, about a spider and a fly.

Mr Parke went to a cupboard, which on being opened revealed rows of drawers. He continued to talk all the time.

" Now, isn't this a cosy parlour, my dear ? And there is this nice chair for you to sit in by the window ; and the arm-chair for you, Sir—be seated, I pray."

Mary Anne looked at her Papa with round eyes. "I don't want to sit down, thank you," she said. "I needn't, Papa, need I?"

"Well, I think you had better do so, my pet," replied Mr Danvers. "Mr Parke wants to have another look inside your mouth, to see if he can improve your beauty. There is nothing to be afraid of—only just a tweak or two. It will be over in a twinkle."

Molly remembered the sad fate of the fly ; but she sat down meekly, for she trusted her Papa, though she disliked spiders, and somehow, or other, kind old Mr Parke had assumed the shape of one in her mind. He came towards her with his hands behind him. The attitude was suspicious.

"Now open your mouth and shut your eyes," he said, smiling at her, " and when it's all over I'll give you a prize."

Mary Anne thought of the jujubes in the glass jar, and did as she was told, without catching sight of the claws concealed in his right hand, as he placed his left hand on the top of her head. But she never forgot what those claws felt like when they wrenched out first one and then the other top tooth all in a minute which seemed like an hour : though she never moved or uttered a sound.

"That's my brave Polly !" exclaimed her Papa. "It wasn't so bad after all, was it?"

Molly couldn't answer. She was feeling sick, and her mouth was bleeding.

Mr Parke showed her the two long tusks he had extracted, which he wrapt up in paper and presented to her, without any jujubes. So that was the prize !

Her Papa gave her a penny for each tooth, to be spent on what she pleased instead of putting it into her money-box. But she felt a helpless victim, and that she had been betrayed by her Papa. So she returned home sadder and wiser than she started out, and wished never to go and buy lavender lozenges again.

5

It was nearly seven o'clock when they reached home and Mr Danvers opened the door with his latchkey.

Mary Anne rushed straight upstairs to the nursery, where she found Charlotte was being bathed and put to bed.

" Oh Nurse, look ! " she cried, as she undid the paper and displayed the two teeth. But when she caught sight of them she shuddered, and felt the horrible wrench all over again.

" Well, I declare ! " exclaimed Nurse ; " was that what your Papa took you out for ? I thought you were going to see all the Durby folk coming back."

Molly poured forth her tale of treachery into Nurse's sympathetic ears while Charlotte was being dried on her capacious lap.

" Those two great gaps in front don't look very nice," Nurse remarked.

" In my opinion they'd best a-been left as they was ; but I s'pose your Papa knows best, and when those two up top have growed down a bit perhaps they will look less like elephant's tusks than they do now. So cheer up ; and you shall have some of my nice honey from home for your supper."

Molly threw her arms round Nurse's neck and hugged her tight. Of all sweet things, honey was to her the sweetest.

" Me too ! " demanded Charlotte, in a state of nudity, as she wriggled into her nightgown. Nurse said " No," so she stretched herself stiff with passion. Without another word she was whisked away and put into her crib, where she could stretch as much as she pleased, with no one to take any notice of her.

" Now, run downstairs, Miss Molly," said Nurse, " and tell Master Roger to come to be bathed. He is with your Mamma in the drawing-room, and I shall be quite ready for him by the time he takes to get here."

Mary Anne did as she was bidden, and Mrs Danvers said as she entered the room :

" I hear you have lost two teeth, poor child. Come here and let me see."

" No Mamma, Nurse has got them upstairs," said the matter-of-fact Molly. " And she wants to bath Roger now."

" I fear that Papa has not been wise in consulting a chemist instead of a dental surgeon," remarked Mrs Danvers as she examined Molly's mouth.

But Molly wanted to forget all about it, so she ran out into the garden to look for Hetty. The plants had been deluged, but Harriet was not there.

" Here I am ! " she called from her bedroom window above. " Come up."

Mary Anne found her sister looking on at the party next door. The click of the croquet balls came in at the window, and Hetty began to talk the moment Molly entered the room. They leaned out of the window together.

" Do come and look at Miss Speergrove's new hat ! She hasn't worn it at church yet. Did you ever see such a thing ? It's as big round as an umbrella. Nurse says she is afraid of her complexion."

Miss Speergrove's muslin skirt was looped up over her crinoline in the prevailing height of fashion. Her fat foot in an elastic-sided boot was placed on her adversary's ball, and she was in the act of croquetting him away to a distant corner.

" The Miss Lanes' crinolines are bigger than any of the others," Harriet continued, " and Carrie Gilston has got on a new striped organdie dress, but only her old pork-pie hat and veil. She will be burnt brown to-morrow. She was trying to hold up a parasol with one hand, and play with the other, but she missed the ball each time. I don't think Mr Hugo is back yet from the Derby."

Nurse now came bustling in. " It's nearly eight o'clock,

young ladies, and time you were undressing," she said.
" I will crimp your hair in four plaits to-night for a birthday
treat, and we will stand by the window and look at the
ladies and gentlemen. But they will soon be going in to
supper I expect. Phœbe has gone to help Bella wait at
table."

" I wonder what they have got to eat ? " said Molly.

" I know," said Nurse. " Susan was busy yesterday
cooking a ham and a couple of fowls and a tongue, and to-day
she has been making tarts and trifles and custards."

" I do wish we could have some of them ! " sighed Molly.

" Well, p'raps you will," said Nurse. " Mrs Lindsey is
sure to send you in what's left to-morrow."

" P'raps there won't be anything left ! " sighed Molly
again.

A bell was heard tinkling from the garden door, and
Miss Barbara was seen to lay down her mallet.

" Now they are going in to supper ! " exclaimed Hetty,
leaning out further to see better.

" Come in this minute, Miss Harriet, and be quiet ! "
said Nurse, taking hold of her by her hair. " You shan't
stand at the window if you let yourself be seen and heard.
Whatever would your Mamma say ? "

" There goes Eugenia Gilston with her young man ;
they have just finished playing," said Hetty. " But Miss
Sumner and Georgina Tregunter haven't got through the
cage yet, and it will be too dark for them to go on playing
after supper."

" It's a pity they don't finish their game first," said
Nurse. " Miss Lindsey and Bella laid it all ready this
afternoon and everything is cold on the table. Now, let
me wash your hands and faces and then get undressed
quickly while I run downstairs to tell your Mamma you
are ready to say your prayers."

Presently Mrs Danvers came up to say good night.

" Have you had a happy birthday, dear ? " she asked, as she closed the lower half of the window.

" Oh, please don't shut it ! " said Harriet.   " It's so hot to-night."

Mrs Danvers tucked her little daughters up in bed together and, kissing them fondly, left the room.   They lay still and listened until voices were heard coming into the garden again.   Then Hetty jumped out of bed.   It was quite dusk.   The gentlemen were smoking cigars, the strong scent of which rose up to the open window.   The ladies were bringing out candles and lamps to illuminate the lawn and enable them to finish their game.

The click of the mallets and balls began again.

" Molly ! " said Hetty   But there was only a sleepy reply.   " Aren't you going to keep awake for the fire-works ? "

" Have they begun ? " asked Mary Anne, sitting up and rubbing her eyes.

" Oh no, not yet ; they won't for a long time.   I mean to run up to the nursery when they do ; we can see them so much better from there."

Mary Anne lay down again and she was soon fast asleep. Even the sky-rockets did not wake her when they began popping and cracking.

Harriet stole upstairs alone and found Nurse undressing by the open window and Phœbe leaning out of it.

" My word, Miss Hetty !   Who gave you leave to come up here ? " asked Nurse in a loud whisper.   " I declare I thought you was sleep-walking !   You gave me quite a fright.   Go to bed again directly."

" Oh, do let me stay, Nurse !   It's my birthday, you know," said Hetty.

" Why shouldn't she ? " remarked Phœbe.   " She won't take no harm this warm night.   It's too hot for bed."

" Well, be quiet then," said Nurse.   " If you wake up

baby and Miss Charlotte I shall have no end of a job to get them off again."

"Oh Phœbe, do tell me about the party next door," whispered Harriet. "Did they have champagne as well as lemonade ? "

"Real champagne, that foamed at the mouth, and coffee to finish up with," declared Phœbe. "A bewtiful supper it was and they've ate up nearly everything. There ain't a scrap over for the kitchen, Susan says."

"And what did they talk about ? " asked Hetty.

"The Derby to be sure ! It was all the Derby," replied Phœbe. "Mr Hugo and his friends could talk of nothing else : and the fine time they 'ad on the race-course. Old Colonel Lindsey was telling some stories in his hoarse voice, of Derby Days he remembered, as made 'em all laugh."

There was a movement in the corner crib where Mary Anne used to lie and listen to the rain beating against the window-panes. Roger occupied it now and he sat up and began to whimper.

"You've been and woke 'im up ! " said Nurse crossly. "Just stop your talking, Phœbe, and if you say another word, Miss Hetty, down you go to bed again." She lifted Roger from his crib to quiet him.

The croquet had come to an end ; most of the company had gone indoors, from whence sounds of music and laughter issued through the open windows. Mr Hugo could be heard singing a comic song, with all his friends joining in the chorus :

> " Champagne Charley is my name ;
> Half a pint o'porter is my game."

"Well, if that don't wake up the baby, nothing else will ! " declared Nurse. But both baby and Mary Anne slept through it all.

VIII. THE RISING GENERATION

" The temper of each new generation is a continual surprise."
ANTHONY FROUDE.

I

IT was nearing the close of another year. The Parson's pew had been provided with a new hassock for the benefit of little Charlotte, who had just reached her fourth milestone.

She began her religious career by protesting aloud when she beheld her friend the beadle coming up the aisle in his official garb.

Mrs Danvers had been obliged to beckon with a rigid forefinger, in the middle of the exhortation, to Maria Swan, who advanced from her seat on the chancel steps, and picking up the frightened child, she carried her through the little door into the churchyard and so home to Nurse.

Now Nurse had been glad to get rid of her, for there was yet another baby in the nursery. No party had taken place in honour of its arrival, for it was only a little girl. She was quietly baptized with parish babies one Sunday afternoon in the presence of the family and the pew-openers and her Mamma's friend, Miss Constantia Markham, who stood sponsor, bestowing upon her the name of Constantia in addition to that of Emily.

Babies were getting too numerous at the Parson's house to be treated individually. There were many calls for economy and self-denial with a family of six ; but proud as their parents were of each child, they had to be regarded as a whole. Nevertheless, they were not destined to be a mere row of peas in a pod. "Nor could you have fore-seen in the folds of a long night-gown the white surplice in which it was hereafter cruelly to exercise the souls of its parishioners, and strangely to nonplus its old-fashioned vicar by flourishing aloft in a pulpit the shirt-like raiment which had never before waved higher than the reading-desk," as Charlotte Brontë proclaimed.

It was a wet Sunday from beginning to end. Waterproof cloaks, goloshes and gingham umbrellas had encased and protected the whole family for the morning service. The Parson never permitted any member of his household to neglect Sunday church-going. He considered it the sound basis of true religion and morality.

When the black gown was worn in the pulpit, and crinolines filled up the pews, there were no daily services in the Old Church; but the parishioners were called together twice every Sunday by the only bell left of the sweet peal that formerly swung in the square tower.

Nurse went off to her chapel in the afternoon, leaving Harriet in charge upstairs, and Mrs Danvers took the two babies downstairs.

Sarah Turke had left some weeks before to better herself in the service of a dignitary of the church in a northern suburb. Nursemaids were luxuries and must be done with-out. Hetty must take her place and make herself useful.

"Let's play at church," she proposed when Nurse had set off, leaving Molly behind on account of the weather.

Molly was dejected in consequence. "We can't play without people," she demurred.

"Oh, yes we can," said Harriet. "You can be a pew-opener and I can play the organ, Roger must be the clergyman, and Charlotte can make the congregation"; but Charlotte objected.

"Nonsense!" exclaimed Hetty. "You must do as you

are told or you will spoil the game. You can pretend to be first one person and then another, being shown into pews by Molly, until it is time for the service to begin."

Charlotte changed her mind. The play-acting appealed to her. She could personate everybody. " But there aren't any pews," she said.

" We can make believe there are," responded Harriet, quickly demonstrating an imaginary family being shown into the nursery fireguard, which unhooked at the side like a pew door.

The game proved attractive. Roger was already erecting a pulpit with one wooden chair upturned over another. He decided at once that the fireguard closely resembled the altar rails in church and must not be utilized as a pew because the Charity children would be seated around it.

" Very well," said Hetty. " Then we must have the chairs, and you must use the linen-basket for a pulpit."

" But I shall have Nurse's chair for a reading-desk," Roger declared.

" Very well then, you can have it," said Harriet, " but the washing-stand must be the organ, and I shall play it now."

Full of confidence in her powers of imagination, she opened the lid that shut everything in and began pulling out and pushing in stops.

" May I choose the hymns ? " asked Mary Anne. And having received permission, she wrote down the numbers of her favourites and placed them with Hetty's hymn-book on the reading-desk.

" Roger, will you pull the bell and keep it going until the clock strikes," called out Harriet, for Roger had disappeared into the night-nursery and was robing himself in Nurse's nightgown.

To toll a bell appealed to him as much as preaching, and full of importance he began clanging on the tin saucepan with a spoon, in the passage outside. But the elder sisters had trouble with the younger, who was tired of being the whole congregation and obstinately refused to be people any longer.

" What will you be then ? " asked Hetty, shaking her.

" I shall be a dissenter," replied the child with decision.

" But dissenters don't come to church," declared Harriet.

" Yes, they do," said Charlotte. " Mr Turke said the organ-blower was one."

" And Papa said he was better than some people who never go to church," observed Molly.

" Then you can be the organ-blower, Charlotte," Harriet decided, " but you will have to get into the toy cupboard underneath."

She seated herself at the washstand and struck up a lively voluntary in a marvellous voice. Then Roger was seen coming solemnly in at the door clad in a nightgown, clasping his Mamma's Church Service in his small hands, which were covered by Nurse's best black kid gloves with the long finger-ends. He knelt down at the nursery chair and closed his eyes piously.

" You mustn't read all the prayers, Roger," whispered Hetty. " It will take too long. Let's have the Litany."

Charlotte was dragged from the cupboard and made to repeat the responses. Then a hymn was given out, and Roger disappeared into the night-nursery. The sisters went on singing " Sun of my soul " in a loud voice until he reappeared with Nurse's black silk skirt hooked on round his neck.

His sisters burst out laughing, but Roger meant to be taken seriously. He clambered into the pulpit and said, " Let us pray."

" Oh, Nurse will be angry ! " whispered Molly. " She didn't wear it to-day because of getting it spoiled in the rain.

"Amen," said Charlotte in a loud voice as the prayer came to an end.

The text was being given out when footsteps were heard coming upstairs. The door opened and the Parson peeped in.

"Oh, Papa!" cried Harriet. "We are playing at church, and Roger is just going to preach. Do come and listen."

Mr Danvers smiled upon them. "What is the text you have taken, my son?" he asked.

"There shall be wailing and gnashing of teeth," replied Roger promptly.

"Not a very pleasant one to preach to little girls upon," remarked his father. "What have you got to say on the subject; and what made you take it?"

"I don't know now," replied Roger. "You have put it all out of my head by coming in; but it was really there, Papa, because Mr Coulston told us the other day that we were all in danger of hell-fire, and Molly and Charlotte were so frightened——"

"That you thought you would enlarge upon it and alarm them a little more, eh?" remarked Mr Danvers.

"Well, that's what preachers do," declared Roger stoutly. "I should like to be a parson when I grow up."

"You said you wanted to be an engine-driver the other day," said Molly.

So I did until now, but I have changed my mind," retorted Roger.

"Let it be made up for good then, and don't change back again," said his father seriously. "Young as you are, you must learn to keep your word, and to be in earnest about such things; you couldn't do better than be a parson, but I can't have you choosing texts to frighten the congregation," and he lifted little Charlotte on to his knee.

" You do," said Roger, " Molly says so. She can't go to sleep sometimes."

Mr Danvers looked amused. " So you think it's a good way of keeping people awake in church, to frighten them ? " he remarked ; " but that is not what a sermon is meant for, my boy. It is a good thing to rouse people into new life and action on the Lord's Day from the dull sloth and indifference into which they are apt to sink at times during the week, and enable them to pursue their calling, strengthened by worship and the words of the preacher."

" I don't intend to be preached to by Roger ! " declared Harriet. " He is four years younger than I am. The idea of his trying to frighten me indeed ! "

" Yes, what an idea ! " laughed her Papa. " You will be a grown-up young lady before we are all much older ; and pray what do you mean to be then ? "

" Mamma says that girls don't matter," replied Hetty, " but I suppose I shall be a mother."

Mr Danvers threw back his head and laughed heartily. " Capital ! " he said ; " and how large a family would you like to have ? "

" At least six," replied Hetty, " and I shall feed them on buns and milk. They won't get anything else."

"'Buns would be nice," observed Molly, " but not milk."

" Then what will you give your children to drink ? " asked Papa.

" I shan't have any," said Mary Anne. " I shall keep cows and pigs and ducks and chickens instead."

" You'll be an old maid like Miss Crispe at Swaffham," suggested Roger, " and I will come and stay with you, and hunt for eggs in the haystack."

" I won't be an old maid ! " declared Molly.

" Yes, you will, I'm sure," teased Hetty ; " and you will

go on making pincushions and patchwork all your life, I know."

Mary Anne resented the idea and protested again.

"Never mind what Pussy says, my pet," said the Parson, "she is only teasing you. Take my advice and stick to your pins and needles, and you will grow up into a useful woman, and sew somebody's buttons on for him some day."

Charlotte began to wriggle off her Papa's knee, since no notice was being taken of her.

"And here's my ugly duckling!" he exclaimed, putting his arm round her. "No one will want to marry her. She has got no nose—only two big eyes, and they don't match."

"And Nurse says she is as obstinate as a mule," observed Harriet.

"And she howls in church when she sees the beadle coming!" taunted Roger.

"Dear me," laughed Mr Danvers. "Whatever will she be like when she grows up?"

"She said she was going to be a dissenter this afternoon," remarked Mary Anne.

"A dissenter indeed! Whatever put that into her head?" asked her Papa. "What do you know about dissenters?"

Charlotte replied by stretching herself stiff and opening her mouth with a howl so loud that no one could hear Nurse coming up the top stairs. The door opened, and she burst into the room exclaiming:

"Now, Miss Hetty, you've been teasing your little sister again I'll be bound, and I'll box your ears for you, that I will!"

And there sat her Master in the middle of them all.

"I beg your pardon, sir, I'm sure," she said, "but how was I to know you was here with all this bellowing going on? And I do say as Miss Harriet is old enough now to know better than to tease the little ones, specially when she is left in charge of them."

" But I am afraid it is my fault this time," said Mr Danvers. " Miss Charlotte has advanced opinions of her own, and I was asking her how she got them. She is what might be called a conscientious objector."

" Why, she's been that ever since she was born, sir," declared Nurse, " and she makes more stir in the nursery than all the rest of 'em put together."

" A very healthy sign," observed Mr Danvers. " A little leaven leaveneth the whole lump."

" And what's my black silk dress doing on the floor I should like to know, Miss Harriet ? and the whole place turned topsy-turvy."

It was Nurse's turn now to object, and she called upon her Master to arbitrate.

" I think, sir, if you was to speak seriously to Miss Harriet it would be a good thing. When she's put in charge of the younger ones she is old enough to see as order is kept, or how can I go to church of a Sunday now there is no nurse-maid ? "

Full of righteous indignation she followed Mary Anne, who had picked up the silk skirt and run into the night-nursery to put it back into the cupboard, where it hung in safe seclusion all the week.

" Here give it to me," demanded Nurse, " and tell me what you've all been up to while I've been gone. Dressing up like you did at your Grandmamma's ain't fit play for Sundays ; and Miss Hetty ought to know better, and so ought you. But there ! she's always leading the lot of you into some mischief or other."

" It wasn't Hetty's fault," said Mary Anne penitently. " She said we would play at church and that is a Sunday game, isn't it ? and Roger was to preach ; so he went and got your dress for the black gown and put it on without our knowing anything about it. Indeed we didn't, Nurse."

" Well, well," said Nurse, mollified. " I hope I shall wear

it to chapel next Sunday and take you with me, so we'll say no more about it. Now run and put the nursery to rights, while I take off my bonnet and shawl."

Molly found the nursery empty. Papa had pacified Charlotte by taking her off downstairs to what he called his den, a snug little room in the basement, where he could write his sermons and smoke his pipe in peace. It was a sanctuary for all sorts of odds and ends ; tools and rusty nails, corks and bits of string, piles of old newspapers and sermons, besides many books, all of which he was confident would come in useful some day.

It was a special privilege to be allowed to penetrate into the mysteries of this sanctum, which was shut off by a green baize door from the sounds above and the smells below.

Mary Anne tidied up the nursery alone, but she was longing to run down after the others. She found Nurse's black kid gloves in the open linen-basket and went to replace them in the little top drawer where Nurse kept all her trinkets and treasures. But Nurse was standing in front of it, regarding herself in the looking-glass while she arranged her Sunday cap of black lace and velvet rosettes over her tight black braids.

" If I had left you in charge now," she remarked as she went to the cupboard and began getting out the tea-things, " I don't say as I should have any fault to find."

" But we were only playing at church," argued Mary Anne, who was feeling rather self-righteous.

" Well, you shouldn't turn solemn things into mischief, which you dursn't do if I had been here. It ain't right," Nurse remonstrated. " I'll give it to Master Roger when I catch 'im, and Miss Hetty too, for letting 'im. Now you may finish laying the teacups and see that the kettle don't bile over while I run downstairs and fetch the babies. Your Mamma has had enough of them I expect, and it's time you elder ones got ready to go down to tea. Miss Harriet shouldn't 'ave run off now, and she knows it. It's just like your Papa to come and take them away with 'im before they've had their 'air brushed and their pinafores on."

2

Harriet had got beyond the limited sphere of knowledge that Miss Manners could impart, and the New Year began with a new governess. Mrs. Danvers engaged a young person of superior abilities to come daily from Clapham, who professed to be competent in foreign languages, as well as in reading, writing and arithmetic.

One morning early in January, Mary Anne was looking expectantly through the wire blind in the dining-room, and just as the church clock was heard to strike ten, she announced the fact that Miss Petifer had mounted the doorsteps and was about to ring the bell.

" What is she like ? " asked Harriet eagerly, running to look over the top of the blind sideways, which she was now tall enough to accomplish.

" Hideous ! " replied Molly in her matter-of-fact way.

The door stood open and Harriet placed herself at the entrance to receive the new governess whom Phœbe was admitting.

" Mamma is in the kitchen ordering dinner," Hetty explained when she had shaken hands. " But she won't be long. Will you please come and take your things off." And she led the way to a small lobby at the end of the passage where there was a row of pegs for coats and hats, and the perambulator was wedged in beneath the tiny window which looked out onto the garden behind.

" There is no mirror," observed the young person, somewhat dissatisfied, " and I cannot tell whether I am fit to be seen."

" Oh yes, you are quite neat enough," said Harriet, regarding her as she led the way into the parlour.

Mary Anne advanced shyly from the window.

" Where is your brother ? " enquired Miss Petifer. " I believe he is to be my pupil also."

" Yes, it's absurd ! " said Harriet. " He is much too backward to do lessons with us. Papa is teaching him Latin in the library now."

Sounds of declensions could be heard through the folding-doors that divided the two rooms. There was an awkward pause, while the governess and pupils regarded each other. The conversation flagged.

Roger's voice was repeating after his Papa :

" Nominative : Mensa, a table.
Accusative : Mensam, table. .
Genitive : Mensai, of a table.
Dative : Mensai, to a table.
Ablative : Mensa, from a table."

" If your brother is backward," remarked Miss Petifer, " it is all the more necessary that he should be properly instructed at once."

" Well, he will have to learn things quite different from us, and he is ever so much younger than I am," grumbled Harriet. " Besides, I don't care to do lessons with boys."

Mary Anne had gone back to her position at the window and announced the fact that the Pessimist was returning from his morning walk.

" And who may he be ? " enquired the governess.

" He lives at Number Five and writes books," replied Harriet.

This mild piece of intelligence electrified Miss Petifer. She flew to the window.

" What privileged children you are to live so near to one so great ! " she exclaimed, as she watched the slouching figure go by. " I hoped in coming here every day that I should catch sight of him occasionally ; but I did not expect it would be so soon ! "

" He goes out and in every day as regular as a clock," said Harriet. " We don't think anything of seeing him. Why do you want to ? "

" Because he is a prophet and I venerate him," replied Miss Petifer. " And so will you when you are older, and can read his books."

" Nurse calls him a cross old creature," said Mary Anne. " He scowls at us when we meet him."

" But there's a worse man than he is," declared Harriet. " He's a poet, and you have to be out late to catch sight of him. Miss Manners says he walks by moonlight, but never in the sun."

" He's an artist as well," observed Mary Anne. " He lives in a large house by the river and keeps a lot of poets there, and wild animals and snakes as well."

" We bowled the prophet off the pavement with our hoops one day and Nurse said that gave him something to scowl for," said Harriet.

Miss Petifer held up her hands in dismay. " What shocking behaviour ! " she exclaimed. " I hope you were punished for it ? "

The door opened and Mrs Danvers entered the room.

" Heads at the window ! " she said ; " Come away at once, all of you. I never allow this, Miss Petifer. What is the meaning of it ? "

The new governess felt confused and left her pupils to explain the reason, which Harriet was ready enough to do.

" I am ashamed that a neighbour should be stared at so vulgarly by my children and their governess. I must ask you Miss Petifer to consider it a part of your duty in training their minds to begin by setting them a good example."

Miss Petifer's fat cheeks turned to plum-colour. Fortunately, attention was diverted by the entrance of Roger through the folding doorway. His braided knickerbockers and tunic hung loosely on him and made him look thin and lanky.

Mrs Danvers seated herself in the arm-chair and drew him towards her.

"This is our eldest son," she said. "My husband is teaching him Latin ; but I shall be obliged if you will instruct him in the modern languages and deportment." Then turning to the little girls, she continued :

"And these are my two eldest daughters. This is Harriet and that is Mary Anne. I fear you will not find them advanced for their age ; but I do not wish their minds to be forced. I consider that discipline and deportment are of greater value when children are growing. A good carriage is essential, and I desire that they should not be allowed to stoop over their dictation and copy-books. Neither may they get into a habit of scribbling, for handwriting is an index to character. Lines must be carefully ruled for them and you must make a point of seeing that they hold their pens properly. I have provided penholders with finger-rests for the purpose. Harriet, get your copy-books from the cupboard and I will show Miss Petifer the need of improvement in your handwriting."

The governess stood speechless, and Mrs Danvers proceeded to say :

"I wish them to hold the backboard regularly every morning, while the lessons are repeated. Little Roger is not so strong as his sisters, so I must ask you to take that into consideration. Harriet, you are hunching your shoulders. It is a dreadful habit . . . You really must be drilled."

Turning again to Miss Petifer, she went on to say :

"They have been reading aloud every morning with me from *Mrs Markham's History of England*. It is advisable to question them upon it ; and I have one word more to say about the geography. I wish you to teach it with the globe.

Harriet will bring it from the library. Now it is time to begin lessons." Then rising from her chair, Mrs Danvers left the room.

3

Miss Petifer's plain face was aglow with something suppressed. Mary Anne thought it was anger, because her cheeks were crimson, and her dull eyes blazed as they followed the retreating figure of Mrs Danvers. But Harriet attributed it to the vision of the Prophet, which to her acquiring mind was of interest. So she at once began asking questions about him.

" To think that you live so near and know nothing of his life-work ! " the governess exclaimed. " I have worshipped him at a distance ever since I read his first book, and at last I have actually set eyes on him ! " No wonder they blazed then, thought Molly, in her matter-of-fact way.

" ' I do not know whether this book is worth anything,' " quoted Miss Petifer, " ' but this I could tell the world : you have not had for a hundred years any book that comes more direct and flamingly from the heart of a living man.' " And her eyes blazed again.

" This is his latest work," Miss Petifer continued, producing from her pocket a closely printed volume and handing it to Harriet for inspection.

" I haven't read any French History yet," said Hetty as she looked at it. " But I daresay it would be a pleasant change from Mrs Markham."

" Papa carries a New Testament in his pocket," Roger sententiously remarked, " and he learns a verse from it every day. He is going to give me one on my birthday, and I shall do the same."

" You can't read properly yet," observed Harriet. " But I could read the newspaper when I was four."

" Mamma said we were to read in French now," remarked Mary Anne. And it was as though she had applied the bellows to the embers of a fire that had died down ; for Miss Petifer's cheeks glowed again, and her eyes blazed, as she snapped out :

" You had best learn to read in your own language first. Your Mamma thinks more about the education of the body than the mind apparently. If so much time and attention have to be spent on your figures and your fingers, you will only be fit for the ball-room."

" We are going to learn to dance," said Harriet. " Mamma said so the other day."

Mary Anne liked listening to what everybody said, without saying much herself. She now decided in her mind that it would be much nicer to be like her Mamma when she grew up, than to resemble Miss Petifer, who was dumpy and round-shouldered, though learned. And if being clever meant having a bad figure and careless appearance, she would prefer to be stupid but nice to look at.

Harriet was keener on knowledge than deportment, and exclaimed, as she brought the backboard from the corner where it was kept :

" Bother the backboard ! Please, Miss Petifer, will you let us read about the French Revolution ? "

The new governess was mollified by this desire to learn on the part of one of her pupils, and she replied :

" Well, let us be seated, and I will give you a short dictation from this book. You may not understand much of it, but it has come direct from the heart of a living man."

When twelve o'clock struck Miss Petifer was loth to rise and take the children for their morning walk. Harriet began putting away the lesson-books.

" Cannot they be left where they are ? " asked the governess.

" No, Phœbe lays the cloth for dinner while we are out, and we practise the piano while she clears away," replied Hetty.

Miss Petifer sighed, and muttered :

" There won't be much work done at this rate, what with holding backboards and ruling lines and playing the piano and going out."

She retired to the lobby to put on her things, and the children ran upstairs to get ready.

" We are to take these notes," said Harriet when she came down again.

" Where to ? " sniffed Miss Petifer. " I think Mrs Danvers should have given me the instructions herself."

" She is teaching Charlotte her A B C," said Hetty. " I know where we have to go, and can show you the way. Molly, you can walk on in front with Roger, and I will follow with Miss Petifer."

And so they set off, but Miss Petifer was sulky and displeased. It was one o'clock when they returned, and a good smell of dinner was coming from the kitchen.

Phœbe let them in, then went below and brought up a very large dish and two vegetables. Having placed them on the dinner-table, she rang the bell. Mrs Danvers descended the stairs, followed by Charlotte, and the governess emerged from the lobby, where she had endeavoured to smooth her hair and ruffled feelings without beholding her dissatisfied face in a glass.

" I hope you had a pleasant morning with your pupils," said Mrs Danvers, as she seated herself at the head of the table, and told the governess to take the other end.

The four children ranged themselves on either side of the table and their Mamma said grace. Phœbe then raised the cover and disclosed a roast leg of pork.

"Hurrah!" cried Roger. "Please, Mamma, may I have the crackle?"

"Not if you behave like that," said Mrs Danvers decidedly. "Miss Petifer, will you cut up this slice for Charlotte and mix bread with it, if you please?"

When all were helped Roger began to chatter.

"Mamma, may we have a holiday next Thursday for my birthday?" he said. "And can we go to the cemetery, please?"

Miss Petifer looked up and regarded him with astonishment. "What a depressing place to spend a birthday in!" she exclaimed.

"No it isn't," said Harriet. "It's very nice, all laid out with paths and tombstones, with texts and all sorts of interesting things to read upon them."

"First we go and count the coffins being carried into the chapel," said Roger, "and then we follow the procession and see them put into the holes."

"Miss Manners used to take us there often," observed Mary Anne, who saw Miss Petifer's face become suffused with colour again as she filled her mouth with food and ate in silence.

Phœbe removed the plates and dishes and put a large milky rice pudding before her mistress.

Miss Petifer disliked milk. Only a few grains of rice fell to her share, and she picked them up delicately with a fork.

"Mamma, look at Miss Petifer! She is eating her pudding without a spoon," observed Roger, ladling up the milk on his plate.

Mary Anne saw the governess fire a spiteful glance at the little boy and lower her eyes.

"Phœbe, have you omitted to lay a spoon to Miss Petifer?" asked Mrs Danvers.

"No, ma'am, she has one if she wants to use it," replied

the maid ; but the governess having eaten the grains, left the milk on her plate.

Mrs Danvers rose and repeated the grace after meals.

" Now you may go a short walk by the river while the table is being cleared," she said, " and then resume your studies until tea-time."

The children ran upstairs to put on their hats, and Miss Petifer retired again into the lobby. She was boiling with indignation.

When she returned to the passage the front door opened with a latch-key, and the Parson entered the house. His genial face smiled upon her.

" Someone waiting to see me ? " he asked, " but I don't think I know who it is."

His voice and smile acted like oil on troubled waters. Miss Petifer's countenance ceased to be ruffled.

" I am waiting to take the children for a walk," she said shyly.

" To be sure ; you must be the new governess then," exclaimed Mr Danvers. " But why are you standing in the hall ? Please come into my study and take a seat." He opened the door and followed her in.

" Now tell me what you think of my bairns ? " he said. " Pussy is sharp and Polly is slow, but the boy is backward, and I have been trying to make up for lost time lately with his Latin. His mother says his mind must not be forced as he is growing too fast, and I daresay she is right, you know : women always are ; but he will have to make his way in the world (she calls it making his mark), so we cannot have him lagging behind other boys of his age."

Miss Petifer felt her soul expanding under the kindly influence of this gentleman, and was about to reply when the children ran into the room.

" Oh, there you are at last ! " exclaimed their Papa ; " but you mustn't keep this lady waiting in the passage while you are getting your things on.   That was where I found her when I came in."

" Oh, that's because she doesn't know any better yet," said Harriet.

" I am afraid it is because you do not know any better, Miss Pussy," replied her Papa.   " You must not forget your good manners."

Harriet hung her head.   A reproof from her Papa was painful to her.

Roger began impatiently :

" Oh, Papa, do listen !   May we have a half-holiday on my birthday to go to the cemetery ? "

" Stuff and nonsense !   What a place to go to ! " laughed Mr Danvers.   " I don't approve of holidays on birthdays. You ought to be working all the harder because you are a year older with a year less to learn in.   And what do you find to amuse you at the cemetery, pray ? "

" We watch the men digging graves," Roger began——

" And I read all the tombstones," said Mary Anne.

" Pish !   Much better be trundling your hoops in the park," decided Mr Danvers.   " Now be off and make the most of the January sunshine."

Miss Petifer went out in a brighter humour with her young charges than she had done before dinner.   A cloud had been lifted from her conscience.   She saw the sun dip down into the mist that hung over the river as they walked along its banks, past the church and under the old archway, where the dockers were filling carts with coke and coal from the barges.

" Shall we meet the prophet or the poet ? " she asked her pupils.

" No, they don't come out at this time of day," replied Harriet.   " I expect they are all fast asleep.   Miss Manners says they prefer the dusk, like bats."

IX. THE DANCING CLASS

I

" I saw then in my dream, so far as this valley reached, there was on the right hand a very deep ditch ; that ditch is it into which the blind have led the blind in all ages, and have both therein miserably perished. Again behold, on the left hand, there was a very dangerous quag, into which, if even a good man falls, he can find no bottom for his foot to stand on.

Into that quag King David once did fall, and had no doubt therein been smothered, had not He that is able plucked him out."

JOHN BUNYAN.

"HARRIET, you must learn to hold yourself better. I cannot have you poking your head forward like that," said Mrs Danvers at dinner one day. She sat very upright herself as she helped the family from the soup tureen. It was Friday, and on that day all the odds and ends in the larder were concocted into " Bouillee " and served with flour and water dumplings floating in it. There was some art required in partaking of it without stooping. Harriet straightened herself, and her Mamma went on speaking.

" I had hoped by now to see some improvement in your shoulders. I fear Miss Petifer has not been giving enough attention to the use of the backboard."

The governess reddened but said nothing.

" You must not allow them to stoop over their lessons," continued Mrs Danvers.

" It is impossible to prevent it if they do so much writing and dictation," replied Miss Petifer. " I should prefer to devote more time to reading and questions on various subjects, but there is not time for everything."

A half-holiday was allowed on Saturday afternoons, and on that day Miss Petifer did not stay to dinner. When next it came round Harriet and Mary Anne were told by their Mamma that they were to be ready to go out with her at three o'clock.

" Mayn't I go with Papa, and Molly with you ? " asked Hetty.

" No, you will both accompany me this afternoon," said her Mamma. " I am taking you to see a mistress in calisthenics and deportment."

Mary Anne would have preferred to stay at home and do some gardening. The elder children had each a strip of ground in which they endeavoured to cultivate all sorts of things, especially radishes and mustard and cress for their parents' breakfast. Mary Anne's plot was in advance of the others for she possessed more patience and perseverance than Harriet and Roger in getting things to grow. Hetty was always trying experiments and making changes, while Roger would dig daily to see if the seeds were sprouting.

It was just the weather for gardening, but when dinner was over the little girls were sent upstairs to get ready, and punctually at three o'clock Mrs Danvers set out with a daughter on each side of her, down the Row to the riverside, and along the Walk to the left.

They stopped before a large old wrought-iron gateway enclosing a house with a verandah, which was covered with a wistaria in full bloom.

When the door opened they were admitted into a spacious hall with a vista of a garden beyond.

They went up the wide stairway and were shown into a long room where three windows opened on to the verandah.

Mary Anne thought she had never seen such a big bare

room. There was no carpet on the floor, and the furniture consisted only of a grand piano and a row of spindle-legged chairs set against the panelled wall.

Presently a lady entered wearing a lace mantilla arranged over her head. She made an elaborate curtsey to Mrs Danvers and expressed herself much honoured by the visit. To which Mrs Danvers replied :

" I received your prospectus, Miss Gaunt, and I have brought my children that you may see for yourself how much their figures require attention. I fear I cannot afford your terms, but I trust that we may be able to come to some arrangement which will make it possible for them to attend your classes."

Miss Gaunt bowed again and replied :

" It depends, madam, on what branches of the art you wish them advanced in. If they are taught privately it will be more expensive, of course, but I have classes for drilling and dancing every week."

" Oh Mamma ! " exclaimed Harriet, " do let us learn to dance ! "

" I wish you to do so later on, Harriet, but your Papa unfortunately does not yet approve of it, and at present I consider the control of your carriage and development of your limbs of more importance."

Miss Gaunt seated herself in an elegant position on the music-stool and smiled serenely. She observed the little girls with interest, and struck a few strange chords on the piano, after which she remarked :

" There are dances which improve both the carriage and the figure. I include them in the exercise classes. The Spanish Katutcha for instance is a very graceful perform- ance."

The dancing mistress rose and advancing into the room she threw herself into a series of slides and contortions, observing when she came so a standstill :

" You can see that it imparts suppleness to the limbs and
elegance to deportment. If you will allow these young
ladies to attend my classes, on Wednesday afternoons, I
will endeavour to meet Madame as to terms."

Mrs Danvers smiled graciously upon Miss Gaunt. She
bade Harriet and Mary Anne go outside on to the verandah,
while she discussed the terms with the mistress of calisthenics.

" Before I can consent to this arrangement," she said, " I
must make some enquiries about your pupils. I am extremely particular with whom my children associate, and
I could not allow them to be brought into social contact
with the tradespeople."

Miss Gaunt inclined her lace-covered head. " My class
is small and select, Madame," she replied, " but I am anxious
to increase the number of my pupils. Perhaps if I give you
satisfaction, you would be so kind as to recommend me to
your friends."

And so it was settled that Harriet and Mary Anne were
to attend the classes on Wednesday afternoons, and as they
walked home by the river, their Mamma came to the
conclusion that Miss Petifer must take her half-holiday on
Wednesdays instead of Saturdays.

There would be no more afternoon walks for Harriet with
her Papa while the classes lasted, or visits to his parishioners
with him for Mary Anne, if they were to do lessons on
Saturday afternoons. Molly liked to be taken to see Mrs
Tart, who lived almost next door to Miss Gaunt, in a small
house called Gothic Villa.

This old lady attended church regularly on Sunday
mornings, clad in an ermine tippet and bonnet to match, on
the top of a coal-black wig in which she looked very forbidding. But Molly's fair round face had awakened a
warm corner in her heart, and she always had ready a
home-made gingerbread, black with treacle, and white
with blanched almonds both inside and out.

The little girl was pleased to go where there was something nice to eat. Her Papa often took her to see Mr and Mrs Whitehead and their daughters, who lived on the King's highway, in an old house set back from the noisy road in a small frontage, with trees.

A good smell of cookery was usually to be inhaled there according to the time of year : such as orange marmalade in the winter and jams in the summer ; not to mention cake-baking and all manner of confectionery at any season.

The very atmosphere was pleasing, as well as the inmates, all the year round. On the massive mahogany sideboard in the parlour, stood a pair of heavy cut-glass decanters with silver labels hanging round their necks on which were ornately engraved, " Port wine " and " Sherry wine."

Mr Danvers did not consider it polite to refuse a glass of wine when it was offered, and Mary Anne was always sure of something good to eat.

Dessert dishes made in the likeness of dark green leaves flanked the decanters on the sideboard, and they were never empty. Apples, oranges and nuts in the autumn and winter—strawberries, raspberries and currants during the summer, the supply never failed, and Molly was given some on a plate resembling a fig-leaf, which was much nicer to eat off than any ordinary plate. If Miss Julia was there, Mary Anne was certain to have more than was good for her. She was the youngest of the three daughters, and a favourite with the Parson, and she made a pet of the demure little girl, admiring her chubby cheeks and golden locks.

Miss Julia was engaged to be married, and on one occasion Mr Danvers asked her if she would like to buy a little girl to set up housekeeping with. Miss Julia blushingly replied that no home could be considered complete without one, and what price did the Parson want for her ?

Mr Danvers said, " Don't you think she is worth her

weight in gold?" And Miss Julia laughed and declared she thought she was.

Whereat Mary Anne burst into tears crying out, "I won't be buyed," and hid her face in her Papa's long overcoat.

2

Harriet and Mary Anne did not look forward with un-mixed pleasure to the calisthenics, for they were to be deprived of their half-holiday in consequence. But novelty and progress were joys to Hetty; while the desire to culti-vate a figure like her Mamma's was paramount in Molly's mind, even at so early an age.

The following Wednesday afternoon Mrs Danvers set forth punctually at a quarter to three o'clock, with Harriet and Mary Anne on either side of her, each carrying brown holland bags which contained their new bronze sandal shoes.

The class had assembled when they entered the room. It consisted of about a dozen little girls, and a few Mammas seated against the wall.

Miss Gaunt advanced curtseying, and conducted Mrs Danvers to the row of chairs where the other ladies were with interest observing the waving of arms and the shuffling of sandalled feet to the sound of the piano, which was cracked and out of tune.

"Now, Mary Anne, do not be shy; it makes you look foolish," said her Mamma, as Molly clung close to her side. "Go and comport yourself to advantage amongst these other children, and you will soon learn to do the exercises as easily, and I hope more gracefully than they do."

"Now young ladies, attention, please!" called out the dancing mistress. "Point the toe and chassez forward. Turn, raise the arms above the head. Turn again, chassez to the right—turn again, chassez to the left ; hands over heads and march round the room."

Harriet and Mary Anne were permitted to stand and watch these evolutions the first time. Then they were placed at the end of the line of pupils and told to imitate their movements.

Expander exercises came next, to the lively tune of " Garry Owen," followed by instruction in the Katutcha, which consisted of curves and bends with the assistance of a fan.

When the class was over, arms, legs and backs all ached. On their homeward way Mary Anne felt that she could embrace the backboard in preference.

Mr Danvers met them on the doorstep and let them in with his latchkey.

" So you have been learning to dance, have you ? " he said with his genial smile.

" No, Henry, they are only doing exercises at present," corrected their Mamma, " which I trust will develop their limbs and enable them to walk gracefully, without swinging their arms and poking their heads forward."

" You can show them how to do that for nothing, my dear," laughed their Papa, " and if they like to come for a walk with me after tea, I will take them to see my friend Miss Wilkins. To look at her, and to listen to her conversation for an hour, will do them as much good as a class for calisthenics, or whatever you call them. She is as upright as the poker, and as argumentative as a lawyer, isn't she Pussy ? " and he pinched Hetty's ear. So after all they had their walk with Papa ; though they did not care to visit Miss Wilkins.

She was a spinster of uncertain age, who lived alone in lodgings with her maid. Her conversation was intellectual, and she was not fond of children.

On one occasion, when Mary Anne and Roger had been

taken to see her, Mr Danvers had a troublesome cough, which interfered with the talking. It disturbed Miss Wilkins' mental equanimity. She rose from her high-backed chair, and unlocking an oaken cupboard which stood in a recess, produced from a shelf therein a glass jar that contained sugar candy. The children had looked on, silent but expectant, while the jar was handed to their Papa, who refused the candy. Then it was replaced in the cupboard and locked up again. Their faces fell: Mary Anne had heaved a sigh, and there was a twinkle in the Parson's eyes as he looked towards the disappointed pair.

Some years later Miss Wilkins died, and in her will she had bequeathed the oaken cupboard and all her learned books to Mr Danvers, in gratitude for his visits. It filled a recess in his library, and the books were placed in a row on the sugar-candy shelf, as Roger called it for ever after.

3

The course of calisthenics was continued throughout the summer months and terminated with lessons in the " deux-temps " and polka-mazurka.

" The thin edge of the wedge, my dear ; I knew it would be so," remarked the Parson to his wife, as he watched his little daughters whirling round together one evening after tea. To which Mrs Danvers replied :

" Really, Henry, they must be brought up like other children in their class of society ; and it does them good to revolve gracefully."

" They have only to copy you, my dear, as I said before, in order to do that," retorted Mr Danvers, beaming upon her as she reclined in the horse-hair arm-chair, stitching one of his cravats.

Mrs Danvers smiled complacently and replied :

" I cannot imagine why you should disapprove of the exercise, since it is countenanced in the Bible and was indulged in by David, whom I have often heard you say was a man after God's own heart."

"Perhaps you have taken me too literally, my love," said her husband. "David was a King and could do pretty much as he pleased, which led to his doing many things he ought not to have done. I maintain that dancing was an undignified pastime in his position ; neither do I consider it a becoming exercise for clergymen's daughters. The money you are paying for their instruction might be spent on things more necessary for them."

"Oh, I wish we could go to a real dance ! " sighed Harriet, as she came to a standstill for lack of breath.

"And have real partners ! " panted Mary Anne.

And in due time these desires were to be gratified.

It was growing dusk one Saturday afternoon early in November. Roger stood with flattened face against the parlour window, where he was on the lookout for the lamp-lighter with his ladder.

Harriet and Mary Anne had been practising duets with their Mamma, and were gone upstairs to get ready for a tea-party to which they were bidden. Roger had also been invited ; but Mrs Danvers considered him too delicate to be out after dark and he was feeling unhappy in consequence.

The muffin man came tinkling his bell down the Row. Bella was waiting at the area gate next door to catch him as he went by.

Roger supposed that he would be obliged to have tea in the nursery as his sisters were going out, and that while they were feasting on all manner of good things, he would have nothing but stale bread and salt butter to eat, with milk and water in a mug to drink. It was beneath his dignity to have meals with the babies, since he was getting on for nine.

Hetty and Molly went out and enjoyed themselves, while

he had to stay at home, and he was quite sure they didn't want him, either. And not to be wanted by anyone was very depressing.

There was the lighterman at last ! He was placing his ladder on the bar of the street lamp opposite and running up it as agile as a monkey !

The gas-light gave a yellow glimmer in the Row. Roger looked forward to being a lamplighter when he grew up, but meanwhile his life was a burden.

He heard his Papa whistling outside and he was aware that he looked in at the open door. But the little boy continued to stare into the street.

" What, all alone ? " said the Parson. " Where is Mamma ? "

" I don't know," replied Roger, " but I am so miserwable."

" Why ? whatever is the matter ? " asked his father.

" I don't know, but I am miserwable."

" Because you are not going to the party ? " laughed Mr Danvers. " Well, never mind ; Mamma knows best. She will take care of you at home while I take your sisters out to tea ; she will coddle you up, you may be sure, and read the *Pilgrim's Progress* to you and tell you all about the Giant Despair. Now run up and tell them I am ready to start."

Harriet and Mary Anne came downstairs clad in their Sunday clothes and carrying the holland bags which contained their sandal shoes.

" Mamma said we were to take these," said Hetty. " Do you think there will be any dancing, Papa ? " she asked, as the front door banged behind them and she tripped down the steps.

" It is only a tea-party and so much the better," replied Mr Danvers. " I expect you will play games and have all sorts of fun ; the dear old Chaplain and his daughters are such kindly people, and you are invited to make the acquaintance of his granddaughters who have lately come from India. But you must not let your high spirits run away with you, Pussy."

They walked along the riverside in the dusk, towards the Military Hospital to which they were bidden for the party. The Pessimist passed them on his way home to tea, and the Poet flitted by like a bat in the twilight, out for his evening stroll.

Each child held a hand of their father's, and Harriet chattered all the way.

" Doesn't he look like a big bat in that black cloak ? " she laughed.

" He was talking to himself, like Nurse does sometimes," said Molly.

" No, he was talking to the river," said Mr. Danvers. " I could almost hear what he was saying."

" Oh Papa, what did he say ? " exclaimed Harriet.

" You wouldn't understand if I told you," replied her Papa. " But one day perhaps you will."

" The river can't hear or understand," scoffed Hetty. " I could."

" That doesn't matter to poets," laughed Mr Danvers.

" Do tell us what he said, Papa."

" Well, let me see : I wonder if I can remember," mused the Parson. " I think it was something like this :

> " O water wandering past ;——
> Albeit to thee I speak this thing,
> O water, thou that wanderest whispering,
> Thou keep'st thy counsel to the last.
> What spell upon thy bosom should Love cast,
> His message thence to wring ? "

4

The Chaplain had three daughters. Miss Henrietta was the eldest, and she kept her father's house. Miss Constantia ruled it ; and Miss Eleanor used it as a *pied-à-terre* when she was not paying visits, for she was the youngest and gayest of the three. Harriet considered them quite middle-aged, because Miss Constantia was little Emily's Godmother, and a great friend of her Mamma's.

Mr Danvers turned in at the big gates that opened on to the private road which led to the Chaplain's house. Another Parson and his two children were waiting to be let in when they arrived. They all peered at each other in the dark.

" Why, King, is that you ? " said Mr Danvers. " So you are doing the nursemaid as well as me. We can be useful sometimes, can't we ? "

Mr King was a widower, and Mrs Danvers had it in her mind's eye that Miss Constantia Markham would make him an excellent wife, and at the same time would be just the mother his children needed. And so she sometimes invited them to meet each other at the Corner House.

An old pensioner opened the door and revealed a large, square entrance hall, alive with people. Miss Eleanor Markham, in walking attire, stood in their midst, and by her side was young Dr Burton, who resided in a big house to himself on the other side of the road. It needed a mistress as much as that of Mr. King.

" We have just been taking a walk in the grounds," said Miss Eleanor, as she shook hands with the two clergymen. " I am glad we have some men to tea. Please go into the drawing-room ; you will find my father there." And she floated up the broad staircase to take off her hat and cloak, looking back at the doctor as she went.

Mary Anne stood silent and observing, while Harriet was busily talking to Katherine King. She saw the doctor put the tips of his fingers to his lips and waft a silent kiss to Miss Eleanor, over whose left shoulder there dangled from her huge chignon a long curl which was all the fashion, and Nurse called a " follow-my-leader." Molly wondered if there was any connection between the kiss and the curl.

A maid took their hats and coats and led the way into a long room, where the table was spread from one end to the other with all sorts of good things, and a large party of children were about to sit down to tea. Mr Markham's grandchildren, Nellie and Constance, sat one at each end of the table, doing the honours and feeling shy amongst so many strangers. But Harriet Danvers on one side and Katherine King on the other, kept the conversation going between them. Mary Anne was satisfied to sit in silence and centre her attention on the feast before her eyes, and she ate steadily from every dish that was handed to her.

At the same time her Papa was being well entertained in the drawing-room. The white-headed old Chaplain sat in his arm-chair by the fire, which blazed brightly on the hospitable hearth, piled with logs cut from a fallen elm in the grounds. He did not take tea, neither did Mr Danvers ; so they talked together, independent of interruption from the circulation of cups and saucers. Miss Markham presided over the silver tea-service at a round table near by, and Dr Burton handed everything to everyone.

A large old-fashioned chintz-covered settee was comfortably filled by Miss Constantia and Mr King, whose hands were uplifted and entangled in a skein of wool they were winding together ; for to be unoccupied at any time was against Miss Constantia's principles.

Miss Eleanor, a little chilly after her walk, found the fender-stool a pleasant position. The fire made a becoming background, transforming her red hair into a flaming golden aureole. Dr Burton drew a low chair onto the hearthrug and subsided into it with his cup.

So Miss Markham was left outside the circle : but she was accustomed to that, and she looked on approvingly, listening to each " *tête-à-tête* " in turn. Presently Mr Danvers rose and went across to her. He dined at half-past six and was obliged to take his departure.

As he walked home in the mist and darkness, he rumi-
nated on the comforts of home life, and hummed to himself
the verses he had quoted to the river.

Later in the evening, when he had satisfied his appetite
and was mixing his whiskey and water, he remarked to his
wife who sat darning in the arm-chair :

" My dear, you shouldn't play with matches ; they are
apt to take fire."

" What do you mean ? " she asked.   " Have I really
struck one ? "

" It looks like it," said her husband.   " Our friend King
brought his elder children and curled himself up on the
sofa, making cat's-cradles with Miss Constantia.   That's a
sure sign of attraction, isn't it? "

Mrs Danvers dropped the stocking she was darning, and
became interested.

" She is just the woman to be mistress of his house, and
those children need a mother sadly," she said.   " Their
manners and deportment are quite neglected, and Constantia Markham is an excellent disciplinarian.   She deserves
a good home of her own, too."

" I should not be surprised if Miss Henrietta is left sole
mistress of her father's house before long," observed Mr
Danvers.   " That fellow Burton is dangling after Eleanor,
if my wits did not deceive me this afternoon."

" Really ? " exclaimed Mrs Danvers.   " I think she might
do better than that.   Such a distinguished looking girl, and
I always admire red hair.   But she possesses no qualities in
comparison with Constantia."

The conversation was interrupted by the entrance of
Nurse in her bonnet and shawl.   She was going to fetch the
young ladies home from the party.

" Please'm, the children are all fast asleep," she said.
" But I left the door open in case of a cry."

And it was not long before the cry was heard. Mrs Danvers hastened upstairs to find Charlotte in a panic of terror, because Roger had come into the room pretending to be a ghost. But his Mamma found him fast asleep in bed. She did not return to the dining-room, and when the little girls came in, their Papa was sipping his toddy in solitude. He smiled at them and said :

" Well, did you enjoy yourselves ? "

" Oh, yes, Papa ! " exclaimed Hetty. " And we danced quadrilles, and Dr Burton danced with us and Mr King too, so we had real partners ! If you had stayed longer you would have had to dance as well."

" Should I ? But I don't know how."

" Nor did Mr. King," remarked Mary Anne. " But baby's Godmamma showed him what to do, and Miss Markham played the piano for us."

" And was that all that happened ? " asked Mr Danvers.

" Oh dear no ! " exclaimed Harriet. " We played at ' Puss in the corner ' and ' Hunt the slipper.' "

" And ' Musical chairs,' " put in Mary Anne.

" But I liked the dancing best," said Hetty.

" And what did my Polly like best ? " asked her Papa, with a humorous glance at her stolid little face and figure, a contrast to Hetty's vivacity.

" The supper," said Mary Anne frankly. " And Nurse came to fetch us before we had finished, and she sent in word that we were to come this very minute, and so we had to get up and go," she added regretfully.

" You greedy little pig ! " exclaimed her sister. " You had two helps of trifle, I saw you ; besides jelly and meringues."

" Well, I did want to have one of those custards in the tall glasses," said Molly with a sigh. " They looked so nice with nutmeg on the top."

Their Mamma entered the room at this moment and said :

" Nurse wants you at once, dears, so run away to bed. Did you enjoy yourselves ? And what are the two little Markhams like ? "

" Exactly like their aunts," declared Harriet, " and they are named after them too. But they didn't talk much."

" You didn't give them a chance, I daresay," said her Papa, laughing.

" Oh, Papa, I hardly spoke at all ! " exclaimed Hetty. " But you should have heard Katie King. She never stopped talking the whole evening."

" And what was it all about ? " asked Mr Danvers.

" My father, the Principal," mimicked Harriet. " She is so conceited because he is the head of St Matthew's College."

" And had you nothing to say about your father, the Parson ? " enquired her Papa.

" No, there are other things to talk about at parties," replied Hetty.

" And does my Polly forget her old father when she is away from him ? " he asked.

" Oh, she thinks of nothing but eating ! " declared Harriet . . . " She doesn't talk at all."

" Now say good night, dears, and go to bed. Nurse is waiting for you," said their Mamma. " Be very quiet, for Charlotte is restless, and Roger has been walking in his sleep again."

5

For the sake of vicinity and the daily visions of her Prophet, Miss Petifer continued her engagement with Mrs Danvers through a second year. During that time she had not endeared herself to her pupils, neither did she feel at all attached to them.

" Priggish, narrow-minded children ! " she declared

them to be, one evening in the privacy of her home, while relating some of their faults and deficiencies.

" Harriet is headstrong and domineering ; Mary Anne is self-conscious and sly, and Charlotte is so self-opinionated and obstinate that it is impossible to teach her anything that she doesn't know already, according to her own ideas. I feel that my efforts are being wasted upon them, and I shall terminate the engagement at Christmas."

At about the same time, Mrs Danvers observed to her husband after his evening meal :

" I am thinking of changing the governess, Henry. I don't consider that Miss Petifer takes sufficient interest in the education of our children ; or that they are advancing in their studies as much as we might expect them to do, and she pays very little attention to my requests."

" Well, you know the best, of course, my dear, though she always seems a conscientious young woman, so far as I can see. But I have been thinking a good deal lately about our boy. He is getting too old for petticoat government. I want to make more of a man of him. It is time we should see about sending him to school."

" Oh, Henry, I cannot consent to his leaving home ! " said Mrs Danvers. " He is too young, and far from strong."

" Pish ! " exclaimed her husband. " It will do him good to mix with other boys, and he has many things to learn in life besides lessons. There is a good Grammar School in the Square, where our neighbour, Dr Wilton, is Head-master, you know. I mean to speak to him about the lad, and it is within an easy walk."

" Oh, Henry ! Think of the winter weather and the fogs ! " groaned Mrs Danvers. " And the child would have to go there and back twice a day ! "

But her husband only said " Pish ! The exercise will do him good."

So it came to pass that Roger was seen trudging off to school each day after an early breakfast in the nursery which was much beneath his dignity, with a new brown canvas satchel slung across his shoulders, in which was secreted amongst books and slate and paper and pencils, a packet of sandwiches or some biscuits, put there by his Mamma.

It was a great adventure, and he enjoyed the novelty and independence. Some of his schoolfellows were rough and teased him because his legs were lanky, and clad in braided knickerbockers. Others, better born, treated him with the respect due to a Parson's son ; and two young brothers named Walpole, who also wore knickerbockers, fraternized with him and struck up a friendship for life.

Harriet and Mary Anne regarded her brother in a new light when he brought his friends home to tea. William and Dudley Walpole were the sons of a retired officer, and their mother being anxious to make friends ventured to pay an afternoon call on Mrs Danvers ; but it was not returned.

In due course another governess was engaged for the rest of the family. Miss Pearson came from Pimlico every morning and entered upon her duties with a cheerful countenance. Her standard of knowledge was not high ; she knew nothing and cared less about prophets or poets : but she could cut out and make clothes with the aid of a pattern, and expressed herself willing to do anything required of her.

With a fast-growing family and a slender income, the Parson's wife considered these qualities of special importance ; and little Robert was added to the number of pupils and sent into the schoolroom to learn his letters of an afternoon, while his sisters practised the piano with their Mamma.

X. THE DANCE

*" One that ruleth well his own house, having his children in subjection with all gravity . . . for if a man know not how to rule his own house, how shall he take care of the Church of God ? "—*Saint Paul.

I

IT was the last day of the year.   Family prayers were over and the three elder children sat down to breakfast with their parents

Mrs Danver settled herself before the japanned tea-tray, which was no longer kept in reserve for parties, but brought into use every day.

Mr Danvers adjusted his stifly starched cravat, which he had tied in a hurry, pulled out his whiskers, glanced over his letters and thrust them aside for the more immediate business of breakfast.

He beamed on his little daughters, seated on either side of him, and helped himself to a boiled duck's egg, cutting off the top with his knife at one stroke. This he handed to Hetty, who scooped it out with a spoon and ate it with relish.

Slices of brown bread were given to the little girls, as being more beneficial for their teeth and digestions.

Roger, released during his holidays from the nursery breakfast, was seated at his Mamma's side, and being regaled on hot-buttered toast.

It was Harriet's privilege to take the letters from the letter-box after prayers and to put them on her parents' plates.

This morning there were two for her Mamma : one was

directed in the pointed handwriting of Grandmamma Jackson ; the other bore the London postmark and had a large gilt monogram on the back of the envelope.

When Mrs Danvers had poured out the tea and helped herself to toast, she proceeded to open this letter.

Harriet's inquisitive eyes were upon her while she perused it, as she intended to ask for the monogram to put in the album that her aunt had given her on her birthday.

Having read the letter through, Mrs. Danvers remarked, " This is an invitation from Mrs Prince, Henry, and I must say I should like to accept it."

" Why not, then, my dear ? " he replied. " Is it a dinner party ? "

" No, it is for Harriet and Mary Anne," said Mrs Danvers.

" And what are they bidden to ? Another tea-party ? " enquired their Papa, as he cut a huge piece of crust from the loaf and helped himself to butter.

" No, it is a dance on the twelfth for their children who are home from school," replied Mrs Danvers. " And as our daughters have been learning to comport themselves, it would be an advantage for them to go out amongst others in their own position."

" Ah ! " sighed Mr Danvers, " that learning to comport themselves, as you call it, will be a fine excuse for many things of which I don't approve."

" Really, Henry, you cannot wish your children to be brought up in social ignorance."

" They are young yet, my dear," he replied, " and there are more important things for them to learn in life than their position, as you call it."

Mrs Danvers demurred. " They are getting quite big girls, and it would be for their good to go amongst children of their own age and class. Harriet is too forward in her manners, and backward where one would not expect it. Mary Anne is absurdly shy when she goes amongst others ;

and there really are no children for them to associate with here."

" Oh, Papa dear," pleaded Harriet, " do let us go to the dance ! You always say Mamma knows best, don't you ? "

The Parson beheaded another egg and this time he handed the top to Mary Anne. Then he said :

" No doubt she knows what is for your good in many ways, she is so worldly-wise you see ; but I want my children to learn early in life what is the difference between right and wrong, and not give themselves up to vanity, which only leads on to vexation of spirit."

" Really, Henry," retorted his wife, " you are giving them the impression that you regard this kind invitation from our friends as sinful. It is only a children's party ! "

" Very well, my dear, perhaps I am wrong ; accept it by all means if you really think it will make them happy," said Mr. Danvers philosophically, beaming at his little daughters, who beamed back again with delight at having gained his sanction.

" At what hour are they bidden ? " asked their Papa, as he finished his second egg and pushed his plate aside.

Mrs Danvers took up the letter and read it through again.

" We are invited for eight o'clock," she said with some misgiving.

" Well, there is an instance of what I say," exclaimed the Parson. " Children ought to be in bed and asleep at that hour, instead of dressing up and setting out to parties."

" It is only for one night, Henry," his wife remonstrated, " and we can leave in time to be home for prayers."

" That I must make a *sine quâ non* eh, Roger. What does that mean ? " asked the Parson, as he passed his cup across the table for more tea.

" Why do you feed that foolish boy on toast ? " he re-marked, in order to change the subject, which was not agreeable to him. " No wonder there is no flesh on his bones. Let him share an honest slice of bread with me." And he proceeded to cut a thick round from the loaf.

Roger shrank from the chunk of bread handed to him and looked for remonstrance from his Mamma. But she sliced and spread it with orange marmalade from her plate and told him to bite it well.

" Mayn't we have some marmalade too, Mamma ? " asked Harriet.

" No dear, butter is best on brown bread," replied Mrs Danvers.

" But the butter is so salt, isn't it, Molly ? " complained Harriet.

" But, butter, buttest," laughed her Papa. " But me no more buts, Pussy ; you can eat it or go without."

Hetty pouted and went without. It was envy of her brother that had prompted her to ask for marmalade, for she was feeling quite indifferent as to what she ate, with the prospect of a real dance before her. She soon changed the subject by enquiring eagerly :

" What shall we wear at the party, Mamma ? "

Mrs Danvers sipped her second cup of tea and replied with complacence :

" You will go properly attired for the evening, of course, and your summer frocks are not smart enough. But Miss Pearson understands dressmaking, fortunately, so I hope she will fit you well."

" There is another instance in point " ; remarked her husband. " You see how one extravagance leads to another. If they cannot go in what clothes they possess, I do not think they should go at all."

" But Papa, we have quite outgrown our last year's frocks, haven't we Molly ? " cried Harriet. " We should be wanting new ones this year in any case."

" And grow out of them again by the summer, eh ? "
said Mr Danvers.

" Well, you all know more about it than I do, no doubt,"
he added, as he leaned across the table, and seizing the teapot, drained it into his cup. " Now, who wants the golden
drops ? "

" I do," said Roger, sidling round to his Papa.

" You don't deserve them," declared Harriet. " You
had marmalade."

" And you had the egg tops," argued Roger.

" But you don't have to eat brown bread like us,"
retorted Mary Anne.

" Oh, but he is the son and heir," laughed their Papa,
taking a large red and yellow cotton handkerchief from
his pocket, and blowing his nose like a trumpet. " Now,
fetch the Bibles, Pussy, and let us read the lessons for the
day."

" This is the last day of the year," said the Parson im-
pressively, as they began to find the places in their Bibles,
by the aid of blue ribbon bookmarkers, made and presented
by their aunts, embellished with strips of perforated cardboard, and texts worked thereon. " To-morrow we begin
another decade ; and to-night we shall all go to church
for a solemn service at eight o'clock."

" That's our bedtime," remarked Mary Anne.

" And it's the same time as we are asked to the party,"
put in Harriet.

" That is so," replied their Papa. " But to attend Divine
worship at that hour is more profitable than to be indulging
in amusement or even in sleep. . . . I trust that to-night we
may be enabled to confess the sins and shortcomings of the
year that is ending, and to make good resolutions for the
one to come, if we are spared to see it."

Mrs Danvers felt the importance of her husband's serious

words. But during the day neither she nor her children found any time for solemn thought.

When the Bible reading was over and the contents of the larder inspected, Miss Pearson arrived, and an important discussion took place in the parlour before lessons began, about making the new dresses for the dance.

"Everything depends on your being able to complete them by the twelfth," said Mrs Danvers, "or I cannot accept the invitation."

"Oh, Miss Pearson, you will, won't you?" begged the little girls. "And we can help with the sewing you know, can't we, Mamma?"

"I don't think your needlework will be good enough," replied the governess good-naturedly. "Of course the time is very short for making two dresses by hand, with all the flouncing you wish for, Mrs Danvers. But I will do my best to get them done in time, if you can let me have the material at once."

"There is not a moment to be lost," said the Parson's wife. "I must go and buy it this afternoon, so that you may begin to-morrow. But I cannot allow the lessons to be neglected in consequence. The children can repeat what they learn by heart, and do their writing and sums while you are getting on with the needlework, Miss Pearson."

Instead of piano practice and duets that afternoon, Harriet and Mary Anne were sent upstairs directly after dinner, to get ready to go with their Mamma to the family draper, whose shop was in the Square, at some distance along the high road and close to Roger's school.

"Hip, hip, hooray!" cried Hetty, seizing her sister by the waist and whirling her round in a waltz as soon as Grace had been pronounced.

"Harriet!" exclaimed Mrs Danvers, "I will not take you to the dance if you behave in such an unseemly manner.

What would your Papa think of you if he were here, after what he said this morning ? "

" But we needn't be solemn till to-night," said Hetty. " And it isn't as though we were going to buy mourning, is it, Mamma ? "

2

Harriet's godmother, who lived at the Rectory before she was born, had given her a brown velveteen coat for the winter, and Mrs Danvers presented Mary Anne with one to match, in order that they might be dressed alike. These garments were kept for Sundays. But as the day was cold they were allowed to put them on.

It threatened to rain when they had walked as far as the King's highway ; so Mrs Danvers held up her umbrella to stop the brown omnibus which was just starting from the yard.

This was a sacrifice to dignity, though a saving of time ; for in the days gone by it was unusual for ladies to enter an omnibus, and the Parson's wife held her skirts high.

To Harriet and Mary Anne it was an untold treat. They trampled up and down in the freshly-laid straw and seated themselves at the end near the conductor. He banged the door to, tinkled his bell, and they rumbled along at a slow pace towards the Square.

" I wish it was David Swan on this 'bus," said Hetty. " Don't you, Molly ? Then we could send a message by him to Maria, about the party."

But she was reproved by her Mamma for calling the vehicle a 'bus, and informed that it was not usual to converse with the conductor.

" Nurse calls it a 'bus," observed Mary Anne.

" And Papa always talks to David Swan," retorted Harriet.

" That is because he is a parishioner," said their Mamma,
" and it is the duty of a clergyman to do so."

When they alighted in the Square, they saw Mr Peters
the linen-draper standing behind the glass door of his shop,
looking out for customers. He bowed low with a gratified
smile, as he held it open for them to enter. This Mrs
Danvers did with the air of having alighted from a carriage
and pair ; and in those days that was just what an omnibus
was.

" Good afternoon, ma'am, very pleased to see you," said
the gratified man. " Walk this way, and what may it be
our pleasure to serve you with ? "

He led them to the further end of the shop, a place of
distinction to which ordinary customers were not invited.

Three high cane-bottomed chairs were pulled forward, on
which Mrs Danvers and her little daughters seated themselves for the afternoon.

It was not the custom in those days to go from one counter
to another for what they required. Everything asked for was
brought forward by the young man who served ; trembling
under the watchful eye of Mr Peters, who hovered near at
hand to see that the Parson's wife was waited on to the best
advantage. He regarded Mrs Danvers as one of his most
distinguished customers ; for she ran up a long bill during
the year, and it was of little consequence if it was behindhand in being paid, since she graced the establishment with
her presence, which meant business.

On this particular afternoon, in addition to the muslin for
the new party frocks, flannel was required for the nursery.
Six different rolls of red and white, of various qualities and
price, were brought out and displayed upon the counter
before Mrs Danvers could come to a decision as to which
was the best value for the money.

Next some warm stockings were needed for Mary Anne,
whose feet were covered with chilblains ; and the latest

fashion in tartan mixtures was handed out for inspection, according to instructions given aside by Mr Peters, although plain grey knit had been asked for.

" Quite the latest thing, I assure you, ma'am," he urged, as the man untied the packets and held up red and green with yellow stripes and circles on approval.

Molly's eyes grew round with admiration as she gazed upon them, and she yearned for a pair in which to show off her fat legs. She had heard her Mamma say one day to Miss Lindsey that Harriet's calves were too thin, but that those of Mary Anne were nicely rounded.

" Good value for the money, ma'am, and they will wear better than the grey," insinuated the assistant, as he dangled a pair of the red with yellow circles before their eyes.

" But they are more expensive," demurred Mrs Danvers. " However, I will take one pair of the tartan stockings for you to wear on Sundays, Mary Anne, and two pairs of the grey for weekdays . . . and now show me, if you please, some white openwork stockings for evening wear, in these young ladies' sizes."

" Oh Mamma, when are you going to see about our dresses ? " sighed Hetty who had slipped away unobserved, to watch proceedings at the next counter, while Mrs Danvers was deliberating over the flannel. She now returned, in the hope of being consulted about the muslin.

" I must buy what is necessary first," said her Mamma, " and then I shall know what I can afford to spend on you. Be seated, and learn to sit still like your sister."

Mary Anne pointed to the tartan stockings with pride, and Harriet said :

" What vulgar things ! I wouldn't wear them. They will make your legs look twice as big, and they are too fat as it is."

The white stockings were more to Hetty's taste and were soon decided upon ; then Mrs Danvers asked to see a fine quality in book muslin. First one and then another width was held up to the light and fingered to examine the texture ; and after a good deal of vacillation, Mr Peters appeared again, and brought the transaction to a close by stating that the muslin at one and eleven pence would wash better than the others. So twelve yards were measured off with a wooden rod before their eyes.

Next came a selection of ribbons for sashes and bows, and the little girls were allowed to choose their own colours. Finally there were white kid gloves to be bought, and a pair for each child with one button to fasten at the wrist, after much stretching and pulling, was declared by their Mamma to be quite the finishing touch to their toilettes.

All the purchases being now accomplished, she rose from the chair, which Mr Peters pulled back from beneath her with a bow, before preceding her to the entrance, where he opened the door with another bow, wishing them all a Happy New Year, and they emerged into comparative darkness from the gas-lit shop, for it was already tea-time.

When they turned out of the noisy streets into the quiet Row, Mrs Danvers said :

" Now dears, dismiss from your minds every thought of new dresses and dancing. Go straight upstairs without disturbing your Papa, who will be preparing his sermon for this evening. Take off your coats and hats and come down to tea quickly. Remember, we are all going to church afterwards."

3

When the meal was over and the table cleared Mary Anne sat down with a pencil and some scraps of paper provided by her Papa for scribbling purposes. She began to draw whole families in flounces with low-necked bodices and short sleeves, all in a row, one behind another, like the children on the mural monument in the church, at which she sat and stared every Sunday.

Presently the bell was heard tolling for the service and she reluctantly hid away her productions in a little desk that she possessed, and went to get ready with her sister.

Harriet was in high spirits. She regarded everything in the light of an entertainment that proved a diversion from going to bed. But Mary Anne dreaded the awe-inspiring hymns and the solemn sermon her Papa was sure to preach on the last night of the year.

The evening was damp and Roger was allowed to stay at home, lest he should catch cold. Charlotte was subject to coughs, but she was determined to go out in preference to bed, and was allowed to have her own way.

Only a small congregation had assembled. The corners of the church looked very dark and forbidding, Molly thought, as they sat in the pew, waiting for their Papa to appear through the little door that led into the vestry.

The white effigy emerging from a tomb in the dim chapel opposite was a veritable ghost; and in the shadowy distance the beautiful figure in marble seemed to have raised herself on the black sarcophagus into a very real attitude of attention between the high pillars, when the City Missionary in his corner close by began to shout the Advent hymn, which the Parson had appointed to be sung.

" Lo-ho, He comums in-in clou-hou-houds de-e-scen-n-ding
        Once for favoured sin-in-ners slai-hain ;
    Thousand, thou-ou-san-nd sa-ha-haints atten-n-ding,
        Swell the triumph of-of-His-is tra-hain.
    Hallallallelujah, Hallallallelujah, Christ aha-happears
        On earth to reign."

Harriet declared when they were gathered round the supper table afterwards, that the noise he made was like the costermonger's donkey braying at night in Pig's Ground The Parson thought so too, though he did not say so, for he had borne the full blast of it from his elevated position in the pulpit.

During the singing of this hymn Mary Anne had glanced furtively over her shoulder into the shadows behind. The small chapel was full of the bones of bygone ages. She observed a quaint pair of spinsters who lived together in a tiny house on the King's highway : one of a small row with little gardens leading up to them. The two women were rocking to and fro to the tune. They looked like gnomes, so distorted were their features and figures under the flickering light of the solitary gas-lamp wreathed in ivy for Christmas.

In reality they were Ann and Jane Short, a worthy couple who worked hard at dressmaking all the week and attended the Bible-class and service, held on Thursday evenings, for recreation and instruction.

A coloured fashion-plate was always displayed in the window of their front parlour, according to the season, and they were patronized by Nurse when she required a dress made.

Mrs Tite sat on the Chancellor's tomb without her crinoline, faced by the two Miss Swans, who were singing each other down through their noses, with clenched teeth and rapturous expressions.

Miss Milman and old George, side by side under the pulpit, swayed and groaned as the hymn proceeded ; all were favoured sinners and ransomed worshippers, or how could they so revel in the terror that the hymn conveyed to the mind and the imagination of Mary Anne ? She tried to picture them rising to meet their Lord in the air, as some of the many saints attending Him ; but it was as incomprehensible as the Trinity to her.

The church was full of skeletons sealed up in leaden coffins beneath the stone floor. She had heard her Papa say so to Mr Redburn. Would they rise with the congregation ?

Mr Danvers had fed his flock on all the mysteries, and led them through all the intricacies of the Book of Revelation, during the last four Sundays of the year, and his text to-night was the final verse in the Bible.

" He which testifieth these things saith, Surely I come quickly. Amen. Even so, Come, Lord Jesus."

When Molly went to bed that night she had waking visions of beasts and other abominations, including churches and candlesticks with flaring lights, and plagues and deadly sins all multiplied by seven.

" Lo, He cometh in clouds, and every eye shall see Him ; and they shall look on Him whom they pierced," kept repeating itself in her brain like a pendulum.

" As a thief in the night," she whispered to herself, while Hetty was snoring by her side. She longed to wake her and talk. But when the first cock crowed in Pig's Ground, she knew that the day was breaking ; the night and the fear of it, was past. Then she fell heavily asleep until Harriet aroused her with a shake and " A Happy New Year."

4

The Emperor Napoleon was called to his account two days before the dance, and the Court went into mourning according to the Royal decree.

Mrs Danvers felt it expedient to follow the fashion ; so all the bows of coloured ribbon that the little girls had taken such pride in making and sewing down the front of their white muslin dresses, had to be taken off and replaced with black ones.

" Oh Mamma ! " pleaded Harriet, " It will be such a lot of trouble for nothing, and the black bows will look so hideous. Need we really do it ? "

" Certainly," replied Mrs Danvers. " In fact, I should not be surprised if the dance is postponed."

" Well, we must be in the fashion, I suppose ! " sighed Mary Anne, as she cut off the blue bows and sewed on the black ones.

There was no intimation that the dance would not take place ; so Mr Worby drew up his cab to the door of the corner house in Queen Anne's Row punctually at a quarter to eight on the eventful evening, and into its straw-strewn interior lightly stepped the little feet in the white open-work stockings and bronze sandal shoes.

The children felt full of importance, wrapped up in knitted shawls carefully held across their bare necks by hands encased in white gloves. Mrs Danvers followed in black velvet and lace.

Harriet and Mary Anne thought she looked lovely when they were not thinking about themselves. But Hetty preferred her Mamma when she dined out in lavender silk and in the white cashmere shawl with the Paisley border gracefully draped round her sloping shoulders.

Molly, with her love of colour, liked her best in the chestnut poplin and bertha of Irish lace, which had been a present from their Uncle Roger for the christening party. But to-night Mrs Danvers was wearing Court mourning.

The cab was quite a state coach for the occasion, and Worby himself looked imposing enough to drive the Lord Mayor, in his voluminous cloth capes and beaver hat.

As they lumbered along towards the Park through the fog, Mrs Danvers spoke a few words in season to her little daughters, who sat facing her on the back seat.

" You both look very nice, dears," she remarked as her eyes scanned an outline of round white faces and well-crimped hair. " I expect you to behave nicely as well. Good behaviour and appearance are of great importance in life. It is your duty to make friends, which you can only do by being agreeable. But it is not necessary to know everyone ; you must learn to discern between the right and the wrong people. To-night you will only meet your equals, and you may not have as many opportunities of doing so as I should wish. We cannot entertain, and your Papa does not approve of dancing and parties. But I consider that going into good society is a necessary part of your education, and I think you are old enough to understand what I mean."

"Yes," laughed Hetty. "We are to make friends with the sheep and avoid the goats, Molly."

"Harriet, you are vulgar and profane," said her Mamma. "I wish to impress upon you the importance of making a good marriage when you grow up, for no lady can earn her own living. Therefore you must marry, and I should like you to make a good impression to-night on Mr and Mrs Prince and their family."

"We are to improve the shining hour with the sheep because we are not meeting any goats ; but I like them quite as much as the sheep," laughed Hetty.

Mary Anne listened to all that was being said, and turned it over in her small mind as they rumbled along. Going to a dance now assumed a different aspect.

The cab drew up before a large portico, with a path of red bunting leading up to it across the pavement.

Worby climbed down from the box and gave a thundering knock at the door, which was flung open at once by a foot-man, and a flood of light from the entrance hall dispelled the foggy atmosphere, illuminating the arrival of Mrs Danvers and her daughters.

A maid was at hand to take their shawls, and they were preceded up the wide staircase by a portly butler, who ushered them into a large reception room where the family were awaiting their guests.

Mr and Mrs Prince, and Edward and Charles and Janet and Jessie, their sons and daughters, advanced to welcome the first arrivals, and Harriet and Mary Anne had the good fortune to be engaged at once for the first dance by the two boys, to the gratification of their Mamma.

It was not long before the room was crowded with children of all ages, their mothers seated round the walls, and elders looking on with amusement.

Mrs Danvers found many old friends to talk to ; the time slipped by all too soon, and when the butler at ten o'clock announced that her carriage was waiting she was reluctant to say good night, for Harriet was prancing round the room with Edward and Mary Anne had just gone to supper on the arm of Charles.

Mrs Prince remonstrated at the idea of their leaving so early.

" I promised my husband to return at ten," said the Parson's wife. " He does not approve of late hours, so we must really go now. Come, Harriet, the carriage is at the door ; say good night and follow me directly."

This was peremptory, for Hetty was polking past her Mamma, who had visions of extra sixpences on the cab fare, and of her husband waiting to conduct family prayers.

Mary Anne was found in the dining-room partaking of roast chicken and champagne. This had to be left uneaten and all the sweets untasted, though she had swallowed an ice after every dance.

Charles offered her his arm most politely to the door of the cab, and regaled her on the way there with a tiny glass of liqueur from a tray on the hall table.

" It will warm you driving home this foggy night," he said with a laugh as Molly obediently drank it off in a dream of delight.

" What a gentlemanly boy ! " said Mrs Danvers as they drove away. " He and his brother are at Eton, where good manners are essential."

" Well, if Charles is a sheep, Edward is a thorough goat," said Hetty, " and he dances just like a kangaroo."

"He is certainly not so distinguished as Charles, but he is the eldest son, and will inherit large property," replied her Mamma.

"After all, we need not have taken off our coloured bows," remarked Molly; "there was no one in mourning but ourselves."

"There is nothing to regret, since you had a pleasant evening and were the more noticeable in black," said the Parson's wife.

XI. SAINT VALENTINE

" The flowers appear on the earth : The time of the singing birds is come."—SOLOMON.

I

THERE was snow on the ground. Roger's holidays were over, and his daily trudging to and from school began again.

It was not long before he caught cold and fell ill. When he got better the doctor sent him to a warm place on the south coast with his Mamma, and the little girls were left in the charge of the new governess.

That was a diversion for Harriet, but Mary Anne took very little interest in her lessons. Her mind was lazy, and she preferred walking out with Miss Pearson who was addicted to looking in at all the shop windows instead of going along the riverside, or crossing the new bridge into the park.

They would traverse the busy highway, and spend a good deal of time admiring the valentines on view in Mr Mac-Arthur's shop.

Molly longed above all things to receive a valentine. They were so exquisitely embellished with baskets of flowers and true lovers' knots, nestling in their cardboard boxes edged with laced paper. Miss Pearson would stand and read aloud all the sentimental verses and the prices attached to each one, while Hetty was absorbed in the latest photographs of her Papa and other notabilities in the neighbourhood.

When Saint Valentine's Day dawned the postman was an hour later than usual, and his knock was redoubled. The cook came running up to receive a packet addressed to her.

"I wish I could have one," sighed Mary Anne as she went in to prayers.

"Nonsense!" said Harriet, sorting out the letters. "Only silly people care about such things."

The cook's plain face was radiant as she came into the room and settled down to listen to her Master reading the Bible, with her valentine hidden away under her apron. "No one looks so happy as she does!" thought Molly. "I s'pose the pork butcher sent it to her; Nurse says so."

Miss Pearson was not so punctilious as Miss Petifer had been, and the children soon learned to take advantage of her good nature.

During Mrs Danvers' absence from home she remained to tea with them, and Harriet did not ask permission to jump up from the table and run to the door when the five o'clock postman was heard trying to squeeze something larger than usual into the letter-box.

She rushed back into the room calling out. "Here's a valentine for Molly, and I was just going to give it to Jane. She has been expecting one all day from her sweetheart."

"What's a sweet-tart?" asked Charlotte. But no notice was taken of her in the excitement of looking on while Mary Anne unpacked her parcel.

It revealed an elegant production, mentally priced at sixpence by the governess, displaying two posies above and verses beneath, as follows:

"IF THOU WILT BE MINE DEAR LOVE
    CONSTANT I WILL EVER PROVE."

Molly blushed deeply with delight. "Whoever can have sent it?"

"Charlie Prince, of course!" said Hetty. "He danced a lot with her at the party, and took her in to supper three times."

" He didn't ! " declared Molly.   " I only went in twice, and then I didn't finish."

" Quite a real admirer then," observed Miss Pearson. " You are beginning early, Molly.   Hetty will be jealous."

" Indeed I shan't ! " declared Harriet scornfully.   " If anyone was so vulgar as to send me such rubbish I should put it straight into the fire."

But Mary Anne did nothing of the kind.   She rushed away upstairs to show her valentine to Nurse.

" Well I never ! " exclaimed the good woman.   " Who did that come from, I wonder ?   Master Roger, I'll be bound. He might have sent me one as well, but I s'pose I'm getting too old for such things."

" What does a sweet-tart mean, Nurse ? " asked Charlotte, who had followed Mary Anne upstairs with her usual curiosity.

" Sugar and spice, and all that's nice," replied Nurse as she bustled about the room, getting ready for the baby's bedtime.

" Did you ever have one ? " asked Molly.

" Ah, that would be telling," Nurse said as she whisked little Emily away with her into the night nursery.

Mary Anne followed her, and continued to ask questions while her sister was being undressed.   She wanted to know who Saint Valentine was, and why he should have a day all to himself, like Father Christmas.

Nurse tried to explain it to the best of her knowledge by saying :

" If you was staying at your Grandmamma's now you would hear all the birds a-singing for the first time this year perhaps, and the wood-pigeons a-billing and cooing, and the blackbirds bowing to their ladies because the spring is coming, and they are choosing their mates to help them build their nests.   But in London you don't see all as goes on, for there's nothing but sparrers, and they can't sing like other birds, and don't do much in the way of courting. They go on getting married all the year round ; but I don't suppose as Saint Valentine has much to do with it."

" Doesn't he like sparrows ? " asked Charlotte.

" He don't take much notice of 'em," said Nurse. " They just make themselves useful picking up the dirt in the streets : that's about all they are good for."

By this time little Emily was stripped and standing in the bath, with her long fair hair done in a pigtail. She was past three years old now, a docile child compared with Charlotte, but blessed with a very decided nose like that of her Grand-mamma Jackson.

Mrs Danvers had been thinking that she must try and manage without a nursery soon, and she had said so to Nurse before she went away with Roger. They did not return home until Easter, and then the delicate little boy was sent to a country rectory, where fresh air could be combined with education.

2

In the summer Nurse packed up her big black box and feather bed, and went home to the farm-house from whence she came just before Mary Anne was born. The little girl was inconsolable. Harriet called her a cry-baby, and told her she was behaving like a child in pinafores.

But then Nurse had petted her more than all the others put together She was the first baby in her charge, and she loved her as her own.

Not long after Molly had passed her fourth milestone Nurse had taken her on a holiday to her home in the country, where the little girl learned to love animals and to delight in the freedom of the fields. It was in spring-time, when everything was young and sweet like herself.

The chickens had come running to her for crumbs after breakfast, and she used to go searching for new-laid eggs in the hay-loft with Nurse. Then if no one was looking she would chase the waddling ducks and geese down to the pond to see them swim, and throw stones into the water to drive them out again.

She had a pet lamb for a playmate whose mother had died in giving it birth ; and one day Nurse took her to the cowshed and showed her a little calf that had been born in the night, which she was allowed to fondle.

Nurse's sister Sarah would let her go with her to call the cows in from the meadow of an evening, and Molly loved to see them being milked. Then the tired horses came back after their long day's work on the land, and she went running out to open the farmyard gate and watch them wading and drinking in the pond before they were led into the stables and rubbed down for the night.

There was the nice cool dairy with the row of brown earthenware pans into which Nurse's sister poured the frothy new milk ; and Molly would look on while she skimmed the thick cream and churned it into butter, which she took to market once a week in a two-wheel cart with poultry and eggs for sale.

Apart from the fascinations of the farmyard there were interests in the old farmhouse to notice and discover. Molly found out where all the good things came from that were kept in the nursery cupboard when Nurse received a hamper from home. Flitches of bacon and home-cured hams were suspended from the rafters in the kitchen, and ropes of onions, together with bunches of dried herbs, hung in the chimney corner.

There was a big cupboard in the best parlour with shelves full of stores that shops could not supply, such as cowslip and elderberry wine, jars of jam made from the fruit that grew in the old-fashioned garden, and honey from the bee-hives that stood in a row at the end of it. Nurse's mother was busy all one fine morning taking a swarm of bees that hung on the bough of an old apple tree in the orchard, which had been all aglow with blossom while Mary Anne was there, and the lambs frisking in the sunshine that glinted through the trees. That was where the apples grew that Nurse was fond of munching in bed at night, after she had put the tin extinguisher over the tallow candle.

Besides all these delights there were kind people to amuse her. Nurse's brother Matthew was a commercial traveller, who came home for Sundays, bringing his friend Mr Roebuck with him. He was quite a buck, with sandy side whiskers as big as antlers. He admired Nurse, but she would have nothing to say to him, in spite of his smart appearance and sky-blue stock. Mary Anne thought him a very nice man indeed, for he brought her lollipops, and would carry her pick-a-back to see the pigs fed on Sundays.

On that memorable visit Nurse had collected a quantity of poultry feathers in a sack which she took back with her and made into a feather bed to lay over the hard straw mattress on which she slept at the corner house ; and when Molly lay awake sometimes and couldn't sleep for thinking of the Day of Judgment, or was frightened by the wind howling in the chimney, and the pigs were squealing on cold nights in the yard at the back, Nurse would let her creep into her bed and cuddle down beside her and share the apple she was eating.

When they had finished munching Nurse would say :
" There now, lie still like a good little girl and go to sleep," which she very soon did.

No wonder with all these dear delights shared and understood between them that Nurse and Marie Anne cried their eyes out when they had to part.

3

The days after Nurse's departure quickly multiplied into weeks and months, threading themselves into years like a string of many-coloured beads, iridescent with light and shade.

Little Emily at five still held the undisputed rights of babyhood, and was feeling quite secure in her petted position. Her Aunt Anna, who was one of her Godmothers, had given her a scarlet merino frock in which she was taken to church on Sundays. It was trimmed with white swansdown, and quite outshone the dull garments in which her sisters were clad. This caused a yearning in the expansive mind of Charlotte, whose uninteresting lot it was to inherit the clothes which Harriet and Mary Anne had outgrown. So while Emily was flaunting in bright red, unfaded and newly made, Charlotte was perforce attired in a dowdy well-worn brown rep trimmed with black braid that had been Hetty's.

This aroused in her bosom a sense of injustice, for she considered herself an individual of some importance. She saw no prospect of having anything new for her very own, and what she wore out for her elder sisters was never fit to descend still further to the youngest.

Charlotte's disposition was not prone to either selfishness or jealousy. But she was a budding socialist and held strong opinions.

Harriet delighted in teasing her two little sisters by repeating a verse to them whenever they were inclined to quarrel over their clothes.

> " How proud we are, how fond to shew
>   Our clothes, and call them rich and new ;
>   When all the time the silkworm wore
>   That very clothing long before."

In spite of this taunting refrain Emily's vanity outran her discretion.

One fine Sunday morning after service, in passing through the church with her Mamma, she overheard herself called " the flower of the flock " by a member of the congregation.

Emily did not understand the exact meaning of this pretty phrase, but she lost no time in investigating the matter.

Jane, the housemaid, discovered her during the afternoon standing on a chair before the big looking-glass in her Mamma's room and surveying herself with complacence from top to toe.

A pomade pot was uncovered on the dressing-table, from which she had liberally smeared her long fair locks. The red merino showed signs of greasy fingers down the front.

" Well I never ! " exclaimed Jane, and so startled was Emily from the absorbing contemplation of herself in the glass that she nearly lost her balance and her dignity.

" Your Mamma has sent me to look for her hankercher which she told you to fetch from off the toilet-table, and to see what you was up to. Come down off that chair this minute ! Whatever have you been doing with that grease-pot ? A nice mess you have made yourself in to be sure."

" Let me alone," said Emily with contempt. " I shall come down when I choose."

" Will you then ? " said Jane, taking hold of her. " I suppose you think yourself a pretty little girl, but ' Beauty is vain,' as the psalmist says, and you had better try and be good, for you will never be pretty with a hook nose like you've got, and it's no use anyone a-saying as you will."

" That is only your opinion, which is of no consequence," replied Miss Emily scornfully. " And my nose is better than Charlotte's little stump, I heard Mamma say so."

" Hers does very well to smell with, if there ain't much of it to look at," retorted Jane. " And leastways, she has got a fine pair of eyes, but yours are just slits."

" They aren't a pair at all, because they don't match," declared Emily. " Papa told her so the other day. One is brown and the other is green. But mine are both grey," she added triumphantly.

" Well, it don't interfere with her sight anyway," retorted Jane, " for she can see through a brick wall. Come now, let me wipe away all this grease before you go down again to your Mamma. Whatever will she say when she sees you ? You've just spoilt your pretty frock."

" I have my own eyes, but you have the nose of your Grandmother ! " said Charlotte, coming suddenly in at the open door. " I heard all you were saying as I came up-stairs."

" Listeners hear no good for themselves, anyways," remarked Jane as she rubbed the grease spots in instead of out, with a towel.

" You are to come down directly, Emily," said Charlotte. " Hetty has come in from Sunday-school, and we have got to say our collects."

" Here, take your Ma's hankercher," called out Jane. " She's been waiting for it all this time to blow her nose upon."

Emily was constantly ridiculed by her sisters and brothers because she had inherited the features and the dignified manner of their Grandmamma Jackson ; but it only added to her self-esteem, for her Papa said that Napoleon Bona-parte (whoever he might be) had been known to remark to his officers that people who were blest with big noses could be relied upon in any emergency, as they were always capable and full of resource. So Jane's remarks carried no weight.

Not many months later Emily's nose, which was decidedly Roman for so small a child, was destined to be put out of joint in the same way that Roger's had been seven years before.

Nurse was coming back again—Mamma had said so— and all sorts of preparations were being made for her return. The nursery was restored to its former estate ; the old wicker cradle that had rocked them all to sleep in turn had been dug out from the depths of the toy cupboard and was being draped anew by Miss Barbara Lindsey, who took little Emily to stay with them next door. Robert went away on a visit to some relations at Croydon, Harriet was sent into the country, and Roger was at the rectory in Sussex.

Only Mary Anne and Charlotte were left at home during the hot summer. They went daily to a small and select class for young ladies near by, which was kept by some members of the congregation who conscientiously instilled into their pupils some small knowledge of the French language, and English history learned by heart.

4

The Parson's house was very quiet in those days. Mrs Danvers lay on the sofa at the open window that overlooked the garden, doing fine needlework. Miss Barbara ran in and out from next door, making herself useful and bringing delicacies to tempt her neighbour's appetite.

Nurse arrived towards the end of June and found an empty nursery with a bassinette all newly done up, behind the door.

Molly was overjoyed at the sight of her. According to Papa she had come on a visit for any length of time, and they were to take her to all her favourite resorts—the Crystal Palace, the Christy Minstrels, the Zoological Gardens, and up the river to Kew in a penny steamboat.

This was quite a matter of course to Mary Anne, but Charlotte was shrewd, and determined to consult her friend Alice Oakley as to what connection there might be in this series of events.

Mr Oakley was the vicar of the adjoining parish, and they lived round the corner in the long straight street that led from the high road to the river. His daughters were much the same age as Molly and Charlotte, and they went daily to the same select school for young ladies, which was at the end of the street.

Mr Oakley carefully preserved a narrow outlook on life. He regarded his neighbour Danvers in the light of an apostle, but he had formed no such high opinion of Mrs Danvers, who was wont to follow the fashions of the day, while his own helpmeet adorned herself with shamefacedness and sobriety according to Saint Paul, and still clung to the crinoline of former years rather than move on with the times.

It was a fine day early in July when the four girls walked slowly up the street together on their way home to the midday meal.

Mary Anne and Charlotte left Virginia and Alice Oakley on their doorstep and crossed the road into the Row. At the corner house there was a noise like a cat crying. Molly looked down into the area to see if her beloved puss, a present from Virginia Oakley, was anxious to enter.

The door was opened by Mr Danvers. His face, which had been grave of late, was beaming all over with smiles, and there was a strangely familiar sound coming from upstairs, which brought back to Molly's mind more vividly the old nursery days than did the return of Nurse.

" What is the cat crying for ? " asked Charlotte.

" Run upstairs and see," said her Papa, " but go very quietly for Mamma is not so well to-day."

The sounds were more decided as they proceeded, and Charlotte whispered, " I do believe it's a baby crying."

And so it was. On the bed in the little room that Harriet had occupied lay a naked newborn child, all alone.

Molly's whole heart went out to it, and at that moment Nurse came from Mrs Danver's room adjoining, bustling in and out just as she used to do in the days gone by.

" So you've come in from school to find a new little brother ! " she said as she lifted the baby and wrapped it round in flannel. "My word, what a surprise to be sure! You never expected one, did you?"

"Yes, I did," replied Charlotte promptly, but Mary Anne was speechless with astonishment and delight. To have Nurse back again, and another baby into the bargain was more than her mind was capable of grasping all at once.

Mr Danvers had followed them upstairs to enjoy their surprise and to have another peep at his newborn son, whom Nurse had now swathed until there was nothing to be seen of him.

"He is our little Benjamin," said their Papa.

"Why is he to be called that?" asked Charlotte.

"Because he is our youngest and our dearest," replied Mr Danvers.

"May I hold him, Nurse?" asked Mary Anne.

The baby lay quiet in her arms while she solemnly rocked him to and fro.

"Are you pleased with him?" asked her Papa.

Molly nodded her head and smiled. A wonderful feeling of responsibility crept over her, while Charlotte remarked that Emily would not be pleased, if they were.

And when the little girl came in the following day from next door and saw the baby lying asleep in her Mamma's arms, her heart did not go out to him at all.

She silently regarded him as an interloper, and held her nose higher than ever.

XII. THE PATH OF TILLAGE

" True, the path of tillage is no easy one ; but it is by the ordinance of the Heavenly Father himself, who was the first to stir the fields by art, sharpening the wits of man on the whetstone of trouble, not suffering His realm to lie motionless in heavy sloth."—VIRGIL.

I

THE elderly lady to whom Harriet was sent was a retired governess, who had lived only in titled families ; and she undertook to mould Hetty's mind and character on an aristocratic basis, besides giving her the benefit and advantage of a higher education than she had as yet attained to.

But she did not succeed in winning Harriet's heart, and soon found herself ridiculed and set at naught in her humble little home.

Hetty had gone away delighted at the prospect of spending the summer in new surroundings, but she quickly came to the conclusion that the country was dull, and began to get into mischief.

Long letters from Mary Anne kept her enlightened as to all that was happening at home, and she wanted to be there. So she made herself more than usually objectionable by mimicking the long-suffering lady to her face.

This had the desired effect. Never in her lifelong career of imparting knowledge, and bestowing a final polish on the minds and manners of the young, had she come in contact with such a flagrant case of insubordination and ill-breeding.

Harriet was sent home in disgrace, just when the whole family were going away, which coincided with her intentions.

A well-to-do parishioner who possessed a house on the

Kentish coast, lent it to the Parson for a holiday, and there they all grew and expanded in the bracing air and genial atmosphere. There was a large garden full of fruit for them to play in, and a pony and a donkey, and a carriage to drive about in. There was also a good-natured house-keeper whose cupboards were kept well stocked with home-made jam which she dispensed liberally.

After the recent birth of little Benjamin, Mrs Danvers remained listless, and was content to let the children go their own way. She took pleasant inland drives with her husband, and left Harriet to look after the little ones. She had boxed Hetty's ears in a fit of impatience before starting on the journey, overcome with all the carpet bags that had to be strapped at the last moment.

In addition to the rest of the luggage there was the new travelling bath, with a lid that refused to close down upon its contents : it was filled to overflowing with nursery necessaries and topped up with the cradle and perambulator.

As they drove along the high road in Worby's cab full to the brim, and Nurse seated on the box with the baby in her arms, Mrs Danvers said to her husband with a sigh :

" Harriet has gained no advantage during her absence from home, either in manners or education ; and Mary Anne is becoming too much of a tom-boy by being always with Roger. I cannot allow it to continue."

The Parson was amused at the idea, and replied :

" My precious treasure, there is no need to worry yourself about her, the companionship is more likely to make a mollycoddle of the boy."

During the holiday Harriet took upon herself the respon-sibilities of an elder sister. Charlotte became her slave, while Robert and little Emily learned to look up to her.

Mary Anne and Roger were left to their own devices, and laid the foundations of decay in their new back teeth at the village sweet shop, which was kept by an old dame called

Mrs Amos. She was famed for sticks of stuff which went by the name of black-jack for a farthing apiece, and lumps of hardbake at a halfpenny. Every penny they could produce went to swell her coffers, except a precious threepenny bit with a hole in it which Molly had long treasured as a gift from her Papa, and finally spent on a shell pincushion for Nurse to take home with her in remembrance of their first visit to the seaside.

2

It was late in September when the family returned to their home and settled down for the winter.

The first thing that took place was the baptism of little Benjamin. Relatives from a distance were invited, and there was a supper party to finish up with. The Parson's mother was too old to accompany his married sister, with whom she now lived ; but Mrs Jocelyn and her daughters came up from their home in Croydon for the day, and returned late at night full of family gossip.

The baby was christened " Benson," after the gentleman who had lent his house for the holiday, and who stood God-father to the little boy, having bestowed a handsome present upon him, not forgetting a gold piece for Nurse.

A trying winter followed this delightful summer. Mary Anne began with measles and went on with mumps. The other children did the same, from Harriet down to little Benson wheezing with bronchitis.

The corner house became a hospital. Nurse had gone home again, and two nurses had to be engaged to wait on the family.

Cousin Lœtitia Gingham came daily in her pony carriage, with faithful Fryer on the back seat, to deposit baskets of dainties and delicacies she brought to tempt the children's appetites.

Mrs Danvers no longer reclined upon the sofa, for Hetty

lay there, long and thin, while her Mamma went from one floor to another administering beef tea and port wine.

It was March before they all met again on the ground floor, and then they hardly recognized each other. Harriet had grown as tall as her father, Mary Anne was all arms and legs, Roger was a bag of skin and bones, Charlotte's odd eyes protruded from a yellow face, and the childish countenances of Robert and Emily were blotched and puffy.

They all with one accord began to quarrel, and continued to do so. The Parson's placid temperament was disturbed; his wife was worn with worry and anxiety; therefore he decided that she should take them away for change of air, on condition that one of them stayed to take care of him.

His choice fell on Mary Anne, who was less likely than Harriet to get into mischief when left to her own devices.

Mrs Danvers took one of the servants with her, telling Molly that this would be a good opportunity for her to learn to be useful at home; and she was quite content to stay with her Papa and the cat.

When left to herself it soon became apparent in what direction Mary Anne's talents lay. To descend to the kitchen and cook a mutton chop for her Papa, and then to hear him say that it was the best he had ever tasted, was more than compensation for being left behind. She learned how to broil a marrow bone and to make a " welsh rabbit " to follow, of which his appetite approved.

Then she tried her hand at cakes and pastry on her own account, and had pangs of indigestion in consequence.

After the evening meal together they would play at chess or draughts until it was time for prayers, when Jane ascended from the kitchen carrying the plate basket to take to bed with her.

Habits of economy were also acquired, for Mr Danvers never allowed anything to be wasted.

" That will come in useful some day," he said, as he made

Molly untie the knot instead of cutting the string on a parcel from the printer.

"You must practise patience, my pet, and by patience you will gain experience : habits carefully acquired in youth will form your character and make a wise woman of you."

"But I don't want to be a witch, Papa, or an old wife," said Mary Anne, smiling at him.

"You are sure to be one or the other some day," he laughed back at her, "meantime you must learn how to be thrifty. That piece of string has served its purpose with the printer, but that is no reason why it should not serve yours or mine to-morrow."

"If you do not want it yourself somebody else will," he said as he blew out a candle which he considered to be burning unnecessarily. And he showed her every morning how to make up a fire with cinders and ashes which would smoulder all day and poke into a blaze for the evening ; then before retiring for the night he would carefully remove the embers from the grate.

"Enough there to light a fire for breakfast," he would say. "If you want to be a good housewife, my child, you must study the art of economy. When I was a gay young curate I went one Sunday to help a neighbouring Rector who was ill. He had an only daughter who, when I was shown into the drawing-room, was removing coal from the fire which had been heaped on carelessly by the servant. Had I not been engaged to Mamma at the time I should have felt seriously inclined to propose to that young lady on the spot."

"Perhaps she would not have accepted you, Papa ; it would have been much too sudden," said Mary Anne, who was beginning to have ideas of her own.

"Well, of that I can't be sure because I didn't ask her ; but we became great friends, and strange to say, she is still unmarried."

"How do you know?" asked Molly. "It must all have been so long ago."

"Because she happens to be your Godmamma," replied Mr Danvers with a nod. "Grandmamma Jackson took you to see her when you were staying at Davenport Hall." And Mary Anne remembered driving to Edmonstone Rectory with her aunts and Grandmamma in the middle of a very long day, without Harriet, who had not been invited.

The Rector, wearing a black frock-coat and a stiffly starched cravat like her Papa's, stood at the gate to welcome them, and a son, all smiles, opened it for them to drive in. The Rector's wife received them in the drawing-room, and Mary Anne had been taken very little notice of. She sat next to her Godmother at dinner, which was a grand midday meal of four or five courses, with a pair of boiled fowls at one end of the table and a roast saddle of lamb at the other. It took a long time to get through, and when it was finished Molly was glad to be taken into the garden to sit under the trees with her Godmother, who read stories to her out of books, "Good out of evil" and "Parables from Nature." Then she gave her the books to take home and read to herself and keep on a shelf in her bedroom.

There were no tiresome lessons to learn by heart now. Delightful pieces of patchwork occupied the time spent indoors, and when the afternoons were fine Mary Anne went for long walks with her father to change books at the library in St. James's Square, and then round the corner to Christie's Sale Rooms to see old pictures and curios for sale.

This was an education for after years, in which Mary Anne took no interest at present, preferring new things to old at her time of life. Then they would walk up St. ames's Street to Piccadilly, where there was another Christie's with a window full of smart top-hats. Mr Danvers generally had his old hat ironed and made to look as good as new while they waited. With a "chimney-pot" all shiny and smooth, the Parson would walk up Burlington Arcade—in at one end and out of the other—leading Molly by the hand and dancing quadrilles with smart gentlemen and gay ladies between the brightly lighted shops, and across into Saville Row, where lived Maria Gilston, who had married a tailor and occupied a fine house there.

Mary Anne did not care for these afternoon calls, and was hungering for tea while her Papa sat talking to his old friend. But the conversation offered no opportunity for refreshment. When the visit was over they would walk up Bond Street if not too late, to the Doré Gallery, where the modern pictures that she admired were on view.

Sometimes business took them to the City, walking the whole length of the Strand and Fleet Street, passing through the old Temple Bar along to Ludgate Hill and into Paternoster Row, where a choice would be made of a fresh supply of tracts for Mr Coulston. If it was too late to walk back Mr Danvers would hail the brown omnibus at Ludgate Hill and drive home for sixpence apiece. Then they would sup together off cold mutton and baked potatoes, finishing the evening with a lengthy and solemn game of chess which lasted until bedtime, when Jane came up to prayers with the plate basket.

3

One morning the Parson came in from his parish rounds and found Mary Anne busy as usual with her patchwork spread out all over the table in the dining-room. She was planning a quilt for her parents' bed as a surprise to her Mamma on her return home.

Romulus and Remus, her cat's first family, were scampering about the room with their mother, who was not much more than a kitten herself.

"Aren't you getting a bit dull, my dear?" said Mr

Danvers. " How would you like to go to a party to-night ?
I have just met the Rector. He told me they had a few
young people coming to spend the evening, and invited you
to join them."

" Oh Papa ! " exclaimed Molly, " but I can't go all by
myself."

" Stuff and nonsense, why ever not ? " he replied. " I
thought you would enjoy it, and I couldn't very well refuse.
It was kind of Mr Church to ask you when he heard that
the others were all away and that you were alone with me,
so you must go, my pet. Besides, it will do you good."

" But, Papa, what am I to go in ? " asked Molly in dismay.

" I must leave that to you, my dear ; you know better
than I do," said her father. " By the by, I went to Worby
on my way back and asked him to bring his cab round to
take you to the Rectory at eight o'clock."

Mary Anne folded up her patchwork and put it away in
perplexity.

If only Papa had said he couldn't spare her ! That, she
considered, would have been excuse enough. And there was
a chop to cook for his dinner to-night ; but she could not
do that and get dressed at the same time.

How could he have imagined her to be dull ? She had
seldom been happier ; but he meant it kindly, and she must
go upstairs at once and see about her dress.

The white muslin had been twice to the laundress ; it was
crumpled and quite limp when she took it out of the drawer.

If only she could find Hetty's pinked out silk sash it would
be something towards a toilet ; but she felt sure it was
locked up in her Mamma's wardrobe, and there was nothing
else to wear but an old black one of her own.

All the afternoon she sat hard at work letting down the
hem of her muslin skirt which she had outgrown, and Jane
did her best to iron out the mark that looked like a thin grey
line all round the edge.

After tea Mr Danvers took her up the high road to get a new pair of white kid gloves at Mr Peters' shop. He glanced at her approvingly as she entered, and remarked :

" You are going to be as tall as Mamma, I do believe, and you will, I hope, have an elegant figure like hers."

Molly was very silent on the way back. She was pondering over her father's words, and wondering at the same time whom she would be likely to meet at the party. The very idea of going without Hetty made her nervous.

When they got in she went upstairs to her Mamma's bedroom to brush her hair and arrange it before the larger looking-glass there.

Jane came running up to help her to dress when she had laid the cloth for the evening meal.

" It will do you good, Miss, to go out a bit amongst young folks," she said ; " you look pale and moped here all by yourself after being ill for so long."

But Mary Anne was lacking in self-confidence, and the young folk at the Rectory were not to her liking. She would much rather have stayed at home and cooked the dinner for her Papa, as he was having cold mutton again, while she was trying to make herself presentable for the evening with the help of the housemaid.

There was no one who understood how to tie her sash as Mamma did, and to pin it carefully behind without letting the pins show. It all took a long time, but when she descended into her Papa's presence ready to start, he screwed up his eyes with a smile which expressed approval as they rested upon her.

" Don't look so solemn, my pet," he said. " Now go and enjoy yourself. The cab is at the door, and be sure to come home in time for prayers. I have told Worby to fetch you at a quarter to ten."

4

Jane was waiting in the hall to throw a crimson silk shawl round Molly's shoulders before she opened the front door in answer to Worby's ring at the bell. It was the only piece of finery to be found in the top drawer of Mrs Danvers' large wardrobe—a relic of the handsome trousseau that had stood her in such good stead.

The drive to the Rectory was short, but Mary Anne felt stifled in the stuffy atmosphere of the straw-strewn cab with both the windows closed. As it rumbled slowly along she thought how excited Hetty would have been at the prospect before her, while she, poor child, was only feeling frightened.

Well, here she was, turning in at the big gates which stood wide open, and there was another cab just ahead. A girl dressed in blue silk was getting out of it, tripping lightly up the steps and in through the open door, from whence a broad ray of light was shed across the dark drive.

" Oh dear ! What a lovely vision ! It must be quite a smart affair," sighed Mary Anne.

Worby clambered down and opened the cab door. Molly emerged and followed the " lovely vision " into the house. She was shown into a small room on the right, where the young lady was surveying herself with satisfaction before a looking-glass while the maid removed her opera cloak.

No notice was taken of Mary Anne, who laid the crimson shawl with its fringed edges carefully on the couch in the corner.

The servant led the way to the drawing-room, where a number of people were assembled.

Mary Anne was thankful to be able to screen herself behind the dainty young lady, who was announced as Miss Beaufort. Everyone came forward to welcome her, so she was evidently a general favourite.

The Rector caught sight of Molly in the background, and drawing her aside to the fire he said :

" It was good of your father to spare you as he is alone now. He was telling me this morning what an excellent companion you are ; but you must try and forget him this evening and enjoy some games with us."

Then he left her standing on the hearthrug and went to shake hands with some people who had just been shown in, whom Molly recognized as a young couple lately come to live at the further end of the Row. They gloried in the new-fangled, double-barrelled name of Sidney-Smith, and attended the big new parish church.

She found a seat in the chimney-corner, where presently her father's friend, one of the curates, espied her. He was a massive man of middle age, with a bronze beard and a head like Hercules.

He stood towering above her, and looking down from his gigantic height he tried to make himself agreeable to so young a guest. His voice sounded to her like a lion roaring, and his conversation, though kindly meant, was beyond her comprehension. She was overawed by him, for in her estimation he was elderly and terribly learned.

Mrs Church and her daughter came across the room to consult him about a charade, and led him away to make the acquaintance of Mr and Mrs Sidney-Smith. So Mary Anne was left alone again, and spent the time in observing the company before the charade began.

She was chiefly interested in Miss Beaufort, whom she now recognized as the daughter of a retired clergyman who had lately come to live in a villa round the corner from the Row. The Rector's son was paying her a great deal of attention. He was an undergraduate at Cambridge now, and Molly remembered with confusion that Hetty had once boxed his ears. It must be very nice, she thought, to be so much admired and not to feel shy or self-conscious.

" But then, I am only fifteen," she concluded, " and Miss Beaufort must be two or three years older."

After the charade games were played, then sandwiches and lemonade were handed round, and before they were finished Worby was at the door with his cab. Mary Anne rose hastily to say good night.

" Papa said I was not to keep it waiting," she explained to the Rector when he began to remonstrate at such an early departure.

" It is not ten o'clock yet," he said. " Perhaps he wants to go to bed early after spending his evening in solitude."

" Oh no ! " declared Molly in a nervous burst of confidence. " We have prayers at ten, but Papa never goes to bed until to-morrow."

" Does that mean one o'clock in the morning ? " laughed the Rector. " Whatever does he do all night ? Is he writing his sermons ? "

" Sometimes he does ; but he smokes a long pipe and reads *The Times* to begin with," said Mary Anne. " Then he often falls asleep, and that makes him later than ever."

5

" Well, Polly, did you enjoy yourself ? " asked the Parson when she ran into the house just as the Old Church clock was striking ten.

" I think I did, Papa," she replied dubiously.

" You are quite a Cinderella, I declare," he said laughing. " And did you meet the Prince ? "

Mary Anne was too matter of fact to care about fairy-tales or her Papa's jokes, and he was for ever poking fun at her in consequence. She supposed he referred to Charles Prince, and she blushed as she said :

" No, he wasn't there. I only had the curate to speak to, and he is more like an ogre than a prince."

" What, my friend Selwood ? " exclaimed Mr Danvers.
" Why, he is good company for anyone."

" Perhaps you think so, Papa," replied Mary Anne, " but
I had rather have been playing chess with you than talking
to him."

Mr Danvers threw back his head and laughed. " I feel
flattered that you prefer my society to his ; but he isn't a
grey-beard yet, and a very intelligent and clever man to
converse with."

" I don't like curates," said Molly decidedly, as she threw
off her shawl.

" Now what makes you say that I wonder ? " asked her
Papa. " Since Mr Selwood tried to make himself agreeable
you ought to adore him, as most young ladies do. I was a
curate once, you know, before you were ever thought of,
and I lived in the Rectory with the old Rector and his wife.
They found me capital company too, or they wouldn't have
kept me. You must not despise curates, for they grow up
into Parsons sometimes."

When prayers were over and Mary Anne had gone up to
bed with Jane and the plate basket, Mr Danvers descended
to the kitchen, where the cat and her kittens were curled up
before the fire. He lit his long clay pipe and sat in the
Windsor chair, thinking of the happy days he had spent at
the Rectory previous to his marriage. There were sons and
daughters, growing up and going out into the world of art
and literature, whose lifelong friendship he made. Their
parents had treated him like a son, and housed him until
he could afford to marry, and were sorry to lose him when
he left them.

XIII. BROMSGROVE HOUSE

" *The fountain out of which the race is flowing, perpetually changes—
no two generations are alike.*"—JAMES ANTHONY FROUDE.

I

MARY ANNE looked pale in comparison with the rest
of the family when they returned home buoyant
and invigorated by sea breezes, and her attitude
was listless.

"She is outgrowing her strength, and needs a change of
air as much as the others did," Mrs Danvers said anxiously
to her husband. "I think I will write to your sister at
Croydon, Henry, and ask her if she will have Mary Anne
on a visit."

"Capital idea!" replied the Parson. "I am sure they
will be pleased to see her, and I will run down with her for
the afternoon ; I haven't seen my mother for a long time."

Molly did not like going anywhere without Hetty, but
she was feeling too languid to care much about anything.
They had been to stay at Bromsgrove House when they
were little girls. It was a roomy old residence with a large
garden at the back, and their aunt and uncle were pleased
to lend it to her brother and his family when they and their
children were away for the holidays.

Molly could remember crying her eyes out on one occasion
because Nurse had been left at home with the baby. Another
time, when she was older, she and Hetty had gone together,
and they found some of their cousins at home with Grandmamma Danvers who lived with them all at Bromsgrove
House.

The boys were rough and they teased her. Mary Anne couldn't bear them, but Harriet fought with them, and their Grandmother birched them all for bad behaviour. She was a brisk little old lady and inspired no awe as did Grandmamma Jackson. She liked to have her son's children on a visit, but she never attempted to improve their minds or straighten their bodies.

Mary Anne scarcely knew her girl cousins at Croydon. They were older than herself and were always abroad at school. Ada and Minnie had come to the christening party with their parents, but they had taken no notice of her, so she felt that she was going to make their acquaintance for the first time.

Her modest wardrobe was packed into her Mamma's black bonnet box again, and Mr Danvers went with her in Worby's cab to the station.

Molly sat very silent all the way. She was dreading the parting from her Papa, who had been so close a companion during the past weeks.

When the train came in and they seated themselves in the opposite corners of the compartment Mr Danvers regarded her with a smile, and presently said :

" A penny for your thoughts, Polly. You look very serious, my pet."

" I don't want to stay away for long, Papa," she replied. " Do you think I need ? "

" That depends on how long they care to have you," said the Parson. " Mamma hopes they may keep you for a fortnight at least, and she knows best, doesn't she ? "

Molly sighed, and Mr Danvers continued :

" You will enjoy yourself when you get there, and fee better, my dear child. They are all so kind, and the girls are sure to try and make it pleasant for you. It was a mistake to leave you alone with your old father ; you have become nervous and depressed. But they will soon cheer you up again, such a merry crew they are. You won't know yourself when you have been there a day or two."

Molly sighed again at the mere thought, and said :

" But they are all older than I am, Papa ; and I hope the boys won't be there, they are so rough and rude."

" They have gone back to school, I expect," replied Mr Danvers. " But your uncle takes pupils for the Army, so there will be plenty of young men about, and lots of laughter and fun, I daresay. So cheer up, and put this yellow boy in your purse for any expenses you may incur ; but bring it back unbroken if you can." And he handed her half a sovereign in addition to the money for the return journey.

" Oh yes, Papa, thank you ; I won't spend it if I can help," she said.

" That's right. Take care of the pence and the pounds will take care of themselves," observed the Parson ; " and to please me still more, you must make up your mind to enjoy yourself. I shall expect to see roses in your cheeks and smiles upon your pale face when you return home ; but roses don't bloom all at once, you know, you must give them time to blossom, and not want to come back too soon."

2

When they arrived at Croydon Station a fly was hired and the bonnet box placed on the roof of it.

They drove slowly along the old High Street and drew up at Bromsgrove House, which stood back from the pavement. Old Mrs Danvers was watching for them from the window of her sitting-room in the front. She opened the door and hopped down the pathway to the big iron gate, chirping all the way like a sparrow.

" Well, Henry, I am pleased to see you again. Come in, come in. The coachman will carry the box," and she led the way to a small room on the left of the entrance hall that was known as the Eagle room, with a fierce-looking bird carved over the doorway.

" 'Tis a long time since you were here," said the little old lady. " And is this Mary Anne ? My dear, how you have grown ! I should not have known you."

" Lying in bed so long has made them all lanky," said Mr Danvers. " Now they want to fill out a bit. You must stuff this one while she is here ; I leave it to you, Mother. She is too dainty. Besides, she has been taking care of me while the others were away, and has forgotten to look after herself, eh, Polly ? "

" Annette will feed her up, you know she is great at that," said his mother. " I often think she is unduly so when I see the big joints she puts upon the table every day : and they disappear at one meal. But the pupils have enormous appetites."

" Just so," remarked her son. " I don't suppose there is any left to dish up in one of your delicious hashes, is there ? And no making a shoulder of mutton last through the week as we did when we lived together, eh ? On Saturday we had it roasted and carved it from underneath ; on Sunday we turned it over and there was a whole shoulder apparently uncut. On Monday we had it cold again ; on Tuesday we ate it upside down ; on Wednesday we hashed it ; on Thursday we curried it ; on Friday we had grilled blade bone ; and on Saturday we began all over again with a fresh one. Very simple, wasn't it ? "

" That was when I kept house for you in your first curacy," said his mother, " and very happy we were, weren't we, Henry ? "

" Polly and I have been practising all the little economies you taught me while we have been alone together, haven't we ? " said Mr Danvers, looking at Mary Anne, who was listening to all they said.

" There is none of that here, Henry," said the old lady.

" Annette says it wouldn't pay to economise with the pupils. And a lot of waste goes on in the kitchen. I do not interfere when she is at home, but when they are all away for the holidays and I am left in charge I show the cook how to be thrifty."

Mary Anne had a lively remembrance of her Grand-mamma's hashes when she and Harriet had stayed with her at Bromsgrove House in Aunt Annette's absence. The old lady used to trot round every day collecting all the scraps of fat and odds and ends of meat from plates and dishes, to serve them up for the midday meal with herbs and veget-ables from the garden.

Molly considered it most unpalatable, and even Hetty with her good appetite had resorted to all sorts of tricks with her cousins Jim and Hugh Jocelyn to dispose of the lumps of greasy fat and stale crusts which they couldn't make up their minds to swallow.

But Grandmamma was sure to find them out and birch the boys, administering at the same time wholesome reproof to Harriet.

Her son-in-law, the Reverend William Jocelyn, trained the minds of his pupils for Army examinations. Twenty young men lodged under the red-tiled roof of Bromsgrove House, but they were only visible at meals. A modern annex had been added to the old building for their accommodation, and a gymnasium at the end of the garden ; so the family were not disturbed by them.

Old Mrs Danvers had plenty to say to her son. When at length she had exhausted her memory and voice, she suggested that they should go upstairs and see Annette.

" She is in the drawing-room and the girls are out, I believe, but they will be back to tea."

So Mary Anne and her father left the old lady for an afternoon nap and went together up the old oak staircase with its panelled walls and twisted banisters, to enter a door that stood ajar on the left of the landing.

They found Mrs Jocelyn seated at the open window reading the newspaper.

" Oh, Henry ! " she exclaimed, " I heard you arrive, but I didn't come down because I knew that Mother would want you all to herself for a while. How are you after your trying winter ? You have gone through a great deal since we last met, at the baby's christening."

" Yes indeed, the house was a regular hospital—sick children on every floor and two nurses in attendance ; but we have almost forgotten about it now, haven't we, Polly ? "

" And don't want to be reminded of it, I daresay," said his sister. " So this is Mary Anne ; grown into quite a young lady I see. Come and take off your hat, my dear," and she led the way through a door on the opposite side of the room, which opened into a bedroom.

Molly remembered it with a shudder as she entered. She had slept there with Hetty on her last visit to Bromsgrove House.

Strange noises had kept them awake at night, and their cousin Jim had told them that the room was haunted. Harriet had dragged the feather mattress from the fourpost bedstead on to the drawing-room floor sooner than sleep in it, and their uncle, coming home unexpectedly one evening, found them lying there under the blankets.

" Why, bless my soul, what is the meaning of this ? " he had exclaimed. " Whatever are you doing on the parlour floor ? "

This was more alarming to Mary Anne than a ghost, though Harriet explained the situation quite at her ease. But Uncle William was peppery.

" Stuff and nonsense. Ghosts, indeed ! Rats more like, and they will run over you if you lie on the floor. The house is swarming with them. I wonder what your aunt would say.

Get back into bed both of you this very minute and don't let me have any more of this tomfoolery. I will spank those mischievous boys to-morrow."

And now Molly was to sleep in this room all by herself!

There stood the fourpost bed against the wall, with its chintz hangings just the same, and the washstand in the corner, and the cupboard where the sounds came from that had frightened her so and kept them awake at night.

Oh, she couldn't bear it—she couldn't!

But a glance out of the window at the garden bathed in warm sunshine changed her thoughts and dispelled her fears for the time being. There was the old apple tree in full blossom, and a blackbird was perched upon one of its boughs singing the gayest of songs. Flowers were arranged on the dressing-table, late primroses and bluebells and violets that scented the whole room. She stooped to inhale their fragrance, then stood gazing out into the garden where everything was bright.

Another door behind her opened onto the back staircase. Someone was knocking at it.

" Come in," said Mary Anne. A servant entered with a can of hot water.

" Will you wash your hands, miss? " she said, " and I will unpack your things while you are at tea."

3

A few minutes later the door leading into the drawing-room opened and Ada Jocelyn entered. This was Aunt Annette's eldest daughter.

" She looks quite old," thought Molly, allowing herself to be kissed, " but she can't be more than twenty-five really."

Tall, thin and staid was Ada, with a shrewd expression and kindly grey eyes.

" Are you ready for a cup of tea? " she asked. " We are

having it in the Eagle room, and I have come to ask you not to take your things off as we are going out afterwards. The evenings are so pleasant now, aren't they ? " And they went downstairs together.

" Minnie and Sophie are not in yet," said Ada. " They went out paying calls, so I will take you to Evensong at St. Mark's. We mustn't sit too long over tea or we shall be late."

Mary Anne was not cheered by this suggestion ; she was not accustomed to weekday services, and she wanted to be with her father as long as he was staying, but she did not like to say so.

They found Mrs Jocelyn pouring out tea at one end of the table, and old Mrs Danvers was scraping butter over sliced bread at the other end. Her son was sitting by her side.

" Ada has taken to attending daily services lately, and she hurries us all through our tea," complained the little old lady. " Do you have them at your church yet, Henry ? They were not the fashion when I was with you."

" I have an evening service on Thursdays in connection with my Bible-class," said Mr Danvers. " No one would come any other time during the week."

" Don't you think they would if you had Matins and Evensong every day, Uncle Henry ? " asked Ada.

" No, I don't believe it," he replied. " It's a new-fangled notion of the High Church party. What sort of a daily congregation do you get here ? I am inclined to agree with my friend Canon Kingsley about silly women."

Ada gave a hesitating reply as she sipped her hot tea, by saying, " ' Where two or three are gathered together,' you know, ' there am I——' "

" Yes, Ada, there you are for certain," laughed Mrs Jocelyn, " and we know well enough who is the second. Is Molly going to make the third this evening ? "

The Parson held up his hand reprovingly. Anything profane was offensive to him, and he was surprised at his sister's levity ; but he went on to explain to his niece that single-handed, hard-worked clergy could not be expected to tack on all those extra services that were coming into fashion nowadays.

" It means keeping a curate, and may I always be able to get on without one," he added.

" The congregation depends on the curate, doesn't it, Ada ? " observed Grandmamma Danvers with a twinkle in her bright little eyes as she handed her another slice of bread and scrape.

Mrs Jocelyn diverted attention from this sly remark by saying :

" Mother dear, I wish you would treat us to a little more butter on the bread or we shan't come and have tea with you again."

The Reverend William Jocelyn came into the room at this moment and warmly greeted the Reverend Henry Danvers.

He was a plain man with a red beard, which caused Molly to shrink when he kissed her. She couldn't bear beards.

" You don't take tea, do you, Henry ? " he said to his brother-in-law. " Come to my study now and have a glass of wine and a cigar instead."

Mr Danvers was agreeable to the suggestion and rose to follow him. Ada rose also, and said it was time for her to start.

" Then I must say good-bye, Polly," said her Papa. " Do you think you can find your way home by yourself if I meet you at Victoria ? I am afraid I shall not be able to run down and fetch you. Perhaps your aunt will see you into the train when it comes to the time."

" One of us will," replied Mrs Jocelyn, " but we don't want to talk about her going back yet ; she has only just arrived."

Mary Anne gave her father a good hug, and there were tears in her eyes which no one noticed, for Ada was tying her bonnet strings and saying good-bye to her uncle, and Aunt Annette and Grandmamma were going on with their tea quite placidly, for it was the only time they could spend quietly together during the busy days in such a large household.

4

Mary Anne was very demure as she walked with her cousin to church, and Ada was somewhat preoccupied for fear of being late. But they arrived in time, and walking up the length of the empty aisle, took a seat close to the reading-desk. There were only two people beside themselves.

The little bell ceased its clamour, and a man of short stature emerged from the vestry and advanced to the desk. Miss Jocelyn rose as though to shake hands with him, Molly thought, and they seemed to share the service between them, reading the Psalms together, while Ada repeated all the Amens religiously, like a parish clerk. She remained so long upon her knees when it was over that Molly's patience was sorely tried.

When at last she escaped from the dim religious interior to the bright sunlight outside her cousin expressed a hope that she had enjoyed the service.

" To ' Come apart with Me awhile ' I find so soothing after ' the daily round and common task,' " observed Ada in a dreamy tone, and Molly wondered whether " Me " referred to the curate or Christ. But she only asked whether the little man was the curate.

" Yes," replied Miss Jocelyn, " and I should like you to know him. He is such a holy man, I always feel the better for being near him. Don't you think he looks as though he dwelt with angels, not with men ? He has such a sanctified expression—such a serene outlook ! "

Mary Anne had scarcely noticed him, for he was completely hidden behind the lectern. She asked what his
name was, and tried to take an interest in him, though she
was thinking of her father, just about to catch his train back
to London.

" Ramsay—Paul Ramsay," repeated her cousin. "Doesn't
he remind you of St. Paul ? He suffers terribly from asthma,
but he read the lessons beautifully, did he not ? "

Molly's thoughts had been far away at the time, so she
could only reply vaguely, but she asked if he was married.

" No," said Ada, " but I think he would be better if he
had someone to take care of him. I know he takes none of
himself."

Then she remained silent, and evidently in preoccupation,
until they came to Bromsgrove House.

As they went in at the gate she said, " We dine at seven,
Molly, and you would like to go and unpack your box, unless
Priscilla has already done it. Don't put on anything smart,
we only wear high dresses for dinner."

Mary Anne had nothing but her white muslin to change
into, and she did not think it likely that her cousins would
call it smart.

She found everything hung up or put away in drawers
by the servant, and she took some time looking for the things
she wanted and laying them out on the bed.

Then she stood at the open window gazing into the garden
while she brushed her hair back, which she still wore raked
off her forehead and hanging long and straight down her
back.

A sound of voices came through the door that led into
the drawing-room, and she heard Aunt Annette saying :

" She has grown quite a plain girl, and she was such a
pretty child."

Then the dinner-bell rang out loud and long, drowning
any further remarks that might have been made, and with a

hasty knock at the door, Minnie Jocelyn rushed into the room.

" Well, Molly," she said, " glad to see you, my dear. Sorry to miss Uncle Henry, but we thought he would be sure to stay to dinner. Are you ready ? Come along then."

Miss Minnie took hold of her cousin and led her into the drawing-room, but the others were already on their way downstairs.

The dining-room was long and spacious, with a French window at one end where Mrs Jocelyn was now seating herself, surrounded by her mother and her daughters. Mary Anne was placed between Ada and Grandmamma Danvers on one side of the table, with Minnie and Sophie facing them. A long line of dumb young men stretched to the other end, where Mr Jocelyn was standing to say grace. Then a volume of voices burst forth and a clatter of plates began.

Miss Sophie glanced across the table at Molly and accorded her a smile, but Molly could not catch the remarks that accompanied it, and the young lady relapsed into silence for the rest of the meal. She seemed to be absorbed in her own thoughts, for she scarcely touched the food placed before her, but sat gazing sideways into the garden with a far-away expression in her blue eyes.

Mary Anne was interested in observing her. Papa had always called Miss Sophie Jocelyn his pretty niece, but why should she give herself airs and look so haughty and distant ? Perhaps she had a headache.

Feeding was the business of the moment. The servants were rushing round the table with well-filled plates of meat and dishes of vegetables.

Mr Jocelyn was carving an enormous leg of mutton at one end, and Aunt Annette was helping a huge dish of Irish stew at the other.

Two thick slices of roast mutton fell to Molly's share, and

while she endeavoured to eat one of them she glanced shyly about her, and scrutinized her cousins.

Minnie was inclined to be fat, while Sophie was a slender likeness of Aunt Annette, who was decidedly stout. Minnie took after her father, with sandy hair which was bundled into a coarse chenille net, and Mary Anne saw nothing to admire in her appearance ; but then she was clever, and she looked it with her keen expression and small green eyes.

There sat Sophie taking notice of nothing, with her nose tilted at an angle of forty-five. Mr Danvers called it a *nez-retroussee*, whatever that might mean, but it certainly gave her a disdainful expression.

Perhaps she was annoyed not to be seated next to the good-looking young man on the other side of Minnie, who was trying to make himself agreeable. Minnie at any rate, like Hetty, had plenty to say for herself in spite of the clatter, but her conversation seemed to be scientific.

The meal was hurried through, and Molly's conjectures melted away when they rose from the table and returned to the drawing-room. There Sophie at once became a different girl. Her face dimpled into smiles as she drew Molly out and made plans for her pleasure.

" We will go to the Crystal Palace to-morrow," she said. " Aunt Jane and Cousin Harry are coming to lunch, and they will like to go with us. They live near here, you know. Harry goes back to school next day. He is about the same age as you, but he is as old for his years as you are young."

Mary Anne remembered meeting him at Bromsgrove House when the boys were at home. She had liked him much better than them, and she was fond of Aunt Jane, who was the widow of Mr Danvers' brother.

" Let's have a tune, girls," said Aunt Annette. " Have you brought any music with you, Molly ? "

" No," she replied. " I only play exercises and duets with Hetty."

" Well, I suppose you have some needlework or something to do ; you cannot sit idle all the evening," said her aunt, who was busily crocheting.

Mary Anne rose and went to the dreaded bedroom, returning in a minute with her patchwork. A noisy duet was in progress on the piano between Ada and Sophie. Mrs Jocelyn expressed interest in the quilt that Molly was making and asked whom it was for.

" I am trying to finish it for Mamma's birthday," replied Mary Anne. " She wants something pretty to put over her when she lies down."

" Is she still on the sofa then ? " asked her aunt. " I can't think how she can find so much time for reclining when she has such a large family to look after."

" She isn't very strong, you know," said Mary Anne.

" Or fancies she isn't," observed Mrs Jocelyn ; " but she had to be up and doing I expect when you were all down with measles and mumps."

Molly looked back to the loving devotion of her mother during that long and depressing period of her existence. How she had waited on them all, and never spared herself night or day.

The duet went thundering on. It was one of the fashionable overtures of the opera. Conversation became almost impossible.

Grandmamma Danvers laid down her knitting and asked for the newspaper. Minnie handed it to her saying :

" You read it all through this morning, Grandma."

" Did I ? " said the old lady. " Well, I can very well read it again, for I have forgotten all about it."

Minnie took up a book, while her mother and Mary Anne worked in silence. And Molly's mind was working too. She was feeling rather resentful towards her Aunt Annette.

5

Harry Danvers and his mother came to luncheon the next day, and went with Sophie and Mary Anne to the Crystal Palace.

Aunt Jane was fond of girls, and Aunt Annette declared that was not to be wondered at since she had no daughters of her own.

It was a beautiful afternoon, and Molly was glad to go with them. Her cousin Harry took no notice of her, being entirely engrossed with Sophie's charms, they went off together into the gardens, leaving Mary Anne with his mother. Perhaps it was rather dull, but then she was accustomed to that. Aunt Jane seemed to divine her thoughts and remarked with a smile, " Harry admires your cousin Sophie immensely. Moreover than that, boys generally prefer girls who are older than themselves, you know."

So the afternoon was passed on the terrace, and while Mary Anne's eyes wandered over the vista before her and rested on the fountains that were playing below, Aunt Jane's busy fingers were mending socks for Harry to take back to school.

The young couple found them there when it was time for tea, which they partook of in the Palace.

Sophie was all smiles now, and evidently enjoyed the attention of her boy cousin. She was quite animated after dinner that evening, and inclined to be confidential.

" Harry is a funny boy, isn't he ? " she observed to Molly. " I am afraid you thought it rather odd being left alone with Aunt Jane all the afternoon. He goes back to school to-morrow, so we shan't see any more of him, and I will take you to gather bluebells in the woods. We will send some to Aunt Agnes if you like."

The idea delighted Mary Anne, and they set off together with baskets after luncheon the next day.

As they walked along the dusty road Sophie said :

" You mustn't expect the others to go about with you. Minnie is awfully busy cramming for an examination, and Ada is occupied at present in casting nets to catch the curate."

Molly looked at her cousin with eyes like interrogation marks.

" Whatever do you mean ? " she asked.

" What I say," said Sophie, smiling.

" Is she going to marry him ? " enquired Mary Anne.

" I expect so, if he asks her," replied Sophie.

" I wouldn't marry a curate," observed Molly. " I can't imagine why she wants to."

" Well, it depends on the curate, I should say," remarked Sophie. " It's time Ada got married, and she is very well cut out for a clergyman's wife. She is thrifty and has plenty of common sense ; besides, she is longing to sacrifice herself, and would stick to him like a limpet."

Molly pondered in silence, and her cousin continued, glad of a good listener. " Neither Minnie nor I are made that way, thank goodness ! Minnie is awfully clever, you know. She is going in for the Higher Local, and means to be a B.A. and teach in a school. She isn't one of the marrying sort."

" Would you like to be married, cousin Sophie ? " asked Mary Anne.

" Really, Molly, that is what I should call popping the question if you were a man," cried Sophie, blushing. " I'm sure I don't know. Well, I don't mind telling you that I've had an offer. One of the pupils proposed to me before he left last term, and Papa was furious. He told him that he didn't keep a cramming class for Cupid."

" Then won't Uncle William consent ? " asked Mary Anne.

" I'm afraid there's not a chance of that," said Sophie, stifling a sentimental sigh. " You see, we are both so young.

He is not even gazetted yet, and Papa has forbidden him to write to me. I daresay he will soon forget all about me, but," she added, shaking her head sadly, " I shall never forget him."

Mary Anne became thoughtful. So that was why Sophie refused to eat at meals and sat gazing into the garden with her nose in the air. She was no doubt thinking of the absent one and imagining herself to be in love. But it was only a little conceit which made her disdainful in the presence of the pupils, for what were the admiring glances of many, compared to an offer of marriage from one ?

They had reached the woods by now and were soon filling their baskets from the carpet of bluebells that was spread beneath their feet. Molly began to feel really happy in such sweet surroundings. The nightingales, which she had never heard before, were singing in the plantation, and the startled rabbits kept scurrying out of their way. Lambs were skipping round their staid mothers in the fields they had just passed through.

To see spring flowers growing in such profusion, and to be free to gather as many as she pleased in the flickering sunshine of the woods, was an ecstasy. She had only seen them before in the baskets of street-sellers, and had occasionally bought a bunch for a penny to take to her Mamma.

The almond trees, lilac bushes and laburnums, with the tall purple iris in the squares were the only things that blossomed in town, after the long winter. But then there was the river ! That was a splendid alternative. No doubt the sun was now dispelling its misty morning shroud and dappling it with flecks of gold, dotting it with pleasure-boats and brightening up the staid old barges, while the soft west wind filled their brown sails and carried them along to their destination without the assistance of a steam-tug.

The country might be beautiful with everything coming

to life again, but after all, it could never be so fascinating as the grand old river in its many mysterious moods.

This sweet contemplation came to an end as they walked through the fields to the road again, having filled their baskets to overflowing.

" Why, you have got quite a pretty colour in your cheeks!" said Sophie. " Come along, we must make haste or we shall be late for tea, and we have nearly two miles to go."

" Shall we be able to catch the post and send off the flowers to Mamma ? " asked Mary Anne eagerly.

" Perhaps," replied Sophie, " but they will be all right in a bath until to-morrow morning if not, and Aunt Agnes will get them by tea-time."

6

When they arrived at Bromsgrove House there was no time for anything but to get ready for dinner, and when it was over Mr Ramsay was shown in to the drawing-room. After a few minutes Sophie disappeared and did not return.

Mary Anne would have liked to slip away too and tie up her flowers into neat bunches ready to post in the morning. She was tired after her long walk, but she stitched away at her patchwork, listening to the conversation carried on by Aunt Annette, while Grandmamma looked at the newspaper and Ada and Minnie played duets on the piano.

Presently they were joined by Mr Jocelyn ; the music ceased and the talk became general.

" What is all this in the papers about spirit rapping ? " he said to the curate. " It seems that men of science are openly declaring themselves to be in touch with departed souls through the medium of tables and chairs."

" There are well authenticated cases I believe," observed Mr Ramsay, " but we are warned in the Scriptures against any such practice."

" I know of nothing in the Bible about table-turning,"

remarked Mr Jocelyn, " but people are ever ready for some new diversion, if you can call it such. I should prefer to let sleeping dogs lie, like old Toby there on the hearthrug. He is for ever scratching himself when he is awake. Fleas are his evil spirits, and he is always raising them. They worry the poor dog to death, but he won't be cleansed from them. Spirits raised in like manner must be evil, and might have the same effect on us if we interfere with them. Let them alone I say."

" I don't agree with you, Father," said Minnie, who was a mass of intelligence and always in pursuit of progress and knowledge. " I can't see why, having reached a certain point, we should remain ignorant on account of religious scruples. According to the Bible, which was written for our learning, spirits can be recalled——"

" But," interposed Ada " if those with spiritual authority have warned us that it is harmful to do so "—and she glanced at the curate—" it can lead to no good purpose."

" Just so, it can lead to no good purpose," decided her spiritual adviser, " even if there is anything in the present craze but humbug."

" Well, table-turning is a science then, and I don't believe the dead have anything to do with it, do you, Father ? " remarked Minnie. " Let us try it. We are just the right number for a séance. That gipsy table in Molly's bedroom will do nicely," and she jumped up to go and fetch it.

" No, no, Minnie, I'll have no table-turning in my house!" exclaimed Aunt Annette. " Sit down and be quiet. I wonder what your Uncle Henry would say to such things ! "

" Well, the Mertons where Sophie and I were calling the other day, told us they made a table spin like a top the evening before, and it rapped out all sorts of information for the benefit of the family. It told them that Jessie would be engaged before the month was out, and that Jack was on his way home from India for the wedding which is to take

place in August. Now, wouldn't it be nice to know that our
Willie who is in the same regiment might be on his way home
too, and possibly for the same purpose ! "

Ada turned red, and laughingly said to her sister :

" My dear Minnie, if the table really entered into such
silly details Jessie was probably influencing it by her own
thoughts."

"Just so, her subconscious mind," replied Minnie,
" which proves that it has nothing to do with the devil."

" Did it happen to mention the happy man ? " asked old
Mrs Danvers slyly.

" There was no need to," laughed Minnie. " Mr Ross is
for ever calling at the house and bestowing his attention
on Jessie."

" And his hands were helping to turn it, no doubt," said
Mr Jocelyn. " So the table, having seen him so often there,
put two and two together."

" Well, they should not have asked it such foolish questions," said Aunt Annette. " These little affairs are best
kept a secret until the happy pair announce it themselves."

Mary Anne no longer felt sleepy. She sat drinking in all
that was said. During the spring, before the family had gone
away for a change of air, a friend of her father's had called
to see him several times in the evening and had sat in the
parlour relating his wonderful experiences at a séance, and
how it led him to believe in a future state which hitherto he
had not been able to do.

Harriet was greatly interested in the conversation, asking
many questions, while Mary Anne looked on and listened.

The gentleman had produced from his pocket-book a
photograph of himself with an impression of his mother long
since dead, hovering in the background. This had haunted
Molly and kept her awake at night.

Mr Danvers so strongly disapproved of it all that he forbade the young man to call any more unless he promised never to mention the subject again.

The visits were not renewed, to the great disappointment of Harriet, who talked it over with her sister at bedtime and firmly believed in the manifestations.

" I'm off now to read *The Times*," said Mr Jocelyn, taking up the paper, " so good night, Grandma, good night all."

The ornate French gilt clock under a glass case on the mantelpiece struck half-past ten, and Aunt Annette began to yawn. Minnie followed her father out of the room, but Mr Ramsay still sat on, and Ada became quite conversational.

Mrs Jocelyn sent her niece to bed, and Molly rose reluctantly. She was feeling too frightened to be alone but did not dare to say so.

While she undressed slowly by the dim light of the solitary candle she could hear the talk trickling on through the closed door. The hands of the little clock that her Papa had given her pointed to close upon midnight, but she could not make up her mind to enter the fourpost bedstead. She tried to draw the dimity curtains round it but found that they didn't meet.

How terrible it would be if, just as she was falling asleep, something was to peep in and mutter at her !

There was the gipsy table in the corner, which had now become an object of terror. Suppose that it began to rap out something in the dead of night ! She was cut off by the drawing-room from the rest of the house. Her aunt's bedroom was beyond it on the other side of the staircase. Minnie and Sophie slept together in a room next to Ada on the floor above.

Molly went to lock the door that led on to the back staircase but there was no key in it. She heard the kitchen clock strike twelve. The servants had gone to bed long ago.

At last there was a movement in the drawing-room. Mr Ramsay must be going. But it was her Uncle William's high-pitched voice that Mary Anne heard saying :

" Lor' bless my soul, Annette, what are you all sitting up for ? What, Ramsay still here ? I thought you were going when I said good night. We are early people and can't lie abed of a morning like you curates."

" I am sure I beg pardon, sir," said Mr Ramsay, " but the time passes so quickly in congenial company that——"

Mr Jocelyn hurried him downstairs and almost kicked him out of the front door, which had been barred and bolted for the night.

Ada sighed as she peeped over the banisters after them on her way up to bed, saying to herself :

" How rude father can be if he chooses ; Paul will never come again ! "

The door was bolted up with so much noise and determination that the whole house vibrated. Mr Jocelyn then returned to the drawing-room and found his wife alone.

" What is the meaning of this, Annie ? " Molly heard him say. And her Aunt replied placidly :

" Just so. It looks as though he meant something, does it not ? "

" Meant what ? To hold a midnight service ? " bellowed Mr Jocelyn. " I don't approve of such things, or incense, or evensong, or any of the silly antics they perform at St. Mark's. I can't think why Ada has taken it into her head to attend the church. She is a sensible girl as a rule. We brought her up on the old Evangelical lines, but they don't seem good enough for her lately. I won't have that man coming here instilling heretical notions into all your heads and keeping you up till midnight."

Mary Anne could hear her aunt laughing as she said :

" William, my dear, how blind you are ! If you had carried off Mr Ramsay instead of the newspaper to your study and smoked a quiet pipe with him he would probably have opened your eyes for you. Poor man, he is nervous and needs a little encouragement. Can't you remember your own courting days ? "

" Courting ! " he shouted. " Who is he courting ? "

" Hush ! you will wake Molly. I sent her to bed long ago and she ought to be sound asleep," said Mrs Jocelyn. " Well, it can't be Grandma, can it ? and it can't be me, for I am not a widow yet, though Mother is."

The light began to break on her husband's narrow horizon.

" You don't mean to say——" he bawled out.

" Don't I," replied his wife. " Well, no doubt he will be here again soon, and stay just as long, unless you march him off to smoke in your study."

Listening with strained ears and senses, Mary Anne could hear her uncle and aunt leave the drawing-room and lock the door behind them.

All was silent now, and she knelt down to say her prayers. The candle was burnt away to the socket when she got into bed, and she lay with her eyes wide open, so wakeful and nervous was she.

Something fell on to her cheek from the canopy above, causing a fresh terror. It ran down her face, and she brushed it away in an agony of fear. Could it be a bug ? She remembered that Hetty had seen one on the white dimity the last time they had stayed there.

In the stillness of the night she lay listening—for what ? and at last it came.

Rap, rap, rap—tap, tap, tap. Was it on the wall ? or on one of the doors ? or did it come from the cupboard ? or from the gipsy table ?

She listened no longer, but plunged her head beneath the bedclothes and heard no more.

7

The eight o'clock breakfast at Bromsgrove House was always a scramble, but Mrs Jocelyn and her daughters usually appeared later, when her husband and his pupils had left the table.

It was nearly nine the next morning when the young ladies came down to find their mother with Mary Anne and old Mrs Danvers seated at the window-end of the long room, discussing the curate and his probable intentions.

Mrs Jocelyn was an easy-going, good-natured woman, and she was feeling complacent at the prospect of a wedding on the horizon.

"Grandma and I have finished breakfast; you are all so late this morning," she said.

"That comes of having visitors, who don't know when to go, eh?" said old Mrs Danvers with a sly glance at Ada, and rising from the table, she went round collecting scraps from all the plates, closely followed by Toby.

"You look pale and sleepy, Molly," said Ada as she seated herself by her young cousin. "Didn't you have a good night? I came and tapped at your door, for I thought you might be feeling nervous after our spirit discussion in the drawing-room, but there was no reply, so I didn't come in as it was so late."

That explained the rapping. Mary Anne felt relieved, and was about to confide in Ada and ask her where she slept, when Minnie called across the table:

"Here's a letter from Aunt Jane. She wants us to join her in a picnic to the pine woods next Saturday if the weather keeps fine. Arthur will be there and is bringing some of his fine friends from town. What fun! Molly, you are specially invited. I daresay it is in honour of you. Of course, we must take some cakes and pies. I must see what Cook can make for us."

" And what shall we go in ? " considered Sophie. " The Mertons are sure to be asked, and Arthur's friends are all such smart people."

" You don't want to dress up for a picnic," remarked Ada. " Am I invited, by the by ? "

" Oh, I suppose so," said Minnie, " though perhaps as Aunt Jane writes to me she fancies that you may be other-wise engaged."

Ada coloured up and said, " I don't see what reason she should have for thinking so, but three is a big enough bunch of girls together, and I have my Sunday-school preparation at five o'clock that afternoon."

" Yes, to be sure, and Evensong into the bargain," tittered Sophie. " Molly, have you got anything cool and pretty to wear ? "

" Only my Sunday dress," replied Mary Anne.

" Which is that ? " queried Minnie.

" The green serge with the steel buttons," said Molly.

" It's hardly suitable for a picnic, especially if it is a hot afternoon," remarked Sophie. " A clean cotton frock would be better."

Molly thought she would rather stay with Ada and attend the preparation class, and go to Evensong afterwards if her cousins were going to be so particular ; but when it came to the day she did not want to be left behind.

A cab was hired at the station to convey them to the pine woods, and a big basket containing all manner of things, from cakes to crockery, was placed on the top. They called for Jessie and Amy Merton on the way, who also had a ham-per to convey, and the horse pulled a heavy load up the hill.

Minnie and Sophie resembled young zebras in striped shades of brown and cream-coloured camlet. They had put on their new spring costumes and straw hats with ribbon rosettes to crown all.

In her own private opinion Mary Anne did not admire these dresses at all : they were so tight at the waist that all the stripes seemed to merge into one. She thought that Sophie would have looked much prettier in the simple white piqué and blue ribbons with the shady hat, that she wore on the afternoon that they went to the Crystal Palace.

The Miss Mertons were dressed up too, and looked out of place for a picnic, thought Molly as she sat in a corner of the cab and said nothing. They had plenty to talk about, and took very little notice of her. She had never been to a picnic before, and did not expect to enjoy herself much. But it was a lovely day, and when they alighted from the cab and trod the soft layers of pine needles under foot, inhaling the delicious scent caused by the warm sunshine on the branches above, she became aware of the glorious music that was going on in the tree-tops lightly stirred by the west wind, and would fain have sat and listened in solitude. It was like the overture of an orchestra, the prelude to a pleasant day.

But she was not left to herself, for her cousin Herbert came forward and attached himself to her for the afternoon. He was a delicate, quiet fellow, who had not long left school and had been wintering abroad for his health. His elder brother Arthur, who was a young man with a very good opinion of himself, made a good host, and had brought his friends from the office in town to which he went daily.

Molly's shyness soon wore off with Herbert, who took her apart to sit under the trees. She became quite loquacious, nd when a gipsy woman came towards them and offered to foretell their future if her brown palm were crossed with silver, Mary Anne thought it was better than table-turning, even if there was no truth in it.

And so she felt quite sorry when the day came to an end, and she found herself walking back to Croydon absorbed in day-dreams, with Minnie and Sophie chattering by her side and carrying the empty basket between them.

" Well," said Minnie, " it was a jolly party, wasn't it ? And I do believe you enjoyed yourself, Molly, though you made up your mind not to, with your reserved manners."

" She found her match in Herbert though," remarked Sophie. " He is just as standoffish—I was going to say stuck-up, but perhaps that describes Arthur better. He does think a lot of himself, doesn't he ? "

" They haven't got anything to be stuck-up and stand-offish about I'm sure," exclaimed Minnie ; " but you take after your mother, Molly. Aunt Agnes is so superior to us, you see, and has brought you up like herself. When we came to the christening party last year we thought you were a set of little prigs."

8

Before Mary Anne went home Aunt Jane invited her to spend an afternoon at Redberry Grove. There the widow lived with her sons in a house so small that there was no room for more than two of them at a time.

The little villa stood detached in a sequestered corner where it got the full benefit of the sun, and looked the picture of domestic felicity. A narrow pathway led up to it from the garden gate, between rose trees, with borders of daisies and forget-me-nots all in full bloom. An early flowering clematis covered one side of the house, aglow with masses of white stars. On the other side was a Gloire-de-Dijon rose already in bud.

Ada Jocelyn consented to accompany her cousin, although it might mean being obliged to forego Evensong for once in a way. She always enjoyed a visit to Aunt Jane, being interested in domesticity and woman's influence in the home.

They found Herbert reclining on the verandah in a wicker lounge that he had brought back with him from Madeira. When he saw his cousins coming in at the gate he rose to meet them.

" Mother is resting after a morning's shopping," he said ; " but she is sure to come down when she hears your voices."

" Oh, please don't let her be disturbed ! " said Ada. " Besides, I want to see Elizabeth, so I will go to the kitchen now."

Elizabeth was Aunt Jane's domestic factotum. She was washing up the dinner things and was not best pleased at the appearance of Ada, for with company to tea she had to change her dress early and be ready with everything in good time. It was necessary to be methodical in order to become a factotum, and this she had been all the years of her service.

Being an old-fashioned servant, she knew how to behave to her betters, as she called them, so she wiped her hands and turned down her sleeves.

" Good afternoon, Elizabeth," said Ada. " We have come rather early as I want to get back in good time, and I find Mrs Danvers is resting, so I have come to see you and get a few hints on housekeeping. I wonder if you would mind giving me the recipe for those delicious little buns you made for the picnic ? My sisters told me how nice they were."

Elizabeth felt annoyed at being disturbed, and she did not see why she should be asked to hand over her " specials " just when she was dish-washing.

But she was too subservient to show any objection : so opening a drawer in the dresser, she produced a cookery book and turned over the leaves with her thumb.

" There it is, miss," she said, pointing to the third recipe haphazard, " and if you will be so kind as to excuse me I will go on with my duties."

Ada produced a notebook and pencil and proceeded to write it out. Then after looking round the trim little spic-and-span kitchen with a longing eye, she returned to the front of the house.

There she met Mrs Charles Danvers descending the tiny staircase which literally led on to the doorstep. Mary Anne was standing half way down the garden path, and Herbert was placing a bunch of forget-me-nots that he had just gathered, into her waistbelt.

" They are getting on nicely together," remarked Aunt Jane when she had greeted her niece. " Being both so reticent, I felt sure they would become friends."

" Yes," said Ada, " and Molly is a nice child when you succeed in drawing her out, but it is rather a task to do so. Is Herbert stronger than he was ? "

" Well, I dare not say so, though I should like to think so," replied Mrs Danvers doubtfully as she led her niece into the little parlour. " He is only just home, and I have not had much opportunity of judging ; but he seems in good spirits, and is always very hopeful about himself. I would like him to see more of you all. It will be dull for him here alone with me all day, and as yet he is unable to take up a profession."

" Poor fellow ! " remarked Ada. " I am afraid we are too noisy a crew at Bromsgrove House for anyone so quietly inclined as he is."

Aunt Jane nodded. She knew very well what they were like ; then she asked how long Molly's visit was to last.

" Oh, she goes home to-morrow," said Ada, " and I don't think she will be sorry to leave us, though we have all done our best to make it pleasant for her. Mother says her shyness is only self-consciousness, which can be overcome and ought to be knocked out of her. She has been to church with me several times and I have found her quite amenable."

" I wish I could ask her to come here now and pay us a visit," said her aunt. " Herbert has taken quite a fancy to her, and she would be companionable to us both. But I have at present no room to put her in, with Arthur at home and Charles coming for week-ends. Moreover than that, she might not care to be here."

" It would do her a lot of good to come and be with you,"
remarked Ada. " What a pity it can't be managed."

Elizabeth came in presently to lay the table for tea, and
Mrs Danvers rose, saying :

" I haven't said how-d'ye-do to Molly yet. Shall we go
outside ? "

The two cousins were nowhere to be seen. Ada and her
aunt walked to the end of the garden path and looked over
the little gate up and down the Grove, which contained two
other miniature residences. A nightingale was singing close
by in the shrubbery ; the lilacs and laburnums with the
May trees made masses of colour against the rich green of
the chestnuts just coming into blossom.

" Where have they wandered to, I wonder ? " said Mrs
Danvers, smiling. She was short and rotund, with the kindest
and plainest of countenances, which showed no trace of the
anxieties of her daily life ; but she kept a cheerful outlook
for the sake of her sons.

They turned and walked up the path again. " Now if it
were Harry," the widow remarked, " I should feel it my
duty to follow them. I don't know what ideas he would be
putting into Molly's head. Moreover than that, he is never
out of mischief. I hardly get a moment's rest when he is at
home. He carried Sophie off last week at the Crystal Palace
and we did not see them again till tea-time ; but then she is
old enough to take care of herself."

" You must be thankful when his holidays are over,"
said Ada.

" Well, I feel it to be more a cause for thankfulness that
he is so full of life and fun," replied Aunt Jane. " Such a
contrast to his brother, who lies there with a book all day
long, disinclined to exert himself to any extent."

They entered the house and found Herbert and Molly
in the parlour talking to Elizabeth.

" We have been looking for you out of doors, and wondering what had become of you both," said Mrs Danvers as she kissed Mary Anne. "How did you manage to get in without our seeing you ? "

"We strolled through the copse and came in the back way," said Herbert. " I have been showing Molly over the house, and she thinks she would like to live here."

"Well, my dear, I hope at all events you will come and stay here when I have a spare room," said Aunt Jane to her niece ; "but as you see the house is only large enough for three people, and there are four in it at present."

Elizabeth had placed a brightly polished silver urn upon the table, and they seated themselves. The tea was fragrant and refreshing. In fact, to Molly's mind, everything was a delight, from the birds singing in the shrubbery to Elizabeth's tom-cat purring on the kitchen hearth.

They had come in through the kitchen, and Elizabeth was busy getting things ready for tea ; but she was rather partial to Mr Herbert, and liked the look of Mary Anne. This courteous young gentleman was not a mischievous scamp such as Master Harry, who had no respect for her, or any reverence for her domain. And when the young lady stooped to stroke the cat, which did not flee from the fender as he did whenever Master Harry appeared, Elizabeth's heart warmed towards her.

Could Molly have peered into the future she might have seen themselves living as mistress and maid, rearing generations of kittens and cats, for Elizabeth was destined to play a larger part in Mary Anne's life than any of her relations round the table that happy afternoon.

9

When tea was over Ada had news to impart to her aunt. Her cousins strolled out again, and Mrs Danvers led the way into the miniature room on the other side of the staircase while Elizabeth cleared away. There she sat and listened with interest to her sedate niece, who was anxious to be the first to tell her of her engagement to marry the curate of St. Mark's.

" A little bird has whispered it to me already," said Aunt Jane.

" But he only asked me last evening as we walked home together after Evensong," said Ada. " Mamma had invited him to come to dinner and have a pipe with Papa, because he had treated Paul like one of the pupils last time he came to call. But Paul never resents anything, and he asked Father's consent, and all was settled last night before he left, and everyone seemed pleased about it this morning except Grandma, who says that though he may be honest in his convictions she doesn't approve of them. But that is only her way."

Aunt Jane had never seen Mr Ramsay, though she had heard all about him from old Mrs Danvers, who was a strict Evangelical, and held the poor man responsible for her grand-daughter's High Church tendencies.

" I shall not offer you empty congratulations, my dear," said her aunt. " I think they are vulgar and merely conventional ; but I trust the engagement may bring you much happiness and not have to be too long. Has Mr Ramsay good prospects ? "

" There is nothing in sight as yet on which to get married," said Ada, " but we both feel he has taken the right step towards it, for he is now more likely to be offered preferment."

" I sincerely hope it may be so," replied Aunt Jane. " Lengthy engagements are apt to become tedious ; moreover than that, the best years are wasted in waiting."

A cuckoo clock was heard striking in the kitchen as Elizabeth carried the tea-things through the open door, and Ada counted the strokes in her practical way.

" Five ! " she exclaimed. " I hope we shan't have to

wait five years ! And I promised Paul to attend Evensong. My dear Aunt, we must be off at once. He will be so disappointed if I am not there. Thank you so much for your kindness and our pleasant afternoon. May I bring him to see you soon ? " And Ada kissed Mrs Danvers and called her cousin from the garden.

Molly was enjoying herself and seemed in no hurry to go, but she noticed that Ada wore the " come-apart-awhile " expression which Sophie wickedly declared came over her sister every day directly after tea, so there would be no escape from Evensong on their homeward way, which led past St. Mark's Church.

As Ada hurried along she imparted her news to her cousin, who had not yet heard it. Ada gloried in the telling of it as they walked together, though she was disappointed at the matter-of-fact manner in which Molly received it.

In the stillness of the church, broken only by the asthmatic voice of the curate, while Ada knelt with folded hands and downcast eyes beside her, Mary Anne wondered how her cousin could have made up her mind to marry him. He seemed such a dull little man. There was no halo of romance connected with him, or anything at all attractive about him, so far as she could see, and yet Ada appeared to have attained the object of her ambition.

Mr Ramsay accompanied them after the service to Bromsgrove House, but he had to hurry back to a boys' Bible-class.

Minnie and Sophie appeared at dinner dressed for a dance to which they went later. They were gay girls, though Sophie persisted in being pensive at meals, and ignored the presence of the pupils, who cast furtive glances of admiration across the table, not unobserved by Mary Anne.

The last evening of her visit was a very quiet one, sitting in the parlour doing patchwork with only Aunt Annette and Grandmamma, who were employed as usual with their knitting and crochet.

Ada retired to the privacy of her room and wrote many letters, announcing her engagement to relations and friends : finishing up with a long one to the Reverend Paul Ramsay for the last post.

And Uncle William did not put in an appearance at all.

The next morning Mary Anne packed up her things in the little square box, feeling sorry that her visit had come to an end.

Sophie volunteered to see her into the train, and accompanied her in a cab to the station. As they drove along they talked about Ada and her prospects of marriage ; but Molly's mind was preoccupied. She had forgotten to tip Priscilla, which on leaving home she had been told to do. And now it was too late, unless she confided in her cousin. Her ticket was taken, a corner seat was found in the waiting train, and then she decided to unburden her mind on the subject.

But Sophie only laughed at her.

" You see, I had no change," said Mary Anne, producing the little gold coin from her purse.

" That would have burned a hole in my pocket long before now," said Sophie, smiling. " I should have spent it all and left nothing for the maid."

" But Papa said it was only for necessary expenses," argued Molly.

" Well, you are a dutiful daughter," said Sophie, laughing at her as the train began to move slowly out of the station, " and one day you will make an excellent curate's wife, like Ada."

These words jarred on Molly as she journeyed home, but she had the satisfaction of her Papa's approval when they were seated together again in Worby's cab.

XIV. " NO NEW THING "

" The thing that hath been, it is that which shall be ; and that which is done, is that which shall be done : and there is no new thing under the sun."—THE PREACHER.

I

A FEW days after her return home Mary Anne was sent for to Mrs Danvers' bedroom. She found her Mamma seated at the looking-glass arranging her hair into a chignon. Her Sunday bonnet lay upon the dressing-table.

" I am going out to pay some visits, dear," she said as Molly entered the room, " and I wish you to accompany me. Your Papa has asked me to call on Mr and Mrs Beaufort, who have lately come to reside in the parish. He is a retired clergyman, though they do not attend the church. I know they have daughters about your own age ; they look ladylike, and no doubt are well brought up."

Molly's face brightened, and she said, " I should like to know them very much, Mamma. The eldest one was at the Rectory party that I was asked to. She is the prettiest girl I have ever seen."

" I am glad if it gives you pleasure, dear," replied her mother as she carefully rested the bonnet on the top of her chignon. " You must get over your shy habits and learn to make yourself agreeable. Go now and put on your Sunday clothes and be ready to start at three o'clock with me."

In spite of her pleasure at the prospect of the visit, Mary Anne felt awkward and self-conscious when she entered the house that was occupied by the new-comers, which was in another row round the corner.

Mrs Beaufort was at home, and received them in a kindly manner. She smiled on Mary Anne, and sent the servant to tell the young ladies to come to the drawing-room. Elizabeth was the first to appear, and Molly felt drawn towards her because she was all arms and legs like herself.

Ten minutes later the door opened again and the eldest Miss Beaufort entered the room, giving evidence of having just left the looking-glass. So trim was her appearance, so pink were her cheeks, so white was her skin, that Mary Anne could only sit and stare at her with round eyes.

After shaking hands with Mrs Danvers, Miss Beaufort advanced towards Molly with a sweet smile, saying, " We have met before, haven't we, at the Rectory ? It was really a grown-up party, and Lizzie was not asked, though you are about the same age I should think."

Mary Anne felt just a little bit patronized.

" It was very pleasant for a small affair, wasn't it ? " continued the young lady, not at all embarrassed by Molly's admiring gaze. " It would have been nicer though to have danced in that lovely room. Gerard tried to persuade Mrs Church to allow it, but she is very particular, and said she couldn't have the furniture disarranged. By the by, you left very early, didn't you ? I suppose it was your bedtime."

" Papa said I was to be home in time for prayers and not to keep the cab waiting," said Mary Anne in her matter-of-fact way.

Miss Beaufort gave vent to a little tinkling laugh, and remarked, " Oh, really ? I am glad my parents are not so strict as that ; but then, you are not yet introduced, so it was quite right that you should not be out late."

Molly felt rather small as the young lady's conversation flowed on.

" I expect you found it rather dull, didn't you ? But the nice big fatherly curate took pity on you. It was a pity that Lizzie wasn't invited as well. Then you would have had someone of your own age to talk to." And Molly felt smaller than ever.

But Elizabeth interposed by saying, " Mr Selwood enjoyed talking to you. He thought you went to the party with Helen, and that you were me at first. We are rather alike, you know, everyone thinks so ; he soon found out his mistake, and said what a nice girl you were, and how well he knew your father."

Helen Beaufort tossed her head.

" Curates always prefer ' bread-and-butter ' misses ! " she said, and strolled across to the sofa where her mother sat talking to Mrs Danvers, who regarded her with approval, and invited her and her sister to tea on the following Saturday before she rose to take her leave.

Mary Anne became quite animated as they turned the corner into the Row.

" Mamma," she said eagerly, " did you ever see anyone quite so pretty as Miss Beaufort ? But I like Elizabeth best."

" She is your own age," replied Mrs Danvers. " Helen is introduced, and that makes all the difference."

" Perhaps so," remarked Molly reflectively ; " but Lizzie will never be lovely like her sister, will she ? "

" She may be quite as presentable in a year or two," said Mrs Danvers. " Girls of that age develop good looks if they pay attention to health and are carefully brought up. But beauty is superfluous when you are well bred, and I must say they have nice manners. I should like you to take example from them, Mary Anne, and try to appear more at your ease in their company. They are coming to tea on Saturday, and no doubt Mrs Beaufort will invite you there as well, so you will have opportunities of improving their acquaintance."

Molly ran up the doorsteps at the corner house, but her Mamma said, " I have another call to pay, dear, and I should like you to come with me."

Mary Anne wanted to go in and gratify Charlotte's curiosity about their new neighbours, but she did not venture to say so. They walked on down the Row to the river side, and turned to the right past the church until they came to another row of fine old houses that had been a great nobleman's palace in days gone by.

The tide was out, and a cluster of barges with their picturesque brown canvas sails furled, lay together on the banks of mud close to the old wooden bridge.

Molly followed her Mamma up the long garden frontage that faced the river, her mind still dwelling on Helen and Elizabeth Beaufort. She was observant but not inquisitive like her sisters, or she might have been interested in the visit they were about to pay. They were shown into a large and somewhat bare room, where an elderly lady sat reading. She rose to receive them, and Mary Anne recognized her as a new member of the congregation, who sat with her son in the little pew so long occupied by Colonel and Mrs Lindsey, who were both dead. Miss Barbara and Mr Hugo had gone away, and there were new neighbours now next door.

Molly seated herself near the window where she could watch the traffic going over the old bridge. She did not care to listen to the conversation as Harriet would have done ; but presently she turned her eyes inwards and saw that there were many strange things to interest her in the room, altogether different to the domestic objects that she was acustomed to at home.

The plain grey walls were decorated with Japanese fans and china dishes in place of gilt-framed pictures. There were fine hanging tapestries and large folding screens covered with paintings of quaint birds in full flight. A lacquered cabinet and some spindle-legged chairs seemed to be the only furniture. She thought it a very uncomfortable apartment compared with the parlour at home, with its chintz-covered sofas and upholstered chairs, the dear old grand piano, and the marble-topped chiffonier. Neither was there any carpet to make it look cosy. The floor was covered with straw matting, and one or two small rugs lay about.

Nevertheless it created a diversion in her mind and aroused her artistic inclinations, which were as yet in a dormant condition.

Mrs Danvers presently rose to take leave, and Mary Anne heard her remark :

" My daughter is fond of drawing. I consider she has quite a talent, if only it could be developed. But our family is large, and our income is small for the education of so many."

" Perhaps she would like to see my son's studio and the portrait he is painting of me," said the sweet old lady. " He is out making sketches of the river this afternoon so we can look in without fear of disturbing him," and she opened a door which led along a passage to a lofty room at the back, which was filled with light from a window above.

A large canvas on an easel faced them as they entered. Upon it was painted the artist's mother, her hands folded in her lap, the same calm expression on her face that she wore in conversation.

" What a wonderful likeness ! " exclaimed Mrs Danvers. " Your son is an artist indeed." Then, turning to Molly, she said :

" You ought to feel interested in this visit, Mary Anne. You have not had the privilege of seeing an artist's studio before. I hope it will inspire you to make the most of your abilities."

Molly became self-conscious at these pointed remarks and said nothing, but she looked around at the curious scrolls and sketches that furnished the bare walls, with more grotesque flamingoes on the wing, and fans set about everywhere, giving bright touches of colour.

As she walked home silently by her Mamma they passed the artist, who was sitting on the pavement making a rough sketch of the wooden bridge. Molly was anxious to stop and look on with the crowd of children who had surrounded him on their way from school.

" No, Mary Anne, I cannot permit you to do that," said Mrs Danvers. " You háve had the advantage of seeing his studio and the portrait of his mother. No doubt before long you may have another opportunity of looking at what he is now engaged upon, in a more finished state ; but it would be unheard of to go and stand in a dirty crowd by the wayside. He would be horrified that ladies should do such a thing."

2

After tea Molly curled herself up on the sofa with her cat and a book. Hetty sat at the piano playing Mendelssohn's ' Leider ohne Worte " on the sweet-toned Broadwood, which was getting rather the worse for wear with all the scales and exercises that it had to undergo.

The music went dreamily on, now soft, now loud, filtering through the simple story of girl life that Mary Anne was reading, weaving new ideas and imagination into her thoughts about the acquaintances she had made and of her visit to the artist's mother, who came with her son from America.

Charlotte had asked many questions about the Miss Beauforts at tea, and was dissatisfied with the scant replies she received.

" How stupid you are, Molly," she ended by saying. " I wish Mamma had taken me as well : fancy, not asking their ages or how many brothers they have, and whether they are at school or college, and if they have a daily governess, and how they like living here."

To which Hetty had made rejoinder in her brusque way :

" Don't be ridiculous, Charlotte. I can tell you all you want to know. There are an even number of sons and daughters. The eldest son is at Cambridge, the second is at sea, and the third is at school. They came from the Midlands, because Mr Beaufort had to resign his living on account of his health . . . though he looks very well I must say. Now I hope you are satisfied ; and pray, what does it matter to you ? "

Charlotte always felt snubbed when Harriet sat upon her, and she retired into her inner self, while Hetty in her turn asked questions about the artist and his mother, who interested her a great deal more than the Beauforts.

Mrs Danvers, pouring out tea at the head of the table, was pleased to see a new expression in Mary Anne's eyes. Something had evidently touched a dormant desire within her to develop her mind.

It was getting too dark to read, so the story had to be laid aside. Molly sat thinking in the twilight, while Hetty's fingers ran lightly over the keys, accompanying herself now to a song :

> " Let me dream again . . .
> Ah, do not wake me,
> Let me dream again."

Her rich young voice, untrained though it was, rose and fell with emotion, and all through the music Mrs Danvers could be heard on the floor above tubbing little Benson and putting him to bed.

The others were preparing their lessons for the next day in the parlour, and Molly knew that she ought to be doing the same. So she laid the cat on the cushion and climbed upstairs to the bedroom that she shared with Charlotte, where she liked to learn her duties for the next day by herself.

" I wish I could do something real in life," she sighed as she opened the books from which she had to commit to memory certain portions by heart. "Hetty can play the piano and sing, but I can only make patchwork as yet. I should like to be an artist, but I don't suppose I ever shall."

3

"Mamma says we may ask the Oakleys to tea on Saturday as the Beauforts are coming," said Charlotte to Mary Anne the next morning when they were on their way to the select private school they attended.

Mr Oakley was the Parson of the next parish, and his three daughters went to the same class every day with the three Miss Danvers. They were all much the same age, and got on very well together until the advent of the three Miss Beauforts, who created jealousy in the hearts of the three Miss Oakleys when they observed the great interest that their friends took in the new-comers.

Alice was in the habit of pouring all her confidences into Charlotte's ears, and Mary Anne would expatiate to Virginia on the beauty of Helen Beaufort and the cleverness of Elizabeth as they walked home together from school.

Louisa, the youngest of the Oakleys, was a little older than Emily Danvers, who nevertheless patronized her, to which she submitted with good nature.

Harriet was the eldest of them all, and preferred to pursue her own way without making individual friendships like her sisters. She did not care to hear them singing the praises of the Beauforts any more than the Oakleys did, and in her opinion they were not more remarkable than other girls ; but Mary Anne declared that she had no eye for beauty.

Virginia had sniffed, and said that she regarded them merely as a pair of dressed-up dolls. And when Virginia made this remark Molly felt inclined to resent it.

"You and Alice are more like dolls than they are, with

your hair in ringlets, and Helen's is turned up," she retorted ; but Mary Anne was always matter of fact.

When Saturday afternoon arrived Harriet went for a long walk with Mr Danvers, so that Molly found herself in the responsible position of receiving and entertaining their guests until tea-time.

She felt quite at home with the Oakleys, but it was a different matter to introduce the three Miss Beauforts into this small circle, and a presentiment that they had nothing in common with these strait-laced daughters of the Church overcame her. As it was, they all stood staring at each other and Mary Anne had to make conversation. This she addressed entirely to her new friends in her anxiety to make them feel at home, which aroused symptoms of jealousy in the breast of Virginia, who looked on, while Charlotte and Alice exchanged confidences in a corner to the effect that they considered Helen Beaufort's manner was stuck-up.

In the hope of creating a general interest, Molly produced her patchwork and spread the half-finished quilt on the table before the eyes of the assembled company, secretly thinking that they would be sure to like it. But Helen said she preferred the new " School of Art " needlework that she was learning to do at South Kensington, and Lizzie only remarked on the time and patience it must have taken to sew the pieces together.

Jane came in to lay the tea, and Mary Anne took her friends into the drawing-room, where they played the piano in turns until tea was ready. That loosened their tongues a little, though the presence of Mrs Danvers on the sofa was rather awe-inspiring.

When Harriet came in she soon set them all at their ease, and there was a great deal of giggling round the tea-table, over which she presided.

Then they went for a walk by the river with a maid in attendance. Mary Anne strolled arm-in-arm with Lizzie

Beaufort, and Helen had to walk with Virginia as Harriet did not accompany them. Miss Oakley then and there formed her undying opinion that Miss Beaufort was nothing more than a little French doll, and this she announced to the others in class the next morning. At the same time Molly began to realize that she had many things in common with Elizabeth, and nothing but lessons with Virginia.

A return tea-party was given the following week by the Oakleys. Virginia wrote prim little notes, and delivered one at the villa where the Beauforts resided, on her way to school in the morning. The invitation was accepted, with the exception of Helen, who was going away on a visit.

These small social events were much looked forward to by the Parson's daughters in the neighbourhood as a relaxation from the ordinary routine of daily life. They afforded very little variety by way of amusement, and not much of interest on which to converse.

The same programme invariably took place at the home of the Oakleys. They were rich in the possession of a rocking-horse, which was ridden by all in turn, and there were always cracknel biscuits with jam in the centre for tea. Mrs Oakley sat at one end of the table effaced by the urn, and Mr Oakley was facetious at the other end, which produced a series of giggles from his daughters if not from their friends.

Afterwards the young people would withdraw to the drawing-room and play at " spillikens." Later on Mrs Oakley would appear and might be prevailed upon to make a performance upon the piano—the only surviving tune of her girlhood, which consisted of many runs and flourishes. Then the young ladies would take it in turns to play their latest achievements for her benefit.

Punctually at eight o'clock maids arrived to fetch them home, and they would say good night with mixed feelings.

These mild diversions were given for the benefit of the

Miss Beauforts. They in their turn sent similar invitations
to the Danvers and the Oakleys when Helen came back
from the country.

"Whatever shall we do to amuse them?" said Lizzie
to her sister.

"They really are so stupid!" exclaimed Helen.

"Well, they are very easily pleased," remarked Lizzie.
"We played at 'spillikens' and 'oughts and crosses' most
of the time last Friday, and they all seemed to be enjoying
themselves very much."

"How absurd! We won't do that here," declared Helen.
"Mother, may we dance?"

"Yes, if you like, my dear," responded Mrs Beaufort,
who generally yielded to her daughters' desires.

"Then we must invite their brothers as well or we shall
only have girls for partners," said Helen.

"I have no objection," said their mother. And so it was
agreed.

4

The next morning when Elizabeth and Nancy Beaufort
were out walking with their maid they met Virginia and
Alice Oakley returning from their class.

"Won't it be fun?" said Lizzie. "Helen is getting up a
dance when you come to tea."

Virginia gasped. "But we have never learned to dance,"
she said.

"Oh, that doesn't matter, we will soon teach you,"
replied the good-natured Elizabeth, "and Mamma says
we may ask some boys."

Alice Oakley was full of giggling good humour. She
foresaw scenes in the family circle which stimulated her
powers of resistance.

After a debate with her sister on the doorstep she resolved
to break this news in a casual manner at the midday meal.

When grace had been pronounced by their father and the cover lifted from a boiled leg of mutton which he was soon busy carving, Alice observed that they were going to dance at the tea-party on Saturday.

Mr Oakley's attention was arrested. He looked at her down the length of the table, and said :

" It is against the rules to speak at meals unless you are spoken to. Children are to be seen but not heard, if you please."

" And to dance," persisted Alice, with her eyes on her plate.

" What is this I hear ? " exclaimed Mr Oakley as he lifted a fork-load of food to his mouth.

" My dear," said his wife nervously, " Alice is only saying that they are to be allowed to dance at Mrs Beaufort's on Saturday."

" Pray, who is allowing them ? We are not," retorted her spouse. " The rules I have laid down for the religious up-bringing of our family may not be violated on that account. If you have accepted this invitation without being aware of the dangers to which it may lead, my dear Fanny, your first duty this afternoon is to wait upon Mrs Beaufort and explain that you have made a mistake."

Virginia gasped and Alice giggled. " My dear," remonstrated Mrs Oakley, " you forget it is the Mothers' Meeting this afternoon."

" You can call on your way there," decided her husband, " and the sooner the better."

Mrs Oakley did not venture to dispute his will. She wore the ornament of a meek and quiet spirit which had been her chief attraction to him on first acquaintance, added to the fact that she possessed a small fortune of her own, which on marriage became his.

After dinner she put on her bonnet which was made in the same period as the crinoline that she had never discarded, and wending her way across the street, turned into the little row where the Beauforts lived. She found Mrs Beaufort within.

Meek as a mouse to all appearance, Mrs Oakley possessed the courage of a lioness in the performance of duty, however disagreeable it might be. She went to the point at once, being in haste to get to the Mothers' Meeting.

" I have called at my husband's desire," she began. " Our children have told us that there is to be dancing at the tea-party to which you have kindly invited them. If that is really the case I am afraid we must decline it as our daughters are not allowed to dance."

Mrs Beaufort expressed her regret and said, " But it is merely amongst themselves, you know. We have not asked a great many."

Mrs Oakley's little side curls were shaking under her poke bonnet but she was firm of purpose.

" Well, we must give up the idea of dancing then and have charades instead," agreed Mrs Beaufort. " It was Helen's suggestion. You see, she is introduced and that makes a difference." But Mrs Oakley knew that it would make no difference in her husband's determination. She thanked her neighbour and trotted away.

5

Mr Oakley was usually in good humour at tea. James, the firstborn of the family, who was a daily scholar at Westminster, always returned in time for it, and general conversation was permitted, provided it was restrained.

" Well, my dear Fanny, did you inform our new friends that we do not dance ? " enquired the Vicar as he seated himself at the table.

" Yes, my love," murmured his wife, passing him the first cup of tea.

" And have you withdrawn your permission for our children to be there ? " he went on.

" Not exactly, my dearest, since Mrs Beaufort kindly said they would give up the idea of dancing," replied Mrs Oakley.

" Ah-h-h-h ! " panted her spouse as he sipped his tea and buttered his toast. He had a habit of closing his teeth and drawing in his breath when moved by any emotion, which was inherited by Virginia in a lesser degree in the form of a gasping sigh. This she now gave vent to, saying :

" Mamma, did you never dance ? "

" Oh, my dear, I can scarcely remember ! " replied Mrs Oakley with some hesitation while her quaint little curls seemed to tremble at the mere suggestion. " Louisa, my love, pass the toast to your Papa."

" I wonder what the Beauforts will do to entertain us," pondered the practical Alice. " They do not care for the games we like."

" I should think not," put in James. " Noah must have played them in the ark."

" My son, that is a profane remark," said his father severely, and James winked across the table to his sisters, who were giggling at the suggestion.

" I believe Mrs Beaufort mentioned charades," faltered Mrs Oakley.

" Oh, that will be something new ! " exclaimed Alice with delight.

But the Vicar opened his mouth and drew in his breath like the Psalmist.

" My dear Fanny," he said, " you surely did not agree to that, knowing how I disapprove of play-acting ? "

" Oh, my dear, I didn't think there was anything harmful in charades," replied Mrs Oakley. " We used often to have them at home when I was young."

" They are traps to catch young Christians in the shelter

of their homes," declared her husband, bringing his fist down on the table and causing everything thereon to quiver. "Acting is the thin edge of the wedge. It leads on to the stage, and the stage is a veritable snare laid by the Devil himself."

Silence reigned for a moment, then with another intake of breath Mr Oakley went on again :

" I must say I am astonished that our neighbour Beaufort, who is, or was, a minister of religion like myself, should permit his family to indulge in these ungodly amusements. It is as well that we should make it plain to them that such antics are not countenanced in this diocese. I shall go and consult my friend Danvers on the subject."

" Father, have you never been to a theatre ? " asked James.

" Yes, my son, I did in days gone by, so I can testify to the iniquity of it," replied the Vicar with emphasis.

" On what grounds ? " enquired James. " There must be plenty of good plays as well as bad ones."

" This is not a subject that admits of argument in my house," declared his father. " Theatre-going inclines to sinfulness and leads to waste of valuable time, during which one is apt to inhale an immoral atmosphere."

" Oh, my dear ! " whinnied his wife, " I am sure you have never done that ! "

" No, my love, I do not speak from experience," said her husband.

" And what have you seen at the theatre ? " asked James, with a furtive wink at Alice.

Mr Oakley inhaled again and replied, " I told you what I saw—the iniquity of it all, and I do not intend to enter into further particulars. I do not go to theatres, neither do I wish you to go. That is sufficient reason for you. We must uphold our principles, my son, and I maintain that dancing and charade acting tend alike to corruption of principle."

x

Virginia here interposed, having seen a performance of *The Forty Thieves* at the Polytechnic.

" But, Papa, Mr Danvers took us to see a play in the Christmas holidays."

" True, my child," said her father, " but I had gone into the question with him closely beforehand, and am convinced that he would do nothing that had any tendency to evil. His views are very broadminded in comparison with mine I must confess, and I feared lest he might be misguided in his desire to give pleasure to young people ; but he assured me that the performance was only a dumb show portraying the simple fairy-tales of our childhood, and that the name of Jehovah could not be taken in vain. No cursing or swearing could possibly assault the ears, and that nothing was to be seen there that would offend the eye."

James glanced at his sisters and said, laughing :

" How about the fat fairy ? She was fifty if she was a day, and her skirts did not conceal her calves."

The Vicar brought his hand down again upon the table and gave himself no time to take breath.

" Be silent, sir ! " he commanded. " We do not mention a lady's legs at table. I presume you referred to her ankles."

" No I didn't," declared James boldly. " I said calves."

Mr Oakley was nonplussed for the moment and hastily swallowed his cup of tea. His wife neighed nervously, for James was daring to joke. She was proud of her only son, and she liked to hear him talk, but he was too much given to playing with edged tools. His parents had designed him for the Church, and he was proving himself to be an intelligent scholar.

Down in the depths of her palpitating heart his mother rejoiced to hear him airing his own opinions.

" My dear Fanny," began her husband—then pausing to gain the attention of his family he proceeded :

" Our children may be proud to possess parents who were

brought up with the fear of God before their eyes, and to be brought up themselves in like manner. Whose grandparents were nurtured in godliness by their parents and their great-grandparents before them. I trust that you may have no vain or worldly desires : that you may tread in the paths of virtue and shun the haunts of vice."

"Oh yes, indeed, my love," faltered Mrs Oakley. "Won't you take another cup of tea now?"

"No thank you, I have finished," he said, and then continued : "Oh, my children, if you could but learn to commune with your own hearts and know what noble company you can make them, you would little regard the elegance and splendour of the worthless. 'Almost all men have been taught to call life a passage and themselves the travellers. The similitude may still be improved when we observe that the good are joyful and serene, like travellers that are going towards home : the wicked but by intervals happy, like travellers that are going into exile.' And now we will sing the 'Gloria' and say grace for what we have received, if you are all satisfied."

"That was a crib from Oliver Goldsmith," whispered James to Virginia as the family rose and stood with folded hands and downcast eyes ; and he muttered in her ear as the singing proceeded :

"Glory be to the Father, and to the grandfathers, and to the great-grandfathers ; as it was in the beginning is now and ever shall be, world without end, Amen."

Mr and Mrs Oakley then retired to the drawing-room above, and the younger generation remained below. As soon as the door closed behind their parents Virginia sank in the arm-chair quivering with suppressed laughter, which quickly turned into hysterical tears. Alice giggled now without repression.

When her sisters became more subdued Louisa asked laconically, "Why shouldn't we dance if the Danvers do?"

" Because your grandparents didn't, my dear, nor your great-grandparents before them," said James.

" I'm sure Ma did before she met Pa, though she didn't dare to say so," remarked Alice.

" Well, I'm not going to bring up children in the nurture and fear of the Lord, to behave like Quakers at a meeting," declared Virginia.

" You are not likely to have any to bring up, my dear girl, except the ten little niggers," remarked James. " Remember you are destined for the Mission field."

" At any rate, *I* mean to marry," exclaimed Alice, " whether Ginny does or not."

" Don't flatter yourself," sneered her brother, " you are far too plain——"

" That has nothing whatever to do with it," replied Alice hotly.

" And what about me ? " asked little Louisa, who was nursing the big black cat.

" You are sure to be an old maid, always cuddling the cat," said James as he opened the door to depart to his studies in the library.

" And so much the better.   I vote we let the race die out."

6

Mrs Danvers was so much occupied with little Benson's babyhood and upbringing that she had no spare time to devote to her elder children.   Harriet became the constant companion of her father ; her energies were given to the choir and the Sunday-school, but her heart and soul went out to music.

Mr Danvers took her for long walks with him in the afternoon just " to work off her steam " as he termed it, and if she had engagements Mary Anne would go with him instead. They were both companionable in their different ways :

Hetty would never, cease talking, Molly was more or less silent and preoccupied.

" A penny for your thoughts, Polly ? " her father would say to her.

And sometimes she replied by gravely propounding a question, such as, " Papa, do you think I shall be able to make a good marriage ? "

" Not unless you break yourself of that habit of twitching your nose like a rabbit," he said, laughing. " But whatever put such an idea into your head ? "

To which Mary Anne replied literally, " Because Mamma has told us we must."

" Well, you are growing very like her, so perhaps you will do as she did. At any rate, she didn't make a bad match, did she ? though I am not prepared to say that you might not do better."

Molly pondered over this remark as they walked down Fleet Street. They had been to Paternoster Row to make a selection of tracts for the following month. The bells of Saint Clement Danes were chiming their sweet old tunes :

" Oranges and lemons, say the bells of St. Clements.
I owe you five farthings, say the bells of St. Martins.
When will you pay me ? say the bells of Old Bailey.
When I grow rich, say the bells of Shoreditch.
When will that be ? say the bells of Stepney.
How do I know ? says the big bell of Bow."

Mary Anne did not reply until they turned into Trafalgar Square. Then she remarked :

" I shouldn't like to marry a clergyman, Papa."

The Parson came to a standstill, threw back his head, and laughed.

" What a funny girl you are ! " he exclaimed. " Look ! the lion on the parapet of Northumberland House is wagging his tail with amusement after catching what you said.

Didn't you see it move ? Then wait until you do. And pray, why don't you wish to marry a parson ? They are respectable men as a rule and make very good husbands. Aren't you satisfied with me as a father, for instance ? "

" Yes, Papa," Molly said in a matter-of-fact tone, " but then I don't want to have any children, and clergymen always have so many."

This remark seemed unanswerable, so Mr Danvers only said, " We must move on or we shall have collected quite a crowd. Everyone is waiting for the lion to wag his tail."

So they crossed Trafalgar Square, always a dangerous and busy thoroughfare, and made their way to Christie's to look at pictures and curios in the sale rooms. This was quite an education in art for Mary Anne, but she could never understand how old masters bore any comparison to new ones.

Afterwards they would turn the corner into St. James's Square to change a book at the London Library, and sometimes find their neighbour, the old Prophet, absorbed in the books he had called into being, oblivious to all else.

In Molly's estimation it was a very stuffy place. The only occasion on which she had found it interesting was when the Librarian took them to a window at the back where new foundations were being dug upon old ones, and the workmen had opened a plague pit. She and Roger had been reading books from the library by Mr Harrison Ainsworth, wonderful romances about old London, and they were fascinated by the horrors they contained.

Here she could see with her own eyes that the novelist had not been romancing. Skulls and bones were being unearthed while they looked on, pearl necklaces and precious stones, bracelets and rings came to the surface. A necklace was brought in for them to see, and Mary Anne pictured to herself the gaily-dressed lady who wore it being cast into the pit regardless of degree, her body heaped upon the cart with the rest when the crier went along the deserted streets at night calling, "Bring out your dead!"

On the way home Mary Anne was more loquacious than usual, and after tea she wrote a long letter to Roger, describing what she had seen and heard that afternoon.

"When you come home for the holidays we must go together to change the books and see them digging up the bones before the pit is filled in again. Just imagine all the ghosts that must have haunted the old houses built on top of it! Papa says they must have been 'unfit for human habitation.'"

Roger, with a morbid mind, read the letter aloud to the few select pupils who were being educated with him at the country vicarage. They were all keen on anything sepulchral, but they laughed the letter to scorn.

"She is taking a rise out of you, Danvers," said Douglas, the eldest. "Tell your sister we don't believe a word of it."

XV. GROWTH IN GRACE

" And God said, Let there be light, and there was light."—MOSES.

I

IT was Trinity Sunday. The sun streamed in through the latticed windows of the Old Church, lighting up the dark corners and gilding the dust on the monuments. The organ began with the National Anthem, to which the assembled congregation sang :

> " Holy and blessed Three,
>   Glorious Trinity.
>   Wisdom, Love, Might.
>   Boundless as ocean's tide,
>   Rolling in fullest pride
>   Through the earth far and wide,
>   Let there be light."

Mary Anne liked it best of the many Sundays in the whole year. It seemed to her to be the beginning of all that was happy and good. She wore a white straw hat and a new dress for the summer, which gave her almost as much pleasure as the sunshine : the glory of the gardens, the green clothing of the trees, the song of birds, the soft south wind. They all appealed to her religious instincts and personal feelings.

The darkness of the winter had given place to light. The terrors of Advent were being outgrown, though the Parson's firm faith in the prophets of old helped to foster them.

Mr Danvers was instant in season and out of season, never failing to teach and preach the Gospel. This morning he took his text from the second lesson for the day :

" Behold He cometh with clouds, and every eye shall see Him."

But it lost its terror at Trinity for Mary Anne. She rose with a light heart to sing the Trinity hymn before the service was ended, and something in those wonderful verses made her feel inspired with a real sense of religion.

" Holy, Holy, Holy ! Lord God Almighty !
Early in the morning our song shall rise to Thee.
  Holy, Holy, Holy, Merciful and Mighty !
  God in three Persons, blessed Trinity !

Holy, Holy, Holy ! all the Saints adore Thee,
Casting down their golden crowns upon the glassy sea.
  Cherubim and Seraphim falling down before Thee :
  Which wert and art, and evermore shalt be.

Holy, Holy, Holy ! though the darkness hide Thee,
Though the eye of sinful man Thy glory may not see,
  Only Thou art Holy, there is none beside Thee
  Perfect in power, in love and purity.

Holy, Holy, Holy ! Lord God Almighty !
All Thy works shall praise Thy Name, in earth and sky and sea :
  Holy, Holy, Holy ! Merciful and mighty !
  God in Three Persons, Blessed Trinity ! "

BISHOP HEBER.

The sun shone with unusual brilliancy. It shed a shaft of gold dust down upon the Parson's pew from the gabled window above. It sprinkled the river with a million saintly golden crowns which spun and danced on the ripple of the tide, in Molly's imagination, as she walked home after church along the shore.

Mr Danvers had given notice of a Confirmation to be held at the new parish church in July, and Harriet waited in the porch after the service for her father.

" I should like to be confirmed, Papa," she said as they walked home together.

" I am very glad to hear you say so, Pussy," the Parson replied. " I have been hoping that you might express the desire of your own free will. I do not wish to influence your decision one way or the other."

" But surely I ought to have been confirmed long ago," demanded Hetty. " Helen Beaufort has been for nearly two years and we are more or less the same age."

" Age has nothing to do with it," said Mr Danvers. " Only the spiritual age, according to your growth in grace and in the knowledge and fear of the Lord."

Harriet was silent for a moment. She never liked to be behindhand in anything, much less in religion.

" Mrs Beaufort told me that all the boys and girls in their village were confirmed at fourteen as a matter of course, the same as being baptised when they were babies."

" That is an argument with which I do not hold," said her father. " In baptism responsibilities are taken for you by your Godparents. At confirmation you must be old enough and thoughtful enough to take them upon yourself. It is not a thing to be treated lightly or as a matter of course when you have reached a certain age. It requires a great deal of careful self-examination. You were admitted into the fellowship of Christ's religion at your baptism, and confirmation means the fulfilment of all that was promised for you by your Godparents. I shall hold a class for instruction and help for those who present themselves, which you will attend and benefit by I trust."

Harriet spoke to Mary Anne about it on their way to the Sunday-school in the afternoon, and also to the younger teachers who were there. She was of opinion that they all ought to be confirmed, if only to enable them better to instruct the young.

" I shall if you will," said Stella Duvale, who was the daughter of a leading actress, and a member of the congregation.

Several others followed Hetty's lead and sent in their names to Mr Danvers, but Molly was too timid and uncertain to speak for herself. She did most things under the control of other people. Now she meditated on the fact that the Beauforts were confirmed before they left their country parish, and that Helen had been allowed to turn her hair up for the occasion and had worn it so ever since. Lizzie had told her so. And in her secret soul Molly felt that this was a point in favour of becoming a candidate.

But when she considered the catechizing that was to take place beforehand, she knew that she had dreaded it ever since she tried to learn the Church Catechism by heart with Miss Manners.

If confirmation was to be as unintelligible to her as the Catechism, she preferred not to become a candidate.

As usual, Harriet made up her mind for her, and when the classes began Mary Anne thought more of the frilled muslin cap with the floating ends that she was to wear on the occasion, than of the Bishop's hands that would be laid upon her head in consecration.

The classes for instruction were held at the church once a week during the lengthening evenings of June. The young ladies sat in a row in the Parson's pew, and he stood at the reading-desk to address them.

Mary Anne, fully aware of her ignorance, sheltered herself under her sister's superior understanding. At intervals she cherished a thought of the new white muslin dresses that were being made for the occasion by Ann and Jane Short ; but before long her interest was aroused by her father, who asked but few questions and explained the mysteries of Holy Communion so clearly that she was sorry when the quiet hour each week was over.

Molly began to realize that she had a soul to be developed as well as a body. Harriet's outlook was more intelligent. She was never at a loss when a question was asked, and her father was obviously pleased at her ready comprehension. The other candidates, with whom she was now brought into closer contact, respectfully called her Miss Danvers, which gave her a sense of importance. She enlisted several new teachers for the Sunday-school amongst them, and formed a great friendship with Stella Duvale, and Edith Radnor, the doctor's daughter.

There were Biddy and Annie Redburn and Mary and Alice McArthur, the printer's and stationer's daughters, whose fathers were sidesmen at the church, as well as the two Miss Wellingtons and Lilla Seaton and Jenny Pilcher, who lived in private houses and considered themselves a cut above trade, and on an equality with the Parson's family.

Annie Cooke, whose mother, the butter merchant's wife, according to Molly's memory, had experienced so much difficulty in bringing her into the world, offered herself for confirmation because the Parson's young ladies were setting the example, and her little brother Billy, now a sturdy lad of fourteen, wished to join the class for boys. John, the elder son, had a big class in the Sunday school, and took his father's place in church by handing round the plate when there was a collection.

Then there were the two dark-eyed daughters of the baker, who lived in the narrow lane over the little shop close to the church. They considered themselves on an equality with the Misses Redburn and McArthur who dwelt in the King's highway; but those young ladies contrived to sit in the Parson's pew with the Misses Danvers and Oakley at the classes, and consigned the others to the pew opposite.

Virginia and Alice had obtained their Papa's permission to be confirmed with Harriet and Mary Anne, and to attend Mr Danvers' course of instruction.

2

Mr Oakley looked in on his friend one morning as he often did to consult him about various parish matters, and to take his advice on the subject of confirmation.

He found Mr Danvers as usual seated in the horsehair arm-chair by the window, reading his Bible preparatory to setting forth on the day's duties.

The Parson was a ready listener and equally ready to poke fun at his friend, who brought his grievances, great and small, to lay them at his apostle's feet. Mere molehills were enlarged into mountains on this occasion before Mr Oakley had finished all he had to say.

A soft tap was heard at the front door, and Mr Danvers got up to answer it, observing as he went :

" The fact is, my dear friend, you do not believe in anyone but yourself and the Almighty."

To which Mr Oakley replied with dudgeon, " I trust I do not put myself first."

" In this case it seems to me that you are doing so, and that you are permitting your Heavenly Father to look on under the impression that He is taking your part. But there are always two sides to a question, you know. That church-warden you are up in arms against has a right to his opinions, and to hold them as strongly as you do yours. No doubt he is an obstinate fellow to deal with, but then, so are you ! And of course he sees things from a different point of view. Probably a basis could be found on which you both might agree, with the blessing of God, and enable you to meet the wishes of the congregation without further dispute."

" That is all very well, my dear Danvers," remonstrated the Vicar, " but he has the impertinence to dispute my authority."

" Pooh, pooh ! " said the Parson. " You take my advice and give him the lead by yielding a bit on your side, and see if he doesn't follow. It never pays to be too exacting, you know, and if the people are tired of the black gown why not preach in your surplice ? After all, what difference can it make to your discourse ? and that is the most important thing."

Mr Oakley inhaled a deep breath which showed that he was unconvinced, and started on another subject.

" I shall be grateful to you, my dear Danvers, if you will prepare my two elder daughters for confirmation. I would not willingly trust their religious instruction to anyone but myself, though I feel sure it will be to their advantage to reap the fruits of your spiritual attainments. I am holding a class myself for youths in the parish and some of the teachers in the school, but I do not wish my children to mix with them. I doubt if any are sufficiently advanced in the fear of the Lord to be confirmed. The young women are gaudy and the young men are godless. My own son has not shown himself in any way the better since his confirmation last year. I can see no improvement in his spiritual condition."

There was another soft tap at the front door, and the Parson moved towards it. But Mr Oakley continued, " I must confess I am disappointed in him, Danvers. He is inclined to be too independent, and I fear he is mixing with an irreligious set at school. What would you do under the circumstances ? "

Mr Danvers blew his nose on his red cotton handkerchief like a trumpet of no uncertain sound, and replied :

" Well, my dear Oakley, I should not be in any hurry for results. Boys will be boys, you know, and growth in grace is gradual, and takes time like growth of body. There are so many temptations open to them, alas, and a necessary part of public school education is to be all things to all men. But the good seed has been sown, although it may take time to come up. The soil easily gets hardened ; perhaps it needs watering. Hoe it with care and dilute it with love."

" I do that daily, my dear Danvers, and yet I see no signs of sanctification."

" Well, my friend, we older men must only lead the younger ones, as our Saviour led his sheep. He did not drive them. We cannot force them to follow, any more than our Heavenly Father forces us. He has bestowed freewill upon us all. As I said before, it does not do to be too exacting—to expect too much—especially with growing boys and girls. Only win their confidence and trust them to do what is right."

Mr Oakley took another deep breath and gave vent to a long-drawn Ah-h-h ! as he passed slowly through the hall. Mr Danvers opened the door to let him out, thinking to himself as he did so :

> " A man convinced against his will,
>   Is of the same opinion still."

An unobtrusive-looking little woman was standing on the doorstep.

" Come in, Mrs Justice, come in ! " roared the Parson. " How long would you stand there without making yourself heard ? I believe you would wait all day. What a fly's tap you gave to be sure ! Who did you think was likely to hear it ? "

" Oh, sir ! " she replied in the meekest of whispers, " but you were busy, you see."

" Not so busy as I shall be with you," declared Mr Danvers, " and Coulston will be here in a few minutes. He is the missionary and you are the Bible woman : of quite as much importance in the parish as he is, though I can't get you to believe it. At any rate, if you insist on effacing yourself, don't efface the Bible."

At which Mrs Justice merely smiled in a deprecating manner and said, " Oh, sir ! " for she understood her pastor's little pleasantries.

3

Mr Oakley crammed his big chimney-pot hat on to his head as he descended the doorsteps, until it covered the back of his neck, and wended his way round the corner to his own house in the neighbouring street, thinking as he went of his friend's advice with regard to his son.

James was certainly studious, and his father was satisfied with his abilities, which were above the average ; but the boy was of an age to resent parental supervision. If he made friends at school he was not encouraged to invite them to his home, nor did he care to do so.

The only scholar with whom he was allowed to be on terms of intimacy was Thomas Armstrong, whose parents were regular attendants at Mr Oakley's church.

Mr and Mrs Armstrong were very godly people. Their family consisted of three sons and one daughter, whom they were bringing up in accordance with the religious views of their Vicar, who never failed to enlarge upon their exemplary conduct to his own children. To them they were objects of derision, and James pointed them out to his sisters on Sundays as Shem, Ham, and Japhet going into the ark when they entered the church two-and-two with their parents.

Perhaps it was on this account that James had but little in common with Thomas at school and preferred to choose his friends for himself. Of them he made no mention at home, and was content with the companionship of his sisters. He preferred the society of Alice as a rule to that of Virginia, who was less amusing, and inclined to be hysterical.

The following Saturday afternoon he obtained permission from his father to go to a cricket match at the Crystal Palace, and to take his sister Alice.

" I was not aware that you cared about cricket," observed Mr Oakley at breakfast. " However, I have no objection if you are home in time for supper and are careful of your behaviour in your sister's company."

It was considered a treat to go to the Crystal Palace, and Virginia felt jealous that her brother had asked Alice, and not herself, to go with him.

The weather was dull, and when they arrived there it turned to rain.

" I think it is only a shower," said Alice. " We can stand under a tree."

But her brother demurred. " There's no fun in getting wet," he said. " Let's stay inside and see what's going on. I don't care for the cricket."

" But you came on purpose to see it," remarked Alice.

" Did I ? " observed James. " Well, that doesn't matter. I believe there's a play going on in the theatre at three o'clock which will be much more entertaining. Let's go and see."

The play advertised was called *Pink Dominoes*.

" What is it ? " asked Alice, picturing to herself the mild game of dominoes that they played sometimes at their tea-parties.

" Something that would make father's hair bristle," laughed James as he made for the box office. " It has been all the rage in town for a long time, and I have been longing to see it somehow. The fellows at Westminster have told me all about it."

" But we aren't allowed to go to the theatre," said Alice.

To which her brother replied, " Oh, never mind ! This place isn't a theatre."

" James, I believe you came on purpose ! " declared Alice. " Whatever would Pa say ? "

" He won't know anything about it if you keep it dark," said James. " But you mustn't let it out to Ginny and Lovey. Come along or we shall miss the beginning."

Y

There was no time to deliberate on what they were doing ; they hurried in and took their seats just as the curtain rose.

When they emerged two hours later refreshment was necessary, and a marble-topped table was selected at Spiers and Pond's restaurant, where time was forgotten as they talked over what they had seen together.

" I say, it was something new ! " declared James as he seated himself. " I shall go to Paradise Gardens next, but I shan't be able to take you with me."

" I should love to go though," returned Alice, " just to see what it is like. I don't believe it's as bad as Pa says."

" That play was pretty bad," remarked James ; " but they always make life out worse than it really is. So does father : he exaggerates everything."

" How can you tell ? " asked his sister.

" From what I hear," replied James ; " but I mean to go and see things for myself, instead of taking other people's word for them."

This seemed to Alice to be quite a reasonable conclusion, but she said, " You won't really go to Paradise Gardens, will you ? Pa would be sure to find out."

" What's the harm ? " argued James. " Old Shawfield of St. John's went one evening on purpose to see all the sin and iniquity that is said to be carried on there, before he denounced it from the pulpit, and quite right too. You see, the Gardens happen to be in his parish."

" Oh, James, how did you hear ? " exclaimed Alice.

" Young Danvers told me he did, because Shawfield went round and consulted old Danvers about it," replied James. " He wanted old Danvers to go too, but he fought shy of it as he's got the proprietor's family in the congregation, and it wouldn't pay to denounce the place before them."

" And what happened ? " asked Alice. " Did Mr Shawfield go alone ? "

" Yes, he borrowed a pea-shooter and a bowler hat from

one of the tradesmen in the parish and spent the night there," said James.

His sister giggled with amusement. "And what did he see?" she asked. "Of course he told Mr Danvers all about it, though I wonder if Charlotte knows and she didn't tell me."

"Oh, he winked at it, I believe," said James, stuffing a bun into his mouth. "Roger said that old Shawfield had to explain to his parishioners that he felt himself justified in doing evil for once in order that good might be the result ; but I believe he went out of sheer curiosity, just as I shall."

"Oh, James, you won't really?" exclaimed his sister.

"Shan't I?" replied her brother. "We shall see ; but I certainly won't be such an ass as to consult young Danvers about it."

"You will tell me though, won't you?" said Alice.

"If you promise not to pass it on to Ginny ; she would have hysterics on the spot," declared James. "I say, what about eating any more?" he mumbled with his mouth full. "I s'pose we ought to be getting back."

They got up and made their way to the station to find that they had just missed a train. James consulted a time-table.

"Confound it ! There isn't another for forty minutes," he said.

"Oh my ! we shall be late for supper !" exclaimed Alice. "Whatever will Pa say?"

"Now don't get nervy like Ginny," requested her brother. "You can tell Mamma we were obliged to have some tea, and I will explain to Pa."

"We shan't get any supper !" deplored Alice.

"So much the better," decided James. "We shan't be so likely to be cross-questioned ; but we had better have some crooked answers ready in case of need."

4

The evening meal of cold meat and cocoa nibs was over when the pair arrived home. Mrs Oakley sat nervously awaiting them in the parlour where the housemaid was clearing the table. The Vicar, shut up in his study, was preparing his sermon for the next day.

" My dears," she said, shaking so that her side curls bobbed and trembled, " how do you come to be so late ? "

" We missed our train by a hair's breadth," replied James, " and there was not another for nearly an hour."

" Your Papa was much upset by your absence at supper. He said it was not to be kept on the table, so Ann is clearing it away."

" Oh, that's all right," said her son. " We had a jolly good tea at the Palace."

Virginia and her younger sister were in the drawing-room above, sewing tuckers into their Sunday frocks. When Alice joined them they asked all sorts of questions about the Crystal Palace.

" What made you so late back ? " enquired Virginia. " Papa was furious at supper."

" We stayed for tea, and just missed the train," replied Alice.

" Well, it's a mercy you haven't missed prayers," remarked Louisa, " or you might have been shut out for the night."

" What fun ! I should have enjoyed that," said Alice, laughing. " Then we should have gone to Paradise Gardens ! " and she ran upstairs to take her hat off.

" I believe they have been up to something, Ginny," said Louisa, " for Alice looks so sly."

" I'll find out when we go to bed," replied Virginia as she took up her Bible to prepare for her Sunday-school class the next morning.

The dinner-bell rang for prayers, and Mr Oakley emerged from the study looking irascible. The servants were assembled with the family when he entered the dining-room, and a quiver of nervous apprehension preceded him.

His eyes were fixed on his son, as he inhaled a deep breath and opened the prayer-book.

" Enter not into judgment with Thy servant, O Lord, for in Thy sight shall no man living be justified."

Then followed the General Confession and the Lord's Prayer, with a thanksgiving for blessings vouchsafed to them during the past week and an appeal for protection from evil and for growth in grace.

The family rose from their knees, and the three servants left the room.

Alice glanced sideways at her father from the corners of her eyes, which were as black as sloes, set in slits above her red cheeks.

Mrs Oakley nervously removed the prayer-book and Bible from the table and replaced them on the bookshelf in the corner of the room. Her husband was regarding his son with severity.

" What do you mean by keeping your sister out so late ? " he enquired. " I stipulated that you were to be home in time for supper."

" We missed the train," mumbled James.

" And pray how did you manage to do that ? " asked his father, " since I told you the time it left the station ? "

" We had tea after the match, and I thought we had plenty of time," replied James.

" Umph !—the afternoon was so wet I am surprised to hear that any cricket was played," grunted the Vicar. " You should not have let your sister be out in rain ; she must have got very wet."

" We were under cover," said his son.

" I am very much displeased at your indifference to my

expressed wishes," Mr Oakley continued. "You have not even professed yourself sorry that you kept us waiting for supper and caused your mother anxiety. I shall not allow you to take your sister out again. Your preparation for school on Monday remains to be done on the Sabbath, which I shall not permit. You put me to the trouble of writing to the headmaster on the subject. Now go at once to bed."

As the young people filed out of the room their parents had the mortification of hearing James mutter to himself:

"Enter not into judgment with thy son, O father, for in thy sight shall no one living be justified."

5

The Bishop came one afternoon early in July and laid his august finger-tips lightly on the well-greased heads of the boys, and the palms of his hands on the caps of the girls as they knelt at the altar rails of the large modern parish church which half a century before had taken over the responsibilities of the ancient edifice by the river side.

During the ceremony the hymn that Mr Danvers had desired his class to commit to memory was sung by the choir to the soft music of the fine organ, and they were able to repeat it as a prayer from beginning to end.

"Thine for ever, God of love,
Hear us from Thy throne above!
.   .   .   .
All our sins by Thee forgiven,
Lead us, Lord, from earth to heaven."

Harriet and Mary Anne were both deeply impressed with a sense of their growth in grace, and in the knowledge and fear of the Lord on this solemn occasion, though Molly's mind was at times distracted by the cascade of frilled streamers that flowed over the shoulders of the tradesmen's daughters in the pew in front of her ; and Hetty's imagination wandered to weddings as being the next likely occasion of kneeling there.

Virginia and Alice Oakley sat in the same pew with them. Their long corkscrew curls and bare foreheads were uncovered, but on the crowns of their heads were pinned plain caps to meet with their father's approval. These were intended to be the outward visible signs of an inward spiritual grace, whatever their natural longings might be.

The gallery above was filled with the relations and friends of the candidates. Parents were on their knees anxiously praying that the Holy Ghost might descend upon their children below as they passed to the altar.

There had been a struggle for the front seats, in which Ann and Jane Short, both small in stature, had been nearly defeated in their anxiety to get a good view of the young ladies who were clad in their handiwork. But Charlotte and Emily Danvers had taken compassion upon them and brought them safely into the same pew as themselves, accompanied by the three Miss Beauforts and their maid. They found they were looking directly down on Harriet and Mary Anne with the Oakleys and others who had attended Mr Danvers' class.

" There ain't no dresses so stylish as theirs," whispered Jane Short to her sister as their eyes took in every detail.

" You're right, Jane," replied Ann, keenly observing them as they filed from the pew beneath to join the long line in the centre aisle.

" Just look at the Miss Oakleys' backs, all in a hump. There ain't no cut nor yet no seam, I declare. That maid of theirs may save herself time and trouble, but she can't make a dress in the fashion. They're just like rag-bags." Then down they went on their knees with the rest of the congregation.

Helen Beaufort said to Lizzie :

" I don't like Molly with her hair done up. It looks much nicer down while she is at such an awkward age."

And Nancy remarked to Emily Danvers :

" Helen and Lizzie wore much smarter caps when they were confirmed, with rosettes of narrow white satin ribbon each side."

To which Emily did not reply at the moment, having been taught not to talk in church. But the statement was not allowed to go unchallenged. On their homeward way she observed that rosettes were more suitable for old ladies' caps and babies' bonnets, and her Papa told them that girls' heads must be suitably covered for Confirmation but in no way adorned.

Nancy tossed her head and replied that of course it depended on the depth of one's religion just the same as in mourning. Emily did not deign to answer this assertion, but her nose went up in the air several degrees.

Charlotte's attention was centred on Alice Oakley, who had talked to her a good deal about confirmation and told her " Pa's views " on the subject. She had also confided in her friend the visit to the Crystal Palace with her brother, and the performance of *Pink Dominoes* that they had seen on the sly. Whatever would her Pa say if he knew ? She dared not confess it to Mr Danvers lest he should tell Pa, and that would get James into further disgrace.

" Did Charlotte think she ought to be confirmed under the circumstances ? "

And Charlotte had replied like a Sphinx, " That is a matter for your own conscience."

And there was Alice now kneeling at the altar with the Bishop's hand upon her head and the wickedest play in London on her mind.

James himself regarded the affair as quite an achievement, and had made his sister promise not to tell. Certainly she had been led astray : it was a heavy weight for her conscience to bear, no doubt, but confirmation would strengthen and protect her from evil in the future.

Charlotte was fond of Mr Oakley because he had singled her out from the rest of her family as his favourite, and gave her presents on her birthday, and encouraged her to talk when she came to tea ; but his narrow views were not in accordance with her opinions.

" It's as though he had one eye open and the other one shut," she said to Alice one day when they were talking things over between themselves.

" And the wrong one open all the time," Alice had replied ; but that Charlotte would not allow.

" Mr Danvers sees things behind and before and all round," said her friend when they were discussing the confirmation classes, " and he makes us see things for ourselves too, whereas Pa can only see things from his own point of view, and that with one eye."

Charlotte came to the conclusion that she had no desire to be confirmed. Her Godmamma, Mrs Leinster, still came regularly to call at Christmas, bringing a small token of remembrance and some interest in her spiritual welfare. It was advisable to leave the matter in her hands as long as possible, she thought.

XVI. THE SUNDAY-SCHOOL TREAT

" I went with them to the house of God, with the voice of joy and praise ; with a multitude that kept holyday."—DAVID.

I

AFTER the confirmation Harriet found another outlet for her energies by arranging a holiday for the Sunday-school.

It was to take the form of a trip down the river to Greenwich, with a dinner and tea in the Park. A steamboat was chartered for the occasion and a day early in August was fixed upon.

Certain poor parishioners and regular attendants at Church were invited ; others who were better off bought tickets, so did all the newly confirmed young people, and a good boatload was assured.

Breakfast was very early at the Parson's house on the morning of the day. Harriet roused her sleeping father and turned him out of bed on her way downstairs.

" You mustn't be late at the church, Papa," she said. " Remember the service begins sharp at nine o'clock."

She found Mrs Danvers in the dining-room making the tea.

" Why did you let Papa lie ? " asked Hetty. " How can he be so lazy to-day ? "

" I did rouse him, dear, but he pulled his nightcap over his face and buried his head under the bedclothes, so what could I do or say ? He was very late into bed last night," said his sympathetic wife.

" That was his own fault," said Harriet briskly as she

looked round the table and helped herself to everything. Her sisters were already there, but the boys were still in bed. It was holiday time, and they did not care for school treats.

Mrs Danvers poured out the tea for her four daughters and saw them start off before she went upstairs to wash and dress little Benson.

Hetty rushed down to the church, but Molly and her sisters went to fetch the three Miss Beauforts, who had taken tickets for the treat.

When they all arrived at the big west door they found Harriet with Stella Duvale, surrounded by a crowd of dirty children and excited mothers.

" Why can't my Bobbie go ? " asked an angry woman.

" Because your Bobbie never came to school until last Sunday," replied Hetty.

" Well, my Martha 'as bin reglar for two months a' more ! " exclaimed another, " and she ain't got a ticket either ! "

" Of course she hasn't, Mrs Chittle," said Harriet. " You know very well that she has been going to the Dissenting Chapel all the winter, as well as to their tea after Easter."

" Well, why shouldn't she ? They invited 'er, and a very good tea she 'ad," grumbled the woman. " I shall let 'er go there again."

" Here's my Pollie, she 'as a right to go to the treat," declared Mrs Martin, pushing her child to the front.

" That she certainly hasn't," replied Hetty. " She was turned out for misbehaviour a month ago, and disturbed the whole school by screaming through the key-hole that you wanted her sister Ellen ! "

" And so I did, miss. There was no one at home to mind the baby ; it wasn't Pollie's fault," complained Mrs Martin. " I sent 'er to fetch her sister, and you wouldn't let 'er in."

" Please, Miss Danvers, do take my little 'Arry," pleaded

a mother with a child on each arm. " He do so long to go on the river along wif 'is brother."

" He is too young, Mrs Coby, he might fall in and get drowned, then what would you do ? " said Hetty. " We can't take the Infant School you know."

The church clock began to strike nine and Mr Danvers came hurrying round the corner, blowing his nose like a horn to let them know he was approaching.

Mr Turke, resplendent in a new suit of clothes, closed the big door after him when Harriet and her friend had re-treated inside, leaving the women arguing and gesticulating on the pavement with arms akimbo.

Within all was orderly. The pews were filled with children in freshly starched frocks, their hair oiled and crimped, the scent of which from so many heads arose like incense to greet the nostrils of the Parson as he took up his position at the reading-desk and gave out the number of a hymn.

" Now thank we all our God, with hearts and hands, and voices ;
  Who wondrous things hath done, In whom this world rejoices."

Harriet, in the organ loft, raised her voice and started the singing. A ray of sunlight glanced through the east window and illumined the faces already glowing with pleasure. The Parson blessed the children in his heart when they all knelt and joined in the General Thanksgiving. Then he prayed for a fine day, a happy day, a day of preservation from harm, both in body and soul, " through Jesus Christ our Lord, Amen."

They all streamed out into the narrow street with the teachers, who formed them into a procession, headed by the Sunday-school banner, held aloft and proudly carried by two of the bigger boys.

A strong force of parents and rejected girls and boys followed them to the pier, where the steamboat lay in waiting.

" How horrid all this crowd is ! " said Mary Anne to her friends as she shrank aside from the people. " Let us cross over the road."

It was a very wide crossing now, and the banks of mud had disappeared. In their place gardens were laid out, with shrubs and gravel walks under the old trees that for years had shaded the river's edge. The slimy water no longer lapped their roots or overflowed into the cellars of the houses during winter floods. The little skiffs and pleasure-boats that used to lay along the shore for hire, and dance upon the incoming tide, were past and gone.

Now the river rose and fell full and broad against massive stone walls that kept it at bay.

It was not so picturesque as formerly, but the artist was at work all the same, catching early impressions of haze and sunlight upon the water ; and the Prophet came stumping along on his punctual promenade, bending over his stout stick. He too had crossed the road to avoid the noisy procession and was scowling at the interruption to his morning meditations.

But what did any one in that happy crowd care for him or his thoughts, which were wrapped up in the past or fore-shadowed in the future ? It was only the present that the children were concerned with as they marched along shouting and singing :

" To spend a happy day ! To spend a happy day !
  We're all a-going to Greenwich to spend a happy day."

" It's like entering the ark," said Lizzie Beaufort when they arrived at the pier and stepped across the gangways in single file.

" The animals went in two by two," remarked Hetty, who was standing by to see that no one passed on without a ticket. " Now, Mrs Tite, hurry up. It's a little too narrow for your circumference, isn't it ? Whatever made you come out in your best bonnet on a day like this ? What you want is a shady hat ; your complexion will be ruined when the sun appears."

" Oh, Miss Danvers, I do wish I 'ad a picture 'at ! Daddy says it's going to be a downright 'ot day," cried Mrs Tite, whose broad face might be pitted with smallpox, but her vanity vied with her vexation of spirit in the conviction that the heavy black bonnet was the correct thing to wear on an outing, even if it cast no refreshing shade upon her open countenance.

Daddy Tite followed her in his shiny old frock-coat and the latest of chimney-pot hats that his pastor had bestowed upon him ; but he confided in Hetty that this was only for show to please the missus.

" My red cotton 'andkerchief will be 'andy for my 'ead as it gets 'otter, miss," he said, passing along the gangway.

Mr Turke in his new livery came next with his second daughter and a second wife. With them were old Mrs Cobb and Mrs Webb, the late pew-openers, and widows, now in the Workhouse. They wore grey shawls over clean cotton gowns for the day out, which the Parson had procured for them with special permission. Harriet gave them a warm greeting as they dropped their respectful curtseys. The gallery pew-opener with her husband, the new organ-blower, and her pretty daughter Susan, who was one of the school teachers, followed with Ellen and Maria Swan, who held their heads too high for wedlock with any man of lesser degree than the City Missionary.

This dream had not yet dawned upon the simple mind of Mr Coulston, who brought up the rear. Busybodies had said in days gone by that Ellen would make him a suitable wife, but he evidently preferred his independence, though he always singled out the sisters for select companionship on these occasions, and drank tea in their parlour when he called with the monthly tracts.

Mr Danvers had been the first to board the boat, and he stood beneath the funnel with a word for everyone as they crossed the gangway.

"You had better secure seats under the awning," he advised all the young ladies in their summer attire when they shook hands. "That will be the pleasantest place by and by."

The beadle said as he paused at his side in passing :

"I never knew, sir, as how you 'ad any children unbeknown to me. Them young ladies with Miss Mary Anne are like enough to be her sisters."

"They are all my children to-day, Turke," replied the Parson with his genial smile.

2

It was a fair bevy of damsels who embarked that morning on the *River Queen*. The sun was gaining the victory over the early mist which predicted a fine day, and as the steamer, beating the water into foam with her huge paddle-wheels, swung slowly away from her moorings, the shouts of the school children re-echoed from shore to shore with :

> "To spend a happy day, to spend a happy day ;
> We won't go home till morning, till morning,
> Till morning, till daylight comes again ! "

The parents looking on from the Embankment waved frantically to their offspring on the boat, holding up the disappointed ones left behind to see them move off. Mrs Danvers stood amongst them with little Benson in her arms. The Parson noticed his wife in the crowd and waved his red cotton handkerchief. He had on his thin black alpaca coat, which was a sure sign of a hot day, and a smile of content lit up his countenance as he glanced around him. But the next moment his quick eye detected impending disaster.

A heavily laden barge was swinging right across the bows of the *River Queen* just as she got under weigh. His heart stopped breathing for a moment, and every kind of thought surged through his brain.

Shouts were raised. What if this happy throng were suddenly to be flung into the foaming water around them? He held his breath, and thought of his wife and all the mothers looking on.

Another second, which seemed like a lifetime, and the collision was averted. The steamer had reversed her paddle-wheels just in time, making more noise than ever, and the barge took a sweeping curve aside.

The Parson breathed again, and a sigh of relief that was almost a sob escaped his lips in two words: " Thank God ! "

" That was a narrow shave, sir," said the beadle, whose eyes had followed those of his pastor, as they were wont to do, with the devotion of a dog.

Daddy Tite had also looked on and gasped aloud.

" It was a very merciful preservation, my friends," said Mr Danvers, and turning to Hetty, who now stood by his side, he said, " My dear, we must give thanks at once for deliverance from what might have been a terrible disaster. Stop that shouting among the children and start the hymn of praise."

Harriet mustered the teachers, and the next minute their voices rose above those of the children, who joined in the hymn of thanksgiving :

> " Now thank we all our God
> With hearts and hands and voices ;
> Who wondrous things hath done——"

Sing they must, and one song was as good as another to them, it all meant joy and praise. When the hymn was ended the old refrain was taken up again by the lusty young voices, and Mr Danvers moved about amongst them, telling the teachers of their merciful escape.

Mary Anne, seated in the bows and talking to her friends, had not realized the danger and wondered what made Hetty suddenly start the hymn again. One of her freaks, no doubt; but she thought it sounded very effective as they glided along the smooth surface of the river.

" Well, this is a petticoat party ! " exclaimed Helen Beaufort, looking around the loaded boat. " I don't believe there's a single young man on board. Why didn't Hetty invite Gerard Church and Harry King ? "

" It isn't a picnic, it's a school-treat," observed Molly bluntly. " Young men don't care for such amusements, even the boys don't. Roger refused with scorn when we asked him to come."

" So did Carol," remarked Lizzie. " I believe he was going to ask Roger to go with him to the Crystal Palace."

" Brothers don't count, of course," continued Helen ; " but I am sure Gerard would have come if he had been invited and so would some of Hetty's friends."

Harriet was here, there, and everywhere, from one end of the boat to the other. She had now worked her way through the crowd to where her sisters were sitting and had overheard Helen's remark.

" Some of my friends ! " she exclaimed. " There are plenty of them at the other end of the boat. Come along and make their acquaintance. I'm afraid we've got no curate on board for you to flirt with, Helen, but Mr Horbury is the next best thing. He's the superintendent of the boys' school, a most earnest young man, I do assure you. And there's Mr Cale, a coal merchant's clerk, who teaches the small boys. He is very bashful and not quite your style perhaps, but he loves to play ' Kiss-in-the-ring.' "

They found Mr Cale performing with pathos upon a concertina. He was surrounded by his class of boys, one of whom accompanied him on a penny whistle to the then popular tune of " Poor Mary Ann." Near by, and holding on to the boat rail with her iron hook, stood Mary-Ann Knight, smiling as ever. She was clad in the same tidy black bonnet and shawl that she had worn ten years before when she had wheeled out the perambulator with Nurse.

The Parson called her his parish perennial, for she came up as fresh as a flower each year, with no visible means of subsistence except an old broom, with which she swept a crossing and managed to keep out of the Workhouse.

Harriet took a mischievous delight in introducing Mr Cale to Helen. He was attired in a black frock-coat which he wore on Sundays, and a brown pot-hat in which he went to the office on week-days. Grey canvas shoes and flannel trousers completed his costume. The effect was expressive of what he considered the correct thing for the occasion.

Mr Horbury looked superior in a white flannel suit and a straw hat. He was more at his ease as the young ladies approached. " Kiss-in-the-ring " did not appeal to him ; he had brought stumps and bats, and was bent on a game of cricket with his boys in the park.

Helen liked moving about the boat. All the girls stared at her, admiring her pretty summer frock and pink ribbons. Those who attended the confirmation class were not a little jealous of her intimacy with the Parson's daughters. They nudged each other as she passed by, and whispered amongst themselves that she gave herself airs and didn't care to associate with them.

3

Molly was the youngest teacher in the Sunday-school and she was too shy to mix with the others. She was happy sitting talking to Elizabeth, with Charlotte and Emily and Nancy near by, all enjoying themselves in their own way.

A school-treat was to them the most delightful form of entertainment that they knew of, what with the early rising, a whole day's holiday, and going late to bed.

A slight breeze had sprung up and was blowing the morning mist away : but soon the sun began to glare, and Lizzie remarked that she would prefer to sit under the awning.

" How long will it be before we get to Greenwich ? " she asked with a yawn. Mary Anne looked at her, and observed that she had turned pale.

" I should like to lie down," said Lizzie faintly. " The motion of the boat makes me feel sick."

" We had better go below," said Molly, full of nervous apprehension, and they made their way to the cabin, where a number of boys were at play. In the noise they were making and the throb of the steam-engines Lizzie quickly developed a headache and turned quite green.

Molly fanned her with a handkerchief, and was glad when Hetty came bustling down the stairway to see what had become of them.

" You will certainly be sick if you stay here," she said. " Fresh air is essential for a headache, and this hole reeks of oil. Come up now and lie along the seats. You can lay your head in Maria Swan's lap. What you want, my dear Lizzie, is something to eat ; I daresay you started without any breakfast to speak of."

But the mention of food put the finishing touch to poor Elizabeth's condition. She tried to rise and fainted away.

" Now, you boys, get out of the way and don't come crowding round ! " said Harriet. " Help me to raise her, Molly ; we must take her up into the fresh air. She's coming round now—that's all right."

Helen appeared on the stairway in search of her sister. " Oh, here you are ! " she exclaimed. " I couldn't think what had become of you. Why, how ill you look, Lizzie ! Whatever is the matter ? "

" She's sick, and so we shall all be if we stay down here," declared Harriet. " You had better go up again at once. We are coming."

But Helen demurred. " The wind blows one about so, I thought it would be nicer down here, one gets so untidy. Is there a looking-glass anywhere ? "

" Yes, I am a very reliable one," replied Hetty. " I can tell you what you look like if you want to know ? "

Helen did not want any of Harriet's home-truths. She was aware of her friend's faculty for making fun of everybody, and the marvellous powers of mimicry that never failed to amuse her friends and relations.

" You ought to lie down, Lizzie," said Helen, turning to her sister. " I will stay here with you : Hetty and Molly needn't remain."

" If you want to be sick that will be a good plan," observed Harriet ; " but I advise you both to come up. You are missing the best part of the river, and it won't be long now before we get to Greenwich. Come along." So saying she took hold of Lizzie and dragged her up the steep stairway.

Everyone was in high spirits on deck. A wind had sprung up, hats were being blown off, and some had gone overboard. Teachers were kept busy in tying them on securely. Daddy Tite had doffed his chimney-pot and wound a red and yellow bandanna about his bald head which his wife fastened in upstanding knots that resembled the ears of a donkey.

The *River Queen* was rushing along with the wind and the tide : waves crested with foam lapped and dashed against her sides caused by the swell of passing steam-tugs and other craft.

Mr Danvers, surrounded by young ladies, stood pointing out the many objects of interest on the shore ; and was telling them all sorts of tales and traditions connected with Father Thames.

Mr Turke was entertaining the ladies of his set in a similar manner but in more hilarious fashion. Mrs Turke and Mrs Tite sat shaking with laughter at the jokes their good husbands were making for their benefit.

" Anyone would think as you was a clown from the pantymine ! " declared the beadle's second spouse.

" And you'll be the pantaloom then ! " said Mrs Tite to Daddy

" And you the Columbine, my dear," returned the facetious old man as he clapped the chimney-pot over the handkerchief to make the ladies laugh.

Mr Coulston sat in the same row conversing with the two Miss Swans on one side of him and the two Miss Shorts on the other. His cackling laugh attracted the attention of the widow Justice who stood at some little distance with her youthful son and daughter. A resigned smile and a faint sigh betrayed her feelings, which were tender towards the City Missionary.

Harriet and Mary Anne were now seen approaching with Lizzie in tow, who was the colour of a duck's egg. The Missionary rose, full of concern, and Maria Swan esteemed it an honour to take Lizzie's head in her lap. Ellen possessed an elegant lace-edged handkerchief which she spread over Lizzie's face, and Molly squeezed herself in between them on the seat.

Mr Coulston then talked in high ecstatic tones on the beauties of nature and the wonders of creation. This was a day to divert his thoughts and those of others from sordid homes and common tasks ; he might be forgiven for showing off to the ladies what knowledge he possessed on the subject, but Mrs Justice, on whose open ears a good deal fell, thought he should have quoted more from the Bible and less of his own opinions.

Presently Greenwich came in sight. Everyone rose to his feet and made a move forward. The great paddle-wheels slackened speed ; the *River Queen* slowed down and drew up alongside the pier.

It took a long time to disembark, and Harriet was the first to cross the gangway with Stella Duvale and Mr Horbury, who proceeded to place the children in pairs for procession as they landed. The banner was unfurled again and they started off like restive animals in search of food.

A marquee had been erected in the park for the party, and when at last this was reached the children threw themselves in rows on the grass and were glad to eat and drink what was given to them. Then they rose up and rushed off to play, regardless of the careful instructions given by their teachers, who were now anxious to feed themselves.

4

The company of elders had retreated into the shade of the tent and taken their places at the long trestle tables which were spread with unbleached cloths and covered with dishes of cold meat and fruit pies, cress and lettuces, intermingled with great jugs of beer and lemonade.

" Now, Molly," said Hetty as she and the teachers filed into the tent, " don't be exclusive. Go and seat yourself with the rest, and leave Lizzie to take care of herself." And Mary Anne was driven into a bench between Mr Cale and his sister.

The young man was feeling the effect of his exertions in handing round meat pies and mugs of water to the children, so he took off his frock-coat and sat upon it previous to partaking of beef and beer in his shirt-sleeves.

Molly was sensitive to her surroundings and lost what appetite she had gained by the fresh river breezes. The baker's three daughters sat next to Mr Cale on the other side, and were not a bit abashed by the deshabille.

Charlotte and Emily, with little Nancy Beaufort, seated themselves opposite, intent on observing the actions of Mr Cale as he mopped his face with one hand and passed the mustard to Molly with the other.

Lizzie was lower down with Ellen and Maria Swan, and Helen was sandwiched in between Harriet and Mr Horbury who though of humble origin was a man who should be susceptible to feminine charms. But it was Hetty who claimed what attention he had to spare from his plate, and his modesty forbade him from addressing Helen at all. He filled her glass with lemonade when he had poured some into his own from a stout white jug that was tucked like a petticoat. Being a rigid teetotaller he had the advantage over Mr Cale, whose thirst compelled him to imbibe too much beer before he partook of beef and bread, so that he hiccoughed without cessation as he stretched across the table to Harriet saying :

" Will you—pass—the mustard—please—Miss Danvers?"

At one end of the long trestle table the Parson presided. He never ate in the middle of the day, but the City Missionary, who sat at the other end, always partook of as much as was possible on such occasions.

A munching silence fell. But food was of no importance to an ethereal damsel like Helen Beaufort ; she glanced up and down the table, observing the whole company engaged in eating a heavy meal on a hot midday, and it disgusted her. She nibbled a small piece of lettuce and became restless.

" We shall have you fainting too if you don't eat something," remarked Harriet, who was plying her knife and fork with energy.

" I think I shall take Lizzie outside into the air," replied Helen. " It is so hot in this tent she might faint again."

" It will be far hotter outside in the sun," said Hetty. " Is she so given to fainting ? A good meal will be much better for her, I know. You haven't had enough lettuce to keep a rabbit alive, and there are speeches to follow."

" Oh, I couldn't eat any more, and I hate listening to speeches ! " exclaimed Helen, jumping up and extricating herself from the narrow bench. She made her way round to her sister who was seated beside the Swans, studying character and sipping lemonade. But she was willing to exchange the stuffiness of the tent for the shade of a spreading oak tree and the cool breeze that came from the river.

Presently they were joined by Mary Anne and the younger sisters, glad to rest and talk while they watched the teachers playing games with the children in the hot sun.

" Do look at Mr Cale ! " said Charlotte. " He has drunk no end of beer, besides eating an enormous dinner, and now he is incapable for the afternoon."

" Wasn't it bad manners to eat in his shirt-sleeves ? " said Mary Anne. " His sister ought not to have allowed it ; but I suppose they don't know any better in their class of life."

" They always have meals in their shirt-sleeves," observed Lizzie. " It must be more comfortable when they can't change their clothes as often as we do."

The young man in question was lying full length under the next tree, with his pot-hat over his face.

" The sun and the beer have evidently taken effect," remarked Emily.

" Look at this ragged woman coming ! " said Helen. " I believe she's a gipsy. What fun ! "

The hag approached the little group of girls, and came under the tree.

" Shall I tell your fortune, my pretty young lady ? " she began, looking at Helen who had risen.

" Don't be silly, Helen," said Lizzie ; but her sister was already holding out her hand.

" Cross my palm with silver and I'll give you good luck,"

said the gipsy ; and Helen produced a sixpenny piece from her purse.

"There's a nice young gentleman dying of love," the old woman began, " but he can't afford to marry, and there's another as rich as can be, but you won't look at him while the other one is near."

Helen blushed with delight as the teachers and girls came crowding round to listen, and the gipsy continued her palaver.

"You will meet a tall dark man before long, and he will be your fate."

"Oh, do tell me when I shall meet him and where ? " exclaimed Helen excitedly, and a voice from the background broke into song :

> "Where and when shall I earliest meet him ?
> What are the words that he first will say ? "

It was Harriet, who had come to see what was going on under the tree, and who buzzed like a bluebottle into their midst.

Miss Beaufort did not like being made fun of. "Don't interrupt ! " she cried impatiently, but Harriet quickly dispersed the group and sent the gipsy away.

"It's stuff and nonsense," she declared, "and we want you all now to come and see the Observatory. Papa is going to conduct a party."

Harriet drove the little group before her like a flock of sheep to where Mr Danvers was standing with Mr Coulston and Stella Duvale.

"Come along, young people ! " he called out. "This is an opportunity that should not be missed. I have obtained a special permit to view the wonders of the universe," and he started off leading the way, Harriet and Miss Duvale bringing up the rear, so there was no escape.

Helen was upset and annoyed. " It was much nicer sitting

talking under the trees," she complained. " I wish Hetty wouldn't interfere so."

" You needn't come if you don't want to," said Molly bluntly, " but everyone else does, and you would be left alone."

" Oh, I shouldn't mind that a bit ! " said Helen. " I have rather a headache, the sun is so hot, and I should prefer to be quiet."

" I shall stay behind too then," said Lizzie, who guessed that her sister meant to go back to the gipsy. But Helen demurred.

" I won't have you staying to look after me ! " she exclaimed pettishly. " I shall be quite happy by myself." But Lizzie protested and stuck to her like a leech after Harriet had reluctantly allowed them to drop out of the personally conducted party.

5

A group of teachers were resting under a tree in the distance, from whence came laughter and exclamations.

" Vulgar girls ! What a noise they are making ! " said Helen, but the next minute her quick eye perceived the gipsy in their midst.

" Let's go and see what it's all about," she added, hastening forward, and Lizzie was obliged to follow.

The baker's handsome daughters were having their fortunes told, and around them thronged a company of schoolgirls. The restraining influence had gone to the Observatory, and the gipsy was making a fortune as well as telling one.

The Miss Bramertons had fine complexions and dark eyes. Helen stood listening, and was not a little jealous of the fates being predicted for them. Her own was insipid compared to the dazzling futures foretold to both. They were not even well-born like herself, but one was to marry a marquis after an eventful career on the stage, and the other was to sail round the world with a millionaire and to marry his only son.

" Do come away," remonstrated Lizzie, but Helen pushed herself forward and succeeded in attracting the gipsy's attention again.

" You must cross my palm in silver twice over, my lovely lady," declared the woman, and Lizzie's slender purse had to be emptied to satisfy Helen's demands as she stood by the gipsy, trembling with excitement while everyone looked on with interest. At least an earl might fall to her lot.

" You won't go far to find him, and it won't be long before you do," predicted the hag. " All the gals in the town will be dying for him, and he will be first for one and then for another until he meets you, and then 'is mind's made up."

" Has he a title ? " asked Helen diffidently.

" Yes, but only a poor one," said the woman. " Just 'is Reverence, my dear. But give me another sixpence and p'raps he'll be a Bishop."

" Helen, come away and don't be so silly ! " said Lizzie, as her sister drew her purse from her pocket again, but no silver coin was forthcoming.

" You can't expect titles for nothing," said the gipsy and she began making advances to Lizzie. " Come, my dear," she wheedled, " it's your turn now."

But Elizabeth shrank from her. She had not yet arrived at the age for coquetry, and so contented was she in the present that she cared nothing as yet for the future.

" You will both be in love with the same man," the woman went on. " And there will be a broken heart, but it won't be his. Now cross my hand again and I will tell you all about him."

There was a threepenny bit in Lizzie's purse that laid there for luck, and to please her sister she produced it. Helen put it in the gipsy's palm.

"You can't expect much for that," grumbled the hag. "I'm only a poor woman and have my living to make."

"But that is all we have to give you," said Helen regretfully.

"Well, you'll never be rich whatever 'is title may be," sighed the gipsy; "but it will be a love match, and you will have a large family to bring a blessing on it." And that was all she could be got to say.

Helen was disappointed and disgusted. She followed Lizzie to a distance, where they lay down under a tree and watched the fallow deer.

"I hate school-treats!" remarked Helen, closing her eyes. "They are such a bore, and there is no one fit to speak to."

Lizzie produced a small sketching block and began to draw the deer.

"It's just lovely sitting here," she said, "and it's nice to see people enjoying themselves."

Helen didn't answer. She fell asleep, and Elizabeth hoped that she would wake in a happier frame of mind.

6

When the party returned from the Observatory it was tea-time. A bell rang outside the tent and the children came flocking from the four corners of the park, thirsty and hot.

"Now seat yourselves upon the grass as they did in the Bible," called out Stella Duvale, who was the moving spirit of the meals.

Everything she said and did was according to the Scriptures.

"Here we have the loaves and fishes," she observed,

carrying a plate of thickly cut bread and butter in one hand and a dish of shrimps in the other. " But what are they amongst so many ? You younger children must be content to gather up the fragments that remain."

" The heads and tails that is," laughed Hetty, who was handing round mugs of milk and water.

" Then there will be no waste or litter, girls," went on Stella to her own particular class. " No doubt the miracle of the loaves and fishes was intended to teach us to be tidy as well as thrifty."

Mary Anne was following in Harriet's wake with a large jug of diluted milk.

" I wonder what has become of the Beauforts ? " she said anxiously to her sister.

" They've gone running after that gipsy woman, you may be sure," said Hetty. " If they didn't hear the bell they must go without their tea."

But Molly missed her friends, and she knew that Lizzie had sacrificed her own inclination by staying behind with Helen.

" Mayn't I go and look for them ? " she asked. " They mustn't miss tea, for they ate no dinner."

" Nonsense ! " said Hetty. " They must take the consequences. It would do no good for you to go and get lost too. Ask Mr Coulston to ring the bell again."

.   .   .   .   .

" Helen," said Lizzie, hastily putting away her sketching book, " Did you hear that bell ? I expect it is for tea, and we are ever so far from the marquee."

" I don't want any tea," replied Helen crossly.

" Well, I do," said her sister, who did not feel inclined for further self-sacrifice, " and I'm sure a cup will do you good. Make haste and come along."

Elizabeth rose and hurried ahead, but Helen followed at a very leisurely pace.

A great clattering and chattering was going on inside the huge tent when they arrived. Harriet and her friend Stella were seated at either end of the tables behind big urns of tea, and were filling cups and passing them along as fast as they were able.

Everyone was in a state of heat more or less. Hats were taken off, bonnet strings were untied, and handkerchiefs were being used as mops.

Helen glided in almost unnoticed, and Mr Danvers made room for her at his side.

"And where have you been, young lady, that you can look so fresh and cool this hot afternoon?" he asked. "You are like a lily-of-the-valley amongst a bed of peonies in full bloom."

Miss Beaufort felt so flattered by this gallant remark that she forgot her ill-humour and began to enjoy herself.

The tea-table was quite tempting with dishes of cut bread-and-butter, fresh green watercress, and cakes and buns all down the centre.

Helen permitted the Parson to make her a watercress sandwich to taste, then returned his flattery by asking for another.

"Now, Mrs Tite," called Harriet from the head of the table, "are you ready for a sixth cup? It's a real luxury to be hot and thirsty when there's plenty of tea going."

The cobbler's wife was still mopping the beads from her brow, and the action caused those in her bonnet to jingle.

"I ain't much given to drinking, miss, but I do enj'y me food," she replied. "Give me tea and s'rimps and I don't want nothing more; but I must be cooled down fust."

Mr Cale had so far recovered himself as to take twelve cups of tea as quickly as he could get them, according to

Charlotte's acute calculations, her far-reaching eye still upon him.

"Six from one urn and half a dozen from the other," she observed to Emily and Nancy Beaufort, seated on either side of her.

"But he has only washed down a few shrimps with it," remarked Emily with scorn.

When at last the urns ran dry and the cups ceased plying to and fro, the Parson said grace and the company emerged into the air again.

On the homeward journey all class distinctions vanished in the genial atmosphere that prevailed. Harriet made herself the centre of attraction amongst the girls and gathered them all round her in a bunch in the bows of the boat, keeping them in ripples of laughter with her fun; and Helen found herself conversing amicably with some of the recently confirmed young ladies, who twitted her about the dark young man.

"It might be Mr Cale," said Lizzie to Molly with a laugh, "but it is sure to be a curate."

The cool breeze on the river after the hot day in the park was refreshing and invigorating; the Misses Swan ceased to fan themselves with their pocket-handkerchiefs as they had been doing all day, it being beneath their dignity to mop their faces like the common herd.

Mrs Tite removed her bonnet and placed it on her husband's head.

The teachers started part-singing at the other end of the boat, varied by the school children's persistent refrain:

"We won't go home till morning, till daylight doth appear!"

And no one was in a hurry to reach their destination, unless it was the Parson, who was finding his alpaca coat a trifle thin towards sundown.

7

When at last the *River Queen* slowed down and headed for the home pier it was getting dusk, and a mist began to rise on the water.

" Time for all children to be in bed," declared Mr Danvers ; but the mothers and babies and sisters and brothers were awaiting them, and loud shouts greeted them from the Embankment.

The banner was unfurled again, and when all were landed it led the way to the church for a thanksgiving at the close of a happy day.

The Prophet, starting for his evening stroll, heard them coming in the distance and beat a hasty retreat up the Row.

Daddy Turke had the church key in his pocket and was hurrying to unlock the big door, when Mr Danvers called out after him :

" Never mind about the lights, Turke, we can praise God in the dark."

It was a mixed rabble that followed them to the entrance, and Harriet hustled them all inside with the aid of the teachers, allowing none to escape home without giving thanks for their safe return.

The last rays of the setting sun were filtering through the western windows of the Old Church. Hetty ran up the dark stairs that led to the organ loft, calling to Stella Duvale, " Come and blow the bellows, we must give the mothers some music."

And when her father had led them in prayer below she was ready to start them in praise above :

> " All praise and thanks to God
> The Father now be given.
> The Son, and Him who reigns
> With them in highest Heaven."

As they sang the sun dropped into the river mist outside. The sweet, soft music of the organ died away and a blessing was given.

Ten minutes later all was silent within the ancient building. The key grated in the lock of the western door and was transferred again to the beadle's pocket.

No light penetrated now into that dim repose of the bygone dead who lay in peace within those hallowed walls.

Presently the moon arose and shone through the latticed window in the chancellor's chapel, casting her luminous rays upon the white lady opposite, " That unstained copy and rare example of all virtue," with her winding-sheet wrapped round her. The effigies of her parents and relations kneeling in perpetual prayer day and night within the shadows are close beside her.

" Ye most incomparable and pious Lady, Ye Lady Jane," wife of the Lord of the Manor in the seventeenth century reposes gracefully upon her couch of touchstone. She gazes across into the darkness on the other side of the church where lie with closed eyes my Lord and Lady of the Manor in the sixteenth century flat on their backs with their baby beside them, he in his suit of richly damascened armour, she in her bonnet and ruff—beneath their canopy of marble—" resting inviolate till all shall arise and come to judgment."

So be it. Their memorials have not perished with them, nor will they while the old house of God exists.

XVII. THE YOUNG PLANTS

" Methinks animals, and even man himself, are like plants ; for we who manure the earth, know by experience that it is easy to prepare all things necessary before we plant. But when that which we have planted is come up, the care and pains we must take about it is very great and troublesome. There is my son ; ever since he has been born his education will not suffer me to rest one moment, but keeps me in continual fear."

PLATO.

I

AT the far end of the King's highway, beyond the precincts of Paradise Gardens, stood an old Georgian house in large grounds, where it was like driving into the country on a winter's night.

Its big windows were ablaze with hospitality and warmth one evening in the New Year, to give light to the various vehicles that were turning through the fine old wrought-iron gateway, and making their way slowly up the drive under the overhanging trees to the entrance.

The front door opened beneath a massive portico with a well-worn flight of stone steps upon which was laid a length of crimson bunting.

The jovial host was Canon King, his beaming bride Constantia Markham, whom he had prevailed upon to become his second wife.

It was Twelfth Night, and Worby's cab was tightly packed as it rumbled along the King's highway, for Mrs Danvers was delighted to chaperone Helen and Elizabeth Beaufort to the party as well as Harriet and Mary Anne. They all managed to squeeze in, and set off in high spirits.

Constantia King called it a schoolroom dance, for it

included young men and maidens, nephews and nieces, boys and girls of all ages ; so Molly and Lizzie were allowed to go, and the confirmation muslins were decorated for the occasion with ribbons and roses.

A blazing log fire gave everybody a welcome in the big square hall, and hot tea and coffee awaited them in the panelled drawing-room which was illuminated with count-less wax candles set in sconces round the walls.

The buzz of conversation and merry laughter was kept going by the assembling guests, who were more or less known to each other, being the clergy and select society of the neighbourhood.

Mary Anne retreated into the background with Lizzie Beaufort, from whence they watched their elder sisters, and observed other girls like themselves being led out to dance.

" Who is Hetty dancing with I wonder ? " said Molly.

" Oh, that is a college friend of Gerard Church's," replied Lizzie. " He is staying at the Rectory. We met him there last evening."

" Did they have a party there ? " asked Molly. " They don't invite us. Hetty boxed Gerard's ears once when we were playing together a long time ago and they have never forgiven her."

But Harriet was soon to be seen whirling through a waltz in Gerard's arms, and Mary Anne and Elizabeth were brought out from their corner and provided with partners also. Mrs King came along, followed by all sorts and conditions of mankind, and Molly found herself being led into the big ballroom by a little man whose knees did not seem equal to supporting his small body, while Lizzie paired off with Harry King.

Mary Anne felt hot but happy when, after a refreshing glass of lemonade and a rest on the broad oak staircase, Mr Parker asked for the pleasure of another dance. He led her back to her mother's side in the drawing-room, where

Mrs Danvers detained him for conversation a little while, and when he left them to seek another partner she remarked to Mary Anne :

" A very agreeable young man, dear, and of good family. He is one of the Parkers of Parkstone, which is near my old. home in Suffolk. I used to go to dances there when I was a girl."

Harriet had joined them now, and broke in with, " What an insignificant little monkey he is ! Molly and he were a funny sight bobbing about in the polka with their knees knocking together. Everyone was laughing at them," and away she went on the arm of someone else.

The Parson's wife felt like a hen with a brood of chickens ; old customs were rigidly observed in those days, and she expected the four girls to return between each dance to her sheltering wing. But Helen and Harriet soon transgressed and were seen no more till supper-time. Then the music ceased and the elders processed to the dining-room arm-in-arm, according to their social status, where the supper was conducted with all the formality of a dinner party.

Canon King led Mrs Danvers to the head of the table, for in his opinion she took precedence of any lady present, having been the one who introduced him to his excellent partner in life.

His daughter did not share her father's satisfaction. She had looked forward to being his hostess and housekeeper when she grew up, and a stepmother did not meet with her approval.

Mrs Danvers congratulated her friend Constantia on the arrangement of the supper-table as they wended their way back to the drawing-room. The feast of good things of which she had partaken, with champagne as the beverage, made her veins tingle with a sense of well-being and happiness. She was proud of her daughters and pleased with their friends. It gratified her to see them enjoying themselves. Few girls in the room were so amusing as Harriet, she thought, and none so pretty as Helen Beaufort.

As for Mary Anne and Elizabeth, they had time in which to develop, and the company was always well chosen at St. Matthew's. She sat down with a smile of content by Mrs Burton, Constantia's youngest sister, who long ago had married the doctor, according to the Parson's prediction, and had brought her boy and girl to the party. Her red hair was still a crown of glory, but her figure was not as elegant as it used to be.

Presently Mrs Danvers realized that it was one thing to bring four girls to a dance, but another matter to take them away. Harriet's high spirits got the upper hand after supper. Helen Beaufort had more partners than she could dance with, so she sat out with one, and although Mary Anne was safe by her mother's side one moment she was gone the next, while Mrs Danvers' eyes were looking after Lizzie.

It was Mr Parker of Parkstone who carried Molly off at the last moment to dance Sir Roger de Coverley. The lively tune had just started, and pairs were taking their places down the centre of the long room.

After a vain pursuit the Parson's wife subsided again into her chair, and her indefatigable friend and hostess came and sat down beside her.

" Oh, you mustn't think of taking your girls away before Sir Roger ! " she exclaimed. " We want all the couples we can get. John has gone to drive them in from the staircase, and declares that he is going to dance it with me. It is the last on the programme, and when it is over will be time enough to think of departing. You will have to get accustomed to late hours, my dear friend, now that your daughters are growing up ; and what fine girls they are to be sure ! "

Mrs Danvers went home feeling as young and happy as they did. It had brought back memories of her own girlhood, and reminded her of when they used to drive miles in the moonlight, with hot bricks on the carriage floor to keep their feet warm.

The snow was falling fast, and Worby, who had strewn his cab with plenty of clean dry straw, sat asleep inside, patiently waiting for his passengers, who presently made their appearance with Gerard Church and his friend, asking for a lift as far as the turning to the Rectory.

They scrambled onto the box seat beside Mr Worby, who managed to make room for them and covered their knees with his horse-cloth.

When the lodge where the Beauforts lived was reached the young men handed them out. Lizzie had the latchkey in her pocket, and the sisters vanished into the house after inviting everyone to tea on the morrow.

It was past midnight when the cab drew up at the corner of the Row. The Parson was reading the paper by the kitchen fire, but he did not hear the wheels for the snow lay deep on the road, neither did the grating of the latchkey in the lock disturb him, or the tip-toeing of his wife and daughters up the staircase to bed, for he was absorbed in the Tichborne case.

2

Helen Beaufort had an elder brother at college and a younger one at school. Both were home for the Christmas holidays and appeared at the tea-party next day. Their parents preferred to leave young people to entertain their own friends, and having shaken hands with the invited guests, they drank a cup of tea with them and retired to the dining-room to read and be quiet.

There was quite a large gathering of young folk in the drawing-room when Hetty and Molly entered. Katherine and Harry King were there as well as Eliza Church and her brothers, with Mr Pembroke, Gerard's college friend.

James Oakley and his sisters were talking to Mr Beaufort by the fireside, and in the centre of the room stood George Beaufort, his eldest son, looking ill at ease amongst so many. He was a shy young man, whose attainments at Cambridge were known to be great, for his family had mentioned them to everybody.

The younger son, Carol, was, in his sisters' estimation, only an ordinary schoolboy. He had been for a walk with Roger Danvers, and they turned up together just in time for tea. Being both of an age, they preferred their own company to that in the parlour, and had a good many things in common.

" Girls are such fools ! " Carol confided to his friend. " They only think of what they look like, and scream if you touch them, and they always run and tell if you do anything that you don't want whispered abroad."

His elder brother, if he did not altogether despise female society, was obviously bored by it. Seated in the midst of these daughters of the Church, George Beaufort was silent and reserved.

His sisters told their friends that it was his nature to be so, though Lizzie said that he liked girls.

Harriet, with her high spirits and powers of mimicry, soon set the fun going and drew him out of himself.

Mary Anne had heard so much about this particular brother from Elizabeth that she was disappointed when she met him, and thought he seemed a very ordinary young man. " But then he is so learned that it doesn't matter what he looks like," she concluded in her mind.

Tea handed round in the drawing-room was a new experience for the Oakleys, who always sat down to table for a meal, and they were feeling rather out of their element for everyone was talking about the dance the night before, to which they had not been invited on account of their parents' prejudices.

James was studying for a classical exhibition and would not have accompanied his sisters if he had not been specially asked to meet the young Cambridge don.

" You must come and make my son's acquaintance," said Mr Beaufort, leading James into the centre of the group. " He can give you a lot of useful wrinkles."

But Hetty was already in possession.

" Why didn't you come to the dance last night ? " she was saying. " It was so jolly—specially coming home in the snow all squeezed into a cab full of tobacco smoke. Worby had been sitting in it all the evening with his pipe going."

" I was at the theatre," replied the young man diffidently.

" Oh indeed ! and what did you see ? " asked Harriet. " *Pink Dominoes ?* How shocking ! "

" Why shocking ? " enquired James Oakley. " Awfully amusing, isn't it ? "

" How should you know ? " challenged Hetty.

" Because I've seen it," replied James boldly.

" Well I never ! And pray how did you get your Papa's permission ? " exclaimed Harriet satirically.

But James, ignoring Hetty's banter, felt very pleased with himself on being drawn into a discussion of the play with George Beaufort and the other young men present. Harry King slapped him on the back, saying, " Good business, old chap ! If you will come out with me one night I will show you a thing or two. What about Paradise Gardens, eh ? "

Alice giggled violently and spilt her tea in the saucer.

Conversation became general now and individual shyness wore off. Virginia Oakley found herself chatting quite gaily with Harry King, unaware that he was quizzing her all the time.

" Shall we have some music ? " suggested Helen, anxious to be asked to sing herself.

Harriet at once sat down to the piano and began to play.

Then she was induced to sing, and one song followed another at the request of the young men. Her voice attracted so much attention that Helen became restive.

She sang with so much pathos that Lizzie's little dog joined in and brought it to an end, to the amusement of all.

" Doesn't anyone else sing ? " suggested Helen plaintively.

" Yes, you do," said Hetty. " Come along, and I will play the accompaniment," and Helen was pleased to pipe out an Italian song that no one understood a word about, with a great many trills and high notes.

" Your voice requires developing," said Harriet when it had quavered to the end. " How many lessons have you had ? I don't think much of your singing master. He shouldn't let you learn a song of that kind to begin with."

Helen could have cried, and she longed to slap Hetty, who was monopolizing Gerard Church a great deal too much. He was now a fashionable undergraduate with a monocle, and cultivating a golden moustache.

Twirling round on the music-stool, Harriet felt like Miss Speergrove at the christening party in days gone by, as she talked first to one man and then to another while they crowded round enchanted by her fun and quick repartee.

" Don't any of you sing ? " she asked at length. But Carol Beaufort was the only one who owned to a voice, and that he declared to be cracking.

So the music wore itself out, and Lizzie came forward with sheets of notepaper and pencils for a round game to amuse the Oakleys.

" Let's play ' Consequences,' " she suggested, to which they all agreed, and a good deal of laughter ensued when the first to be read aloud stated that Harriet Danvers met James Oakley in Paradise Gardens and he invited her to go with him to *Pink Dominoes*. The consequence was that they got engaged, which everyone declared to be a risky proceeding.

The Rector's daughter was prudish and did not approve of this kind of amusement, so she informed her brother that it was time to be going.

" Oh, don't break up the party ! " cried Helen, " the fun is only just beginning."

But Eliza was the eldest of the family and she was firm. She bade her brother remember that they were to dine at half-past six that evening on account of the " Penny Reading " at eight o'clock in the Parish Room.

" Oh, bother the ' Penny Reading ' ! " said Gerard. " What an unearthly hour for dinner ! " But Eliza carried him off to the annoyance of Helen and Hetty, who had to relinquish his friend, Mr Pembroke, in consequence.

3

A few days later a hard frost set in and the Parson fitted his family with wooden skates and conducted them each day across the old bridge into the park on the opposite bank of the river, to teach them the art of balance and progression on the frozen surface of the artificial lake, where in the summer they went to feed the ducks and wildfowl.

Mrs Danvers clothed her children sensibly in grey homespun and wrapped them round in scarlet cross-overs, knitted by their Aunt Anna. Harriet complained that they looked like charity children compared with Helen and Lizzie Beaufort, who were careering on the ice in fashionable fringed cloth mantles and fur-trimmed hats in company with the Rector's sons.

Eliza Church watched them from the bank, being too nervous to skate herself. The Oakleys stood near her, attended by Lydia their maid, looking on and shivering, conspicuous with red noses and chilblains. Mr Oakley did not accompany them. He considered skating as improper an accomplishment for young ladies as dancing, and he had a bone of contention to pick with his friend Danvers on the subject next time they met for encouraging his daughters to waste their time in what he called immodest antics.

Roger and his school friends helped Charlotte and Emily along, but Harriet and Mary Anne preferred to struggle by themselves. It was galling to see Helen and Gerard Church skimming past them so gracefully, but the Beauforts had all learned to skate in the country.

Molly became obsessed with a desire to swing along by herself as swiftly as Lizzie did, and being of a persevering disposition she succeeded in her endeavours before the thaw set in ; but Hetty soon tired of it, and turned her attention to other things.

Harriet had ambitions of a more important nature than skating. She had decided to Be, to Do, or to Suffer, as for instance : To be a great singer like Jenny Lind ; or a hospital nurse like Sister Dora ; to do great things in either profession as the case might be, and, if need be, to suffer the righteous anger of her relations in consequence.

Her mother's frequent lament was, " I cannot conceive how a daughter of mine can dream of dragging our name down to the level of the lower classes ! "

" Then I must change it," Hetty would retort. " I suppose if I don't marry I shall have to earn my living sooner or later. Molly is treading on my heels, and Charlotte and Emily are looming in the background, besides the three boys to educate and send to college."

" Harriet, though you are my child, it grieves me to say that you always had a disposition to be vulgar," said Mrs Danvers in a tone of resignation. " I cannot imagine where you get such ideas. It must be from your associates in the parish. Papa has made a great mistake in allowing you to have your own way so much. I always said so ! "

" Come, come," put in the Parson, who had been listening to the little contretemps with amusement while he sipped his whiskey toddy after dinner. " We mustn't let matters go too far. You are very young yet, Pussy, to be thinking of such things, and we can afford to keep you at home a little longer I fancy."

He smiled good-humouredly upon his daughter, and ladled some of his weak beverage into a wineglass for his wife, to revive her drooping spirits after the exertion of putting little Benson to bed.

" But, Papa, you forget that one has to be trained for a profession, and it's of no use unless you begin young," remonstrated Harriet.

" And where is the money for the training to come from I wonder, if we can't afford to keep you ? " said her father.

" Really, Henry, I cannot think why you should argue with Harriet ! " exclaimed Mrs Danvers. " It is not worth while. Of couse, we could not hear of her adopting a profession, even if we had the money to train her."

" My dear, the training would do her no harm," said Mr Danvers. " She must work off her steam somehow."

" Well then, may I try for a Scholarship at the Academy of Music ? " asked Hetty eagerly. " If I get one it would probably cover the expenses of my training."

Her father smiled and said, " That depends on what it would lead to—if you got one."

" It would mean free training for the profession," replied Harriet promptly.

" That I will never consent to ! " declared Mrs Danvers with decision.

" Well then, may I go and be trained at a hospital for a nurse ? " sighed Hetty. " That would cost nothing, and I must do something in the world."

" It would be worse still," said her mother. " You must be content to stay at home like other girls, and help me with the younger ones until you are old enough to marry. There is nursing to be done, and music to teach here, besides the necessity of setting your sisters a good example."

" Oh, Papa ! " cried Hetty in desperation. " Why mayn't I go out and do something ? There are such limitations at home, and I don't want to be married : I want to be free to do as I please with my life."

The Parson paused before he replied, and ladled out another wineglass of toddy. Then he said, " Well, at any rate, I see no harm in your trying for a scholarship if you want to," adding with his humorous smile, " It's ten to one you won't get it."

His wife moaned in despair. " It is always the way : I have no voice in the matter ! "

" That depends, my dear," said her husband. " Let her get the scholarship first."

4

And she did get it. There was an anxious interval of preparation and an exciting hour on a certain day when she sang with her usual self-possession before the great *prima donna* and her husband, the president, at the School of Music.

Harriet had more than her share of assurance to carry her through the world, and she came home radiant to dinner.

Some days later the Scholarship was offered to her on condition that her voice should be trained for professional singing.

The same evening Mr Danvers called Hetty down to his den for a talk.

" Papa, you won't let Mamma stand in the way, will you?" she began eagerly. " I should just love to be a public singer ! Think of the money I could earn, and the good I could do with it ! Send the boys to college and be off your hands myself."

" Yes, my dear Pussy, that sounds all very well to look forward to," said her father presently as he drew long puffs at his pipe, " but there are other things to be taken into consideration, you know. Mamma and I would not like our daughters to earn their own living, and we trust that it may never be necessary for them to do so."

" But it will be necessary as far as I can see ! " urged Hetty emphatically. " There are too many of us, and we are poor enough as it is, all growing up together in so small a space. There is nothing dishonourable in earning one's living that I can see, and I don't care a fig for what people think ! "

" But Mamma does, and you know she is always right," said the Parson. " We are proud of your talents and of the honour you have gained at the School of Music but we fear what it might lead to, my pet, and the musical profession is not exactly suitable for a clergyman's daughter."

" Why ever not ? " demanded Harriet. " What difference can it make whose daughter I am if I can cultivate the talent God has given me ? "

" That is your way of looking at it," replied her father, " but Mamma and I see things from a different point of view."

" Oh Papa, I thought you were going to be on my side ! And now you have gone over to Mamma's way of thinking. It is so old-fashioned and narrow-minded ! " groaned Hetty. " If I don't take this chance I shall never get another, to have my voice trained, or anything else."

" But it would not be honest to accept the training under the conditions on which it is offered, since we do not wish you to become a public singer, my pet," remonstrated Mr Danvers. " It would throw you into another class of society altogether, besides being a great tax on your time and strength. Ask your friend Stella Duvale what her mother has to say on the subject."

" But Mrs Duvale is an actress, not a singer," retorted Harriet.

" Yes, and she has gained a foremost position by sheer hard work as well as talent," replied the Parson ; " but she will tell you that singing for the profession may lead on to the stage, and is very little apart from it in its demands."

" Oh Papa, I can't sit still with folded hands and wait for nothing until it is all too late ! " declared Harriet.

" Don't be impatient, my dear girl. There is plenty of time for success and happiness in life ; you are very young yet," said her father, tenderly stroking her hair as she sat on his knee.

" But I am not too young to make a beginning, and I shall be miserable if I mayn't," cried Hetty. " I've always wanted to sing, and now that I've got the chance you won't let me take it ! I shall never get such another. Oh, it is too bad ! " and she jumped up and beat her hands together, pacing the little room.

Mr Danvers tried to calm her. " I am very grieved, dear, to disappoint you," he said, " but you will be grateful to us one day and see that we were right. It would not be for your future good if you accepted the Scholarship on those terms, and it would be contrary to your upbringing if we were to allow you to do so. Your whole outlook would be changed, and you would have to sacrifice your class and position in life."

" I shouldn't mind that a bit ! " declared Harriet. " One class is as good as another. It is only when it comes to marriage that it matters ; but if you won't let me accept the Scholarship I shall marry the first man that asks me, whoever he may be."

Her father smiled. " Well, I hope he won't put in an appearance yet awhile," he said. " I don't know what I should do without you, my pet, but when he does present himself I trust he may be worthy of you and make you happy."

" And suppose he never turns up ? " retorted Hetty.

" Am I to wither away on the virgin stalk like Miss Wilkins for the rest of my existence ? "

" I can't exactly see you doing it," laughed Mr Danvers, " but that need not worry you, my dear child. Good wives are always in demand when the time comes."

" It's all Mamma's fault ! " cried Harriet passionately.

" No, no, it isn't," said her father. " She is most anxious that you should have scope for your abilities, but in acting for the present we must think of the future, and we talked it over for a long time together, as well as consulting Mrs Duvale on the subject."

" And pray what does she know about it ? " asked Hetty.

" She has a life's experience to speak from," said the Parson, " and she admitted that it was a hard one. She told me that she prayed every day that her daughter might never have to follow her profession."

" Stella hasn't got the talent, or she would I know," said Harriet.

" That may be God's way of answering her mother's earnest prayer," replied Mr Danvers, " but you belong to us, and we can't bear to disappoint you. Try and think kindly of your parents, my child : we are acting for the best, and you must be guided by our wisdom and discretion until the right man comes along and claims you for his own."

Harriet loved her father too well to doubt his wisdom or his word ; but she had no reverence for discretion. Feeling that there was nothing more to be said she submitted to his tender embrace and went to her bedroom. She threw herself full length upon the bed and burst into a torrent of tears. Molly, on her way upstairs, heard her sister in distress. She guessed what it was about and quietly closed the door, wondering why Hetty couldn't be content with life as it was, instead of wanting to cram it with responsibilities.

5

Since the visit to the artist's mother, Mary Anne had laid aside her patchwork and was spending all her spare time in learning to draw.

Lizzie Beaufort had constructed a little studio of her own on the first floor landing in their house, and with her mother's consent she invited Molly to share it with her whenever she could come round the corner. This was a real delight to both the girls. Mary Anne managed to find her way there for an hour or two every other day, and received some instruction from Elizabeth, who was pleased to have so painstaking a pupil.

One morning in the spring Molly was sitting in the parlour window steadily copying with fine strokes in pen and ink an illustration by Gustave Doré that she greatly admired in a large book of poems by Tennyson.

The door opened behind her and someone entered, but she was too much engrossed in her drawing to look up. She thought it was her father who came and stood over her, and she felt sure of a word of encouragement from him. But a strange voice said :

" Why do you copy such stuff ? Pen-and-ink work is good practice, but get something better to spend your time and talent on."

Looking round in astonishment, Mary Anne beheld the artist behind her.

" Is it too early to see Mr Danvers ? " he enquired. " I want him to sign a paper for me," and at that moment the Parson entered the room.

Molly left it, feeling crushed. She had admired the picture of the knight in armour riding on the coal-black horse through the dark shades of the long avenue that led up to the mediæval castle, and thought it so romantic. Now it was condemned by a real artist. She would never look at it again.

If it had not been for Lizzie's kind encouragement she would have abandoned art and taken to patchwork once more ; but Helen Beaufort, who was learning the new Art needlework at South Kensington, condescended to show her the various stitches to be acquired, so she took up that instead.

Virginia Oakley did crochet work in her leisure hours, but Mary Anne was not inspired with any admiration for the antimacassars and toilet-tidies that she made. To imitate Helen and Lizzie became the object of her daily life. She had never felt any desire to be like Virginia or Alice Oakley, with their prim manners and corkscrew curls, but if Lizzie Beaufort wore her hair raked off her forehead with a circular comb she was pleased to do the same.

When Roger came home for the holidays he brought his schoolfellows to the corner house and was allowed to invite them to tea, which made a diversion for his sisters. Harriet would preside at the tea-table, with her hair done up behind, and poke fun at everybody. But on these occasions Mary Anne became conscious of her extremities. This she confided to Charlotte, with whom she shared the old night nursery as a bedroom, while she brushed and plaited her long fair hair and tied it in a pigtail before the looking-glass that Nurse used to regard herself in.

This fashion did very well for the schoolroom, but when young gentlemen came to tea it seemed unornamental to Molly's developing mind.

Charlotte, pallid and pert, would reply with disdain and decision, " As if boys cared what we look like ! They don't come to see us."

She was always an individual to be reckoned with. Her opinions were not to be gainsaid when she chose to express them. Her body was small, but her head was large, and furnished with big brown eyes that pierced her opponents through. She possessed a memory that carried her back to the year in which she was born, and she had an answer for everything.

Douglas was the schoolfellow who took most kindly to the corner house and its family life, for he had no sisters, and his parents resided in lodgings at Bayswater. But Browne and his cousin, Fred Gray, were the sons of rich City men who fared sumptuously every day. They found the *ménage* at the Parson's table too homely to suit their tastes.

"I like your sisters, Danvers, and your jam isn't bad, but your butter is beastly," Fred confided in Roger, and Roger repeated it to Hetty as a joke.

"Oh, he likes us, does he, better than our butter ! Well, he won't like *me* if he comes again." But he didn't.

Roger diligently pounded away on the piano when he was at home, and his friend Douglas had a voice to develop, so Harriet did not have all the music to herself. The old Broadwood was seldom silent. Mary Anne played perpetual tunes ; Charlotte and Emily practised scales and exercises during the day, as their sisters had done before them ; and on Sundays after tea they would gather round the piano and sing hymns to Hetty's accompaniment.

That was a happy hour, and when it was over they would rush upstairs to get ready for Church, and file off in pairs down the Row to evening service.

Harriet had lately been promoted to sing in the choir, and Roger began to look upon the family pew as a nursery for the little ones. He referred to them contemptuously as "the kids." When Douglas was with them the two boys went up to the gallery with Hetty, and sat in the choir seats in front of the organ. Miss Speergrove still reigned supreme there, but she was getting bronchial, and seldom appeared at church in the evening, so Hetty's clear contralto took the lead.

There were new members in the choir now, though some of the older ones still sang on. Isabella Sussex had ascended to the gallery from the pew behind the Parson's, though she cawed like a rook ; but her father had replaced her departed mother by marrying Miss Chaine, the grocer's sister, and he no longer needed his daughter's company there.

Young men and maidens filled up the gaps that time had rendered vacant, their fresh voices contributing to the sweetness of the singing that their Parson loved to listen to. In the Springtime, when the early sunshine lit up the ancient building, and the organ pealed out his favourite anthem, he would look up with a thankful heart that the darkness of winter was over.

> " And the choirs that dwell on high
>   Swell the glory of the sky, Alleluia ! "

The organist would pull out all the stops when it came to the mountains, and drown the voices.

> " Here let the mountains thunder forth sonorous.
>   There let the valleys sing in gentler chorus, Alleluia ! "

Then he would push them all in again, and Miss Speergroves's tremulous falsetto could be heard filtering through Harriet's rich contralto.

> " To God who all creation made,
>   The frequent hymn be duly paid, Alleluia !
>   Wherefore we sing, both heart and voice awaking,
>   And children's voices echo, answer making, Alleluia ! "

And the Parson caught the echo in the family pew beside him.